Third Degree Burns

Michael Patterson

Copyright 2018. All rights reserved.

The Author has asserted his moral right to be
identified as the Author of this Work.
No part of this book may be reproduced, stored in a retrieval system,
or transmitted by any means, electronic, mechanical, photocopying, recording,
or otherwise, without permission from the author.

All characters in this publication are fictitious
and any resemblance to real persons, living or dead,
is purely coincidental.

© Michael Patterson 2018

Cover design and layout by
JAG Designs

ISBN: 9781980580775

"I could have been a giant, said the bonsai tree. But someone bound my roots and held me down. I could have reached the heavens, said the snowy owl. But they clipped my wings and kept me on the ground."

- Brian Bedford

Prologue

Thursday 21st January 2016

The largely unoccupied car park sat at the foot of Edinburgh's Arthur's Seat. An immense peak that was once described by the novelist Robert Louis Stevenson as, 'a hill - for magnitude; a mountain - in virtue of its sheer bold design.' The agreed location was virtually outside the richly decorated, wrought-iron gates of Holyrood Palace and directly across from the infamously designed and way over budget Scottish Parliament.

Not exactly a meeting place one would call remote or inconspicuous. Yet this was where the seller was keen to do the deal. Clouded gunpowder skies overhead, alternated between drizzle and hail. In primitive, pessimistic Scotland it seemed like your typical, quintessential weather - a rain soaked gateway to the weekend. Any foolish tourist silly enough to venture out in the first place, would now be quickly splish-splashing his or her way back to their overpriced Edinburgh accommodation.

At fast approaching ten minutes past four, available parking posed no problem. The two cars drew close and parked side by side. They reversed cautiously up to the fence of the Queen's official residence and faced out toward the ancient, looming volcano in the heart of this bustling, historic city. Leaving enough adequate legroom for individuals to stand behind their respective vehicles, money was soon exchanged. That transaction was then quickly followed by one car boot being routinely opened and a guitar sized case taken from the back seat of the second vehicle, being placed delicately inside. Having just parted with substantial funds, the scruffily dressed, dark haired man then went to unveil his purchase. Nowhere to be found was a Gibson L-5, Martin D-45 or Fender Telecaster. However, as he pulled back cautiously on the sturdy metal zipper, every single tooth click was obviously music to his ears. A satisfactory smile and nod of his head was soon offered. For a few brief seconds he stood proudly, staring with deep affection at his newly acquired Barrett M99.

Desperate to try it out, he shook the sellers hand, concluded the private deal and immediately headed eastbound out of town. No strap or plectrum - would be required.

ONE

"As the wise old pigeon peeled his eye and the nettles and the weeds began to sigh. The daddy longlegs said 'my-oh-my.' Are we ready for the reel in the flickering light?"

- Christy Moore

That evening, sets of six swung ecstatically around the dance floor. Hair flowed, sweat poured and testosterone was Canadian barn dancing with the best of them! Easily at this point, seventy to eighty high-spirited individuals were giving it all they had. Rousing reels, jubilant jigs and tranquil waltzes had already taken place. So it was now the turn of laughter, excitement and boisterous fun to pulsate it's way majestically throughout the room. Interlocked at the elbows, partners at regular intervals were being hoisted high and thrown wildly off their feet. They were quite literally paragliding over and above the dance floor. The smiles made it abundantly clear for all to see, that this was a popular time of year in Scotland. Another sixty or seventy bodies were currently resting in seated areas, drinking at the bar or unwinding in their partners arms. As they all looked to regain a second wind, yet another lengthy queue was waiting anxiously to get into the highly popular club. Capacity was probably around the two hundred to two hundred and fifty mark. Tonight it was bursting at the seams! In its previous life it had been a large car showroom, catering for Mercedes-Benz and Jaguar. Now, with really very little work having been required in converting it. It was THE place in Edinburgh to party.

Robert Burns, born on the 25th of January 1759, was proudly regarded as the national poet of Scotland. Each and every year his birthday was faithfully and reverently celebrated throughout the world. From Japan to Russia, the U.S.A to China - dedications, suppers, dancing and impressive recitations would all be in full swing in the coming days for this lyricist, farmer and excise man. Official 'Burns Suppers' were often seen to be boring, stuffy and ostentatious events. Traditionally they were held for the male species only. With each man trying desperately to outdo the other - either in the speaking or drinking stakes.

These days however, people, especially students, want to actively be involved and celebrate his life. Or if truth be told, their own lives. Most, really don't care a jot about the Ayrshire lad. And although recognising him as a great talent of his day, opinion is most probably equally divided on his current role model status and in his treatment of the 'fairer sex.'

Ultimately these particular weekend groups are out on the town partying and want to go somewhere to enjoy themselves. So in and around the 25th of January, that is either done by attending some outstanding musical concerts held to honour Rabbie, or like here in this old revamped warehouse, where he would be hero-worshipped through music and dance. And no ordinary, shallow form of dance either, but that of a high energy, traditional Scottish ceilidh! A ceilidh would typically represent one large gathering - A party or the like, at which singing, dancing and even occasional storytelling would comprise the usual forms of entertainment.

"Take your partners, for the Gay Gordon's," the band leader cried.

Hands were soon joined and held aloft. Male and female, girl with girl and guy with guy. You could hold anyone's hand at a ceilidh. The four piece band were in fine form. Those sitting this one out were still actively participating by stamping their feet furiously. The two accordionists, drummer and fiddle player were clearly accomplished. The main hub of the miniature arena was bouncing. Hands were red raw from clapping. Swaying bodies perspired like water fountains. This was a unique venue and the crowd recognised that and loved it. Even those in the neighbouring residential property had no complaints. Often, they never heard a thing!

"What do you think?" The girl was asked.

Tiny beads of perspiration ran smoothly down her neck, arms and legs. From her waist down she wore the briefest of tartan mini skirts. In equal measure, it was both alluring and revealing? Also, it was visually very distinct in the Clan MacLeod colours. Those were a very recognisable yellow and black, which was why it would often be referred to as the 'bumble bee' tartan. If one looked extra closely though, a faint red line running effortlessly through the material, could also be detected.

Again the quiet voice asked, "So, what do you think?"

The tartan clad lass responded cheerfully. "And you say that they're free?" She double checked.

A smile accompanied the nod. "You just need to walk with me to the car to pick them up. I'm heading off right now, if that's okay. I have one more model named Gillian meeting me this evening. She may actually already be there. So if you can just collect them from my car, that would be a great help and save me a double journey back inside."

The "No problem, that sounds like a plan," was accompanied with a cheerful expression. Excited and with a vibrant, powerful spring in her step, she gracefully approached her new friend's mode of transport. Thirty seconds later, her throat had been garrotted with ruthless precision. The energetic, enthusiastic bounce was long gone. She now lay brutally still, cold and motionless. The significant stench of dried blood and death already hung in the air. The rank odour of murder circulated from within. She had been butchered and discarded without a second thought. Thrown into the back of a dust covered, chalky, functional, seven year old commercial vehicle. Already there in attendance and with rigor mortis about to make an appearance, was her equally, specially chosen modelling companion for the evening, Miss Gillian McLean.

A full twenty-four hours of relative calm had passed before the booming voice echoed out:

"Fair fa' your honest, sonsie face, great chieftain o the puddin'-race! Aboon them a' ye tak your place, painch, tripe, or thairm. Weel are ye worthy o' a grace, as lang's my airm."

Members of Lothian Police had gathered for their annual Burn's Supper and it was in its infancy. Ally Coulter had recently retired and was no longer a fully fledged part of the force. However, he had been invited back especially for tonight because of his 'haggis addressin' skills.' He was in full flow and held court majestically, as raucous laughter followed after each one of his exaggerated verses, or wildly animated arm gestures.

As Coulter made a large mound like movement with his hand over his plate, he accompanied it with - "The groaning trencher there ye fill...... " On cue, Ally then grabbed his unsuspecting buttocks firmly. " ...... your hurdies like a distant mill."

More drunken guffaws ensued. Glasses clinked merrily and whisky odoured palms were being beaten steadily and loudly on tabletops and onto sturdy, sweat stained shoulders and backs. Several legs hastily made their way toward the bar, determined to replenish their low stocks in the spirits department. Other upstanding members of the force strode keenly back for second helpings towards Katie. Katie was the gorgeous female serving up this year's delicious fare. Her small hand-written sign at the front of the kitchen serving hatch, simply stated: 'Mmm delicious. A recipe never to be repeated. Get it while you can!'

The evening was still relatively young. Triangular, tartan bunting hung decoratively from the walls of the hotel's largest function suite. Whilst large oversized Saltire flags merged happily with passionate, red lion rampant's and festooned the room. It was an area that was already bustling and crammed with many of Police Scotland's so-called finest. Although, to Steven Murray, the atmosphere felt rather surreal. It was as if everyone was searching for some much needed light relief, and for many tonight, that solace would no doubt be found at the bottom of a glass. For others, it would require the emptying of a whole bottle or two. Young DC Andrew 'Kid' Curry had just downed his third whisky. He was looking rather on edge Murray observed from a distance. The 'Kid's colleague Susan 'Hanna' Hayes, just shook her head vehemently and offered a look of genuine disappointment toward her partner.

The mixed mood in the room could have been forensically traced back to earlier in the day. To when several of the officers in attendance, had been present at a belated memorial service for one of their previous DCI's. The occasion itself, had not been recognised or sanctioned by the force and the man in question was most certainly not being honoured. But many of his ex-colleagues felt as a mark of respect toward his family, the very least that they could do was to put in an appearance. Murray, who had been a close family friend for years was treated like a pariah. He even received a face full of musty, cloud coloured spit for his trouble. The avalanche of glob was delivered, courtesy of the so-called grieving widow. She remained exceptionally bitter about everything. So considering it was Inspector Steven Murray that had brought her husband to justice and ultimately held him to account, he may personally feel he got off rather lightly.

Six months previously, Detective Chief Inspector Keith Brown had been awaiting trial for corruption, money laundering and a range of sexual assault charges. As a high ranking police officer for several years and still seen by many in the Scottish judicial system as a man of good standing. He was, like all, assumed innocent until proven guilty - and having been assessed as being of no imminent threat to others - he was subsequently and correctly released on bail.

The twist in that particular tail though, was the fact that seven other accused alongside him as part of the TIME/

ABC Casino case, were also members of the Scottish legal system. One judge, four lawyers and two staff from the Procurators Fiscal office. 142 people in total had been arrested in connection with the sex trafficking ring that had operated throughout the UK and were still awaiting trial. Numerous others on a variety of membership lists were still being investigated and vetted.

Needless to say, James Baxter Reid was not one of them. He was never caught on camera and managed somehow, yet again, to evade the police that raided the scene. Murray suspected that he WAS most likely handcuffed, then escorted down to the front door and off the premises by one of Lothians finest. But sadly, possibly one that earns a little extra on the side each month, aiding and abetting the affairs of one 'Bunny' Reid. Once safely outside, the handcuffs had no doubt been removed, and as they say… the rest is history!

Anyhow, three short weeks ago, after Brown's arrest, the disgraced DCI set off on a quick, five minute car journey. The brief drive from his plush upmarket Colinton residence, took him to his desired destination at Edinburgh Park train station. It would be from here that several months later, cats, dogs and various other four-legged vermin, would still be picking up and licking at the remnants of his bones. Those fine, slender, near invisible slivers that had been missed by trained forensic officers, after Keith Brown had went head to head that morning, with the Glasgow bound ten-forty express train

TWO

"All is quiet on New Year's Day. A world in white gets underway. Nothing changes on New Year's Day. I will be with you again. I will be with you again."

- U2

As he leaned deep in thought against the busy function room doorway, DI Murray pondered the famous words of the individual being honoured during the evening and how they related directly to the late Detective Chief Inspector. The so-called 'gentleman' that we reverently call our National Bard had penned... *'Should auld acquaintance be forgot and never brought to mind?'* Definitely food for thought Murray reckoned.

Speaking of food - Coulter finished off his vocal rendition and visual masterclass with a crystal decanter clasped tightly in his right palm. Of those present, probably only his close friend and confidante Steven Murray knew that it was filled with 'apple juice!' This clearly made Coulter's monologue even funnier to his old pal. Because 'Ally' appeared to be getting more and more tipsy with every passing word. As the retired detective carefully put down the expensive looking transparent container, he remained silent for an impressive three second pause. He had the whole crowd's attention now, exactly as he had planned. And to finish off his delivery with style and panache, the bold 'Ally' Coulter, now swaying merrily from side to side, held his glass high above his head and voiced slowly and deliberately: "Auld Scotland wants nae skinking ware - that jaups in luggies. But if ye wish her gratefu' prayer - Gie her a Haggis!"

Glasses were quickly refilled and raised. Officers (those who still could) stood proudly, and unitedly raised their glasses high into the air once again and offered the immortal centuries old toast: "Tae a Haggis!"

Whilst the well behaved members of Her Majesty's constabulary had been enjoying their annual Burn's Supper. A short distance along the coast...

'Her name is Rio and she dances on the sand...'

Her arms did not seem to be in rhythm with the music. They were flailing wildly and had an uncontrollable recklessness to them.

'Just like that river twisting through a dusty land.'

Her legs also struggled to keep the beat. They were tapping ultra fast and too frequently. Randomly and indiscriminately lashing out.

'And when she shines she really shows you all she can.'

In fairness to Debbie Griggs, when you have an exceptionally thin nylon wire squeezed tightly around your neck and it's choking you to death - It is normally impossible to sit very still!

'Oh Rio, Rio dance across the Rio Grande.'

Adjusting the strap on her shoe, she had only just relaxed and sat back in the front passenger seat of the van. She had been told they were parked at the rear of the club so that they would have privacy for the photographs. At the time that seemed to make sense to Miss Griggs, who had been busy flicking her locks and getting prepared for her exclusive photoshoot.

Here she was, yet another kind samaritan. A volunteer model willing to help out a complete stranger, only to be ambushed by the deceit, depravity and evil of the world. As soon as she placed her dark hair upon the headrest, within a second, the flex, cord or whatever it was, had been thrust firmly around Deborah's tender throat from behind. That was when the librarian's feet first began to break into a frenzy and go berserk. The underside of the glove compartment took the brunt of it. As her bare shins continually rattled off it, blood quickly began to pour steadily from those wounds due to the ferocity of her striking out. Her body raised from her seat. She seemed to be levitating, such was the pressure and force being applied from behind. The young woman writhed hysterically and struggled incessantly. Determined not to be beaten, she then groped desperately at the air for something, anything at all to lash or smash into her assailant.

At that moment, her right hand connected to the handbrake.

- 'Click, click, click,' - Like her throat, the brake became tighter and even more intense. As if in autopilot, her fight or flight response again kicked in. For whatever reason and in unison, she immediately pushed the button in with her thumb, and the lever down with her forearm. All parties appeared to hesitate for a brief second. The wire relaxed, her legs seemed to freeze and the car... Nothing.

I'm going to die, she thought. Then as the depth of the cut in her neckline increased, as her gurgling, frothing and choking intensified, a strange sensation was felt. The vehicle had been parked on a slight slope. The handbrake had been released after all and gradually it had begun to roll forward. Was it really happening? Perhaps it was just events continuing to spin around in her mind. But no, ever so slightly, her senses confirmed it was most definitely moving. Griggs sputtered, coughed and exploded with saliva as she desperately tried to spit out coherent words or make sounds. By now though her attacker had relinquished their grip on the wire and was furiously wrapping both hands back around the handbrake. One almighty pull… TTRRRRRR, and it was back pointing sharply at the darkened grey, ever threatening sky above.

Having just experienced the fight scenario. The endangered curator of literature was now in full flight. She had managed to open the door and had stubbornly scrambled out, sure and adamant that she was surviving this evening. Her legs though were unable to hoist her to her feet. Paralysed through fear, nervous energy or whatever, she tried once again to stand. It would be close. No one was around. She had instinctively dragged herself up and was making her way back around to the front of the club. The sound of the van's engine purred softly and intimidatingly in the cold night air. As Deborah Griggs reached the bottom of the small gradient her mind was gone. She could no longer interpret fact from fiction. As the powerful purity of the headlights came toward her, she thought she had initially sidestepped being part of a Stephen King novel. Where in reality, she was now right at the centre of the horrific plot.

Would the driver/photographer have time to reassess his plan? Would he stick to his routine or were things going to have to change?

Lee Child was famous for writing his 'Jack Reacher' series as he went along. Changing the start, middle and end as he wrote. He found it exciting and empowering. He was in control of all the suspense and it ensured that he never gave away any of the storyline, as it changed so frequently from day to day and hour to hour. If and when the need arose, the British born author could take you by surprise, as his thoughts and plan of attack would change frequently... at the final second!

The attractive female soon had her answer. The vehicle never slowed. It's lights only seemed to intensify as it increased its speed and headed straight for the bedraggled and desperate, half dead woman. In one last hopeless act of audacious despair, Griggs held her trembling, badly injured, yet well manicured hands out in front of herself - desperately seeking more powerful help. Internally begging, pleading and praying mercifully for the oncoming van to stop. By now the heartless driver could see her bruised and battle scarred body. Her hands and legs were covered in a rich blanket of crimson. The stream of blood had seeped continuously from her neck wound, across her chest and flowed down over her marked thighs. Deep cuts and abrasions to her injured wrists, knees and ankles contributed to the overwhelming squall of red.

In an instant it was all over. The lights faded, the sound of the engine died down and the driver at the very last moment...... swerved violently and avoided the maimed reveller.

A last minute reprieve. What were the chances? A loving God or Lee Child? Either way she was so, so grateful and would be at church that Sunday and purchasing a few 'Jack Reacher' novels, by way of hedging her bets!

It's scary the driver thought. To think that one day we're going to have to live without our mother or father, or husband or wife. Or that one day, we're going to have to walk this earth without our best friend by our side, or them without us. We really should appreciate our loved ones while we can.

Having just given someone an instant stay of execution, our driver continued to ponder - *Because, none of us are going to be here forever.* "Tha neart teaghlaich, mar neart arm, na laighe na dìlseachd," they offered.

It had taken our learned librarian a few extra seconds to compose herself. She had initially dropped to her knees with acute discomfort and tightly closed her swollen eyes. Badly marked, bruised and bloodied and still fighting relentlessly for air, she began to slowly rediscover herself. She was alive and realised fully, just at that moment, in that instant, how lucky she had been and how thankful she was. Diminutive tears of joy, relief and gratitude slowly began to trickle briefly down her gasping cheeks. Just how close to dying had she actually come? Did her last gasp prayer make a difference? If so, and that was how quickly and efficiently the Lord answered prayers… she would be in attendance every week from now on, not just this coming week!

Aching from every joint and intent on protecting her neck from the prevailing wind and elements, she hobbled around the corner more determined than ever. Determined firstly to alert the police. Determined to bring her attacker to justice and finally, determined to let her loved ones know just how much she really……… BANG!!!!!

Deborah Griggs' ravaged frame was dramatically thrown ten to fifteen feet, high into the chilly evening air. The van had accelerated upon impact and had no lights on. The callous driver checked carefully once again that there was no one visibly around. They then immediately jumped out from behind the steering wheel. At pace they walked over toward the twisted limbs that lay motionless on the deserted roadside. This depraved individual firstly checked to ensure there was no pulse. Then, hurriedly placed something in the region of her lap. One would guess that the crazed psychopath had turned out to be a Lee Child fan after all. Poor Deborah Griggs - not so much!

Only a minute or two could have gone by before a group of keen partygoers with a mission, each one desperately in need of a nicotine fix, vacated the premises. Together they stumbled across the broken body, interspersed with fragments of shattered glass. At least one of the group had the wisdom, good sense and sobriety to call the emergency services.

The police did nothing to help me all those years ago. But I'm not bitter, I believe fully in sharing. Tonight they are all entitled to a small piece of the action 'that jaups in luggies!' They will have to head off home soon. I suspect they are going to be in for a very busy and eventful few days.

It was two hours later and the self-indulgent hero worshipping was beginning to wind down. The Blackhall House Hotel on the Leith waterfront had been chosen mainly due to the fact it had a wonderful function suite. One the perfect size for hosting a State banquet. Fortunately there was no royalty in attendance. However, many in 'officialdom' were bleary-eyed and sat passed out at their gold upholstered seats. Others were slumped forward with 'neeps and tatties' in their hair. Two or three had vanished to the bathroom to throw up once again. Upset stomachs they claimed. Their overindulgence with the alcohol never even got a mention as a possible culprit. A young PC had vomited over the tartan Axminster in the adjoining lounge, and those actions registered a full seven out of ten on the amusement scale with DI Murray. He reckoned that sallow faced constable would definitely get 'carpeted' in the morning. Ironically no doubt, by one of those perfect role models currently displaying 'haggis' highlights! The sheer travesty made him smile. He then carefully continued to monitor proceedings around the well established hotel. 'Established,' could easily have been the operational code word that evening for - 'old and rundown.'

An assortment of suit jackets that didn't match trousers were being drunkenly entered into. Some with ill fitting shirt sleeves protruding. Others with individuals wondering just how much they'd eaten, as their *'weel-swall'd kytes were bent lyke drums.'* Thus numerous jackets were unable to be buttoned up. As one of the very few sober individuals on the scene, Steven Murray found it hilarious to watch these shenanigans. He soon discovered that there was even a select few amongst his police hierarchy who genuinely, after several toasts, could not understand how this uniquely Scottish dish - had made them magically slur their words!

"Inshpecktur shir," one overly familiar colleague greeted Murray, slapping him emphatically on the back. "How's shings. That rare wis a night no great eh? Dis that Burns guy shtill write the odd word ur two? Whit de ye reckon big man… Does 'e?"

Murray was certain that in his own grog filled mind, that smiling young man with the honey-roast glazed eyes was indeed speaking the Queen's English. However… before he could finish that thought, Coulter had stuffed a wad of fresh smelling business cards into his old boss's hand.

"What do you think Stevie boy?"

Murray's instant thought was, at least I can understand what you are saying!

"Looking good Ally. They give off an essence of excitement. So no regrets then?"

"With the retirement you mean?"

Murray nodded.

"No, no the time was right Steve. I'd had a good run, I've got a healthy pension and this new adventure will allow me to keep my hand in. And you are right, it is exciting. I should have possibly taken this step sooner!"

Murray stared at the selection of colourful, glossy blue cardboard pieces in his hand. He picked one up, turned it over and began to read it as if announcing the latest cinema blockbuster. "Coulter Investigations. Private Detective for Hire. With not a minute to waste - We'll be on the case!" Ally's mobile and email completed the text on the card.

Both men's eyes met up - fully recognised, 'corny' when they heard it… and laughed loudly in unison.

Then as they physically bent over in merriment, Murray's phone rang. It was two minutes after 11pm. He answered it, briefly responded and put it away again.

"Need to go 'Ally,' that was 'Sandy.' In good old Taggart terminology…"

"There's been a murder," Coulter finished off.

"Indeed there has," Murray said. "Speak to you soon."

"Remember," 'Ally' shouted. "Quick as you can… There's not a minute to waste!"

He could hear Steven Murray howl with laughter as he quickly exited out the doorway.

As the Detective Inspector drove at speed toward Ocean Terminal, where the Royal Yacht Britannia was berthed. He momentarily reflected on Sergeant Robert 'Ally' Coulter, their friendship and what the future held for him. These past twelve months especially, had been challenging to say the least. It had been just over a year ago that 'Ally' had witnessed first hand, his friend and partner DC Tasmin Taylor have her throat cut. That had clearly been traumatic for 'Ally' and took its toll, as it would have for anyone. The Sergeant had tried to quit then, but Murray had encouraged him to take some well deserved gardening leave and re-evaluate everything. Since his return though, which had been infrequent at best. He had only managed a few weeks on, then a few weeks off. His demeanour, his nature, his bubbly personality and even his charismatic style had dramatically changed.

Murray, his friend for over twenty years had probably noticed it more than anyone else. His passion, his enthusiasm, his dogged determination seemed to have gone off on vacation and never returned. So in October, after helping sign off on all the DCI Brown/Anderson/Latchford sex ring fiasco, he then handed in his three month notice. That made his intention, official. This time DI Steven Murray never tried to dissuade him. Both parties remained silent. They knew it was the correct course of action and their special bond survived intact. On the 31st of December 2015 and after three decades in the job, the hands on the clock struck midnight. Sergeant Robert Coulter retired and on that New Year's Day - his life was to change forever.

THREE

"Ocean Drive - Don't know why you're so blue. He left you black and blue, without a word of explanation."

- The Lighthouse Family

In a small lane just off to the west of the sprawling Sir Terence Conran designed shopping centre in the port of Leith, lay the body of twenty-two year old Gillian McLean. Forensics officers had arrived twenty minutes before Murray and one of their familiar tents signalling death, had already been established and set up.

Several miles east along the rugged coastline, in a densely populated forest on the outskirts of North Berwick, another tent had also been erected. The lone occupant of this particular canvas would be staying overnight however. Throughout the evening, at regular intervals, he would double check to ensure that no one else was in the vicinity. Back under cover he sat wiping, cleaning, calibrating and adjusting. A quiet, delicate low ping from his phone informed him that he'd received a text. It read: *Glasgow flat now ready. Proceed as planned.*

A row of four smiley faces and a thumbs up completed the message.

Back at Ocean terminal, Murray had looked to get an early update from Sergeant 'Sandy' Kerr. He soon spotted his good friend, head pathologist Dr Thomas Patterson retrieve equipment from his car. With his beautiful Irish brogue the doctor would often be referred to as 'The T'inker.' This was due, like many of Irish descent to their uncanny ability not to pronounce the t.h. in t'ose words!

"On shift tonight then Doc?" Murray asked.

"Well, sure I'm not out here for a bit of late night shopping Steven am I?"

"And a very good evening to you also. Ya moanin' faced, grumpy, Irish rat-bag!"

Both men grinned, glad they had gotten their normal pleasantries out of the way early. On his return back to the starched white forensics tent, Murray then met up with DS Sandra Kerr who had just arrived on the scene, along with DC Joseph Hanlon. Nods were exchanged between the trio of officers. 1, 2, 3 - Greeting over.

"Gillian McLean - age 22, trainee teacher," Kerr informed them. "Currently was on a placement nearby at Craighall Primary School. She lives in a flat at Portobello."

"Lived!" Hanlon gently added.

"Well, yes," Kerr agreed solemnly. "Obviously."

Whilst the forensics team scraped, prodded, photographed and measured. The three detective's took a few quiet moments to make the scene personal to them. They viewed the body carefully. She was blonde haired and wore only a silk top and shoes. Kerr was still uncertain as to whether the deep blue garment was meant as a daring short skirt or a classy, fashionable blouse?

"No jacket, handbag or phone Sarge?" Hanlon questioned.

"Well, no…" Kerr began.

"Because she was DUMPED here!" the Inspector added wisely.

"Certainly looks that way sir. However, her purse was only a few feet away. Possibly thrown out after her," Sandra Kerr suggested. "That was what gave us photographic proof of who she was."

"Clumsy or deliberate? Either way they obviously wanted us to be able to identify her quickly. Do me a favour Sandy," Murray continued. "Ensure that Hayes and Curry are both in bright and early in the morning. Get them doing some legwork around here. CCTV monitors, street cams, maybe a little door to door. Unlikely we'll find anything of note I know. But worth checking out nonetheless."

"Will do sir."

The hands-on Inspector continued to delegate tasks. "My dear 'Sherlock,' get your deerstalker looked out and at first light tomorrow start digging."

As DC Hanlon offered a thumbs up to his boss, Sandra Kerr headed off and all three were back at their respective homes within the hour. It was officially Saturday - 1.10am.

A month earlier, the well educated Gillian McLean had treated herself to a special festive Christmas gift, although it was for this upcoming Springtime. She was preparing to spend 16 days volunteering at a kid's school and orphanage in Kenya. That gift was all about giving. Her upbringing was all about giving. Gillian McLean was all about giving. She loved and adored children. Hence her lifelong desire to be a schoolteacher. It was either that or 'Mary Poppins' she had figured growing up.

Having been brought up in upmarket Giffnock, a leafy suburban town in East Renfrewshire, she was the fifth child in a large family of seven. Four girls and three boys born alternatively. What wonderfully balanced planning by her considerate parents. Her incredible mother, Anna, had stayed at home throughout her married life to bring up and raise the 'magnificent' seven." And she had been in her element doing so. Her father Bob on the other hand, was Gillian's role model, mentor and inspiration. He had taught in the well respected Eastwood High School for over three decades. Even throughout Gillian's teenage years there. Unfortunately however, during the school holidays of 2013, just as a new, modern, state of the art school building was set to open in the August, Robert Halpern McLean passed away. A massive, fatal heart attack at home in his favourite armchair on a late July evening was to see him depart this mortal earth.

One calendar month later, in their new 'Giffnock Academy' premises, over 700 people attended a memorial service for the man. There was standing room only in the 'spanking' new assembly hall. Pupils past and present had gathered to pay their individual respects. Former colleagues and fellow teachers were amongst those in attendance. A select few of his ex-students had been out of school for over a quarter of a century, but their most inspiring and favourite teacher 'Mr McLean,' had kept in touch with them throughout the various stages of their careers and family life. He had never stopped caring. He was an exceptional role model and an exceptional man. The overwhelming number of individuals desirous to be at his service and to lend support to the family, bore true unexaggerated testimony to that fact.

None of the McLean children stayed at home any longer and the two youngest were currently both students in halls of residence. Anthony was busy studying at St. Andrews and the baby of the family, 'Sam,' short for Samantha, attended Abertay University in the City of Discovery - Dundee.

Heartbroken as her grieving mother Anna was at receiving the shocking news regarding the death of her daughter, Murray was also later informed that she was somewhat relieved, that her late husband did not have to experience this awful anguish and pain.

"All Gillian ever wanted, was to continually help children fulfil their undoubted potential," the distraught mother had confided in the two west coast officers who broke the news to her at her home in Giffnock. "To help them gain a self-believe in themselves. Instill a quiet confidence and determination to succeed. To enable them to find their own voice, to speak up, to offer an opinion. To simply be courageous and bold. She was a giver you know," Mrs McLean had again reiterated before becoming inconsolable.

Those scenes, quotes and news had all been relayed back to DI Murray. A man that believed 90% of all teachers were givers. You really had to be, he thought. Otherwise you would have never entered into that profession in the first place. However, that also made him instantly reflect and ask - Why then do people join the police force? As the right and left hand sides of his brain were about to enter into a frenzied debate on the matter, Murray shut them both down as only he could.

"Oh what fun we had, but at the time it seemed so bad. Trying different ways, to make a difference to the days. Baggy trousers, baggy trousers, baggy trousers..." Madness he thought, sheer madness.

Lying back, shattered, on his leather settee. He was about to set off on another emotional rollercoaster. His cauldron of thoughts turned quickly to finding justice for that young girl's family. She had been most definitely a giver. So, 'giving back' answers to her family, was the very least the broken system could offer up in return. Now crystal clear in his mind and actions, the debate was over before it had even really begun!

A certain young master Murray was always regarded in High School as the official 'class clown.' From those early teenage years however, he would often remark on - How the persona of a clown fascinated and informed him. It was the colourful, yet dark character's constant change of emotional and physical balance. How he was able to go about as an unhindered perpetrator of chaos. The DI loved that description - 'perpetrator of chaos.' It was quite simply as if the rules of society did not apply. The Inspector then introspectively reflected carefully on several of his recent actions and wondered if his own alter ego was beginning to apply those same parameters? For Murray, whose star sign was Libra, was it time to measure his own internal scales? The legendary figure of the clown epitomised the creative balance between disarray and resolution. Was the west coast maverick, yet again about to make another highly dubious decision. One that he would later come to so fully regret?

The drowsy voice on the other end of the line was angry.

"Murray what the… I was sound asleep man."

The Detective Inspector let him have his expletive filled rant. After all, it was in the very early part of the morning.

"Are you quite finished?"

Several more choice obscenities were hurled through the phone line.

He allowed one last volley of abuse before loudly interrupting. "I have a job for you!"

Silence.

"You, you Mr Murray? You have a job for me?" The man repeated. His voice was slow, deliberate and uncertain at what he was actually hearing.

"Is your hearing failing you these days Ray?"

Another round of silence.

"Ray!"

"Aye, I'm here Mr Murray." He slowed again. "It's just…" He was wary…

"Do you want the job or not Ray?"

In an irrational tone the voice offered up: "In fairness Mr Murray, normally I'm only keeping you in the loop with anything I hear for a bit of pin money. I don't usually get work offers from you and certainly not the kind of job proposal I suspect you're looking for. I take it, it is a…"

"It is!" Murray cut in. "So meet me at our usual spot. Two o'clock later this afternoon."

FOUR

"You've got a friend in me, you've got a friend in me. When the road looks rough ahead and you're miles and miles from your nice warm bed. You just remember what your old pal said. Boy, you've got a friend in me."

- Randy Newman

As dawn broke on the Saturday morning. Dense, heavy cloud had all but disappeared and East Lothian was experiencing some bright blue skies overhead. Although it had to be said, it was bitterly cold as the wind whipped in from the sea. The athletic looking man, kitted out in army fatigues chose two large, aged beech trees that were reasonably close together on the outskirts of the wood to pin his posters upon.

Historically the offering on displayed would have been: 'Lost cat,' 'Lost dog,' or even 'Reward offered.' However in more recent times, we have come to expect: 'Overweight?' 'Revolutionary diet shakes!' 'Earn thousands - call now!' Realistically though, temporary bulletin boards in remote Scottish woodlands would never actually help discover the whereabouts of 'little Trixie, ugly Rover or assist greatly in big Senga's weight loss.

However on this occasion, the solitude and isolation was ideal to try out Mr Barrett, his newly acquired friend. On show was a male face. Nothing more, nothing less. No header, no title, no detail or instruction. A small photograph had obviously been enlarged to standard A4 photocopy size, the 'Print' button called into action and *hey presto!*

As the first fierce whip sounded, the non-threatening face on the crisp, photographic sheet, instantaneously disintegrated. The shooter then impressively swivelled his shoulder toward the neighbouring tree. He was easily two hundred metres away from what had been a happy, smiling countenance on the xeroxed paper. A slight adjustment by finger and there once again, was the red laser dot he had adapted the rifle to accept. It was directly centred on the image forehead. Another deafening 'crack,' echoed throughout the barren woodland, as the second bullet exploded at speed and safely entrenched itself in tree number two.

Mr Barrett, the M99 in question, was a single-shot, long range precision rifle. By no means would it have been the man's first choice. But given the time sensitive contract he'd accepted, the powerful weapon would suffice. Generally speaking it would have been used in the main, for so-called 'hard' targets like armoured vehicles, convoy patrols, etc. 'Soft' targets, such as individuals hiding behind seemingly invincible brick walls however, would also be in for an almighty and often unwelcome surprise, when these big, bold, bad guys were fully unleashed.

After helping the forestry commission cut down four more beautiful scenic trees, his practice session was over.

Elsewhere the razor was drawn delicately across the skin. This had become a favourite time of year. The police had no clue what was going on and tonight would be a busy one for them - 'Tha neart teaghlaich' was then uttered in Scots Gaelic.

The violent, ear piercing sound of shattered glass was heard first. Then officers in the nearby corridor held their breath in anticipation at the time honoured expected follow up - loud abusive shouting, complete with expletives and unsavoury language! A second or two passed quietly. Oh well, maybe not they...

"Giant freaking poppadoms!" Came the angry, yet almost polite yell. The high pitched, nasal voice continued furiously with, "Pastel coloured verrucas." Before finally trailing off more timidly with an apologetic, "Biloxi blues!"

Different, very different Steven Murray thought as he walked cautiously toward the office and nodded a number 71 (this should be interesting). He was familiar with some of the quirks and traits of his female colleague in the room. Especially her continual challenge to eradicate bad language from her vocabulary.

She had joined the force when it was top heavy with male counterparts and to become one of the boys, she ended up speaking like them. Much to her own personal regret. Over the years Murray had been involved in several cases with her. Mainly when she had been a DI based in Musselburgh. That was when she had started to offer up alternative words in place of crass obscenities. In the politically correct world that we currently inhabit, there is no place 'officially' for abusive or filthy language. And considering on first meeting her, you would think butter wouldn't melt in her mouth, it was refreshing to hear some of her latest substitutions.

Murray's delicate, yet rather hungry stomach growled intensely. He had deliberately missed breakfast and headed straight into work for an early start on his latest case. It must have been the thought of those 'giant poppadoms,' he smiled. With a two o'clock lunch meeting already scheduled, he would chew some gum and hold off until then. Although, with an almighty headache looming, that was possibly not such a great idea.

Starting today, unusually on a Saturday, DCI Barbra Furlong had been transferred in full time to take take over from the late departed and discredited Keith Brown. The team had coped admirably throughout the latter half of the year. Having been allocated a couple of acting DCI's in the interim. They had both covered for approximately three or four months each and that was when the bad habit had been formed, or resurfaced may have been closer to the truth. The waiting for the volley of verbal abuse to follow suite from the aforementioned room. Unfortunately, the bottom line was that those on temporary secondment were never really fully invested in the team. And as such, they simply held the fort and as is often the case, left behind a rather dispirited, poor legacy.

"There will be a brush in his cupboard. Sorry, the cupboard Ma'am," Murray quickly corrected. "DCI Brown liked everything spick and span. I think you may find every cleaning invention known to man hiding in there."

The broken vase lay smashed to smithereens across the carpet, as a rather red-faced Barbra Furlong stood in the centre of the room, feeling rather exposed. Her elegant, thin, uniformed frame was in the midst of apprehensively placing down a large and mightily impressive bouquet of gorgeous flowers.

"Ah, DI Murray isn't it?"

She knew fine well it was.

"At your service," he bowed and gallantly rolled his arm. "We thought it would be Monday before we saw you Ma'am?"

"Please call me Barbra, Inspector," she offered in a friendly, understated manner.

And that's not going to happen, Murray thought to himself.

"Yes, yes, Steven isn't it? Most people expect you to start on a Monday. But everything and everyone is so busy catching up with the weekend backlog and preparing for the week ahead. So here I am, two days early. Ready, willing and able."

"And I see that you've got off to a smashing start!" Murray felt comfortable enough to joke.

His new Detective Chief Inspector bowed her head in his direction, smiled sheepishly and whilst gesturing toward the mess on the floor said, "Well actually, this could all be attributed as your fault DI Murray."

Murray's eyes widened and his shoulders froze. He had no idea where this was headed.

"Thank you so much for the flowers," she then added. Pointing instantly over at the black leather chair in the corner of her room. And there, sure enough, sat yet another very distinctive and artfully arranged, luxurious bouquet of exquisite blooms. In fact, they were twice the size of those she currently held!

"That was very, very generous and exceptionally thoughtful of you. Though, there was really no need," she added.

It was DI Murray's turn to feel slightly awkward, vulnerable and extremely exposed. Had this anything to do with the 'Call me Barbra' remark?

He soon became rather flushed in response. "It was the least WE could do," he emphasised. "From ALL of the team," he felt the need to reiterate. "WE are ALL looking forward to working closely with you Ma'am and congratulations on the promotion." His voice had accelerated rapidly as he concluded. "Now let's get that mess dealt with. First things first!"

Murray vanished into the 'cleaning' cupboard like a shot. Sure enough, inside there was a matching brush and pan that would cope admirably with the shards of broken glass. And no surprise, lo and behold there was even a replacement ceramic container for the other flowers. Murray immediately lifted it out and placed it carefully on to her desk.

Calmer now, her voice was warm, smooth and informative as she extolled: "Did you know Inspector, spick and span was first found in Samuel Pepys' Diary in 1665?"

The vase was tall, bright and breezy. It would be the ideal replacement - just as Steven Murray now knew DCI Barbra 'No Bleedin' Swearing' Furlong, was also going to be!

In the previous twelve months Murray's squad had lost two valuable team members. To promotion and pregnancy he was okay with. Premature death whilst working in the line of duty... not so much!

Tasmin Taylor had everything to live for. Killed without a shadow of a doubt by James Baxter Reid. However, Mark Ziola one of Reid's trusted lieutenants, copped a guilty plea to all his crimes and there were no further proceedings taken against the newly suited and booted career criminal. The man with the Polish ancestry, died only eight months later of cancer. A diagnosis that he had only co-incidentally been given, one month before he pled guilty to the series of murders that Reid was wanted in connection with.

More recently, Detective Constable Machur 'Mac' Rasul had been guilty of sheer inexperience, naivety and over enthusiasm. His dogged determination to prove himself to Murray and his new colleagues, ultimately became his downfall. Although a large African spear, viciously impaled in his upper torso, was the actual culprit.

This Monday coming, two full days after DCI Furlong officially started, would also see the arrival of Rasul's long overdue replacement. Murray recognised that DC Linda Rennie had managed admirably for five months. But that was always to be on a temporary basis, as she herself then went on maternity leave two weeks ago. As the Inspector sat purposefully at his desk going over the paperwork for his newest team member. He knew that Sergeant Sandra Kerr would also be genuinely excited to hopefully have a long term partner once again. A line that her loving husband Richard was not overly keen to hear her express!

Scanning briefly throughout the pages of Glaswegian Detective Constable Allan Boyd's paperwork, Murray suddenly felt a presence at his side.

'Sherlock,' had arrived.

"Morning!" DC Hanlon offered, with a bright and breezy demeanour.

Murray nodded (a long number 26 - delighted to see you also).

"Couple of relevant issues sir. The first of which is a bit of background on our young trainee school teacher."

"I'm listening." Murray said keenly, as he ran his lengthy fingers across his chin. He had always come to expect something that little bit extra from DC Hanlon's background checks. So he proceeded to sit forward in his chair, elbows on knees and hands being rubbed in anticipation of the juicy bits.

"Sitting comfortably?" Hanlon checked as he rested against Murray's desk for support.

"Get on with it Joe. Some of us have real work to do," he snapped.

Steady on. Geez what rattled his cage Joe Hanlon thought. Not like him to be so abrupt. Even on his bad days he is generally well mannered and courteous. Hanlon then unfolded his arms and began.

"Gillian McLean. Twenty two. Lived in a rented, one bedroomed flat in Rossie Place, Portobello. Had been there roughly six months. Originally from Giffnock in Renfrewshire. Brought up there from birth. Her late father was a school teacher. She was the fifth child in a family of seven. She has, had," he corrected himself, "three sisters and three brothers."

"And?" Murray said.

"And what?" Replied 'Sherlock.'

Murray gave him a look that would have frozen molten lava!

"And her mother Anna is on her way here today to identify the body."

"And…" Murray again said knowingly.

Detective Constable Hanlon rose up from the desk, stared Murray in the eye and forcefully delivered. "And when are we going out for lunch today?" he smiled.

That threw him. He certainly wasn't expecting that. Nor was he ready for it.

DI Steven Murray now looked rather guiltily at 'Sherlock.'
"Aah, yes, lunch," he hesitated, gnawing at his lip and making an apologetic face.

"What! You can't make it. Do you have a hot date?"

"Well, something like…"

"You do!" Hanlon jumped in.

"It's not really…"

"Furlong? I'll bet it is! It's with DCI Furlong," he announced in a none too quiet tone. Causing others in the office to sharply turn around and offer questioning looks.

"What! No! Of course not."

Several more pairs of eyes gazed upon them. They had heard. Clearly heard, the mischievous suggestion.

"You wily old fox you. She's just through the door. First flowers, then…"

"No, I never sent her flowers, I wouldn't." He paused awkwardly, "I mean I would, but I didn't…"

Joe Hanlon had suddenly went silent and was now looking over DI Murray's left shoulder toward the doorway.

Murray's shoulders slumped. He had seen this happen so often in the movies. People entered into frantic dialogue, compromising things were said, even awkwardly misconstrued and they then continued to dig their ditch deeper and deeper. Whilst during all this time the focus of their remarks, the main attraction and star of the show, was stood larger than life, silently poised behind them. They had indeed been listening intently and had been privy to every single embarrassing word spoken. The DI knew at that moment, that this was going to be absolute torture.

Detective Constable Hanlon quickly lowered his head and uttered, "Sir!" As he brushed passed his mentor and made his way smartly out of the office.

Detective Inspector Murray meanwhile, could only raise his shoulders, broaden his chest and accept the inevitable. He blew out his rosy red cheeks and offered, "Ma'am," as a starting point, before turning around to greet... to greet... to greet no one!

The only figure belonged to one grinning Joseph Hanlon. He stood, leaning smugly against the doorframe and sighed: "Ahhh, that was good. So good, so refreshing - So enjoy your secret rendezvous," he then offered dismissively. Just as he went to head off, he stopped suddenly, as if only realising a possibility. He then slowly turned back around and asked DI Murray one more question. And although short, it was posed in a concerned and genuinely thoughtful manner.

"Is it Jayne Golden?"

Murray's whole demeanour changed instantly at the mere mention of the lady, who months previously had begun to steal and repair his broken heart. Only for her to disappear, before being allegedly involved in the DCI Brown/sex slave case. To what degree, that had never been fully established. The Inspector turned sharply toward Hanlon and stared him in the eye for several seconds before finally responding. He initially went to open his mouth, but decided against it. He simply shook his head in a saddened, rueful manner.

"Sorry, for bringing that up sir. Apologies," Joe muttered, now feeling stupid.

Murray shrugged and had already forgotten the embarrassment that DC Hanlon had inflicted upon him thirty seconds previously.

"Oh, before I go. Just one last thing regarding Gillian McLean."

Murray's eyes narrowed.

"She had been a Renfrew and District highland dance champion in her teenage years. Hope that helps."

As the mischievous Joseph 'Sherlock' Hanlon rapidly ran for the hills! DC Allan Boyd's personnel folder came flying through the air like an Exocet missile, with it's sights fixed firmly on its target!

FIVE

"My heart was broken, my heart was broken. You saw it. You claimed it. You touched it. You saved it. While the Chief puts Sunshine on Leith - I'll thank him for his work and your birth and my birth."

- The Proclaimers

At 11.30am Mrs Anna McLean had arrived to identify her daughters body. Sandra Kerr had been assigned to accompany her.

The female officer met a restless Mrs McLean in the warmth of a police interview room at the station. As the lady from the outskirts of Glasgow sat down. 'Sandy' could see by her uncomfortable body language that she was confused by where she was and who she was meeting with.

"Sergeant, I don't understand," the grieving mother said, as she opened her palms to encircle the room and question her surroundings.

"Relax yourself, let me explain things for you Mrs McLean. Firstly though, was your travel through from the West okay?" Kerr asked by way of deflection.

"Sure, yes, no problem," the woman said. Nervously wringing her hands on every syllable. Her eyes still darted warily around the room.

"You know we could have come to you to do this?" The police officer established.

"The identification? Yes it was explained to me. By

photograph, but not the body," she confirmed softly. "However, I wanted to see my Gillian one last time," her voice quivered and trembled.

Sandy' was just grateful that Gillian McLean had not been savagely beaten to death. Her face had remained largely unscathed and she would be the picture of peaceful contentment that her mother had hopefully imagined.

"You know that identifying a body in real life is really nothing like that on TV or film," Kerr told her in a positive manner. "They would have you believe that you'd be led into a cold, stainless steel morgue and a body would be pulled out of the freezer right before your eyes."

The mother listened intently, carefully taking on board the sincerity of the remarks.

"And that is only after some highly tattooed, multi-pierced, Bruce Springsteen fan, turned the volume down long enough on 'The Boss,' to treat your loved one's corpse like a frozen Hawaiian pizza."

A faint glimmer of a smile surfaced on Anna McLean's face. She had really appreciated the officers attempt at keeping things honest and grounded.

By midday DI Murray had recalled Hayes and Curry from their investigative duties in and around the Ocean Terminal development at Leith. Their early morning checks had felt, at least so far, fairly unproductive. Initially, this was often the case and was to be expected at the outset of any major inquiry. Although Hayes had informed him that they had come across one particular roommate that had not returned home on the Saturday.

"A Miss Deborah Griggs sir," she confirmed. "She goes by Debbie. She's a full-time librarian at the small community library on Restalrig Road."

"I know exactly where that is," Murray nodded. "Friendly staff and a good range of books for such a small community hub," he digressed.

"The thing is," 'Kid' Curry then added. "We literally only chapped on that door less than an hour ago sir. Even her flatmate thought that she had possibly just not ventured back in from wherever she had ended up the night before!"

Inspector Murray wondered where Curry had ended up that same evening? Would he be over the drink drive limit if tested right now, based on his alcohol consumption last night?

Susan 'Hanna' Hayes had asked Debbie's friend Amanda, to call her and at least let them know she'd arrived home safely. 'If I don't hear from you by tonight,' 'Hanna' had said. 'Then I promise to follow up later and phone you personally.'

The anxious girl gave the detective her mobile number. But had then smiled at her and whispered, "yeah, right!"

After this scheduled meet with Steven Murray, DC Hayes would begin with a reminder text and prove her wrong.

Murray himself, was personally delighted with what they had achieved so far. Lots of locals in the area had been spoken with, statements taken and one or two possibly worth following up with. Others, like the missing guinea pig and the old granny not back from the shops yet, maybe not so much he considered. Memories, they knew from experience on other major cases, often need to be reminded, jogged or asked several times before recollections resurfaced, and, or people became more willing to be involved.

Praising his diligent officers profusely, he offered: "Individuals are always reassured to see a police presence in and around their local area. Especially when anything untoward like this happens."

He updated them regarding Gillian McLean and the fact that her mother was currently with Sergeant Kerr. He then also asked them to outdo Hanlon with the relevance of her highland dance credentials.

"By the way," he sneakily added. "DCI Furlong would like to see you both on Monday afternoon."

Both halves of the western partnership sighed. Hayes dramatically rolled her eyes, whilst her angst-ridden colleague simply looked heavenward.

"Please take note, 'Hanna' you're down to see her at one o'clock sharp. Drew you're then scheduled for thirty minutes later. May I suggest you consider sucking a mint or two in advance of that meeting." Before either of his detectives could react to that barbed comment, Murray added with the cheeky grin of a naughty, mischievous schoolboy -

"Enjoy!"

The Cockatoo Bar and Restaurant was located in the southeast side of the City. Situated on the Old Craighall Road it was positioned only a short distance from Musselburgh. A firm favourite with the locals. It remained quiet, without being out of the way, remote and seedy. It had a strong family feel, child friendly play area and was within walking distance for Murray's lunchtime companion this afternoon.

Striding in rather wearily from the car park and through the front door, Ray Armour had been an unofficial snitch that Steven Murray had used for many years. Ray had notably been a tall, thin, unassuming man in his earlier years. A martial arts expert by all accounts. The ageing process though had been reasonably kind to him. He only had a slight stoop these days. His half century here on earth had also bulked out his midriff of late. Greying, matted hair and deep tanned frown lines across his once angelic face completed the look.

Dublin born Ray was a fixer. Whatever you required, the Armour of old could certainly get it for you. Murray had been helpful to him on a couple of occasions during the years. Once, when his sister had died a few years back without insurance, the Inspector had helped out with some of the associated costs, etc. Since that time, a strange bond of some sort had formed between them. Although neither of them really knew what their relationship was. Murray always reckoned that with Ray's help he had kept some seriously bad men off the streets for longer. Whereas one Raymond Armour Esquire, was just truly grateful never to have seen the inside of a prison cell. Especially one with several inmates that he had helped put there in the first place. So the Dubliner always reckoned he owed DI Murray. It was as straightforward as that. Throughout his dodgy years, Armour simply worked on a commission. Depending on the job, he got an agreed percentage. More often than not the circles that he mixed in were just bumping off each other, so Murray never got involved. He never went investigating who was after who. He just left them to it. Today though, using the proverbial, 'It was going to be a different kettle of fish altogether,' Murray smiled. Furlong he reckoned, would even know where that saying came from. His smile at that point, widened into a large satisfying grin.

"Let's get down to business," the detective suggested.

"I don't want to know," Armour clarified.

"Well - make sure you don't open the envelope then!" Murray rebuked him.

At that, a short brown haired waitress began to wipe their table. The two power brokers remained silent as she did so.

"Thank you," Steven Murray offered as she made to walk away. "It's nice to be nice," he continued. "You should try it sometime Ray," he snapped.

"Are you okay Inspector? You don't seem your jovial self. Well, what I mean is you are saying the right things, but your tone, your body language, you just seem…"

"I'm fine," he cut in. "I need this done sooner rather than later."

Murray handed across the seemingly 'highly confidential' envelope.

"It's got the agreed amount, name, enclosed photograph and some background info and work details, etc. Okay?"

"Mister Murray, you know that this is a one off attempt price I got you? It's a quarter of the normal cost. If someone intervenes, your target resists, there is a mix up, delay, whatever it may be. There is no comeback, no refund. You know you would need to pay the full price for another attempt? And you are good with that?"

Murray inhaled slowly and deeply. "I understand Ray. I know the score. Just go make it happen A.S.A.P."

Ray Armour acknowledged Murray's instruction with the raising of an eye.

"Things are already in place Inspector. However, and I reiterate, I have no wish to know whose name is inside that envelope," he added cautiously. "But I do think that once and for all, we are all square after this. So I suggest we go our separate ways on completion of this deal?" His voice seemed to crack slightly with emotion when he added in his Dublin lilt, "I don't know what you have gone through or dealt with recently Mr Murray. But I never thought that you would ever be the one sitting opposite me. The one handing over the envelope and the instructions. I am genuinely, so, so sad that it has come to this. Life sure gets crazy confused and mixed up at times." He shook his head disbelievingly and made to stand.

"What are you doing? We haven't ordered yet,"

"I think I've lost my appetite," the once hardened career criminal offered. "Take care Mr Murray. It was interesting knowing you."

The rather dismissive, weatherbeaten man proffered Murray, his long, thin gaunt hand. The Inspector observed it carefully for a second or two and just when it appeared as if his long term informant was about to withdraw it, Steven Murray stood upright and clasped it strongly. The troubled police officer placed his left hand on top of their grip in a gesture of sincerity. He shook it firmly and with gratitude offered, "Thank you, thank you for everything over the years Ray."

Murray then reflected on his often used thought - When choosing between the police and the criminals, it can often be difficult to tell who is a God and who is a monster.

The weary, disillusioned Ray Armour cut a sorry figure as he exited. His mind was abuzz with the possibilities of whose name was contained within the envelope. Although in recent times, there was really only one man Armour concluded, that had been an ongoing continual thorn in the detective's side. One that he had not managed to detain at Her Majesty's pleasure for any lengthy tenure. Instantly into the Irishman's mind came the evil opponent, the direct rival and unwelcome nemesis, Murray's very own Lex Luthor. None other than the rasping, gravel voiced degenerate - James Baxter Reid himself.

The Inspector would never see or speak to Raymond Armour ever again, that was the deal. For DI Murray this was a one-off attempt. It would either be successful or end in dismal failure. There would be no turning back and definitely no second chances. Whatever the result, he would live with the consequences. Although on reflection, that statement wasn't quite true!

The pretty young waitress then returned with notepad and pencil in hand.

Murray spoke slowly. "Fish and chips please. Mushy peas."

As the last piece of crispy batter was being used to soak up the small remaining pool of vinegar from his plate, a vibration in his pocket alerted him to an incoming text. 'Another murder,' had been auto corrected to 'A mother murder.' They may both be correct he thought.

Last night was successful. Two down. Not sure who will be the lucky target this evening, but at least I know where I am going and how tonight's audition will turn out. People love to model. "Tha neart teaghlaich, mar neart arm, na laighe na dìlseachd dha chèile," was whispered gently.

SIX

"Give me a Leonard Cohen afterworld, so I can sigh eternally. Sit and drink Pennyroyal Tea, distill the life that's inside of me."

- Nirvana

The latest body had been discovered at the rear of The Starbank Inn on the A901, westbound from Leith. Through anyone's guess traffic on a Saturday in that part of the city, it was safe to say his journey would take him between fifteen minutes, possibly even up to half an hour. He knew a delay was inevitable as soon as he opened his drivers door. As it allowed just enough space and time for his imaginary four-legged companion to leap in swiftly and jump across onto the rather inviting passenger seat. After his sharp tone and manner in the restaurant, it was no surprise that his black dog was looking to accompany him for the rest of the day.

Heading off to Starbank Road, part way between the Trinity and Newhaven districts. Murray's mind began suddenly to transition into sixth gear. Over thinking, over deliberating and over complicating matters. Sadly so often, it can be the slightest trigger that sets it off - a criticism, a throwaway remark or dismissive body language. Most people can laugh it away, ignore it or have been totally oblivious to any reference or nuance in the first place. But for Steven Murray (at times) it can make him re-evaluate his whole persona and existence!

He questioned: What value does he offer? What purpose does he serve in even being here? Then the why this and how come? Finally the who's and when's break forth. Suddenly and without warning, that is the precise moment the dangerous, depressive, suicidal thoughts re-emerge and kick in. From hiding away from the world innocently under a blanket, to shaking and crying uncontrollably. No further desire to enjoy or experience tomorrow then becomes your focal point. Others outside of the community who suffer from these destructive cognitive ideas will never really, truly grasp, just how these tendencies fluctuate wildly and impact instantly upon the life of the sufferer.

With that said however, Steven Murray during his more lucid hours, recognised fully, the heartache, hurt and distress that immediate friends and close family of sufferers must go through. Not knowing from one moment to the next what they may be planning on doing to themselves. Continually concerned, anxious and worried. What a vicious, cruel, unbearable cycle both sides go through. For Murray, like thousands of others, the darkness appears as quickly as a window blind being pulled closed.

This made him reflect back to a fortnight earlier. It was late on the Friday evening when he had returned home and immediately scribbled a few personal lines in his journal. A collection of thoughts that had been nagging at him all day long. Impressions that he had magically, yet sadly transformed into a four line poem.

It read:

Today at the tragic murder scene - Was I Dr Jekyll or Mr Hyde?
Depression is living in a body that every day solely fights to survive.

Physical strength is one thing - being careful not to simply crash and burn.
But mentally tortured every 24 hours, with a mind that tries to die at every turn!

He loved his music. For most people it would be a nice accompaniment to their day, for Steven Murray it had become his unseen partner. It was a vital health supplement, an invaluable lifeline and coping mechanism for him. It assisted him in his daily fight. However, that may be at eight-thirty in the morning and by ten past ten, less than two hours later - His life meant nothing to him. At that point he would be genuinely happy to once again depart this earth forever. Hollow, empty and alone inside, this generous man so full of enthusiasm and fun one minute, would then retreat meekly to take off his mask.

This mask was the false persona that he used to hide behind to get him through each day. Not false as in deceitful, devious and duplicitous. But rather, it was a protective camouflage to shield himself away from the world. It allowed him to fit in, sometimes to escape and even more often than not, to help him match up to others expectations. Because again and again, the problem was simply that. He would think of himself as not good enough. That everyone else around him was better. They were cleverer, wiser, more articulate and better educated. He could so easily recognise the wonderful strengths and abilities in others, but sadly not in himself.

If an enterprising factory actually produced those masks, their order book would be bursting at the seams. Staff would be on constant overtime, working 24/7 trying fiercely to keep up with popular demand.

The simple point is that the width of that line between life and death can vary greatly. And for many vulnerable individuals in the busy, bustling, social media, celebrity and success driven society that we currently find ourselves in - the price of inclusion is often too much to pay.

As the Inspector arrived at the popular Starbank Inn, many parts had already been cordoned off with forensics tape. There was, as to be expected a large police presence in attendance. Two unexplained deaths, murders at that, within twenty four hours. The general public would be alarmed. Other people were also deeply concerned. Those other people would be his bosses. This could be a public relations disaster if not handled correctly. And even having Murray himself, assigned to the case was the wrong call several of his superiors would feel. However, undeterred the experienced DI arrived, parked on an inside road about thirty to forty yards away and as he straightened his vehicle kerbside his mobile sounded. With his engine officially switched off, the informative update began.

"Doc, what have you got for me?"

"Not a great deal at t'e moment Steven. Time of death would have been between seven and nine on T'ursday evening. T'e poor woman had been cruelly garrotted, possibly with some form of fine wire. Electrical cable and fishing lines are two of the most commonly used, but we're still working on t'at for you. She was t'en unceremoniously dumped by the roadside. And when I say dumped, I quite literally mean dumped. From the numerous abrasions and vast bruising on her body, arms and legs, it would appear quite clear t'at she was probably pushed out from a moving vehicle of some sort."

"Okay. T'at's helpful Doc." Murray offered up, mimicking his accent, as he often would.

"Yes, yes, very good Inspector."

Doc Patterson was well used to Murray's levity. Over the years he had become convinced that it was how Steven Murray attempted to protect himself from the seriousness of certain situations. To outsiders though, he had recognised that it must often come across at times as wholly inappropriate. After that brief reflection, the T'inker paused.

"T'ere is one more t'ing. Rather unusual to say t'e least."

"Go on, what is it Doc?" Murray sat up in his car seat, steadying himself to listen intently.

"Literally attached, it was superglued in fact to the inside of her left hand. I'd guess to make sure it never left her grip or smashed when she was pushed out."

"Superglued to her hand?"

"It was a little silver compass."

"A compass!" The puzzled Inspector then exclaimed.

"Yes, about the size of a ten pence piece. Tiny."

"He is sending us a message Doc. And was keen to ensure it arrived unscathed. He's communicating with us. Interesting, very interesting indeed," Murray surmised.

"Glad I could help," Patterson crackled down the line.

"Doc, you are amazing. Keep up the good work. I need to go, I need to get to the scene. By the way, who do you have here?"

"Danni, should be en-route Steven, if she is not already t'ere. I'll let you go. Bye."

As Steven Murray went to offer a goodbye, the phone line had already been hung up.

One minute later and walking around to the back of the pub, he could see that his favourite female pathologist had most certainly already arrived. The rather bland 'Angel' in the white SOCO suit,' was none other than American, Dr. Danielle Poll.

However, before he could reach Danni Poll, a voice he'd recently become familiar with echoed out warily over his left shoulder. Should this give him cause for concern moving forward he began to wonder.

"Steven," was the only proper word spoken. And although still warm, smooth and informative, it was at least three octaves higher than he normally recalled it. He could feel a chilly, vocal tirade of 'non-swearing' about to be unleashed. Dare he turn? He did. And the force of the volley overwhelmed him, nearly sweeping him clear off his feet!

"Flame throwing Sassenachs! Rear-ending Admirals and Buckaroo Banzai!!!"

The Inspector nodded. "A few spicy new ones there to add to your repertoire Ma'am," he smiled.

"How can you joke at a time like this," she stated animatedly. "And I told you it's Barbra." She then began encircling Murray, as if in search of hapless prey. Next instant she chirped up firmly with - "It's my first day, and we have more dead bodies in Scotland making an appearance than we have Tory MP's! What's going on Inspector?"

Ah, it's 'Inspector' now, he thought wryly to himself.

SEVEN

"I'm stuck on you. Been a fool too long I guess. It's time for me to come on home. Guess I'm on my way."

- Lionel Richie

Police Constable Robert Richards and his partner had arrived first on the scene. They had been literally two streets away dealing with a local disturbance when the call came in. Murray had asked Richards to update him. The young officer, who was probably in his early thirties began nervously as he retrieved his notebook.

"The body had been discovered shortly after noon sir."

"As late as twelve o'clock?" Murray questioned. Struggling initially to understand why not sooner?

"It was simply the first time that any member of staff had had the need to use any of their outside bins," Richards explained. He then paused, as if waiting for the Inspector to question or comment further on this.

Although Steven Murray's anxious wave of his hand clearly indicated… 'go on.'

"That was really it sir. Her body was discovered in between the waste bins, alongside her handbag."

"Her handbag?" Murray confirmed. "Photo ID, cards, etc, all in place?"

The officer nodded. "It would appear so sir. We cordoned off the area immediately and waited for the SOCO officers and yourselves to arrive."

Inspector Murray looked over the diligent man's shoulder as he spoke. Slowly he took on board a panoramic scan of the murder scene.

"The new DCI was first to arrive," Richards continued. "She had seemingly been along the road at Ocean Terminal checking how things were at the scene from earlier in the day."

Had she really, Murray thought. Furlong must have left the station right after he went for lunch then. Because he could remember quite clearly giving her a wave as he went to exit the building. He then surveyed the crime scene car park. It had space roughly for about seven or eight vehicles. Murray could not be wholly accurate, as only half of it had marked bays and was easy to gauge. However, the remainder had obviously had resurfacing work carried out in recent years and replacing the line markings had possibly been an extra cost that was considered no longer required. These were skip sized containers Murray observed. Their large, heavy obtuse doors sloped down at an angle. Set close together, the rim of each unit came very close to touching. However with both becoming narrower at the base, there was enough space to hide or dispose of a body in the gap between them. Unsurprisingly, the green bin was for recyclable products, whilst the dark grey dealt with the majority of their general waste.

PC Richards, who had remained at his side, interrupted his train of thought with, "It was when the member of staff opened the darker container sir, that she became concerned.

Again DI Murray remained silent. This time dropping his head to the side and the widening of his eyes became the clue for Richard's to continue.

"Placed delicately on top was a yellow and black skirt," he said. "As she lifted it, the staff member soon discovered that it was covered in what appeared to be blood. Alarmed and stepping further back she then noticed the heel of a shoe. Then, when she unfortunately discovered it was still attached to an actual body, that was the moment all hell broke loose!

"I bet it was," Murray shrugged.

"She then screamed intensely at the top of her voice, non stop. Her whole body violently vibrating by all accounts. Another staff member was alerted by those cries, before calling ourselves."

The unfortunate employee that discovered the body was currently on the edge of the ambulance tailgate being treated for shock.

"She had literally only just stopped shrieking when she spotted the paramedics arrive sir. When we got here, her eyes were wide with horror. Her mouth rigid and open, her chalk white face gaunt and immobile." Lifting up his left hand he then demonstrated as he continued. "Her fists were clenched, with blanched knuckles and the nails digging deep into the palms of her hands."

"They would have appeared to be her knights in shining armour," Murray perceived.

"Absolutely. No one previously had been able to calm her down, or stop her hysterical animated actions."

Inspector Murray understood fully that this had been a terrifying and traumatic event in this woman's life. She may not have been in imminent danger herself, but witnessing a dead body for the first time had induced such a strong emotional response, that it was vitally important that she received the correct professional support of the ambulance crew at this time.

Police Constable Robert Richards had waited patiently in front of his Inspector for further instruction.

"Thank you constable," Murray generously offered. Aware that PC Richards had read those last couple of sentences directly from the statement that he had taken from the girl when he first arrived.

"Her name?"

"Sorry?" The uniformed man replied.

"The poor deceased's name?" Murray gently encouraged.

"Oh, of course, sorry sir, I never thought. Her name was Melissa. Melissa Margaret MacLeod.

Once again the Inspector's mobile sounded as he waved to PC Richards. This time it was 'Kid' Curry.

"Sir," he said enthusiastically. "Gillian McLean was ceilidh dancing at 'Thistle Do Nicely' on Thursday night."

Hanlon's discovery of her childhood talents had proven helpful right enough. Just as DI Murray would have guessed. 'Kid' Curry had been on speaker, so when Murray gestured suitably toward Hanlon, his young Chief Constable in the making, got his meaning straight away.

"I'm on it boss!" he said, before scurrying off.

"Her friends and neighbours never saw or heard from her on Friday," Curry continued. "The head teacher at the school where she was doing her placement was surprised that she had never turned up without informing them. That seemingly wasn't like her. She had been well liked and appeared to be a very conscientious young lady. We unfortunately left her in tears."

"Who?"

"Mrs Park, the Headmistress. 'Hanna' had to spend ten minutes comforting her before we could leave."

"You might end up in tears and in need of comfort also Constable Curry." The face on the other end of the line was beginning to scrunch up and look confused, when his boss further added. "It's been awhile since I last heard it used, but you might want to ditch 'the Headmistress' tag. I thought I was the one that always dug the 'PC' ditch for myself Kid?"

"Yeah, I actually thought it sounded wrong as I said it..." He went to further excuse himself, but was abruptly halted.

"I'm in a rush at this end. Anything further? Or was it just a dance update?"

"Eh, er, no, well, actually yes, I suppose!"

"What are you on about Kid?"

"Inspector," a voice said clearly and assertively. 'Hanna' Hayes had learned quickly over the past eighteen months that Steven Murray liked his officers to be positive and straight talking. To speak with vibrancy and expectation. Whatever the heck that meant, she was still working on it!

"Sir," she hastily continued. "Outside the dance area, in the hallway where the queue forms, there is a large open notice board. Lots of personal ads, contact details, professional services and the like offered." Hayes also knew, or so she thought, how to play him at his own game. To leave him hanging and wanting more. She had gently placed the worm on the ...

With a wide playful grin, DI Murray sounded startled. He raised his voice and asked hurriedly, "Are you telling me

61

'Hanna,' are you seriously telling me, that our first victim," Murray broke into a posh accent at this point. "Our young 'Prime of Miss Jean Brodie' school teacher, was supplementing her income" - The last five words were uttered in pure Glaswegian harshness - "by being on the game?"

"Oh my, oh my, oh no!" Hayes now thoroughly embarrassed, blushed. So much for clear, concise, communication, she thought. Help! Her cheeks had turned bright red. She was flustered and although she was not in the presence of her superior officer, she was mortified.

"Hanna, Hanna, DC Hayes" Murray yelled. "I'm joking with you."

DC Hayes blew out her cheeks rapidly and sighed with relief. Although her chest still heaved heavily for several remaining seconds.

"Oh my," her Inspector reaffirmed to her. "You'll need to learn to play the game a bit better than that."

Curry who had been listening on the speaker, was now doubled over in laughter at his colleagues humbling humiliation. Although that would have never have been Steven Murray's deliberate intention.

"Good try though," her Inspector encouraged. "So what are you two actually telling me?"

"It's the green stuff sir. What appears to be paper, found under poor Miss McLean's fingernails?"

"Uh huh," Murray interjected slowly from his throat.

"On the notice board we found a postcard sized advert, with the exact same bright fluorescent colouring."

"The exact same colour? Surely it could match hundreds of other business ads or promotional literature 'Hanna?' What makes you thi…"

"There are discernible scratch marks on the card and the left hand edge is missing sir," she jumped in excitedly. Trying, possibly just too hard to make up for her earlier 'carrot and stick' approach.

"And the contact details for the advertiser are about to follow I assume?"

"I've already forwarded them to your phone sir," Andrew Curry shouted in the background. He then flipped his own mobile closed, before drawing a large number one down an invisible blackboard. All this for the benefit of his now, none too impressed colleague!

Murray, feeling rather more upbeat and relaxed after the phone call, turned around and got the fright of his life. For the briefest of seconds, he thought he had seen a ghost. In actual fact it was the still very much alive body of forensic pathologist Dr Danielle Poll, complete with her Arctic white SOCO suit on.

"Did I startle you Inspector?" she asked in her silky sweet American accent. Her immense grin, showed that she seemed to being rather enjoying the occasion. Possibly too much for Murray's liking.

"What can I do for you Danni," he asked.

"Oh no, don't be playing mind games with me Steven. I think it is very much, what I can do for you Inspector," she stated whilst holding steady his gaze. "I wasn't sure when you would be leaving. But I figured you'd be interested to know this before you left."

"And THIS being what exactly?" he asked with a rather tentative smile.

He was a million miles away from expecting what he heard next.

"Melissa MacLeod was given a nephrectomy!

"A what?" exclaimed Murray.

"A nephrectomy."

An uneasy silence soon accompanied the blank expression.

Danielle Poll then stated in layman's terms. "Both her kidneys had been removed."

"Pregnant Pink Piglets!" cried Furlong. Who had just come within earshot. She backed that one up shaking her head with, "You great son of a Presbyterian goat!"

Poll stared at Murray in a serious, 'should I be concerned' way?

"It is a very long story. I'll tell you someday," Murray assured her.

The troubled Inspector ran his right thumb and forefinger across the middle of his lips. Starting wide they slowly slid inwardly toward the centre. As they met up, Murray pondered and offered.

"Both kidneys you say Danni? Possible organs for sale thing? Just random? A point to prove?" He lifted his hands away from his mouth and shrugged. "Any initial helpful thoughts or ideas whatsoever?"

Poll cautiously considered his questions for a second or two before responding. She then steepled her hands to her lips. This gave her a very professional air. She then spoke with insight and displayed a remarkable wisdom beyond her years.

"Firstly, I would say the time of death was late evening on Thursday." She paused insightfully, giving her police colleagues time to absorb her words. "Not random - definitely deliberate. Precise, but not professionally done. Proper surgery would take between two and three hours. This took two or three minutes - ruthless and harsh, so not for resale! If pushed? I suspect it was done to send out a message."

The others remained gobsmacked.

She trailed off with, "When, where or what that message may look like, I can't tell you."

It was now Murray's turn to nod. "You have told us plenty to be going on with Doc. Appreciate it. Remind me again the approximate size of a human kidney Danni?"

Danielle Poll answered cheekily by holding up her two clenched fists, whilst taking a boxing stance directly in front of the Inspector.

"About four or five inches long. Roughly the size of one of these," she smiled. As she playfully jabbed Murray on the chin.

Again, he was rather taken aback by the Doctor's jovial spirit. But he loved to witness character and individuality in people. So privately, he actually admired the pathologists style. We are all different, he reminded himself. Then entering into the good natured sparring role play, he held Poll's left wrist above her head. As if announcing to the world, the latest winner of a championship boxing fight. The trio all smiled briefly. Surprisingly, that included DCI Furlong.

DC Joseph Hanlon had virtually just returned back at his Inspector's side. "Like you no doubt suspected sir, Melissa

MacLeod was in attendance at the 'Thistle Do Nicely' ceilidh also on Thursday evening."

Murray's nod did seem to state… 'as expected!'

'Sherlock,' continued with his feedback. "Several eyewitnesses interviewed in relation to the Gillian McLean case remembered the girl with the short yellow tartan skirt. And one of the doormen identified her from a photo I sent him by text."

After that though the Inspector's appreciative nod, soon turned into an uneasy shake of the head. "My gut tells me Joe that the message had already been delivered and we somehow failed to receive it."

Concerned looks covered each of their faces.

Thank you once again Danni," Inspector Murray courteously offered.

He began to walk away as Doctor Poll coughed. It was one of those familiar 'attention seeking' coughs. An utterance that indicated - I still hold the superior hand, I know something you don't know and wouldn't you dearly like to?

The wily, astute Inspector ascertained all of the aforementioned from that single vocal note! He was intrigued and took two, 'you have my attention' steps back toward her. Sternly, he now held her gaze deliberately and nodded only once. Interestingly without any word being spoken at all - She got his message also!

"She had a child's building block glued to the inside of her right palm."

"Glued you say? Just like the McLean girl," Murray mused

"Just to keep it in place and ensure we didn't miss it?" was DCI Furlong's question.

"I believe it would be exactly for that reason," Poll agreed. "There certainly would not appear to be any other motive currently that I could think of." The young pathologist ventured to ask - "Was that helpful? Was it even a clue?"

"Oh it was most certainly," the Inspector vented. "First a compass and then followed up with a child's toy building block. Nine times out of ten the person that commits these heinous crimes is playing with you," Murray affirmed. "A little bit like your cough a few seconds ago."

The young American began to blush.

"They reckon they hold the upper hand. They feel superior and in overall control, so they then also feel obliged to drip feed you clues."

"Seriously?" Poll said, more surprised than ever and her embarrassment clearly growing.

"Absolutely," replied Murray. "Ironically, it will be the glue that bonds them. Assuming the tests on it come back positively. However, more importantly given that both girls had disappeared from the same local ceilidh and that they have been discovered only a few miles apart, within hours of each other. I think it is safe to say we have the makings of a serial killer on our hands!"

Danielle Poll, pragmatic as ever. Took the statement in her stride and nodded.

Murray turned knowingly to his right. His newly promoted Detective Chief Inspector, one Ms Barbra Furlong had also taken it in her stride. Although, she had stormed off at an alarming pace, muttering something about… 'Furry Jury Janglers!'

EIGHT

"It's in the paper every day. I see it in the headlines and I feel so sick. As another life leaves this world, 'Do we even have a chance?' We are all human. Let's start to prove it."

- Anti-Flag

It was always a horrendous task, being assigned to break the news of the death of a family member. West coast officers had dealt efficiently and quickly with Gillian McLean's mother in Giffnock and unfortunately that would stay with those men throughout their careers.

Steven Murray couldn't recall how many murder scenes he'd attended, major incidents he'd been involved with or the totalled times in court over the years. But one sorry, sad, statistic that was forever stored away in a special, ring-fenced filing cabinet in his screwed up mind, was the number of families that he had informed of that life altering and soul destroying news. Although probably lower that many would think. It was ultimately far too high at 16.

On exactly sixteen separate occasions, he had witnessed a multitude of reactions to receiving that knock on their door. Grown men would break down and crumple before his eyes. Others would stare blankly and simply say, "Oh, right, thank you!" Many would shriek and howl, lashing out furiously. For those next thirty seconds you would be their punch bag and absorb all their blows, their frustrations, their disbelieve at what they had just been told. Then as their energy levels drained and a deep realisation to the reality of the situation struck them - Tears would flow and they would weep freely, as they reached out to embrace you tightly. In an instant, you had transformed from a deliverer of evil - into their pillar of strength and their much needed beacon of hope!

He remembered with deep anguish as a young police constable in Renfrewshire, going to a home in the outskirts of Paisley and chapping on the door of the premises. It was a fairly isolated, remote farm cottage on the edge of a country road and the man that answered looked like a stereotypical farmer. Flat cap, heavy jacket, waterproofs and green wellies were his apparel as he opened the door. His only daughter Rachel had disappeared a fortnight earlier. The poor silver haired man with the rosy red cheeks and bushy eyebrows was at his wits end with worry. His wife, the girl's mother, had died three years earlier from cancer. Father and daughter just had each other now.

Rachel was thirty-seven years old and had never married. She had been a legal secretary in Glasgow city centre with a large corporate firm. But after her mother's funeral, she immediately moved back home to look after her heartbroken father. She mainly helped do his books and generally assisted as best she could around the farm. As an inexperienced individual, it was only Murray's second death notification. His stomach was in complete knots. Today as he recalled the experience, he felt physically sick. For after breaking the tragic details to the man, the shell shocked father had simply walked off to his tiny, linoleum floored kitchenette. There he simply lifted his shotgun and placed it under his chin. On hearing the ferocious bang, Murray had fallen to his knees and cried both vocally and tearfully. Instantly he had fully realised his schoolboy error. He had allowed the recipient of such devastating news to go off on his own straight afterward. Murray had never forgotten that experience and had fine tuned his approach accordingly over the years.

"We have all had a busy, sombre day," he told DC Hanlon. "And we are going to be rushed off our feet for the foreseeable future Joe. However, I need you to call our western duo back and have THEM break the news to Miss MacLeod's nearest and dearest, asap."

"Are you sure? I don't think they have done this before."

"I know for a fact that they haven't Joe. That's exactly WHY I'm extending them this opportunity, harsh as it may seem."

"I fully understand sir. I'll speak to them and make sure they do it before they go off shift and as soon as is practical. We don't want the family kept in the dark any longer than possible either."

"Thank you Joe. You're a good man. I've got a couple of other quick calls to make, before we go follow up on that business card."

DC Hanlon nodded. He could see for himself today that Detective Inspector Steven Murray would be occasionally 'walking his black dog,' on and off all afternoon.

DC Joseph Hanlon decided that there was no time like the present. So while Murray made his catch up calls, 'Sherlock,' did likewise.

"DC Hayes," came the enthusiastic response.

"Hanna," it's Joe Hanlon here.

"Oh, hi Joe, I've just spoken with…"

"Yes I know. It's just he forgot to ask you something and he has now kindly delegated that task to me."

There was a silence, then… "I'm listening."

"DI Murray would like you and 'the Kid' to break the news of Miss MacLeod's death to her family… and in person."

"What!" Hayes exclaimed. This time in a rather less than enthusiastic manner. "But neither of us…"

"He is fully aware of that also. I think you will find that is why he is asking you to take care of it. All part of your career development," Joe said with a knowing smile in his voice.

"Ye, thanks for that," Hayes said rather tersely.

Hanlon then went on to ensure that they could make it a priority before their shift ended. Stressing the mental anguish the family would be going through. So the sooner the better. Also reiterating that this all came from DI Murray and that he was simply the duly appointed messenger on this occasion.

DC Hanlon signed off with a considerably more genuine. "Good luck Susan!"

Phone calls concluded, the senior partnership drove off at pace to speak with the owner of a rather unique, bright green business card!

Afton Drive was only two minutes away. It was a clean, middle income, nineteen eighties housing development. It comprised of a host of one, two and three bedroomed flats. Each with their own private garage below in the forecourt. Two under-age drinkers hid their cans of lager as the officers exited their car. Instantly recognising them as plain clothes police. Access to the third floor, where number 53 was located, was by ground floor lift or a centrally located indoor stone stairwell. With health and fitness in mind, the Inspector set the example and headed off up the stairs.

"Evening," Joe Hanlon offered, to the bearded male taking the steps two at a time on his way down.

"Alright!" he replied, sliding effortlessly between Police Scotland's finest.

Two minutes later, Murray gently sang, *"knock three times…"*

Bang, bang, bang went Hanlon's fist on the door.

"On the ceiling if you want me…"

His young apprentice had matured greatly these past 12 months. There was no greater sign of leadership, than one who helps develop and bring forward other leaders. And DI Murray had done just that with aplomb!

The front door was eventually, cautiously opened a mere couple of inches, with the security chain still very much intact.

"Police Scotland sir," Murray assured him with authority of voice. And just to be on the safe side, his official warrant card was thrust forward toward the lone eye behind the door.

A few mechanical noises, assorted chains, snibs, bolts and mumblings later and the door was opened more fully. Standing inside was a man Hanlon reckoned to be in his late twenties, possibly veering into early thirties. 'Sherlock' shook his head ever so slightly at the man's facial hair. In his DI's rather dated, 'Shortcut to Guilty Parties Handbook,' this individual was wearing a wafer thin goatee beard and tiny narrow moustache. So it was official. He was a guaranteed paedophile! His darkened eye sockets, nicotine stained fingers and dishevelled hair did nothing to convince the jury otherwise.

Thankfully 'Sherlock' did not have a 'Trial By Appearance' annual subscription. Mainly because with a face that matched Rodney Trotter in looks, he himself would likely be behind bars doing a seven to ten year stretch!

"Mr Jordan?" Murray asked.

"Aye, aye, that's right," the man replied wearily, rubbing his tightly clenched fists deep into those blackened hollows on his face. So deep in fact, that DI Murray wondered if his skeletal knuckles would ever begin to resurface. With those 'badger' eyes - Was he desperately trying to burrow his way out of his present predicament? It was as if he was stalling for time. Keep rubbing, keep rubbing he could tell himself, the police will be gone when I stop. When his bony, delicate arms dropped to his side - the two official bodies remained real. Very real indeed. His scrawny, match-stalk figure was kitted out in a navy blue towelling dressing gown, complete with matching slippers. Both items were branded impressively with a distinctive Four Seasons logo.

NINE

"Depending on your viewpoint, this place is blessed or cursed. And in the years I've lived here, I've seen the best and worst. In scores, in droves, the living and the ghosts, the streets of Edinburgh mean the most to me."

- The Proclaimers

It was fast approaching five o'clock and darkness had already been in attendance throughout the City of Edinburgh for easily the last hour. Based on that, DC Hanlon's curiosity was aroused and he remarked.

"Late night last night? Or early to bed this evening sir?"

It took the bedraggled figure a few seconds to come to terms with that question. Then when he had actually sussed out what had been asked of him. He looked at 'Sherlock' warily, through clouded bloodshot eyes and mustered up in his finest nasal vibrato -

"Yes and yes."

"Could we come in Mr Jordan?" the Inspector asked firmly. Before taking one almighty, assertive step forward, with an air of authority that was never going to take no for an answer.

"What? Eh, sure, yea whatever," the man in the robe stammered. Undoubtedly still in 'hangover' mode. He nervously gestured to them to proceed down the hallway. Murray, unsurprisingly, had already done so. Their host had only half opened the door because the large assortment of coats, overalls and jackets hung behind it, had made it difficult. Below them a further selection of sporting goods, boots and shoes which were obviously normally discarded there, had made it extra hard to open the door any wider.

"Do you need us to firstly slip off our shoes sir?" Hanlon considerately asked in his normal helpful way, having also noticed the vast selection of footwear behind the door.

Murray scowled uneasily at this overly thoughtful gesture. Because he was already ensconced in the warmth of Jordan's sitting room. He relaxed soon enough though as he heard their welcoming, local miscreant respond.

"No, no, you are both alright. Make your way through."

All three men sat in the cosy, intimate living room. Rugby trophies and awards seemed to surround them. Someone obviously excelled at the game in their earlier years. Murray had already guessed that the property was a three bedroomed flat. The decor was more upmarket than down. The colour scheme deep and rich. Varying shades of purple seemed to give the apartment a 'Royal' feel. The swirling patterned carpet had a deep pile, but was most definitely more Premier Inn than Marriott. A unique range of inspiring and eye catching prints adorned the hallway. Pictures of young female models on catwalks, close-up shots of their feet, legs and ankles. Those black and white bespoke images appeared to be very modern. They were certainly in direct contrast to the religious, God like picture that hung precariously above the electric fireplace in the room they currently sat.

Paradoxically in comparison to the tidy flat, the 'hobo' host asked, "How can I help?"

"Sir, it so happened we came into possession of one of your business cards earlier today and we won…"

"Stop, stop, stop," the man dismissively threw up his hands. At that, his robe swung open and both officers automatically averted their eyes and instantly checked the ceiling tiles for clues!

Jordan laughed, strapped himself back in and apologised for the wardrobe malfunction. Joe Hanlon was beginning to alter his opinion on 'Trial By Appearance.' For as far as he was concerned the homeowner would be facing twenty years inside, if that little episode happened again he'd decided. Although unintentionally, he had also spotted something rather concerning about the man's body.

"Sorry officers, I butted in because I don't use business cards in my line of work."

"You don't!" Both officers exclaimed in surprised unison. Hanlon and Murray suddenly exchanged concerned glances. This was not good.

"And you only find me in this state today because this is my one day off work this week. I was out extra late last night and sadly I'm now paying the price, believe me. But business cards, no, no not me I'm afraid. Someone's sent you here on a wild goose chase!"

Murray pulled his head back in surprise slightly, before offering the young man a rather quizzical look. Jordan had obviously spotted his unease and puzzled expression.

"It was a popular phrase my mother used Inspector," he voiced, as he ran a nervous hand through his greasy, unkempt, tousled hair.

Murray then gave him a 'get out of jail' card. It was played in the form of an understanding nod (a number 31). But the experienced police officer was genuinely getting an uneasy feeling about this man.

DC Hanlon immediately handed over his phone. It displayed the picture of the damaged card. Joe even enlarged it, so that the writing was more clearly visible.

"Do you recognise that sir?"

The tired man smiled. "I do constable. And I see what has happened," he stammered.

Why the nerves? Murray again wondered. The two officers stood patiently waiting for him to elaborate.

Eventually he realised the silence was aimed at him. "Oh, right, sure, absolutely. It's one of my dad's cards."

"Your father?" Hanlon questioned.

"Correct. My dad. That's what I said. We all have one!"

DI Murray let Mr Jordan's more assured attitude and cocky response initially slide. Although he wanted quickly to regain the upper hand.

"So a grown man such as yourself - Is still living at home with his dad?"

Hanlon suppressed a delighted grin, as a rather humbled 'hobo' looked downward and tugged uncomfortably at the bow of his gown.

"It was a rhetorical question. No need for an answer Mr Jordan. However the following do require some grunts, groans and or nods… Okay?"

Murray had not only raised his voice, but also the pace and intonation of his speech. Hanlon continued to learn, marvel and appreciate the ease at which Steven Murray could accelerate up through the gears when the need demanded. He also knew full well, that although his experienced superior gave the impression of having these outdated, politically incorrect biases. It was really just a 'grumpy old man,' 'Mr Angry act.' An opportunity to vent, to let off some steam and express opinions that most people these days dare not say. Hanlon recognised that Murray trusted him with these private, personal violations of modern day life and was grateful for that. He also knew his wise Inspector required proof before labelling individuals. However he did like to mess with people!

"What is your Christian name sir? Does anyone else apart from your father, sorry dad live with you?" Sarcastically and in an awful broken English/fake French accent he added. "Can you just confirm Papa's first name is Max and what he does exactly for a living?" Then, rather angrily and just for good measure, the Inspector signed off with, "Oh, and does a bear crap in the woods?" Murray used all of his six foot one frame to deliberately overshadow the smaller man. Joe Hanlon had witnessed this routine often over the last year.

"All in your own time son," Murray added in a demeaning, belittling fashion. Possibly just crossing the line and that wasn't like him. Especially for no good reason. 'Sherlock' knew there was something off today. Something troubling him. Where did he go and who did he meet for lunch? That was the key.

Joseph Hanlon duly noted down all the bog standard responses from the poor soul. The scarecrow from the Wizard of Oz really shouldn't have went with the attitude. The 'assumed guilty, until proven innocent' paedophile's name was Craig Alexander Jordan. It was only himself and his dad Max that lived there currently. Max was a builder, a stonemason to trade.

Craig's final feeble reply was, "And I don't think we have any woods around here officer," he said seriously.

Steven Murray sighed and shook his head in disbelief. I'm getting too old for this, he thought to himself.

Before making their way from the apartment the detectives discovered from the son, that Jordan senior had been plying his trade in the London area for the past few weeks. He was busy as part of a team involved on a major renovation project there. The officers had his information from the business card and 'Sherlock' dialled the number.

DI Murray asked, "Do you mind if I take a picture of your religious print? There is something about it I find rather mesmerising and intriguing."

Hanlon winced.

"Are you for real? That awful hideous thing! By all means if you must. It's my dad's. It's called 'Ancient of Days' and it's certainly ancient. He's had it for years."

The attempted phone call had went straight to voicemail. They had never called that number initially, because it was only a short drive from The Starbank Inn to the Jordan's flat. They were always going to call by in person and unannounced.

A relevant message was left for Max Jordan to return their call as soon as possible. As for 'the bearded paedo,' as Murray referred to him (in his mind at least). It had been established that he was 32 years old (slightly older than the Inspector had guessed). It had also came to light that the Four Seasons poster boy, was the manager of a Top Shop fashion outlet. Unfortunately for Jordan junior, that did not seem to help his case. It would appear his retail store was based in the Ocean Terminal Shopping Mall, less than 100 yards from where the school teacher Gillian McLean was found dead.

Well what do you know Murray reflected.

As they navigated their way down the stairs from Jordan's flat, Hanlon vocally erupted. Murray heard passion, energy, determination and enthusiasm all in equal measure be offered up by 'Sherlock.' Alas, what he never heard was proof.

"He's definitely hiding something," he yelled. "Totally quaking in his boots! Or naked feet to be more precise. He was too helpful, gave us too much attitude, too much flaming everything!" Joe Hanlon jibed.

"Are you not just peeved off because he flashed you?" Murray asked in an amused manner.

Hanlon blushed and continued to gesticulate wildly with his arms and hands in the air. This was done in a gesture that clearly stated - 'Oh, why did you bring that up, forget it, never mind. If your not going to take this seriously…'

Murray laughed as if the sound was on a loop system. It was a machine gun howl that fired out at regular intervals. A few moments later however, as he began to calm down, he did reassure his still relatively inexperienced colleague with…

"I absolutely agree Joe," he said sincerely. "There was something seriously amiss in that home. Our 'munchkin' buddy was most definitely covering something, or for someone. At the very least, he omitted to pass on information that he knew could have been potentially helpful."

Joe raised his eyes in surprise and was about to break into song at this good news of support. His Inspector's proactive musical influence was definitely rubbing off on him!

Inspector Steven Murray though continued with, "I'm afraid that it may have been more than nervous energy and cover up. I got a real sense of fear Joe. He was certainly riddled with guilt, of that I'm sure. The bearded Mister Jordan is involved and responsible for something serious. We just have to figure out what!"

TEN

"I was a miner. I was a docker. I was a railway man between the wars. I raised a family in times of austerity, with sweat at the foundry - between the wars."

- Billy Bragg

Driving the reasonably short distance from Edinburgh to Whitburn in West Lothian, 'Hanna'bal Hayes and 'Kid' Curry had sat in silence. Both anxious and nervous, but resigned to the task ahead.

63 Lector Terrace was a traditional three bedroomed council house. Built probably in the early nineteen seventies, Susan Hayes had guessed. A tidy hedgerow at the front, short garden path and concrete slabs with the occasional weed growing through completed the look.

Detective 'Hanna' Hayes may have been suffering with tiredness, because her first thoughts were maybe rather unkind. It was a nondescript house, in a nondescript street, in a nondescript town! And we were about to turn their lives upside down.

Answering simultaneously, both faces at the door appeared to be in their mid-sixties. This would later be confirmed.

"Mr and Mrs MacLeod?" asked Curry, whilst extending his warrant card. "Police Scotland, may we come in."

A consoling arm was tenderly extended along his wives shoulder, as DC Hayes broke the news. Irene MacLeod wept quietly as her husband pulled her close.

Several minutes passed before the emotional silence was broken.

"What happened to her?" he asked quietly.

Both Hayes and Curry had agreed in transit they would not mention her kidneys being removed at this point. No family needs to hear that initially. If doing so was wrong, they would happily take the flak together.

"It would appear she was attacked. Either at or on her way back from a ceilidh sir," Curry stated.

"Was she? You know…" asked Stuart MacLeod hesitantly.

"At the moment sir, it would appear that your daughter was neither raped or sexually abused. That would need to be confirmed of course, but early indications say she wasn't."

The parents hug, became even tighter on that news.

DC's Hayes and Curry stared directly at one another, both guiltily thinking - No, not molested as such… but her attacker gutted her kidneys out!

Melissa's parents stayed a whole five minute walk away from their beloved daughter. Both at opposite ends of the deserted, desolate, run down High Street that the officers drove through on their way into town. The Whitburn Coat of Arms greeted you on a signpost as you entered in off the M8 motorway. The town's rather dated, uninspiring motto was - 'Onward.'

As both serving police officers looked out at their dreary surroundings, they wished they could have done just that! In fairness to the much forgotten wasteland called Whitburn. It had been an old, working class mining town and when

Polkemmet Colliery - their large coal mine closed in the mid eighties, the town had spiralled on a downward trajectory ever since.

Mr and Mrs MacLeod were a rather resigned couple 'Hanna' Hayes thought. Resigned with their lot in life and what the world offered. Resigned to the fact that their daughter was gone, but pragmatically asking, "So what can we do to help?" Amazing as this was, the two detectives had been taken by complete surprise. However on the plus side, the background information required on her upbringing, childhood and career just flowed and flowed. They would have to carefully dissect what they felt would be relevant and suitable. But ultimately, they had been provided with an abundance of details to be going on with. When a Family Liaison Officer joined them fifteen minutes later, it was time for Hayes and Curry, *the two most successful 'detectives' in the history of West Lothian,* to depart.

'Hanna' Hayes had contacted Amanda, the flatmate of Deborah Griggs by text on their way to Whitburn. At 4pm her response to DC Hayes regarding her friend was:

'Not home yet.' Two hours later, after they left the MacLeod home it read: *'Getting really concerned.'*

A further twenty minutes after that and driving east, along the deserted M8 motorway, they soon merged onto the A720 city bypass. At 6.35pm as they reached Sheriffhall roundabout, her next text read:

'No one knows where she is. I am sick with worry.'

Having an actual conscience, generally discouraged in the force, was in fact one of the major traits DI Murray actively encouraged. Susan 'Hanna' Hayes then called Amanda direct.

She told her that her bosses and police colleagues all knew about Deborah's no-show. She then further informed her that they would all be keeping a vigilant eye out for her at the pubs, clubs and various locations that many of them had been assigned to visit with throughout the evening. 'Hanna' Hayes also promised that she would personally visit with her tomorrow with an update. And hopefully if 'Debs,' as Amanda called her, returned home before then, normal service could be resumed.

An all too familiar howling, damp, wet and miserable wind was swirling wildly throughout the cobbled streets of Edinburgh. It had just turned 6.50pm as Hanlon and his Inspector returned to Murray's car which appeared to have been parked under a flickering, faulty street light. Darkness was in full effect and passers-by could hear both men sing…

"R. E. S. P. E. C. T - Find out what it means to me - R. E. S. P. E. C. T - Take care, TCB."

Kudos to Joseph Hanlon, Murray thought. He had all the moves and little nuances, fair play to him. At that, a small vibration in his trouser pocket was cue enough for -

"No rest for the wicked," to be uttered.

"Perhaps that was a favourite saying of your mother also?" Hanlon quipped.

Murray viewed the screen and could clearly see who was calling. He was about to give Joe a clue, but Hanlon's guess came in quickly.

"Is that him boss? This should be interesting."

"Hello," the voice said. It was rich and textured. "Is that Inspector Murray? This is a Mister Jordan, Max Jordan." His tone was very pronounced and proper. It was just not the accent Murray had expected to hear.

"A Constable Hanlon left me a message to call you on this number."

It was exactly similar to when you listen to radio announcers. You have an image of them forming in your mind. You listen to them regularly, and then… WHAM! One day you see an actual picture of them and think, wait a minute that can't be right! They don't look like that! That's not correct! What do you know? You pictured them all wrong. They were taller, shorter, thinner, larger. Blonde - not brunette. Glasses - not contacts. Had a wavy perm… no, no, no it should be cropped. And how was I to know they were black!

"Sorry, yes Mr Jordan. Where are you sir? We really need to meet up with you in person."

Alarmed at this response, Max Jordan exclaimed, "What has happened Inspector? I'm just off a flight from London. What's wrong? Are my family okay? How did you get my number? What was so important?"

DI Murray had tried initially to interrupt. But Jordan's raised voice was emotional and emphatic. Steven Murray allowed him to finish and in hindsight he was glad he did.

"Everything is fine sir, I assure you. We are just making some enquiries into a murder investigation and…"

"A murder investigation! How on earth does it involve me? I've been in London for the last few days. I'm a builder Inspector. I'm currently working…"

"On a renovation project! Yes, yes we are well aware sir. Your son told us all that. But we would like to speak to you nonetheless. When do you return home?"

There was a brief silence at the other end. Max Jordan was

mulling over the Inspector's words. A murder investigation. They had spoken with Craig. Why did he give them my number? What had HE done?

"Sir, Mr Jordan! Did you hear me?"

Steven Murray knew fine well he had heard him, but he was rattled about something. A rather more timid, passive voice returned to the phone line.

"I return home tomorrow morning Inspector."

"Then I will look forward to speaking with you again tomorrow evening then sir. Only this time in person. We'll be in touch. See you then," Murray stated in a firm, yet friendly manner.

"Tomorrow. Sure. Yes. See you then," was mumbled back in a less assured manner.

During all of this time, DC Hanlon had remained attached to Inspector Murray's side. Getting the gist of the conversation based on the one-sided commentary that he had been privy to hear.

"So we are back here tomorrow to see Daddy Bear?" Hanlon offered.

Murray nodded in the affirmative and then yelled, "Get me PC Richards immediately 'Sherlock! It's urgent."

The Detective Inspector then gave a wry smile to his colleague, pointed toward the stairs that they had just came down and announced…

"Yes, indeed we are back tomorrow 'Sherlock.' But right now," he added adamantly, "We are going to see who's been eating my porridge!"

DC Hanlon as was often the case, had no idea what his boss was on about. But Murray had already turned back toward the Jordan's flat and was now taking the stairs two at

87

a time. What had Daddy Bear said he wondered. His Inspector had a renewed strength and vigour. He was excited, with an extremely smug smile on his face.

"We are coming for you," he cried out above the clumping sound of their shoes on the concrete.

"Coming for who?" Hanlon questioned, several steps behind his boss - "Goldilocks?"

A few seconds elapsed before the larger than life Steven Murray set foot on the Jordan landing once again. Possibly disturbing the neighbours, his voice boomed impetuously.

"Not Goldilocks DC Hanlon. But one lying little naked scrotum pole!" he yelled.

Detective Chief Inspector Barbra Furlong has most definitely got a lot to answer for Hanlon reckoned, as a wide grin beamed across his face. She has also greatly enhanced the entertainment levels. For the second time that day, 'Sherlock' raised his hand to the door as Murray sang out.

"Knock three times…"

ELEVEN

"Dear Sir or Madam will you read my book? It took me years to write, will you take a look? It's based on a novel by a man named Lear. And I need a job...... so I want to be a paperback writer."

- The Beatles

Back at the station, Curry and Hayes reviewed their notes. They both agreed that they got off lightly breaking the news to those parents. On the other hand, had it been younger individuals on their own, or if it had been a husband, wife or partner, they reckoned they would have been way more distraught or torn up.

"There was nothing untoward there," Curry said.

The MacLeod's daughter had been a bank teller at the local RBS branch in Whitburn. It had been her home throughout all her 42 years. Attending both Primary School and High School in the old mining town. Throughout her teenage years she was a regular ball girl at Whitburn Juniors football matches. She had been their biggest fan since age four. That was when her father had taken her along one wild, wet and windy Saturday afternoon, Irene MacLeod made a point of clarifying for everyone. Sweet, fresh-faced Melissa from that day forth was not only hooked on football, but her local side! All the players, staff and social club members were well aware of Melissa Margaret MacLeod.

An average, academic student at school, she had no real aspirations in life. Got a job in the bank at seventeen and had been there ever since. Steady, solid, reliable. Contented to live at home up until her mid-twenties. Then she eventually moved out to share a flat with an old female friend from schooldays.

"The boss knew we would get nothing from speaking to the parents. It was all about us breaking the news. Giving us that responsibility and seeing how we would react to it wasn't it 'Hanna'?"

'Hanna' Hayes shrugged her shoulders and gave a rather disheartened smile. "It would appear so," she added. She ran her finger under the final draft of what they had typed up - it read:

That arrangement lasted for about two years, before her flatmate married and left to start a new life with her husband in West Yorkshire. With fifteen years having passed, Melissa had remained in the same two bedroomed flat ever since. She herself never married and her two elderly parents, if mid 60's could be considered elderly, stayed at the opposite end of the High Street from her.

At this point, the officers genuinely wondered whether either of them would be invited to do the eulogy at her funeral, given the current depth of background details they had so far ascertained!

In summary, it would seem that Melissa MacLeod had ventured into Edinburgh on her own. This would appear to be a regular twice monthly thing.

A flirtatious ex-bank colleague from several years ago had introduced her to ceilidh dancing, Stuart MacLeod had told them. Like the football many years previous, she instantly loved the whole experience and had attended many different venues over the intervening years. But since 'Thistle Do Nicely' had opened up, no where else got a look in.

Their shift done, both Hayes and Curry headed home.

"Officers! I thought we were done?" a rather more alert Craig Jordan responded, as he opened his front door for the second time that evening to two of Police Scotland's finest.

"So did we Mr Jordan," Hanlon shrugged.

"What changed?" Jordan asked anxiously. Biting at his lip and tugging at his ear.

Cover up, deceit and lies. This poor man didn't do them well 'Sherlock' smiled.

"I happened to speak with your father. That is what CHANGED," clarified Inspector Murray. "You've made me climb back up all those stairs and there must be easily three or four hundred of them," he exaggerated. "So it had better be worth it."

Shaking his head in a rather bemused manner, Jordan remarked dismissively, "There is a lift you know Inspector. Plus…" he then added sheepishly, "There is only about forty or so steps. And what had better be worth it?"

Oh-oh. Still with the attitude, Hanlon recognised. He's gonna regret that yet again, he thought silently to himself.

"Our guided tour of your house. Just like your daddy promised."

"Yeh, yeh, good one Inspector, but I don't think so." He shook his head adamantly.

"We've already seen half of it. What is your problem Mr Jordan?" Murray threw out there.

DC Hanlon then couldn't resist the opportunity for a dig. "Got yourself some sexy, illegal thongs you don't want us to find sir?" His smile was wider than the span of the Golden Gate Bridge.

The Inspector however was in no real mood for messing

about. "Two people are dead you little tosspot. Stand aside and let us in. You told us only you and your father stayed here."

"And that's right," the man nervously agreed. Licking furiously at his lips and scratching the back of his thumb, also seemed to drastically reduce his credibility with regard to telling the truth.

"Please…" Murray said from halfway down the hallway. This time he was inspecting the modern chic photographs on the wall. Interesting he thought, as he admired the signed artwork.

"You can't just come in here and…"

"Arrest him DC Hanlon," Murray barked.

"What!"

"What!"

Both men shouted over each other.

"Remember your wardrobe malfunction earlier young man?"

Craig Jordan froze.

"We are charging you for indecent exposure. Sorry, but we really have no option."

"You are kidding. This is harassment."

"Indeed it was sir. Sexual harassment! Were you trying to bribe two police officers? Because I don't think I'll ever be the same again."

"You're both enjoying this aren't you? You're disgusting."

"WE ARE disgusting?" Murray broke into his west coast pantomime voice and raised it substantially. "We're not the ones swingin' it around like an Indian elephant son. You could 'ave taken someone's eye out with that thing! Possession of a dangerous weapon Joe, add that to the charges."

Hanlon was in seventh heaven. Desperately he tried not to burst a gut as he approached at pace. He had his wrist restraints at the ready. Then, just as 'Sherlock' grabbed the man's left arm and swung it forcibly behind his back, over and above Craig Jordan's protestations - a voice of reason spoke calmly.

"That is unless we can resolve the situation amicably? Maybe whilst you escort us throughout your property sir. What do you think?" DI Murray offered with a friendly, resigned look.

An air of prolonged silence prevailed.

Hanlon focused on his boss.

Jordan glanced over his shoulder at 'Sherlock.'

While the overall architect of this untimely raid, Detective Inspector Steven Murray, scrutinised every move of 'John Merrick,' aka The Elephant Man!

"You had better be quick," Jordan announced.

Hanlon released his grip, put his restraints away and added, "Absolutely, I'll boil the kettle shall I?"

When the door to the first bedroom swung open, Craig Jordan looked guiltily toward the floor and Joseph Hanlon gave a knowing look to his Inspector.

Murray then ran his tongue under his bottom lip in an effort to remain calm.

He spoke impatiently. "Care to enlighten us Craig - as to which of you two men sleep in this room?"

The aggrieved Jordan's face was a combination of anger and embarrassment.

"I did not lie to you," he said defensively. "You don't understand."

"Excuse me!" 'Sherlock' scolded him, whilst looking over at the lavender and pink duvet set on the single bed. Hanlon then read several of the iconic quotes that had been carefully hand written with pastel shades onto the 'arctic' white walls. Two of which were done in peach, the other finished off in a beautiful shade of green. Above the velour headboard it read: *You know my name, not my story. You've heard what I've done, not what I've been through.* Several of the other sayings decorating the room were more familiar to DC Hanlon. Including the iconic verse scrawled high above the doorway as you exited the room. It was the mint green one - *Stop looking for happiness in the same place you lost it.*

"She doesn't live here," Jordan repeated.

For the first time doubt crept into DC Hanlon's mind. Had Murray got it wrong about this man? He now heard him speak with a more resigned air to his voice. No longer feeling the need to pretend or protect. Had that been it all along? Not about him being caught out, but about protecting someone else? In those two lines - 'I didn't lie to you; She doesn't live here,' Joseph Hanlon heard... Let me explain.

'Sherlock' offered, "So is it a girlfriend or co-worker or maybe..."

"It's his sister!" Murray interjected. "What's her name? Linda? Laura? Lisa?"

"Lucy," Craig Jordan stated quickly, in a startled, shocked manner.

"But how..."

DI Murray interrupted Hanlon, before he even began. "Every one of those prints in the hallway are signed by an L. Jordan and even with my limited detective skills, I figured it didn't stand for Max or Craig! So, elementary my dear

Hanlon," Murray grinned. "Go check on that kettle Joe. I think Mr Jordan should put on some clothes and freshen up also. We could be a while. What do you say sir? How does a hot brew and some crunchy 'honesty' hobnobs sound?"

The young man tugged again at the cord on his flapping dressing gown, rubbed the back of his hand against his chin and blinked in the affirmative. He then made his way back along the hallway to the bathroom, before offering up a rather hollow sounding, "Give me a minute."

Murray at that moment felt inspired to sign up for the unguided tour. What a master he had become at enabling those opportunities to present themselves!

Twelve minutes later, face washed, feeling refreshed, alert and with it, for the first time that day, Craig Jordan sat opposite both men and took one deep, sharp almighty breath.

"Any exciting plans for tonight Craigie Boy?" Murray asked gruffly . "Or are you still trying to get last night out of your system?"

"Well…"

Before Jordan could get past that first word, Murray's hoarse voice continued at speed with, "Out of curiosity, what did last night and the night before even look like?" The words pumped out faster than 'the Flying Scotsman!'

"Do you mean, like where was I those two nights?"

Sharp as a rubber cricket bat Hanlon acknowledged, by way of closing his eyes and counting to three. He also reckoned whoever came up with that cricket bat saying should be shot. However on a more serious playing field, as he began to closely monitor Jordan's interaction with his boss he genuinely wondered at the authenticity of Craig Jordan's 'thick Scottish persona.'

He was the manager of a top retail outlet and alongside those quality photographs in the hallway, hung at least two graduation certificates for Business Management. One was from college, the other a University degree, and both were awarded to a Mr Craig A. Jordan. This guy was more than capable Hanlon considered. Earlier, he was deliberately trying to deceive or fool them into thinking that he was fumbling and thick. The cover up part was accurate though, Hanlon reckoned. More importantly, it was something Craig Jordan felt worthy of covering up. His 'one sandwich short' routine was a clearly defined distraction... but again, from what?

Hanlon's visual perusal continued. There was plenty of quality literature scattered throughout shelves, tables and bookcases. This home was without doubt, a place of learning. This was not a family of couch potatoes. So why the charade, the over the top pantomime act from Jordan junior? *The Godfather; A book on Nostradamus; Roots; The Pelican Brief and Treasure Island* to name but a few, adorned nearby units. Contemporary, classic and iconic. There was no way 'Craigie Boy' had not read those or at the very least had been influenced growing up in a household of people that did.

At that precise moment, 'Sherlock' instantly recalled one of DI Murray's favourite mantras - 'Leaders are Readers.' For his part, Joseph Hanlon preferred the more all encompassing - 'Leaders are Learners.' He felt it was far more contextually accurate. He then also vividly remembered how only six months ago Steven Murray had sat him down and gave him a thirty second overview on succeeding in the force. It was not what Hanlon had expected. Because the simple key factor his Inspector had informed him… was reading!

Initially Joe Hanlon thought he was pulling his leg. But by the end of the half minute discourse, he'd got it. So much so, that to this day he could still remember it word for word. The fact that he'd recorded it onto his mobile phone may also have been a key factor! Listened to regularly ever since, as Hanlon scanned the further array of novels and textbooks in the Jordan's cosy flat, he could hear the 'Play' button in his mind begin once more.

'Reading gives us access to experiences that are not our own Joe. It exposes us to how other people approach problems in business and in life. And you know what DC Hanlon? This then gives leaders more options to make better decisions. Through reading, individuals are exposed to different perspectives that may encourage them to take a new or unique approach to conflicts. It also helps promote tolerance of views outside of their own. Reading Joe, is without doubt the best possible way to become a better leader. Go find some great biographies, best sellers and stories from people you respect - You won't regret it. You'll be Chief Constable in no time!'

"Both nights you were home, that's what you are telling me and sticking with?" Murray questioned, disbelievingly.

Hanlon had been totally oblivious to Craig Jordan's response. He had tuned out. He'd been too busy with his English literature observations and wondered if DI Murray gave that 'reading lecture' to all his team? Now he was fully back in the game. Just in time to witness 'Craigie' boy's buffoonery act continue.

"Well, no, obviously last night I was out. I mentioned that earlier, possibly I had a bit too much to drink."

"Possibly!" Hanlon added, as confirmation of the fact.

"So, Thursday night home. Friday you're getting blitzed," the Inspector stated. Before adding, "With whom and where?"

More scratching, eye blinks and rubber mouthed motions preceded his nervous and tentative response. "No one, and at the dancing he offered with another perfectly timed hand running through his recently showered locks.

Inspector Steven Murray closed his mouth firmly and inhaled powerfully through his nose. He then calmly exhaled through his mouth just as his phone rang.

"I need to take this sir," he offered to Mr Jordan. He then nodded (a 41) to 'Sherlock.'

DC Hanlon hastily offered some friendly advice to the boy with the attitude.

"Sir, I believe my superior officer rather successfully at the moment and who knows how long that will continue, is trying desperately to restrain himself from throwing you head first through that nearby window! I would encourage you to be a bit more informative in future please. I have no desire to wipe up the mess from downstairs."

The Inspector thanked his fellow officer for getting back to him and hung up. Wow, that's impressive Murray thought. Having still managed to overhear 'Sherlock's' living room performance. Joe Hanlon's perfectly polite, yet threatening manner was a joy to behold!

Craig Jordan then began to miraculously sober up. He seemed to be weighing up Hanlon's remarks and offsetting them against the possible consequences 'Sherlock' referred to.

"I was at the Ceilidh club in Seafield Road last night. Both my sister and my dad were away elsewhere on Thursday evening."

"Dad in London. Lucy at?" Murray enquired.

"Who knows! It's like I tried to tell you earlier, it is actually just me and my dad. She occasionally sleeps over these days, but not often." His eyes failed to meet any of the officers during those last comments.

A simple fact that did not escape either Hanlon or Murray.

"My phone call Mr Jordan. It was from a PC Richards."

Jordan's face went redder than an Aberdeen football shirt!

"Yes, I thought as much. We'll see ourselves out…"

TWELVE

"He's gonna lock himself up in his room, shutter the windows and bolt all the doors. Wrap himself up in his Wall Street cocoon, he's painting the ceiling, the walls and the floor."

- The Boomtown Rats

The large hands on the statement making clock above the drinks, had just turned to six thirty that Saturday evening. The thin, willowy figure dressed in smart designer jeans and a bold orange v-neck sweater, stood at the bar awaiting her order. She was also busy chatting on her mobile at the same time. Who said women couldn't multi-task? The irony in that being, the JD Wetherspoon's pub that she was currently frequenting was called - The Alexander Graham Bell. Duly named after the Scots born inventor of the telephone. Nearby, literally a stone throw away in South Charlotte Street was his birthplace. In four years time, in 2020, it would be the one hundred year centenary of Bell being made a Freeman of Edinburgh.

The bar itself was bustling. Weekend crowds, a mixture of tourists and locals swelled its ranks. A cacophony of chit-chat, conversations and lively banter, continually rose into a deafening orchestral performance!

"Miss Cardwell?" The voice from behind asked abruptly. There seemed to be a hint of the North-east in his accent, Newcastle or Sunderland.

"Miss Christina Cardwell?" He repeated rather aggressively.

At 5' 10' she was certainly no shrinking violet and with her four inch heels on, she towered above both men.

The distracted barman found himself preoccupied preparing her drink. There would be no rest for him for a while, as a row of impatient customers waited two deep at the bar. The leggy blonde had taken her phone down from her ear and her conversation with her mother instantly ceased. No 'goodbyes,' 'see you soon' or 'I love you' had been offered. But she did manage in hindsight, to say what would later become five very prophetic words.

She knew who they were. She had encountered them often enough, growing up in and around the crime riddled streets of lower-class Leith. Mainly her familiarity with them was through the brother of her mother. He'd been a product of the local council's foster system and only in his late teens did he track down and reunite with his sister. They had been previously separated for over a decade.

"It's about your Uncle pet," the man told her.

A Geordie then she guessed. Pet this, pet that. How's it going pet, that'll be a'right pet. The tall, cropped haired Tina Cardwell smiled and expressed gruffly...

"They must have more mini zoos in and around Gateshead, than anywhere else on the planet!"

Both offered a confused look at each other.

The smaller of the two men, then added with a Scottish lilt. "We need you to come with us right away. It's serious."

As the barman returned to the counter, complete with what looked like a Coca-Cola mixer. His voice began with, "That'll be ……"

All three had gone.

"Who's next?" he added professionally.

It was several miles west, at the opposite end of the M8 motorway, where the quiet stranger exchanged a substantial monetary deposit for a house key. A bog standard 'Yale,' as they were known in the UK. An old, previously used, discoloured copper one to be precise. Marked and scratched it had obviously seen many tenants come and go over the years. What a mass of sinister and unique stories it could tell no doubt, as it once again opened the imposing portal. Modern electronic pass keys hadn't quite made the transition to this particular group of rather sadly neglected flats quite yet!

A keen eyed observer could spot dates carved on many of the buildings in the area. These inscriptions testified to an era of great expansion in Glasgow. This particular run-down tenement was nearly ninety years old and housed eight other properties in the block. Two on the ground floor and three on each of the other two levels. This short term let was for the centre flat, on the middle landing. It was the ideal location for his needs.

As the less than trustworthy looking landlord exited the small, dingy, one bedroomed hovel. His latest tenant promptly bolted the graffiti riddled door behind him. As soon as he had done that, he almost immediately turned off the room light, purposely walked toward the bay window, undid the central latch, got both his large, muscular, tattooed hands in below its frame and pulled it firmly up about ten inches. Quickly, cool air began to circulate the room. Each breeze dragged with it, the stench of poverty and a long gone, industrial past.

Events were getting closer and becoming more real at the passing of each day. The M99 was soon lifted from its protective case and ceremonially set up. Its detachable bipod, with its clever adjustable legs gave it two inches to spare below the opened window. The barrel and laser were then gently inched out into the fresh evening air. His neck relaxed and was gently rested at a comfortable angle against the cool, brushed steel. An elongated finger was then positioned lightly on the trigger and he appeared superbly confident as he gazed through the perfectly adjusted telescopic sight. The projected 'hotspot' was soon aimed at a random female approximately 100 yards away. The regular sized white carrier bag that she carried was being colourfully enhanced with a red dot dancing diligently across the plastic. The tensed finger then eased away fully from the sensitive trigger. His head lifted and sixty seconds later the aged, rotting window was closed. The armed transient sat back down in a composed, collected manner and uttered faintly to himself…"The perfect view."

His Model 99 had been designed for one thing only: to get the job done. It was rugged, reliable and uncomplicated. With its brilliantly simple design, hard-core construction and surprisingly few moving parts, it offered match-winning accuracy time and time again. Each round fired was a fine balance of science and skill. The M99 had become known as much for its dependability, as its versatility. Once again the nomadic professional felt the need to tidy up and lubricate the trigger housing, having disconnected it firstly from the barrel. A nylon bristle brush was then made to work its magic on the locking lugs, with the bolt face being cleaned thoroughly also.

Afterwards in true celebratory fashion, the hired gunman threw his two feet back up onto the sofa, laid back casually and smiled. The expression was long, calculated and ruthless.

Just like his trusted partner... Mr Barrett!

Back on the east coast as the evening continued, a gun had been thrust aggressively into Tina Cardwell's blood ravaged mouth. Agonisingly breaking three of her lower front teeth. Her left eye, presently the size of a table tennis ball after several horrendous beatings, had swollen shut and looked dangerously close to exploding. Veins and tiny blood vessels on the outer eyelid acted as an intricate road map to hell. Every shade of black and blue had been applied to her bare legs, hips and upper body. Naked, she had been tied securely by what looked like an old tow rope to an aged, rustic, broken down wooden chair. It's archaic high back worked perfectly for this violent, seemingly senseless torture. The trio of bodies appeared to be located in a seedy, badly lit, disused lock-up or garage. Fumes from petrol, grease and oil oozed at regular intervals from the pores of the crumbling, dilapidated brickwork. Recent graffiti, screamed out aggressively from each wall and a dated, five foot long fluorescent strip light flickered randomly above their heads. How electricity still ran through the unit was in itself a minor miracle.

The other work of God currently taking place in that Parish, was the fact that the tender, thin, fragile thirty-two year old mother of three was still alive. Her body which had been persistently pounded, now appeared limp and lifeless. Brutally and savagely battered to within an inch of her life. She had been continually struck and thumped with bare fists. Oversized hands that belonged to two demonic cowards with diamond edged knuckles had repeatedly swung down upon her. The bulk of the damage had been inflicted by their large, sharp, penetrating rings. Her once beautiful, flawless face with cherished pale complexion and dimpled cheeks had been torn, gashed and cut to shreds. Like a cheap fabric dress, it had been ripped violently and discriminately as blow after blow reigned down fiercely. So much so, a stranger would no longer be able to tell if it were a White, Black, Asian or Oriental figure that was flopped unconscious in front of them. Never mind, male or female.

"Why Aye Man!" the Newcastle thug muttered cockily as he stood upright and proudly puffed out his chest. His bulging Geordie finger gently and slowly caressed the trigger. He never hesitated. One clean squeeze and Christina Cardwell's brains exited stage left, high across the discarded 2011 Michelin wall calendar. As policemen go, these two were certainly more 'Monster' than 'God.' However, Cardwell had assumed by their mannerisms, dress and features that they WERE members of Her Majesty's finest. She had never asked to see any proper form of I.D. Though needless to say, the small compact revolver that the short Scotsman had concealed in his pocket would still have convinced her to leave quietly. Her last statement earlier in the evening to her ageing mother, would never now be fulfilled. Ironically, the five innocent words that ended her conversation with her mum were quite simply - "I'll give you a bell!"

Having returned home at nine forty-five on the Saturday night to the stillness of his own lonely four bedroomed property. It was now fully two hours later and after much turning and tossing, Murray sat up wide awake in bed. His hair was all over the place. He was at least grateful though to still have some. A receding hairline and baldness did not appeal. His chin sagged forward, tears filled his eyes. Who knew the reason behind them? By now it had struck midnight. It was a new day. Could it be as simple as that? In recent years he had realised that there needn't ever be any specific reason.

He quickly scanned through yesterday's news on his iPad. A 29 year old family man had collapsed and died after returning home from his daily morning run. Murray's stomach churned painfully as he read that. He hated life. He craved to cocoon himself away in the privacy of his home. To effectively shutter the doors and barricade himself inside. Then through the wonder of the Internet, immerse himself in all that was good, uplifting and inspiring in the world. Conversely if possible, he'd then filter out all the bad, depressing and awful events from around the globe. At that moment, he simply wanted to blast out his 'feel good' music and live in his own stress free utopia. Heavenward he would look up, rub at his stubbled face and utter, "please take me."

Once again he was exhausted. He almost always felt tired before it was time to freshen up, dress and put on another five star performance for the world. A world in which he was only an isolated, tiny, minute particle. Nature, nurture. Success, failure. Rich, poor. Sane or insane? Murray's generous heart was breaking. He had failed so many and so often he would tell himself. Never mind bipolar, Murray saw himself as a polar opposite in relation to how so many other people viewed him. They witnessed a man of laughter, joy and bright spirits. An often larger than life character. One bringing out the best in others and continually inspiring them along the way. In recent years, a man that loved to travel, make friends and experience new adventures and cultures. A strong, principled man of integrity and faith. Again Murray clawed desperately at his hair. Clumps of it came away, uprooted and entangled in his ragged bitten down nails. Looking in the mirror, Inspector Steven Murray felt sick on a regular daily basis. The reflection he was aware of - Was of a self-centred, selfish individual. A man of low moral standing. A cheat, a liar and a weakling. A man that had gotten thus far in life with his charm and wit and very little else. In recent months he had sorely wished he had taken that early morning train journey instead of DCI Keith Brown. But once again he was too much of a coward. Even although everyone else would have reckoned it was the easy way out. For Murray, no way out was easy - for the moment, sadly, he was living proof of that!

THIRTEEN

"Emancipate yourselves from mental slavery. None but ourselves can free our minds. Have no fears for atomic energy. Because none of them can stop the time."

- Bob Marley and the Wailers

In the early hours of Sunday morning...

Sleep had went rather well or as well as suspension of voluntary bodily functions normally can. Murray had managed a good five and a half hours. Which was about the norm for him these days. Over recent years he had saw the marked change. This had occurred for several reasons. But the catalyst had undoubtedly been the tragic death of his wife and subsequent break up of his beloved family.

The healthy, yet often challenging to achieve: Eight hour - wake up blissfully refreshed sleep, was the first to fall by the wayside. Then after a few months that had further decreased to around seven hours. So instead of sleeping all day and feeling depressed the Inspector in the words of one of his favourite eighties bands XTC, had actually found his *'senses working overtime.'* His mind would then be ablaze with ideas, suggestions and theories in regard to his current caseload and every last ounce of energy and resource would be channelled down that particular outlet. In the last few years though, that duration had joined forces with the new 'Even

Less Sleep Company' and together their recent merger created the unstoppable: '5 Hours Will Do' Corporation! Murray in recent times had figured he got 30% less sleep, but had become 50% more productive. At least that was how he sold it to himself.

This morning Edward Sharpe and the Magnetic Zeros *'Home'* had been replaced in the shower, as they had been for the previous four mornings. Was this a shift in power? The Scandinavian Avicii, had never been on Murray's musical radar before. The Swedish DJ, known for his modern dance tunes would not have been in the sphere of sound that the detective normally ventured. However, he had caught the inspiring music video that accompanied the song and was instantly hooked.

'The Nights' spoke about the endless possibilities of what you could achieve in this life and the wonderfully wise words of a father to a son. It's impact was such that Murray now considered it one of his all time top ten songs. One day he thought, he would actually get around to listing those tunes. But at the moment he was far too busy energising himself for the day ahead. With his hair already washed and rinsed and his body currently lathered in the aromatic coconut and lime shower gel - he was primed and ready. And so began his vocal exercises...

"Hey, once upon a younger year, when all our shadows disappeared, the animals inside came out to play."

His docile eyes closed tightly as he allowed the powerful shower to blast away and awaken all his senses.

"Hey, when face to face with all your fears; Learned our lessons through the tears, made memories we knew would never fade."

In an animated, brisk fashion he continued to sing

cheerfully whilst rubbing eagerly away the last remnants of bubbles and froth from his refreshed, muscular legs. He was still in good shape for a man of his age and as he stepped from the glass doored cubicle, he had just began the poignant chorus of the song.

"One day my father - he told me, 'Son, don't let it slip away.' He took me in his arms, I heard him say, 'When you get older, your wild life will live for younger days, think of me if ever you're afraid.'"

As Murray dried his body vigorously, he began to slow down and then ceased the process altogether. He had stopped singing. Over the past few days and several dozen listens, he had realised this was the part that required no accompaniment. These were the words that struck him on the very first listen and were still the most relevant to him each day. The uncredited singer echoed...

"One day you'll leave this world behind, so live a life you will remember. My father told me when I was just a child, these are the nights that never die."

Murray had previously wiped away all of the excess moisture from his newly re-energised body. His overtly fluffy, white cotton bath towel had been replaced carefully back over the warm, tall, wall-mounted stainless steel radiator. That was when the small melancholic teardrop decided to make it's early morning appearance. An index finger was alert to the dawn raid and was quickly despatched to resolve the issue. Departing the steamed up bathroom and with his accompanying iPod on shuffle, next up was the recently relegated Edward Sharpe and his Magnetic Zeros. As he walked along his beige carpeted, upstairs corridor his neighbour's and the surrounding community were soon treated to...

"Home, let me come home. Home is wherever I'm with you..."

A text had been received by him earlier in the morning. It must have been while he'd been gyrating wildly in the shower area he reckoned. Now having arrived at the station, he had just noticed it! It was from Furlong. First thing on a SUNDAY morning! And she only started yesterday... oh joy, he thought. But he couldn't have been further from the truth. It wasn't directly about work, or at least not this case Murray could be certain.

It read: *Just a heads up - DCI Cleland from Complaints needs to meet you - Monday after lunch. Barbra.*

It certainly took them long enough Murray considered and it was the last thing he needed right now. But probably more worrying than everything that may involve, was the fact that she had signed it 'Barbra!'

Dave Cleland operated out of Glasgow. He was an experienced officer. It would be interesting.

Both DC's Hayes and Curry were due in for 10.00am that Sunday morning, given that 'Hanna' Hayes was heading back to visit with Amanda, Deborah Griggs' room mate.

Murray had pondered over the best course of action on how best to address Andrew 'Kid' Curry. During his recent sleepless nights he had put the early 4.00am rises to good use, or at least he hoped he had. On his arrival at the station, the Inspector was made aware that Drew was in the building.

The 'Kid' was busily eating what appeared to be a runny amalgamation of spaghetti bolognese and ravioli. Or was it possibly even a heavily disguised lasagne Murray considered. The Inspector had long since stopped using the staff canteen for that very reason. He may in professional terms be considered a detective. But eventually, especially in recent months, when he lined up the 'usual suspects' from the kitchen - he had no idea who was who, or what was what!

"Sir!" Curry blurted out. Caught unawares by his superior officer, he instantly went to stand.

Murray quickly shook his head, placed his hand on his constable's wrist and uttered, "What are you doing Drew? Sit back down. Since when do you have to stand to attention in my presence?"

The young officer blushed profusely. "Sorry sir. Nerves I guess."

"I guess," Murray considered. He then watched as Andrew Curry continued to eat vigorously. He made no attempt to make eye contact with his Inspector. He was focused fully on his plate, but his previous passion for his meal seemed to have had deserted him. His fork now began to play with the sauce around the rim. From time to time he would flick broken strands of spaghetti back into the centre of the dish. Twirling, twisting and serenading his pasta, Curry was simply stalling for time Murray concluded. So here goes he said to himself…

"How did your chat with DCI Furlong go?"

"Ye, ye, alright I suppose," he said. Looking up briefly with a…

"You have a piece of spaghetti stuck to your…"

Before Murray could finish, Curry had wiped at his face fully with a napkin. He continued to dab at the corners of his mouth as his Inspector continued.

"What does alright look like? Does that mean she praised you? Was happy with your work and offered support and encouragement? Or was it an 'alright,' as in you really need to pull your socks up, start making better decisions or she would kick your 'Fuddy Dumplings into the middle of next week?"

The 'Kid' smiled. He knew Murray hated ambiguity. His partner 'Hanna' Hayes was older, more experienced and she got the whole speak with clarity, communicate clearly your intent, etc, etc. Andrew Curry on the other hand just needed that little extra reminder from time to time.

Today Detective Inspector Steven Murray had sat down beside him to give him what would ultimately be as far as Murray was concerned, his first and final reminder. He was aware that the young detective had recently broken up with his fiancé Judy, after having been together for about three years. He was noticeably drinking to excess and his new wardrobe of clothes had given DI Murray some real cause for concern. He paused for a few seconds before proceeding.

"Do you remember Gerald Anderson, Drew?" He ask inquisitively.

Curry wondered where this was heading. He suspected that his Inspector must have had a good reason to sit beside him. Especially given Murray's well documented disdain in recent times towards the in-house eating area. Still looking quizzical and curious, the young constable looked up warily to confirm a few things with his DI.

"From the case involving DCI Brown a few months back? That Sir Gerald Anderson?" he asked curtly. "The dead businessman that tried desperately to escape from the casino by sliding down a pole that no longer existed?"

At that last description, Murray winced slightly. He had maybe helped influence that particular decision more than he should have. Everybody makes mistakes at work from time to time and police officers are no different he considered. Most of the time, they can be corrected with coaching or counselling, an honest apology or a sincere promise not to make the same mistake twice. Even Murray got that officers must be held to the highest ethical standards though, and so sometimes those mistakes can rise to a level that require a full internal investigation and possibly severe disciplinary action. Hence his upcoming meeting with Chief Inspector David Cleland from the Internal Investigations Unit. An extremely busy unit, whose workload had increased tenfold throughout the last year alone. Happy days!

DC Hayes was also in bright and early. After being contacted late on the Saturday night long after her shift had ended, she no longer had the stomach or desire to sleep. Several of her colleagues were aware that Hayes had put Deborah Griggs on a watch list. At least two fellow officers recognised the similarities and contacted 'Hanna' directly. Once again the deceased's identification was left with the body. The killer definitely wanted these girls identified as soon as possible. The Friday evening blood and debris incident had now been officially designated a murder scene. Initially it had been put down to a panicked hit and run incident. As such, the surrounding area had now been cordoned off accordingly. Forensic teams and police officers were already busy at work on it. The T'inker, Doctor Thomas Patterson had been called in specially to carry out the postmortem examination.

This time being cut free from the woman's bruised and damaged palm, was a rather poorly made, cheap yet colourful, soft fabric toy. The Doc stated for the benefit of his recording process - 'That it appeared to be a rat or some form of rodent.'

By mid-morning on that busy Sunday, the dead body of a friendly, local librarian lay cold, alone and motionless on a table in the city mortuary.

Back in the equally hygienic canteen, a description that DI Murray would most definitely have raised an eyebrow or two at.

The Inspector openly admitted, "I've made plenty of mistakes in my time young man. But hopefully I have made up for them. That in the intervening years my actions have proved that. In banking terminology - I have made many, many, more deposits than withdrawals."

Curry nodded.

"I see you nodding Andrew. But do you really get what I mean?" Murray's voice sounded exceptionally serious. Possibly even verging into threatening. "Problem was 'Kid' I had no one to turn to or confide in. I needed my very own Police priest! Not only a mentor, but someone willing to take confession now and again. Someone, but not the bosses, that I could trust!"

This time Curry's nod was more vigorous. His eyes locked firmly with the Inspector's. His look this time said, 'I understand, I truly do.'

"Often when we start out toward our destination, we can be naive and forgetful. We may even come across a couple of minor setbacks and our end goal may seem further away Drew than ever. Trust me when I say that is the normal path. We often think other people don't encounter those same challenges, hurdles or roadblocks. Well let me tell you my young friend, and be fully aware that I regard you as my friend," Murray generously offered, "They do! More than you would ever know, they go through and face similar oppositions."

DC Andrew Curry had done extremely well in his short career in the police so far. Partnered with a steady, solid colleague in Susan Hayes he'd been nurtured wonderfully, tested frequently and continually encouraged. All whilst part of DI Murray's close intricate team.

He had carried out his duties well in breaking several major cases and was accordingly recognised for the role that he had played. Today however, Murray was making a stand. The 'Kid' had to grow up, step up and take responsibility for his actions or he was out. Not only from Murray's team, but if some of his suspected hunches were correct, Curry would be out of the force and up on charges!

Murray stood up sharply from the table and suggested, "I'll be your priest 'Kid.' But know that it's a limited time offer… Do you understand?"

One final penitent nod was offered up by Detective Constable Andrew Curry.

FOURTEEN

"An honest man's pillow is his peace of mind."

- John 'Cougar' Mellencamp

Murray had tried desperately throughout the last twenty four hours, ever since Craig Jordan told him his sister's name, not to think about a certain pop song of the past. He had failed miserably!

The 1970's hit ballad written by Shel Silverstein had played constantly in his mind, at least twice an hour throughout the whole day. This time as 'Sherlock' and his Inspector 'Lestrade' made their way up the staircase, *Knock three times* had been replaced vocally with, *"the morning sun touched lightly on the eyes of Lucy Jordan!"*

It was close to eight o'clock when the door was opened. That was the agreed time they had scheduled when Joe Hanlon had spoken with Max Jordan on the phone earlier that day at lunchtime.

Glossy warrant cards, longer than normal handshakes and pleasantries were exchanged. Thus allowing into the warm confines of the Jordan's intimate flat an air of trepidation, anxiety and guilt. It was given time to marinade and simmer gently, before being brought gradually to the boil.

Max Jordan wore a salmon pink, v-neck sweater with dark designer jeans and rustic brown leather shoes. He carried himself well. With a healthy confidence and on first impression it would appear, without his son's arrogance. That certainly was the early, initial vibe picked up by Murray. Although maybe a tad heavy with the aftershave and no shirt or t-shirt under his cashmere top was an interesting choice for someone of his era. Someone trying to appear more macho than he really was? He looked to be in and around the same age bracket as the Inspector himself and that was never a look that was IN! However it was always a look for someone's ego, someone out to impress. That, coupled with a dash too much of the smelly stuff aroused quickly the Inspector's curiosity. *'Splash it all over,'* Murray heard in his head. Yet another 70's flashback to a group of sporting celebrities selling you 'the great power' of Brut aftershave. So who was he trying to score points with? The look between the two officers confirmed that they were both asking that same question. Smiles all round.

Two faces waited in the background. One familiar to both of the detectives, the other about to be.

"And you must be the infamous Lucy Jordan?" Murray posed as a question whilst stepping forward to shake her hand. Then thinking about the nineteen seventies pop song *The Ballad of Lucy Jordan,* he then added for a bit of fun - "I've been thinking about you all day." He was simply trying to mix things up to get a reaction and it certainly worked. Both father and son looked shocked. Lucy herself appeared rather stunned, her mouth agape. Hanlon shook his head in despair, before desperately trying to rescue the situation.

"DC Hanlon, Miss Jordan. How do you do? It's nice to meet you." He then added as mischievously as his Inspector, "You do look familiar though. Maybe it's because your brother has told us so, so much about you!"

"I nev... " Craig Jordan stopped himself.

Glares, smoke signals and alerts were dispatched immediately between all three family members in a variety of encoded messages. Hands through hair - Eyes closed and blocked with fingers - Arms crossed - Ears pinched - Bodies leaning away from each other - Feet being repositioned. Oh my goodness, Murray thought. Bring a body language expert in here right now and they would have a field day. His deliberate little slip of the tongue previously, was already turning up the temperature.

Hanlon cleared his throat. "Mr Jordan, actually both Mr Jordan's can I sit with you in the lounge, while DI Murray speaks with Lucy privately please."

All three men then casually headed toward the sitting room as Murray opened the bedroom door to the pink and white palace. Question is: Did it belong to Snow White or an Ice Queen?

The Inspector watched carefully as Max Hanlon's daughter slowly manoeuvred her way past him. Confidently she prepared to hold court. Not unlike DC Hanlon, Murray felt sure that there was that slight something about her that he recognised. What was it he questioned to himself. Was it her informal manner? Maybe her graceful movement? Her smell? He couldn't quite put his finger on it, but it would come to him, he figured.

The detective for the second time in two days, stared at the bright walls and the artistic quotes of various fonts and sizes that surrounded them. The rose petal designs on the fluffy, cotton pillows sang out to him. This could certainly be a room for refuge or comfort one minute, then an intimate chamber to inspire and uplift the next. Shelter and safety or flight and creativity in equal measure. Murray imagined himself in this space. The owner of this domain most definitely endured bouts of melancholy, mood swings and misery. How it manifested itself would be interesting for Murray to hopefully ascertain.

"No one wants to experience pain," the confident female voice stated calmly. "But at times there would seem to be no other way to teach us some of the valuable lessons of wisdom, humility, patience and endurance that we, each of us, need to experience in this life. Don't you think Inspector?"

Murray thought actually, that those were very profound words from one so young. Obviously this young lady was academically astute. Certainly more naturally capable than her older, delinquent of a brother he soon concluded. Whatever it was, Steven Murray had obviously taken a very strong dislike to her male sibling.

"Hurt and pain can come to us all in a multitude of different ways though Miss Jordan."

"I agree Inspector."

At a few inches shorter in height, Murray would have put her at around 5' 5'.

She paused deliberately, before fully catching the officer's gaze and with sincerity she offered slowly: "Sometimes - it - is - deliberate - and self inflicted."

At that moment, it felt like Lucy Jordan was peering deep into Murray's very character. Into his deeply troubled heart and soul. Were they kindred spirits? Aware of each others colourful past? Or due to some common personality flaws was it just that they could relate and empathise with one another!

"At other times," Lucy added, "It's a natural result of mortality."

The detective, impressed, nodded in full agreement.

"Your father's green business card Miss Jordan. How did it come to be…"

"He'd have had no idea where they were distributed," she duly interrupted. "Craig did all that. I'm not sure anyone apart from my brother even had access or knew where all the business literature was even kept. Dad would give him cash in hand every other week to ensure his help in regularly advertising his business."

"Really?" The DI sighed.

"Really!" Lucy echoed. "At his work, at the dancing, wherever and whenever. It was a few extra pounds for Craig and a winner for everyone."

"I see. Thank you for that. What is it you do yourself Miss Jordan?" Murray added curiously, but really just trying to establish some sort of rapport with the girl.

"Further education Inspector. Can't you tell?" She pointed to the vast array of books and literature on all the shelves. As well as the pile of test papers and essays on the table top in front of her. "To supplement my loans, I've worked in a store in Princes Street since I was seventeen. Flexible hours that I can work around my studies."

Quickly, he then abruptly asked, "How is it, sharing with two men?"

That really seemed to take the young student by surprise. She appeared to hesitate slightly before refocusing.

"Didn't they tell you that my mum died about a decade ago? So I am well used to it by now."

Used to it she may have been. But something in her demeanour said that it hadn't been easy. Murray felt a double whammy unexpectedly surface.

"How did you cope back then? Had your poor mother been ill?

Lucy was taken aback. "She died in a fire," she said without emotion. Her eyes turned back toward the various quotes on her walls and she began to scan them. You could see her revisit specific memories as she scrolled across each segment of lyric.

"Do they represent periods in your life?" Murray softly quizzed.

Miss Jordan's chin dipped in acknowledgement.

The tall police officer could at least understand that connection he thought. "Who is Margaret Mead?" he then asked. Her name was attributed below one of the distinct quotes.

"All different years actually," the young female responded positively. "Mead was an American cultural anthropologist. I discovered her in High School. She was prominent in the United States throughout the 1960's and 70's."

"Really," Murray nodded. "I have never heard of her."

It was as if she wanted desperately to say more, but was aware that her family members were nearby. She would cautiously look toward the door every few seconds. And although she spoke articulately and confidently, it was more than apparent that she seemed wary and apprehensive. Murray would possibly go as far as to say, afraid.

"Are you sure you are okay?"

She nodded and quietly whispered, "Love all Inspector. I find it best to simply love all!"

An admirable quality Murray believed, before stating. "Can I just ask what happened yesterday? Why did PC Richards and his colleague have to pay you a visit?"

Lucy Jordan visibly flinched.

Bingo, DI Murray thought.

Her slender shoulders slumped and her smile disappeared rapidly, as worry, concern and misgiving all visibly streamed across her twenty-something face. What had this poor girl endured? What had she gone through these past ten years? Why the need for the overkill of comforting and inspiring lyrics? Why does she no longer sleep there very often? How does she cope now? When did it stop? The Inspector froze, looked with measured compassion at the frightened individual in front of him and asked himself… Had it even stopped?

Was this the reason for her brother's unease, nerves and caginess? Could he possibly be riddled with guilt? Scared of what his sister may say? Was that why in front of her earlier, he made a big deal about not telling them anything? And she was not being angry and aggressive with him. She was being defensive, scared and wary for the protection of herself and what may be revealed.

Lucy Jordan sat perched hesitantly on the edge of her bed. The shade of the quilt cover and floral patterns matched those of her now bloodshot and tearstained eyes. Everything appeared raw and fresh and that worried DI Murray deeply.

A positively helpful trio of encouraging questions then instantly flew from his lips. "Do you need to report something Miss Jordan? Would you like me to get a female officer in attendance? How can I help you?"

She shook her head and pulled her knees close together. "No, you mustn't. It's fine. Everything is fine," she pleaded.

"I suspect everything is far from fine Lucy. But I need you to make a statement."

"I'd like to be on my own now Inspector."

"Miss Jordan I…"

"My own, please," she said raising her voice.

DI Murray held up his hands in mock surrender mode. "Okay, okay, I'm going next door. But I need you to please remain in here whilst we speak with your brother Craig in the living room."

"You can't say anything Inspector, he'll……" She went quiet

"He'll what Miss Jordan?" The Inspector took the chance and repeated, "What happened yesterday?"

Between continually biting her nails and rubbing at her thighs, her nerves were getting too much for her. She breathed in, put her fingers to her forehead and closed her eyes. She then began to slowly recite one of the numerous quotes adorning her wall space. "It's okay to leave now… It's okay to leave now… It's okay to…"

Murray got the message and quietly exited the room. She had been afraid, maybe not for her life, but definitely for her health and safety yesterday. She had experienced it all before on a regular basis growing up, that would be why she called the police. Initially, Murray had thought that it was surely just a coincidence that Max Jordan's card was on the dead female. Now, however, he was not quite so certain.

"You sit on that chair Joe," Murray said, having joined the others. He pointed over to the large, leather seat in the corner of the room. Observe carefully and I will check in with you at the end."

Obviously today was to be a tutorial Hanlon acknowledged. Although disappointed, he was willing to accept this supporting role. It was to be an exercise that was over shortly. In three minutes to be precise. A first round knockout! That doesn't happen too often these days Murray thought. He had begun by producing recent photographs of each of the first three dead individuals. Those photographs were interspersed by a random selection of other females.

Sadly for Craig Jordan things were not looking good. Murray had shown him about eight photographs and on each occasion that a murdered girl was shown, the Inspector knew for definite that Jordan had recognised her.

For Gillian McLean - his face contorted.

With Melissa MacLeod - his eyebrows knitted tightly together.

And as for Deborah Griggs - Jordan's forehead furrowed!

Accompanying each of those tiny, distinct movements though, was a more traditional tell. One that he had hoped Joe Hanlon had also identified.

Suddenly the varnished, eight-pane living room door swung wide open. And there as bright and impressive as a rainbow after a storm, stood the bold and brash Lucy Jordan.

"Miss Jordan, I thought I'd asked you to…"

"Fancy a bite to eat. Anybody want anything? I was feeling rather peckish."

"No, you are fine," Murray responded brusquely on behalf of all."

He then nodded. A singular, intentional two inch drop of his chin. A facial expression that ensured Detective

Constable Joe Hanlon followed the self-assured Jordan lass through to the kitchen.

"Want anything?" She once again asked DC Hanlon, her mascara and make-up badly affected by obvious tears from earlier. 'Sherlock' was determined to check with Murray later, exactly what had happened and what was said in that room. For the moment however, he simply shook his head as she pulled open the fridge door.

The refrigerator light soon revealed the fact that each of those in the house, Max, Craig and Lucy all had separate shelves for their refrigerated requirements! In mutual surprise and respect Hanlon carried out a brief scanned inventory of their respective goodies. Taking care to ensure the female of the species was none the wiser. Fresh fruit, yogurts and salad produce seemed to occupy their father's area. While Lucy appeared to have lots of slim Tupperware containers storing a variety of runny minced produce or soup. Craig meanwhile, obviously liked his cooked breakfasts and fry-ups. As eggs, bacon, black pudding and an assortment of sausages took up most of the other allotted space.

Back in the sitting room an obvious question had to be addressed. "Is there anyone who would want to set you guys up?" Murray bluntly announced.

"Frame us you mean?' Max Jordan exclaimed.

Murray again asked openly. "I'll be perfectly honest with you both. It seems rather too convenient to me that a business card belonging to you sir," he said pointing at Max Jordan. "Was attached to the main notice board of the dance premises. Especially given that you were not even supposedly in the country at the time."

"What do you mean supposedly?" Max Jordan sulked.

Murray felt the need to consider further. "Unless they were just trying to get us to focus on you guys for something else entirely?"

Uneasy glances were exchanged between father and son.

"Then from under the dead girl's fingernails we recover what appears to be exact traces of that card. Forensics of course in time will have to confirm that for us. But it looks definitive at present."

"Exactly Inspector," my thoughts entirely, said a much more relieved Max Jordan.

"The interesting fact though, is it didn't even go down like that," added DC Hanlon, who by this point had rejoined them.

The Jordan family yet again remained silent. But this time stood rooted to the spot, intrigued.

"Earlier today I watched the CCTV footage from outside the club where the queue forms." 'Sherlock' then continued, "And you could see quite clearly the advertising board from the beginning of the night. At that point there was no sign of any bright green business card. None whatsoever. So someone had deliberately scraped it with the deceased's fingernails and then tore off a corner in advance. It had been placed there well after the event. We were meant to find it. And it was meant to ultimately lead us here. But again I ask - Why?"

Silence all round.

Inspector Murray re-iterated, "So once more I ask you sir. Is there someone with a grudge? A disgruntled client? Someone you owe…"

"And they have murdered someone to get back at my dad? Are you really seriously suggesting that?"

"Well actually, no Craig. But alas, sadly, the evidence is."

Both father and son shook their heads.

"What about your own specific relationship with each other?"

The officers stared at him. "What are you suggesting?" said the son.

"Believe it or not young man, I am actually trying to help. Trying to establish some firm alibis, a basis of trust so that we can move forward. Help me out here."

A further quarter of an hour and several dozen questions later, the officers visit was over. Each family member had been invited down to the station tomorrow to make and sign official statements. This was mainly at DI Murray's behest and in part to ensure another private chat with the vulnerable Miss Lucy Jordan.

FIFTEEN

"The language of love has left me stony grey. Tongue tied and twisted at the price I've had to pay. Who's that girl running around with you? Tell me, who's that girl running around with you?"

- The Eurythmics

Sunday early evening: 8.30pm...

After ceilidh dancing for over ninety minutes the free-spirited Maxine McDonald's smiling, rosy red cheeks were embellished with glowing beads of radiant sweat. Hands on hips, body to the side, one foot in front of the other and long flowing locks of auburn hair.

"How's that?" she shouted enthusiastically.

Her snap happy photographer friend offered her a positive thumbs up. Before clicking the camera shutter a few more times.

"You said these are free right?"

From behind the lens of the camera, the voice quietly confirmed, "Absolutely. However would you like to choose two rather than one?"

"And the catch being?" said the bubbly redhead.

"Bondage!" Came the reply.

"What?"

"No one is willing to let me put tape around them Maxine. But it's the in-thing. Very Fifty Shades... dark retro fashion.

Whatever that actually means or looks like to the current 'hip' magazine editors."

"So what does it look like to us tonight?" Asked the girl currently freezing on the pavement at the side of the portable studio. "Because I would most certainly love to go back inside soon and round off the evening with a few more lively dances."

"We could go for a bondage on the move scene and just strap you to the passenger seat for two minutes, take a selection of shots and leave it for me to work my photoshop magic later!"

She seemed to be considering that offer whilst continually pushing down at the front of her olive green zig zag skirt. It was obviously not her preferred length and made her feel very self conscious.

"You know what? Just take a second one anyway. It's okay, you've done brilliantly already. Thank you so much."

"What! Seriously? Really? Are you sure?" Maxine beamed. "That would be great." She then hesitated slightly. Reciprocity had kicked in as planned. And right on cue... "Okay, I'll take those two," she said. Pointing at two specific containers in the back of the van. She then paused once again before adding, "But let's take the extra five minutes and get you those award-winning bondage shots!"

She then smiled, quickly jumped into the passenger seat, strapped up her shoes, pulled her long patterned white blouse out from inside her short skirt and ruffled her already tousled hair. She was ready.

By this point the camera had been put down. Grey duct tape had been wrapped tightly around her ankles, was currently being rolled three or four times around both her midriff and the leather seat at her back.

"Can I put on this zip tie for effect?"

"Sure, absolutely," Maxine said cutely and innocently. Possibly not fully realising what it was, where it was going to be placed or the simple foolishness of taking that chance. Her eyes retracted as it was gently placed over her head.

"We'll leave it hanging loose. It's really just for effect."

"Thank goodness for that," she said with a much relieved smile.

Again the shutter clicked furiously into life. The focus was altered. Maxine McDonald made faces. She pretended to be terrified. The lens got up close and personal. Creative images from the side and below. From behind her neck the loose end of the tie was being promptly adjusted. Click... Click... Click...

"That's too tight," she cried hoarsely, struggling to breathe. Suddenly she realised that her arms and chest were unable to break free from the tape. Her ankles were also bound and securely fixed to the adjustment bar at the front of the seat. Panic immediately began to set in. For the first time her mind exploded with a frenzy of lamentable questions.

Click. What had she done? She'd been stupid!

Click. When would she ever see her family again? Never!

She then stared panic-stricken into the rear view mirror. The figure directly behind her smiled innocently. It was the familiar over straining, evil grimace of every dysfunctional, warped psychopath.

"Can you feel the magic?" Her assailant asked menacingly, before quoting, *"Tha neart teaghlaich, mar neart arm, na laighe na dìlseachd dha chèile."*

Make pretend horror, turned instantly to fully fledged fear. Maxine's eyes bulged from their sockets. She attempted to stretch and grab franticly for her throat. Unable to get leverage, her nails slowly broke apart one by one as they clawed relentlessly at her own neck. The innocent girl was now simply desperate for any kind of air. A gentle breeze, a wind, some form of cool exposure to suck and inhale into her gasping lungs. She was determined to survive this assault and wake up and see tomorrow.

Click…Click…Click… Her eyelids flickered and closed.

With her airways constricted, she managed one final gasp. The obstruction though was too great. No room to swallow. Her neck swung and concertinaed violently. "Uh, uh, uh, kee, ko, kee," was the final sound uttered.

Yet another click… It can't end like this - was her last remaining thought.

Her delicate throat shredded. As if attacked by a rugged cheese grater. The assortment of rasping noises ceased. Her aggressor gave one final solitary tug and silently her head fell forward - Click!

Mid evening, Sunday 24th at Heathrow Airport:
He sat comfortably with one leg crossed over the other. Alternative stripes of sky blue, navy and white appeared on his socks at the bottom of his worn out khaki chinos. An uncoordinated look apparently. The Krispy Kreme t-shirt was tousled and sweat marked. The iPhone sat peacefully in his right hand as he scanned through numerous messages and texts. A bright smile appeared on his face as an excessively large lady nearby, felt the immediate need to announce to everyone her upcoming arrangements for the

weekend. The reason for the wide faced grin was due to the fact that he had on his high end 'Beats' by Dr Dre headphones and yet, could still clearly hear her busy 'food filled' schedule!

The aged, carpeted waiting area was filled with tablets, computers and assorted phones. Some remained idle whilst being charged, others very much connected to a variety of wires hanging from attentive earlobes. Several were ultra expensive. Many more simple, cheap and cheerful airline giveaways. Everyone with no exception, clutched some form of electronic doo-da!

Even as high calorie, exorbitant sandwiches were being constantly unwrapped and their so-called 'quality ingredients' frantically wolfed down with expensive, overpriced water - No one spoke. (With the obvious exception of busy weekend lady!)

In the silence, phones were being monitored constantly. Devices scrolled, books read and texts sent. The only physical exertion, alongside tapping numerous buttons involved the downing of liquid refreshment. Favourites included water, coffee and fresh orange juice. Although do not forget the cherished choice of the large, oversized woman. She of course slurped continuously on a massive Diet Coke of all things. Occasionally, someone even took physical activity to a new level by visiting the toilet!

Pastries, biscuits and chocolate bars helped enable sticky fingers to slide energetically up and down on keypads. Jeans ripped at the knees, jogging bottoms, cowboy boots hiding under canvas trousers. Assorted bags, satchels and impressive miniature tanks disguised as four wheeled suitcases sat on seats or at the feet of their tired, bedraggled owners. A terminal gate pulled everybody into the mix. An extensive variety of intriguingly wonderful characters.

As you travelled to the departure gate, more computer screens were operated and hands ran through assorted hair at varied speeds. Some smoothly, some ruggedly, many scratching, others gently curling and twisting. Contagious yawns were offered, whilst lengthy notes were taken - possibly confidential business ideas or simply daytime doodles - who will ever know? People appeared to be speaking to themselves - and then you'd spot the thin wire rolling down from their ear. Others spoke in distressed, volatile tones and then it was several seconds later before you saw the scolded child begrudgingly waltz into the shot.

Lips were wiped. The tiny wafer thin napkin was given a severe workout at each side of the man's mouth. His sunglasses hung on the edge of his 100% cotton Primark V-neck jersey. His black trainer/cum shoe repeatedly tapped as he once again looked anxiously at his watch. Meeting someone?

The teenage girl's hair was purple and extra long. 'Down to her waist easily' was a fellow passengers guesstimate. Doc Marten boots were back in fashion and another female had a black and white striped blouse to accompany her pair. Her companion wore a short, cropped, black leather jacket and miniature black matching rucksack. Two other young women re-lived their teenage years by making imaginary telephone calls on actual bananas, and then began imaginary ice skating on the grubby woven floor surface. They were obviously trying desperately to keep boredom at bay. As over the P.A they heard the latest announcement delay their departure time even further.

One individual however sat calmly awaiting his flight. Richly inked tattoos adorned every part of his left arm. He wore a sleeveless t-shirt and was slightly on edge. The menacing skulls, serpents and resplendent crests on show returned to the shadows after the call over the tannoy system. He too now knew that it would be at least ten o'clock in the evening before he would set down on Caledonian soil.

At nearly 11.00pm in Portobello, the ceilidh energy levels were being ramped up. 'McNamara's Band' had merged feistily into 'Nellie the Elephant' and the dancing was in full swing. The vibrant fiddle player had regaled everyone previously with a set of high octane reels and this was now his band's last number before a well deserved break. A lively 'dashing white sergeant' had been followed earlier in the evening by the ever popular 'military two-step.' And any armed forces link between the two, had probably been lost on this youthful, energetic Territorial Army reservist who was currently revelling on the packed, crowded dance floor. Having dropped the T.A branding in 2014, our disciplined party goer was now travelling one way at great speed toward the interval on the non-stop 'Flying Scotsman!' Sadly, for 19 year old student Laura McKenzie, her return journey was about to be cancelled.

A large, almighty cheer was offered, accompanied with a genuine round of applause for the band. It had been such a generous reception that the ever smiling drummer had gotten carried away and threw his sticks out into the crowd thinking that they were finished! As a long line instantly began to form at both the toilets and the bar, the 'beatmeister' was already frantically searching for a spare set. Smiles and continual head shaking from his other band members were on offer and when the second accordion was laid to rest and they meandered from the stage, a quiet voice was heard to murmur - 'Ya eejit!'

Laura McKenzie had joined the army cadets as a young, yet mature, 13 year old schoolgirl. Brought up in the rough, tough, working class suburb of Stenhouse, she had been inspired by her father Allan. Allan George McKenzie had served his country for nearly twenty years, having joined the Army straight out of school as a naive seventeen year old. Two years ago when Laura left school she had immediately enrolled in an evening class at college for travel and tourism. Through the day she worked full-time at a large Swedish furniture retailer in the Loanhead area of the city. When you factored in her Army Reservist schedule, you got a good idea of the dedicated, determined individual that she was. So when she saw disappointment and upset on the face of one of her dance partners from earlier in the evening, she was proactive enough to step forward. She had watched several others make gestures toward the individual, but offer no actual support.

"Are you okay?" She asked touching them on the elbow.

The crestfallen face looked up at her. A faint look of recognition came over it. Before hesitantly questioning - "I danced with you earlier, didn't I?"

"Correct. Guilty as charged," she joked. "Are you doing okay? She repeated. "You look a bit down."

In a gentle slow, exasperated voice the response was, "Would you believe I'm actually here for work? And I'm struggling to get just two people to model for me."

They spoke for a further five minutes. Animated arm gestures were plentiful. Nods of understanding were given and received and plenty of celebratory, busy, engaged dancers never gave them a second look. The opening chords of 'The Rose of Allendale' began to get the gathered crowds back up onto the dance floor, just as a second successful sale of the evening had been concluded.

As Laura McKenzie innocently departed quietly through the outside gates, her newly acquired friend presented her with the most beautiful, scarlet red, silk flower.

SIXTEEN

*"Now sark rins o'er the Solway sands and Tweed rins tae the ocean.
To mark where England's province stands - such a parcel o' rogues in a nation."*

- Robert Burns

Monday 25th of January. The birthdate of Robert Burns.

Murray arranged via a brief, early morning text conversation with Hanlon to venture out that evening for a catch up meal. He had even included a little cute smiley face. Oh, how Inspector Steven Murray embraced modern technology!

The arrangement was put in place for seven o'clock that night at 'The Lodge.' The aged, historic premises were located just off St. Anthony Place in Leith. Murray understandably, did not want to be too far away from all the action and had evidently chosen a new restaurant in that murderous part of the city, his colleague had assumed. It seemed like a new eating establishment opened every ten minutes or so in the centre of Edinburgh. 'Sherlock,' although surprised at the invite was curious to go along and find out exactly what was on the menu being offered up by both 'The Lodge' and DI Murray!

Only ten minutes after sending the initial text, his alarm sounded and signalled the start of a new week. An incoming message was then received. Aha, Hanlon's response he thought. Alas, it was not. It was from Furlong. It was advance notice from his DCI that he was now required at the station for 11am and not 1pm as previously arranged. *No excuse, no apologies and she knew she could count on him,* were the exact words that she used. Good psychology there he thought. He quickly replied with a crisp, yellow thumbs-up.

Throughout her first couple of days their new Detective Chief Inspector planned to host a series of meetings with members of Murray's team. And as helpful as it was to find out a little bit about each of them and try to gauge their individual strengths and weaknesses. It was really to reassure them collectively of her support and moving forward, her expectations of them in return.

By the end of her early morning Monday meeting with DS 'Sandy' Kerr, Furlong felt she was now fully clued in on the daily workload of a full-time officer with one year old twin boys! She quickly learned just how much of a priority it was for her Sergeant to have a steady routine. For DS Kerr to be super organised and prepared. Planning and scheduling well in advance were of vital importance to her. She had witnessed many officer's marriages breakdown over the years and she was determined not to be part of those statistics! Furlong had never married. To many inside the force, she seemed like a career cop. In no time at all, she had ascertained 'Sandy' was an Olympic champion in each of those aforementioned disciplines. So much so, that when Kerr stood up to exit the room DCI Furlong felt confident enough to state:

"Sergeant."

Sandra Kerr turned hesitantly to face her boss. A slow, gradual, sincere smile appeared on her DCI's lips before she spoke. When she finally did so, it was to quietly offer up some words of gratitude.

"Thank you so much for the flowers. They were very much appreciated."

Instantly Kerr responded with, "I'm sure I have no idea what you're talking about Ma'am."

"I figured that you might say that. But thank you anyway."

Kerr nodded, blushed and hastily beat a retreat to meet up with her new partner.

DC Allan Boyd was a short, five foot five, ginger haired Glaswegian. He was easily mid-thirties, loved a bit of friendly banter and was a straight talking in your face kind of character. Character being the operative word. Because as much as Boyd wanted to be a part of a united team and strived to live by the motto: 'Thick as Thieves' - On first impression it was easy for Sergeant Sandra Kerr to confuse his mantra with that other well-known, west coast saying: 'Thick as Mince!'

Immediately after meeting with her, they both went to take the lift to the ground floor. Three people were already inside when they stepped forward. Kerr, as one normally would, turned to face the door. DC Boyd walked straight forward and faced up to the back wall. He remained facing in that direction for the four remaining levels they travelled down. Two further people joined them, and ALL were rather unsettled by the time the lift reached the ground floor.

DS Sandra Kerr's head was spinning. This was going to be a nightmare. Boyd was a few fries short of a 'Happy Meal!'

she'd concluded. He may have accompanied me down on one, but his personal elevator doesn't go all the way to the top floor, she thought inwardly.

"Detective Sergeant Kerr," he said cockily in his harsh, blunt, guttural west coast tone.

"Yes, DC Boyd," she replied rather disheartened.

In a wizardly accent, reminiscent of a Scottish Gandalf, Boyd slowly shared his wisdom with her. "I'm a good police officer you know. However, my talent lies in unsettling people. Letting them think they have the upper-hand. Because then, they instantly dismiss you. Just like you have already done!"

DS Kerr blushed slightly. Feeling caught out and rather ashamed.

Boyd's voice became stronger and even more pronounced. His shoulders tensed and he threw his head to one side as he announced in desperate diva style - "They disparage me because I'm short... ginger ... and gay!"

Startled, Sandra Kerr froze and stared at him. Along with thirty other staff and visitors entering the building.

"See, got ye again!" His shoulders dropped and his voice returned to normal. From being Bilbo Baggins' friend one minute - back to plain old Glaswegian 'Taggart' the next!

"So just to clarify - I'm not gay. But as ma big buddy Meat Loaf sang," (he got down on one knee) ..."*Now don't be sad, 'cause two out of three ain't bad.*"

Sergeant Kerr exhaled, shook her head in utter disbelief and offered Detective Constable Allan Boyd the tiniest glimpse of a smile. In turn, he then stood up, leaned forward to shake her hand and said.

"Nice to finally meet you Sandra Kerr and welcome to my world." Imaginary fragments of broken ice lay shattered... strewn across the tiled flooring.

It had only just gone 9.40 am when DI Murray was caught chatting to DCI Furlong in between her scheduled interviews as Hanlon approached rather cautiously.

"And ensure you don't turn up late Steven!" the constable heard the remark. More of a statement than question.

At first the Inspector thought that 'Sherlock' was possibly feeling in awe or rather intimidated by his new female superior. But that proved not to be the case. As he soon discovered his apprehension was for a totally different reason entirely.

"Ma'am, Sir," Hanlon offered. "Sorry to interrupt, but..."

"Just spit it out," Murray encouraged.

"Yes, well," Even now Joseph Hanlon felt awkward.

"What is it Joe?"

'Sherlock' Hanlon straightened his back. Looked Murray straight in the eye and blurted out:

"The unfortunate individual whose head was delicately blown off sir."

Murray shut his eyes instantly in anticipation of what was to follow.

"She is or rather was... 'Bunny' Reid's niece!"

"What! What! No!" His Inspector then exclaimed this mantra several times. On each occasion with his hands firmly fixed on his forehead, whilst birlin' around in circles. A move that had taken him several years and involvement in many fraught situations to perfect.

"You are having a laugh," he eventually added. Competing desperately for airplay with his DCI.

A certain, rather vocal Barbra Furlong by this point was in full flow with, "Desperate Dolly Mixtures and Saint Francis of Assisi," operating on a loop system.

DC Hanlon hastily knelt to tie up a shoelace, although he wore slip-ons. He found his new Chief Inspector's attempts at 'not swearing' exceptionally humorous and he was trying fiercely to stifle his laugh.

"After all these years and I never once looked into his extended family," Murray voiced. "So Tina Cardwell was related to Edinburgh's current number one bad guy," he vocalised. "Someone, somewhere, never did their homework!" Or did they? He then privately questioned to himself.

"You will need to nip this in the bud now Inspector," his DCI managed in between mutterings about sticky, sugar coated candy and great Patron saints of our time!

Murray immediately found a quiet location and hit speed dial. It took only two rings before it was answered.

"Inspector Murray," the voice rasped with a wide, arrogant grin.

Murray paused. He began to nod his head. Realising that Reid was fully aware of his mobile. How come he recognised my number?

The low, deep, growl continued with, "It's been a while Steven. Are you still feeling lucky? Playing the tables?"

Murray said nothing.

"I thought you might get in touch today."

"Oh, is that so." Murray replied. "How come?" He paused slightly. "You already know, don't you Bunny?"

The slow, husky, gravel edged tones continued. They became louder and faster as he spoke. "Of course I know. I knew last night Mr Murray. Do you really think my sister was not going to contact her only brother as soon as she discovered that her daughter, his beloved niece, had been found murdered in HIS city, at the hands of a psycho. How many in the past two days is that?"

Murray remained silent, but listened intently.

"This madman is going to pay Inspector and I think experience would tell you, I am most definitely a man of my word. Isn't that so?"

He gifted those carefully chosen words to hang menacingly for several seconds in the air.

"I would suggest 'Bunny' that we need to meet up. I think we have a problem. Maybe even a couple of problems to be more precise."

Reid's resonant harshness continued. "And that would concern me how exactly? The last time I met up with a couple of your officers, it didn't end too well. Poor DC Taylor. Which reminds me. How is your buddy Sergeant Coulter coping? I hear our 'Ally' is just plain old Mr Coulter these days."

Murray pondered his response by covering his phone with his left hand and thought carefully for a second or two. The wheel was spinning... Red or Black? Odd or Even? The ball bounced to and fro. Tell him or not? What's it to be? Click, clack. Up and down. It fell. Landed. A decision was reached!

"It's not him Bunny!"

"What?"

"It's not him," he repeated. He left a few seconds, before confirming, "We believe there are two killers!"

It was now Reid's turn to pause. After several, elongated moments his demonic tone offered, "Okay, let's get together and meet up Inspector."

Before Detective Inspector Murray ended the conversation, he added, "By the way 'Bunny,' I'm sure that loving sister of yours did contact you. However, seeing as we only informed Mrs Cardwell earlier this morning, I wonder who really gave you the information last night?" He finished with, "I'll be in touch."

As he reappeared back in view, DCI Furlong wasted no time in asking, "So what did he say?"

"He's going to get back to me Ma'am. Joe let's be going," he instructed Hanlon.

"Remember," the female voice sounded after him sternly. "11.00am with Complaints."

As a gesture of acknowledgement Murray waved his hand without looking back.

"Complaints?" Hanlon enquired.

Steven Murray's facial expression said... Enough talking!

Twenty five minutes after leaving the station Sergeant Kerr and Constable Boyd had arrived at the Silverknowes district in the north west of Edinburgh. The specific address was located on Muirhouse Parkway. The home sat directly opposite the east section of the popular Silverknowes golf course. Parts of the house's exterior roughcast had flaked off rather seriously from the gable end of the 1970's building. The gate hung precariously on its hinges and the garden path seemed to offer more weed than the local High School!

It was plain even for these two detectives, to see that it had once been a modern, pretty home. However time, wind and weather had taken their toll. Now it was just in desperate need of some special TLC. Sadly, they knew for certain that the owner's day was not going to get any better.

The doorbell rang and within five seconds it was flung open. A forty-something female had answered. Naturally pretty, but without make-up. Her casual attire of tracksuit bottoms and sweatshirt seemed to act as makeshift 24 hour pyjamas. Nervous energy greeted the two 'Irn Bru' bottles on their arrival. There must be very few red haired officers paired together!

"Mrs McKenzie?," the female voice asked firmly, yet politely.

"That was quick. Thank you so much. I was in two minds to call or not. You hear all sorts. You get worried. When in actual fact it's probably nothing at all."

The concerned officers could hear the alarm and panic in her voice. This was not good. But it explained her tone, body language and shabby dress sense all in one go.

"Can we just clarify your concerns and what you said exactly when you called," the shorter of the two officers offered.

Nice one Kerr thought. Well played.

Showing his warrant card he continued, "I'm Detective Constable Boyd, Mrs McKenzie and this here is my experienced better half, Detective Sergeant Sandra Kerr."

That was when Kerr smiled and offered her warrant card for inspection also.

"Yes, follow me. Come this way," she said. "And I don't need to see your I.D it was me that called you remember?"

SEVENTEEN

"All lies and jest. Still, a man hears what he wants to hear and disregards the rest."

- Simon and Garfunkel

Whilst driving at speed over to the sealed off lock-up that Christina Cardwell's body was discovered in, 'Doc' Patterson rang Murray with a little bit of highly fascinating information. The Inspector would initially tell Hanlon and get him to text the details to the rest of his squad.

"It was the haggis they reckon," Patterson stated. "Only it wasn't! It wasn't haggis Steven."

"I'm not following you 'Doc.'"

"T'ey examined it by running tests on the biles of sickness from three of our own officers - each came back with the same result." The 'Doc' then explained it in scientific gobbledygook. Complete with fancy medical terminologies and details. But basically, the bottom line was that it contained traces of human kidney.

"You're kidding," Murray exclaimed.

"Sadly, I'm deadly serious Steven."

"Melissa Margaret McLeod's kidneys I would assume?" Murray slowly offered up.

"We believe so," the 'Doc' responded.

"So it was an early clue. Just like I thought, the wheels had already been set in motion. It was always part of a bigger picture," Murray then remarked in a casual, satisfied manner.

"Again, it would appear so," Patterson added.

"Thanks again Tom. Speak soon no doubt," and Murray hung up.

Constable Joseph Hanlon watched as his mentor played with notion after notion in his mind. The way we all try to regularly decipher, decode and interpret the thousands of messages, codes and alerts that come our way on a daily basis. No matter your job or career - Every twenty-four hours TV, newspapers, internet, radio and personal communication all vie for our precious time. Currently this relentless killer had Steven Murray's undivided attention.

Rubbing thoughtfully at the base of his puckered lips and stubbled chin he quietly offered, "All of it had been pre-planned. The murders well executed, literally. But it was the range of clues that were organised and detailed. I would put my money on there being absolutely no link between any of the deceased whatsoever. The recipient could have been anyone."

He was right Joe Hanlon thought. Anyone in the world!

The disused premises where Tina Cardwell's body had been recovered, threw up nothing new. And even just thinking about her last moments alive and the unbearable pain that had been inflicted upon her, made both officers wince at the very thought. The gruesome twosome set off once again through the busy streets of Edinburgh and arrived back at the station just before 10.58 am. Exactly in time for 'Barbra' to give the Inspector a 'cutting it fine' shake of the head.

"You're unbelievable - Room 2," she then added.

One minute later and he heard low, dulcet tones extend him an invitation.

"Please, take a seat, Inspector." The voice was akin to 'Bunny' Reid on steroids. Guttural, but perkier. More Morningside, than Muirhouse! This giant of a man at around six foot four, and that was just across the shoulders, would have to be dragged kicking and screaming from his job in the next couple of years. Detective Chief Inspector David Cleland was nearing his fourth decade in the force.

'Ruby, Ruby, Ruby!' Murray blasted internally to himself. Before opting for the more sedate option of: *'Ruuuuubbbbyyyyy...don't take your love to town.'* Yes, Cleland was certainly more Kenny Rogers than Kaiser Chiefs! Forty years, wow! Sadly, that was a whole Silver Wedding anniversary longer than his actual marriage itself had lasted. His partnership with his deranged wife Suzy ended at the fifteen year mark. Both were acting police officers, so their relationship almost inevitably appeared doomed from the very beginning. Shift work, drink, abuse and extra marital affairs certainly didn't help matters much either.

As he pulled his chair closer to the desk Steven Murray reflected on his own personal connection with Cleland. He knew both the man and of the man. Never close associates inside or outside of work though. But both familiar with each other and their respective careers. Their paths had crossed several times. Working together during the years on many cases and in more recent times during complaints procedures involving fellow officers. Today however, the deeply troubled Inspector was that fellow officer! Oh, the vast difference just a few short months can make.

Inspector Steven Murray's musical mind then instinctively took over. Reflecting on how an inexperienced police constable, patrolling and walking the beat in and around the murky Leith docks in 1976, the very arena that Murray and his cohorts currently found themselves playing in, would have returned home after his shift to listen to the riveting, exciting 'pop' sounds of that particular era. Wholesome, humorous, singalong tunes that consisted of the large flared trousers belonging to Brotherhood of Man, Dr. Hook, Showaddywaddy and the almighty Wurzels! However, less than a year later, a slightly wiser and more streetwise PC Dave Cleland would have locked horns with another generation of sounds altogether. Rebellious, opinionated and surely damaging to one's health by all accounts. Welcome to the new world order of The Stranglers, The Sex Pistols, The Damned and The Clash. Within a matter of weeks and months and a quite different musical experience altogether was about to play out in UK pop culture.

It was all a matter of timing. Like Elvis, The Beatles and St. Winifred's School Choir - being in the right place at the right time made all the difference. This was the evolving experience that Steven Murray had most recently experienced and not in a good way. More Jedward than Jay-Z!

Papers were shuffled, ruffled and placed one on top of the other. Then the whole process gone through again and again. It literally was only a few short months ago that DI Murray and his team were being applauded and commended for their diligent efforts and good works in bringing down a huge child trafficking ring. A predatory group that had been growing and extending its reach for years and years. A sick membership that included many Crown Office and Procurator Fiscal staff, including lawyers, sheriffs and clerks. And not forgetting their very own Detective Chief Inspector, formerly in the early years with the 'e,' Keith Brown!

The plaudits had come and gone. Well earned internal praise, positive press coverage and numerous grateful parents finally being given closure. All had had their season. But with prominent, wealthy businessmen and notable members of the establishment also being caught up in the teenage sex scandal, now for whatever reason, seemed to be the ideal time to redress the balance. Commendations had been put on hold and were safely tucked away into dusty drawers and redundant filing cabinets in the meantime. In the last few months, *'Save all your kisses for me,'* had been replaced *'Under the moon of love,'* by some straw-sucking country bumpkin's *'Combine Harvester!'* And Detective Inspector Steven Murray was about to be tossed well and truly underneath it. Torn deliberately and impeccably to shreds. Inevitably not quite doing justice to The Clash's - *'I fought the law and the law won.'*

The official papers were given one final shuffle. Legs were crossed, fingers run under chins and heads tilted to the side. Murray could not help himself. He mirrored every movement his divorced colleague made and for such an experienced officer, he was still certain that Cleland was none the wiser. The DCI then placed his hands on the desk in front of himself. Right over left. Murray did likewise.

"Inspector," he offered.

"Chief Inspector," came the reply.

"Well?"

"I'm well sir. Yourself?"

"Yes. Well Steven, thank you."

Cleland withdrew his hands and sat back.

Murray did likewise and smiled to himself.

"Something funny Inspector?" Cleland asked. Rather taken aback by his subordinates facial expression.

"No sir. Apologies, I was just thinking about a combine harvester!"

The Chief looked perplexed to say the least. He then turned to the third person in the room. Sat by Cleland's side, this investigating officer had an exceptionally elongated, vase like face. His cold, chiselled, cheekbones didn't help matters and his purposeful ears would have made him an appropriate winning trophy in anyone's book!

Murray could not remember ever seeing anyone with a longer, more protruding chin. Although there was one chap he briefly recalled. But that was in a 'Hall of Mirrors' at a carnival on Edinburgh's Leith Links over a decade ago he smiled. Today he was staring at the obvious result of an intimate relationship between Celine Dion and 'Shergar!' It was as if the poor midwife had called continually for his mother to 'push, push, push,' and forgotten to yell 'Stop!'

Slim Jim had been introduced earlier as Inspector James Mare (another horse reference) from Dundee. He was unfamiliar to Murray, because the Inspector was sure he would have remembered him... there was just something about him!

"Combine harvester you say?" Mare questioned. "You do understand this is an extremely serious situation YOU find yourself in? Are you in some way taking the Mickey, Inspector Murray?"

"No, no, of course not sir," Murray declared flippantly. A more serious manner and professional tone being adopted as he continued with, "I wouldn't possibly think of horsing around in your presence sir! Would I Chief Inspector?"

Mare eyed up Cleland. The DCI ignored the question and simply picked up the sheets of paper in front of him. He then rifled them together yet again, banged them twice two handed on the cheap formica surface and finally sat them accurately at the edge of the desk. He lined them up at the corner with both edges, long and short, matching the corresponding outline of the desk frame. Was that OCD or just a neat freak for the sake of it?

Meanwhile back in the Silverknowes district, Mrs McKenzie had led her visitors through into the front sitting room. A small, rather dated gas fire was on at low. It's flame flickered directly in the centre of a 1980's fireplace, constructed from grey, marbled Fyfestone. This was a popular look three decades ago. A host of framed family portraits adorned the said mantelpiece and walls. A well used red dralon settee sat opposite the gentle orange flame and both officers had been invited to sit. Now seated delicately on the edge of the sofa, the female officer spoke calmly.

"Thank you Ma'am. As Constable Boyd said, would you mind just repeating to us what you said when you phoned up." Kerr reiterated.

"Ma'am? Seriously?" The women's face screwed up uncomfortably at this. "My name's Theresa. Most people call me Terri." She then pulled at her hooded 'Just Do It' top and rubbed her hands furiously up and down her trouser bottoms.

"Terri it is then Ma'am," DC Boyd added with a reassuring smile. "I'm Allan."

She offered a gracious nod. Then the silence reminded Theresa McKenzie that they were waiting for her.

"Sorry, sorry, yes sure. I told them that she, that is Laura, my Laura, hadn't returned home from last night."

"And Laura is?" Kerr asked to confirm.

"My daughter. My daughter Laura, I told them this on the phone. Like I said, normally I just turn over and go to sleep. But I usually hear her come in at some weird hour in the morning. Then when I awoke this morning…"

The woman began to become tearful. Her speech slowed and she felt her legs go from under her. She instantly sat next to the Detective Sergeant on the edge of the vintage settee. Knees inward, her fingers ceased playing on her thighs. It was as if she had been operating fully on adrenalin and in one foul swoop it had been drained and sucked vehemently out of her.

"By any chance would that be Laura's father in the photographs?" Boyd asked enthusiastically. Trying desperately to re-engage the worried parent.

Terri McKenzie paused and looked up at him. A slight sparkle, a generous glint even seemed to magically reappear in her eyes. "Were you in…"

"The Royal Scots," Allan Boyd said. His voice only just above a whisper. "Eight years," he added.

"I see," the woman said.

Her eyes were now fixed rather forlornly at her hands on her lap. Both of which were clasped on her knee, as her thumbs circled one another.

"Is he on active service currently?" Sandra Kerr asked innocently.

Constable Boyd's head dropped as the question was asked. He already knew that most soldiers wives do not put up snapshots of their husbands if they are still alive. These were important keepsakes, significant moments and treasured memories put out on display for public recognition. They were intended as a mark of respect and to pay tribute to a special individual. Through a series of continual elbow nudges, Detective Constable Boyd quickly and discreetly encouraged Sgt Kerr to move closer to the homeowner's side. This was in anticipation at what was coming next. His eye movements, through the power of persuasion basically lifted Sandra Kerr's palm and slowly rested it upon Theresa McKenzie's trembling hands. Tears now accompanied her broken emotional voice and in a soft, staccato rhythm, Mrs McKenzie, 'Terri,' continued.

"Laura was only 8 when a coffin returned home instead of my husband from Iraq in 2005," she told the two officers. "He was only 36. We thought we had our whole lives to spend together." A single, despondent tear ran down her cheek. "He was an Allan also," she declared, offering a connective smile at the male detective. "Two l's though."

"Me too," Boyd said.

"He was always proud of that fact," she nodded.

The officers sat in silence. This was going to be hard. This poor, distraught woman just wanted to unload, to take her mind off her missing daughter.

"It was during Operation Telac," she continued. "Did you know that was the codename for British operations in Iraq?"

It was actually Operation Telic! Boyd reflected. But he simply nodded, as 'Sandy' Kerr cautiously shook her head.

"My Allan was killed on the 30th January 2005. Eleven years ago next week."

DC Boyd went to interrupt. This can't go on. We need to stop her, he thought. But the opportunity passed.

"It was when a Hercules transport aircraft was shot down between Baghdad and Balad. There was only ten actual servicemen on board at the time. Sadly, Laura's father was one of them. They all died."

After that highly personal comment there was a lengthy emotional pause. You could tell that she was finishing off and both officers remained perfectly still and silent. An immediate offering of their respect. There then seemed to be an element of closure developing. One that you suspected Theresa McKenzie had never quite allowed to surface previously. Finally, for some reason today, she was allowing the memories, hurt and grief of the past to be put to rest.

"I never, ever wanted Laura to join the cadets. But it was her ambition, her dream. If truth be told, it was her way of 'keeping the spirit of her dad alive,' she would always say. Can you help me?" She pleaded with the officers. "I don't know what I would do without her."

This time, yet another single, solitary tear slid down Sergeant Sandra Kerr's makeup as a thousand others fought for room in the pit of her stomach. And again, as if in silent salute to the decorated soldier, DC Boyd lifted one of the iconic photos from the mantelpiece and placed his other hand on the shoulder of Theresa McKenzie. With the uncertainty and not knowing, she was about to sob for the remainder of the day.

EIGHTEEN

"Where am I to go, now that I have gone too far?"

- Golden Earring

"Sir Gerald Anderson, Inspector Murray. Any thoughts?" Mare gestured a flowing hand into the air, as if trying to politely entice a poisonous snake to appear from a large wicker basket.

Murray instantly envisaged the snake. His particular mental image was of an impressive artistic hybrid. One with a large majestic King Cobra like face, coupled with the giant body of a rugged Anaconda. Open - Stretch - Close. A three second disappearing trick and you would be gone. You slimy, unlikable, big-eared Stretch Armstrong! In his limited interview time with him so far, the Inspector had already taken an immediate disliking to this man.

It had nothing to do with him being part of 'Complaints.' It was his - 'Guilty 'til proven innocent' style. His brusque manner, dismissive tone and arrogant assumptions. Then again there was also something about his…? Behave, he told himself. Although pretty certain that that counsel would not be heeded.

"Steven. Inspector Murray," DCI Cleland offered. "These are serious allegations. Emergency responders are saying you never reacted when told about a man jumping from the rear of the casino premises. It was as if you were already fully aware. No curiosity as to who it was or when and where exactly it had taken place. You seemed in no rush to assist them or tell them how to get vehicular access to behind the property."

Murray shrugged.

"Really Inspector?" Mare contributed unhelpfully.

"Inspector?" Cleland encouraged.

Murray was aware of how to play the game. Good cop - Bad cop. Volatile - Charming. Obnoxious - Pleasant. He had no idea if they appeared in this partnership together often or not. But they were either very good at it, or their own personalities shone through and made it one hell of a winning combination. Due to his relationship over the years with David Cleland, Murray wanted to be more helpful. But his own personal army of demons in relation to this case made it extra sensitive for him to respond. Maybe also, because he knew the truth and no matter the justification, wasn't quite able to handle or embrace it.

"Why would he have chosen that option?" Mare barked.

Not even the common courtesy of addressing him by rank. The Inspector remained silent. He had thought about this often in recent months. He had fully recognised that he may indeed, absolutely, have been responsible for Anderson's death. Had he once again crossed that fine line? Had he deliberately encouraged the knight of the realm to take a certain escape route?

"One officer in particular, although not certain, thought he saw the deceased running from his office whilst you were stood at its doorway."

Anger growing, Murray now felt the great need to jump in and contribute more fully! "It was total bedlam," he stated animatedly. "Bodies running all over the place. People shouting, screaming, naked girls being rescued! Do you remember that part you friggin' obnoxious …"

"Inspector Murray!" Cleland warned.

"Rescued and probably saved from sexual slavery and predatory deviants," he continued - "You don't seem to be mentioning that too much!"

"Steven," David Cleland offered in a translation that bore all the hallmarks of 'steady on now!'

Murray's volume continued to rise, "Handcuffs, restraints, orders shouted, confusion reigned and nobody knew what was going on. However, someone *'thought'* they may have recognised me? How convenient. Really! I swore blind that a certain James Baxter Reid was central to the whole melee. Yet his name eventually never appeared anywhere on the arrest sheets. Funny that!"

"What are you implying?" The pleasant, sweet, good guy asked.

"I'm not implying anything sir. But I can tell you for a fact, that 'Bunny' Reid was there that day."

Again his volume increased. "I heard him. I saw him with my own eyes. Although possibly in the same way that your one, isolated and confused officer supposedly witnessed myself at Anderson's office. Yet, surprise, surprise when the bodies arrived at the station, there was no Reidmeister."

"Inspector Murray may I suggest you…"

"No you may not!" he affirmed as his fury and intensity increased. He did though feel inclined to put forward an alternative. "However, may I suggest you respectfully for once shut your mouth."

The seriously unhappy Inspector 'Mare' made to buck, but was successfully reined in by his more experienced handler. The Chief Inspector had witnessed Murray's passionate outbursts on numerous occasions over the years and was probably mildly surprised that he had managed to hold it all in up until now.

"You may go Inspector Murray. Thank you for your help and cooperation," Cleland added in a polite, yet official tone. He then offered his colleague a nod that said - get out now Steven while you can!

DI Murray stood abruptly, took a step into the face of his accuser, pursed his lips tightly and cast a, 'go on I dare you,' stare directly at his opponent. He struggled to remain composed as his chest heaved furiously. His heartbeat thumped rapidly, sounding like a bass drum in a psychedelic marching band.

"Inspector," DCI Cleland shouted. This time gesturing encouragingly with his head toward the door.

DI Mare mumbled gruffly under his breath. His reddened face displaying an intent unhappiness.

"Sir," Steven Murray spat through gritted teeth. Before disappearing angrily at pace down the lengthy corridor.

One minute later, he was scrubbing his hands intensely at the gents. The Detective Inspector tried desperately to calm down. He didn't normally do stress. He didn't do anxiety and he most definitely never pushed 'the Robin Williams obsessed,' crooked businessman off any ledge. He cautiously then reconciled himself with, not physically at least. Were his actions contributing factors? Well, he would concede that as being a very different question entirely. He thought that surely Anderson would have plainly SEEN that the fifty foot high fireman's pole, that many of his perverted brethren had previously used to flee from the salacious den of iniquity had already been cut down at the 40 foot high mark. It left behind only the top section still adjoined to the fire exit doors of the casino. For Sir Gerald Anderson though - apparently not! In the media savvy world that we live in - He should have gone to Specsavers!

In fairness it had only been cut down earlier that afternoon by the fire service. And that was seemingly in direct response to a request from a senior police official two days previous, both in writing and by phone. Mysteriously however, in the aftermath, the named officer did not even seem to exist and the corresponding paper trail went nowhere! DI Murray's cheeks flushed red at that particular thought. Before he once again reconciled himself with the fact that 'Gerry,' could easily have come quietly. He could have allowed himself to have been cautioned in the large scale roulette room where the bulk of the arrests were made. But, no, no, no, he had to ironically scurry off to save his skin. Adrenalin pumping, heart racing and only one thing on his mind. Which was to successfully leap onto that pole and to escape capture, humiliation and ultimately, a lengthy jail sentence! His body was then found twisted, torn and broken. He was thought to have died instantly on hitting the ground. Had justice been served?

Was Detective Inspector Murray responsible? On that… the jury was still out!

It was now 11.40 am and Craig Jordan had arrived as requested. A junior officer had just located the Inspector washing his face in the bathroom. His blood pressure had not noticeably decreased. Oh dear, it looked like the continually worried retail manager with a definite secret to hide was about to receive the whole wrath of Murray's pent-up frustration and anger!

"Five minutes you say sir. Okay, thanks. I'll let them know." The constable then made a sudden and hasty retreat from the Gents. Inexperienced he may have been, but he was no fool. Even he was well aware of the fury still displayed upon DI Murray's face.

As the Inspector later made his way toward the interview room he witnessed the father, Max Jordan, enter through the main door of the station. A cordial nod of the head was exchanged between the two middle aged men.

"We meet again Craig," Murray offered up as his opening greeting, on entering into the room. "Thank you for calling by," he then casually added.

"Did I have a choice?" Jordan shrugged dismissively. "You said we all had to give statements." A crooked shake of the head and rapid eye rolls accompanied his shoulder exercise.

"Does it feel small in here to you?" Murray asked.

Craig Jordan intensely looked around the room. What was this man talking about? He screwed up his eyes and hesitantly peered at the Inspector, but remained silent. The room was bare. Old matt painted magnolia walls that had seen better days and a black plastic wall clock that ticked faithfully in the background.

Witnessing his confusion, DI Murray felt obliged to help out.

"The walls," he said menacingly. "Don't you feel them slowly moving inch by inch toward you?"

Jordan licked his dried, cracked lips, pulled saliva from the depths of his throat and swallowed.

"You see, we've got you Craig. With every second that passes, we are closing in on you!"

The head continued to shake. Tiny flakes of dandruff jumped for safety.

"What the, are you on about? You've got this all wrong. It's not what you seem to …"

"Well put us right," Murray exclaimed, as he took up his seat. He then continued with his voice raised. "Now. Currently. This your best chance young man. Because I can assure you that by this afternoon son, I doubt you will ever see the inside of a dance hall again!"

Joe Hanlon had deliberately remained quiet and still. He was loath to comment at this stage. As he sat straight opposite the Top Shop boss, he had now been joined by the Inspector at his side.

"Honestly, where to start Mr Jordan?" Murray flippantly posed the question as he leaned across the desk, right up close into his gawky, anorexic looking face. "You love the ceilidh circuit don't you? You were in attendance at all the dances where the girls went missing."

Murray's limbs took on a life of their own at this point. He almost always spoke with his shoulders, arms and head all becoming somewhat exaggerated! Then he inquired politely, as his hands clasped together and his head rested gently on the back of said fingers.

"Interestingly though, did you know that blouses bought on a credit card belonging to you, matched up exactly to those worn by the murdered girls?"

The head shaking began once again.

"I think you did. That is why last night, when shown those images, you grimaced, winced and shook your feet furiously."

Hanlon nodded in agreement. Now fully understanding the significance of watching under the table from afar. Lesson learned. He then felt compelled to offer something into the mix.

"Your artistic photographs in the hallway," he added. "Did you know that we took your fancy modern camera into evidence? We found traces of blood on the case. It's not looking good Craig."

"No, no! What are you doing?" Jordan pleaded. "That's not… It's not… Oh what's the use?" he trailed off.

"Behind your front door," the Inspector continued. "It was a mess of jackets, sports good and equipment."

Jordan sat bolt upright and sighed. "This was never about signing any statements was it? I think we are finished here Inspector."

"We thought at first it had been a fishing line. Thankfully yours was intact Mr Jordan."

Craig Jordan nodded. "See!" he said in a relieved manner. He then proceeded to throw his arms up into the air in a self congratulatory way.

He should have held back on those celebrations. Because then Murray added fuel to the fire.

"Our forensics team, sadly however sir, have narrowed it down to another piece of sporting paraphernalia. Did you know Craig that your tennis racquet was missing two strings?"

Once again the man's tortured head, fell forward into his outstretched hands. He could not believe what he was hearing. This was not happening to him, he thought. Now the room definitely seemed to be getting smaller by the minute.

"Are you arresting me Inspector?" the scrawny, rawboned man asked. "Because if not, then I am out of here." He uttered the words and the two local police officer's waited patiently. But he made no effort to leave. It was as if all the power from his legs had been drained. He wanted to stand and exit, but clearly five minutes earlier his muscles had already ran out and deserted him.

"You did all your father's advertising," Hanlon affirmed. "You had quick and easy access to the very business cards that when we first met you, you fully distanced yourself from. Only the killer would have been able to ensure scrapings appeared under the deceased's fingernails. Which would then inevitably only lead us to one place… your home."

"Aaah, the great double bluff! Was that what you were going for Craig?" Murray concluded excitedly. "Surely it must have been. It was all too easy. The police would never think you that stupid. Someone was obviously setting the Jordan's up. Just like I assumed. Yes, someone was fitting you up! Well played young man."

Craig Jordan stared straight through him. Was it contempt, disdain or a tired, weary look of defeat and acceptance? Hanlon was unsure which. It genuinely felt like the fight had gone out of the accused man. He had no need to continue to defend himself. The jury had returned their verdict and he was willing to accept the consequences.

"There was no denying that you recognised all three girls last night when we showed you those photographs. Is that not right?" Murray queried.

Jordan's head had yet again been accompanied by two hands as it gradually twisted and turned.

Murray knew that he had deliberately instructed 'Sherlock' on the Sunday evening to sit away from the others in the family home. Joe remembered at the time feeling marginalised. But it very soon dawned that it was for him to learn and recognise specific body language. Because as each one of the dead females were shown to Craig Jordan, DC Hanlon could quite clearly see his reaction under the table. The man's feet tapped furiously. His leather heels were hoisted like a ship's anchor, and he must have ended up with friction burns on his thighs based on the speed his palms rapidly ran up and down them. Now although not rocket science, in interrogation circles those were very clear indications that at the very least something was amiss!

A temporary, fleeting silence had extended over the room. It was about to be broken by a surprise instruction from Steven Murray. The often flamboyant and maverick Detective Inspector waved his right hand in Jordan's direction and stated calmly: "You are now free to leave Mr Jordan. Travel safely!"

NINETEEN

"Life kicked in with all its might, but my strong heart it wouldn't break. I got kicked around and broken down. I took all that I could take."

- Imelda May

After lunch Murray brought 'Barbra' up to speed with the Craig Jordan interview and the latest developments regarding 'The Complaints' and their ongoing enquiries. Laura McKenzie certainly was in the right place at the 'wrong' time. But thankfully there was no body at this point.

"Honest thoughts Steven?" she asked.

"About the McKenzie girl?" He confirmed.

On Furlong's nod, he immediately offered, "She's dead Ma'am and it's all about where her body will be recovered from and the accompanying clue or clues."

"Dodgy Dancing Dinosaurs!!!" His DCI merrily exclaimed, turning and twisting in her seat. "Can't you at least sugar coat it occasionally Inspector?"

He raised his hands in a manner that clearly stated - No, and you did ask!

"We were lead straight to the Jordan's flat Ma'am. That was just too easy. Even although I believe the daughter has been or maybe still is being abused in some way."

Scared initially to ask. Furlong eventually blurted out, "By the father? The brother? Or both?"

"Who knows! But the brother for definite," the Inspector stated emphatically. "Craig Jordan is a slimy character. He is clearly hiding plenty. I am certain that below the surface, something unsavoury clearly lurks with that one." Murray then re-emphasised. "And again, whether that is TV license evasion or his personal collection of designer handbag magazines I don't care! But we need to find the common denominator and preferably sooner rather than later."

Just at that, a polite knock at the door and a young female constable entered. "Sorry to disturb you Ma'am, but there is a Miss Jordan here to see DI Murray."

"Thank you," DCI Furlong acknowledged. As her office door was closed back over, she looked placidly across the desk at Murray and queried, "Anything else before you chat with her? If what you suspect is happening Steven then you will need to engage with her cautiously and tenderly. Basically you'll need to tread on eggshells around her." His DCI abruptly pulled a befuddled face. "Do you think you can manage that?"

No sooner had such a serious question been asked and her Detective Inspector duly answered. He stood upright and looked stern-faced at his superior officer. He then stood to attention and reached out both his arms and sung. Yes sung!

"I want you; I need you; But there ain't no way I'm ever gonna love you."

DCI Furlong blushed. Her cheeks gave off an immense heat at that precise moment. She turned briefly to scour the room to ensure no one else was around. She glanced over at the large bouquet of flowers in their vase. Had her Inspector taken leave of his senses she wondered. There can be no office romance nor flirtation. What had happened to cautiously, tenderly and eggshells?

"Now don't be sad ... 'Cause two out of three ain't bad."

Her complexion had turned bright scarlet at one point. But it was now beginning to fade as the familiar lyrics dawned on her and she eventually got her Inspector's musical message.

"Now don't be sad; 'Cause two out of three ain't bad!" Murray crooned one final time and his arms gracefully dropped back to his side.

Silly serenading over. The so-called senior, experienced officer exited the room. DCI Furlong then felt reassured and comfortable enough to finish off with a few offensive, highly explicit lyrics of her own.

"Rickety man-sized buckets!" she pleaded.

DC Susan Hayes was last to enter the room. 'Hanna' had been sent for by Steven Murray who by now, was already safely ensconced opposite Lucy Jordan. Barriers and defence mechanisms were already entering into play for the young female. Arms were crossed. She peered out nervously between flowing locks that covered one half of her pale, freckled face. The collar on her bright red rain jacket remained turned up. As if to protect her from the elements she was now about to face indoors also. The two officers certainly had their work cut out lowering this particular drawbridge.

Whilst waiting on the arrival of Constable Hayes, Miss Jordan had already given and signed her statement regarding her own whereabouts for the nights in question. At the end of which, Detective Inspector Murray had added that he felt sure she could help them with a couple of other outstanding pieces of business, and that his female colleague was on her way. About twelve minutes had passed since that one-sided conversation.

"Hi, I'm Detective Constable Hayes," 'Hanna' said confidently, whilst offering her hand.

Lucy Jordan's arms remained firmly crossed. Although she looked up warily and gave the female constable a polite, courteous nod.

"What is this Inspector? Why am I still here? I thought you said I could help with further enquiries?"

"And you can, absolutely," he assured her.

Just a short distance away, a few rooms along the corridor. A familiar, husky, baritone voice rasped from the grubby handset.

"I pay you to get results."

The intonation was deliberate, the message clear.

"Get him off my back and off this case or you'll assume room temperature quicker than a baby's bottle!"

"Lucy you had started to tell me about your mother last night. What actually happened?"

A swift flick of her recently highlighted hair was offered, followed by a squint and a rather bemused look. "I don't understand how this helps you with your current enquiries into a dead girl at some pub."

"Inspector Murray tells me that it looks like your family are being fitted up," 'Hanna' Hayes interjected. "So background, family circumstances, jilted boyfriends would all play a vital part. Hundreds of pieces to fit together Miss Jordan. You understand that right? And at the moment we are desperately trying to just locate the four corners and the outside edges."

Nicely put, Murray thought. He then led with, "Okay, what about your own relationship with your brother?"

"It was a fire," she quickly responded. Overly keen once again to steer clear of any sibling discussion.

'Hanna' Hayes took a mental note of what her superior officer did there. Well played she thought. Years of wisdom and experience at work.

The evasive female pulled her chair closer to the desk top. She now swept her fringe back and pulled a hairband from her pocket to keep it in place. She had become more relaxed and comfortable. Murray had observed that Hayes closely mirrored her every action. A procedure guaranteed to undoubtedly firm up their bonding.

"What kind of fire Miss Jordan and when did that occur?"

"It was a decade ago. We were in our teens. It was at our old home. They reckon that it was started by a lit cigarette falling onto the floor whilst mum was asleep."

Suddenly that was when Lucy Jordan paused. A look a fear, unpleasant recollections, memories of some sort came flooding back. Murray had witnessed it a thousand times before. For Hayes it may have been less, but today, certainly just as apparent.

Jordan's unblemished hand on top of the desk began to tremble. Her gentle, subdued voice began to quiver with emotion as she tried desperately to continue.

"Lucy," Hayes said softly, resting her own hand on top of Miss Jordan's. "It is okay, we are here at your side. You are safe."

As if not fully recognising where she was, Lucy Jordan nodded her head. At least acknowledging the constable's encouraging words of comfort and support.

"That's when everything changed. Our world was turned upside down," she softly whispered. Every second word then disappeared into silence. "He would work, work, work and then leave us alone. Eventually when he did return, he would be totally blitzed. Very much the worse for wear. Wasted in a lazy, drunken stupor. He would stink of beer and had no idea what was going on under his very nose, in his own house," she said disgustedly. "He was no longer interested. Even in the beginning when I tried to confide in him. He was too busy with that other love of his life."

"Which was?" Murray asked.

Lucy Jordan shook her head.

Was she referring to the drink Hayes wondered. Or was there a mistress on the go? That would make sense DI Murray surmised. If he was having an affair however, so much for always working away from home to support his family. Many people all suffer bereavement and loss. The Inspector's offbeat mind, his latent curiosity was now piqued by this latest information. How come this man, the father, had been so badly affected? What had brought about the sudden change? Why would a previously loving parent, unexpectedly switch off from his own family and neglect them when their mother was gone? Suddenly, Murray's abdomen walls began to tighten and knot. The initial, hollow pain began to grapple, twist and stretch at his innards. It rose from the pit of his stomach, scorching every gastric muscle as it travelled. He felt nauseous. Was he asking those questions of Max Jordan? Or more possibly of himself?

Both the father and his daughter were free to go ten minutes later. All three had given their statements and were able to resume with their normal daily schedules. Protecting

Lucy Jordan had now become a priority for DI Steven Murray. But they needed proof. Hard facts and evidence.

For their supposed catch up meal, both men arrived at about five minutes to seven. Murray having calmed down sufficiently in the intervening few hours had already parked roadside, as Hanlon duly nipped in front of him and reversed. A good-natured, regular handshake took place between both men and Inspector Murray turned to point out the property.

"Oh, right," Hanlon mumbled. He tried his best to raise a smile, but was unsuccessful. Maybe the food would make up for it, he thought. As they approached the door the A4 card pinned to the woodwork seriously began to impact on Joe Hanlon's appetite. A black marker pen had scrawled the words - 'Burns Supper - 7.30 pm Tonight!'

High above the doorway however, was a beautifully dated copper plaque. It simply read: 'Trafalgar Hall, Leith.' They had now been met at the entrance by a man who seemed to be a friend of Steven Murray's. At the very least, a known acquaintance.

Across the street, a blacked out car window was gliding up to close shut. Not invited to the party, it looked like this interested onlooker was settling down for an hour or two. Whatever time it took, this individual would definitely still be there later in the evening, when the two police officers ventured outside again.

Back at home in nearby Bonnyrigg, new boy Allan Boyd had no immediate plans to journey back outside that night. Boyd had become a fairly reclusive individual since leaving the forces and he never liked to talk about his time in the army much nowadays. It involved too many painful memories. His outgoing bravado and larger than life character was exactly that - a character! It was a mask and protection from the world. A role he'd taken on in recent times to help him cope. Never kid a kidder they often say. So it will be interesting to see how Murray and Boyd collaborate together, or not, with so many similar individual traits. Only time will tell.

Boyd was glad however that earlier in the afternoon the fact that he had served, had been established with the missing girl's mother. He felt it gave them a bond, some mutual ground to travel together. Her pain at losing firstly her husband Allan as a casualty of war, then years later, desperately hanging on to the hope that her beloved daughter was still alive.

"Ye, ye, that's the right address." Boyd said into his mobile. "I'll see you there about nine fifteen. Don't be late. I'll definitely owe you big style for this mate. Cheers."

Slipping his phone back into his jeans pocket, Allan Boyd continued to load up an assortment of garden tools into the boot of his car. Those were followed by various painting accessories, including brushes, rollers, trays and actual tins of paint. He had tracked down about four or five different shades. Each with differing amounts in their respective pots. With the back seats folded down, some stepladders, garden shears and refuse sacks finished off his intensive checklist. His shift began at 2.00 pm tomorrow. So alongside his friend, he'd have around four solid hours to accomplish the jobs he had scheduled. Rex, his building buddy, had assured him it was doable. A tight itinerary, but doable nonetheless. And that between them, they'd give it their very best shot!

TWENTY

"It could be a spoonful of diamonds, could be a spoonful of gold. Just a little spoon of your precious love satisfies my soul."

- The Yardbirds

Back at 'The Lodge,' the heating inside was limited to say the least. The solid parquet block in the hall reminded Hanlon of his old High School gymnasium. The lacquered floor covering had definitely seen better days. But right now in 'Sherlock's' mind he was back in his P. E. outfit doing some circuit training and running at speed vaulting over a piece of gymnastic equipment. That particular nostalgic memory was abruptly halted by a bony elbow to the ribs.

"Joe are you even listening to what Chris is telling us?"

No, Joe Hanlon thought. But at least I now know our host's name was Chris. As introductions seemed to have been deliberately avoided at the doorway.

Christopher was big, bulky and broad. If you'd been told he was in training with Scotland for the Six Nations International rugby tournament starting next month, you'd not question it. He was currently giving them some background on the actual building itself.

"Being a major port in the nineteenth century, it was not surprising that Leith provided men for the crews of the ships engaged in the Battle of Trafalgar."

No doubt press-ganged, Hanlon thought to himself.

"In commemoration of that great victory at Trafalgar Bay and the many fine men from this area that were involved, it was decided to form a new Lodge. It was to be named 'Lodge Trafalgar' and here you have it. You may also have saw on your way in, above the entrance, cut in the stone, the Leith Coat of Arms?"

Both men nodded.

"And above it, the motto… Persevere."

Whilst talking, their 'Prop Forward' host, as elegantly as someone at 6' 3' can, had guided them to their exclusive table for two at the top of the hall. A table that Hanlon figured had just been set up and created especially for them whilst the historical tour of the premises had taken place. 'Sherlock' had also already assumed that there would be no menu required for their main course tonight. Haggis, neeps and tatties he guessed would be making their standard appearance. As throughout the world this Burns Night, hundreds of thousands of others would also be enjoying the aforementioned trio of delicacies.

Assured in the knowledge that Detective Steven Murray did not do social events and guided tours on a whim. There then must ultimately be a very good reason for them both to be in attendance at yet another celebration of the life of Ayrshire's favourite son. So this evening, to get to the real truth of their visit he thought to himself, he was most definitely going to have to… 'Persevere!'

The makeshift dining area on the premises looked to be catering for between 100-120 hardy souls. The portable tables could seat eight comfortably and each had been decorated with a pre-cut paper table cover, red tartan napkins and a small, elegant floral centrepiece. An A4 trifold leaflet sat at each place setting. It had been carefully positioned between the white plastic knives and forks. At the other end of the spectrum though were the top quality, crystal whiskey glasses. They had been positioned at every place setting on each table. Obviously nothing was to spoil the taste of one's favourite Malt. Alas for DI Murray and DC Hanlon they wouldn't know. For two small plastic tumblers had been hastily positioned on the outside of their soup spoons to cope with their chosen beverage.

As the heavy rain outside began to fire down from above. Water pellets bounced dramatically onto the misted front windshield of the car parked opposite the Trafalgar House 'restaurant.' The male occupant had been sat impassively for nearly an hour. Having figured out earlier what function was being catered for via Google, he reckoned another sixty minutes or so would suffice. Even longer, if both men intended to stay for each of the almost obligatory toasts. He continued to wait patiently. An assortment of music helped him stay alert. There was no real need to sit at an awkward angle facing the door all evening, both their cars were parked across the street from him. And as much as the beautiful Scottish weather had tried in vain, it had not managed to fully obscure them from his view. He took out a further cigarette and settled back for another shift.

"Wee, sleekit, cowran, tim'rous beastie. O, what a panic's in thy breastie! Thou need na start awa sae hasty, Wi' bickering brattle! I wad be laith to rin an' chase thee. Wi' murd'ring pattle!"

Between their starter and their main course the company had enjoyed a wide selection of Rabbie's poems. Each one applauded and washed down with a time honoured dram.

This current rendition had been the third and there was still one more to go when suddenly, from way out of left field, Joe Hanlon raised his voice and blurted abruptly.

"Who do you visit at Barlinnie sir?"

DI Murray's plastic cup fell from his lips. He coughed, spluttered, half swallowed his tongue and duly showered his fresh orange juice across the table.

"Sorry about that. Maybe I should have timed it better," came Hanlon's rather embarrassed and timid excuse for an apology.

A moment of awkward silence was exchanged between the two men. During which they duly soaked up the 'Sunny Delight' excess with their bold tartan serviettes. Murray wiped delicately and steadily at his shirt and trouser leg. Possibly and probably buying himself some extra thinking and response time. Joe Hanlon though, was unrepentant. He had grown substantially in confidence these past few months and the man mainly responsible for that was now sitting in his line of fire. Directly across the table his Inspector scrunched up the sodden napkin and placed it firmly inside the empty plastic cup. As he looked over thoughtfully at Joseph Hanlon, his chest tightened and his breathing became more intense. His tongue then caressed every tooth as he began to bite nervously on the inside of his bottom lip. Finally, after a long considered pause and studied observation of his young Detective Constable, two words emerged as a question…

"The Doc?" Murray asked gently.

A slow, deliberate closure of both eyes from Hanlon accompanied with the slightest of head movements forward, answered positively. "It was last year sir, when he was battered and left for dead and ended up in the hospital. He shared it with me."

"And you have known all this time and said nothing!"

"Until now," 'Sherlock' added. "He just wanted someone to be there for you, if he didn't survive."

"But he did survive," Murray remarked. More of a rebuke, than a grateful acknowledgement.

"Patterson said you'd visited faithfully all these years. Regularly, once a week and yet the prisoner would never see you?"

Phrased as a question, Murray responded with a resigned shrug of his shoulders and a quiet, "Correct." He then went to speak, but thought better of it.

"Go on sir," Hanlon encouraged.

"Well," he hesitated once again, before finishing. "They have still to confirm exactly the date and time, but he is due out in the next week or so."

'Sherlock,' smiled, began to nod and offered up a rather insincere, "Really!"

DI Murray stared at his young protégé. "Really… What does 'really' mean? What is your problem Joe?"

"Well this certainly helps me understand your recent stern-faced grumpiness. But how I was ever meant to differentiate that from your normal surly faced days I don't know."

"Careful, son. Thin ice approaching."

Joe Hanlon knew this, but skated on regardless. "Eight months ago, during the Cindy Ann Latchford case. When her father confessed to his involvement on video."

"What about it?" Murray asked sceptically.

"He said you could relate to his late wife's hit and run sir. That you knew what he was talking about. Where he was coming from."

This was where Joseph Hanlon upped the tempo. He had learned after all at the hands of a master. "You more than anyone sir, continually encourage us to be honest, to be upfront, to be truthful and sometimes downright blunt with people. Don't pussyfoot around you say. Care and candor you spout."

Hanlon paused for a breath and to ponder for a second.

"Is it all for show sir? Is it direct from the 'Do as I say, not as I Do,' Henderson Handbook?"

DI Murray appeared genuinely hurt by that last statement.

"The thing is though sir, I don't believe that it is all an act. I've watched you take control on numerous occasions. Time after time you lead by example. You encourage, you cajole, you gently persuade and influence. The bottom line is..." Hanlon then assertively raised his voice - "You care. You care too much for your own good. Even when you walk away, more often than not you go to work behind the scenes helping people in your own loyal, yet discrete style."

Steven Murray now lowered his head. 'Hard and confrontational,' as many of his doubters may think him. He'd often struggle to keep his emotional side under wraps. At that, a tender compassionate lump came to his dry throat. He had trained 'Sherlock' well and the young widower was not pulling any punches tonight.

"I have watched you be straight talking, honest and upfront with many people. However, I have also spent enough time in your company, to know that you do it with a sense of love and respect for the individual sir."

Murray began nervously to rub at his hands.

"With a genuine desire that they might grow," Hanlon continued. "That they would emerge from the experience, wiser and stronger for it. I have witnessed first hand, the behind the scenes good deeds and acts of selfless charity that you carry out."

His superior gazed at him through reddened eyes. Moisture began to well up and his tongue made an all too fleeting appearance between his hushed lips.

Hanlon carried on passionately. "Caitlin Bell, Iona Hynd, 'Mac' Rasul's special police fund to name but a few. Heck, even my own wife's upgraded coffin and our returned flat deposit," he stated firmly. "Did you think I didn't know? Do you really believe that your colleagues are oblivious to the wonderful things that you do for others? It's the foolish, unkind things that you try to do to yourself though sir. That is what concerns them most." Hanlon then pointed angrily at Murray's chest before unleashing, "Your selfish, feeble and cowardly attempts to take your own life!"

Tears now streamed openly down his Inspector's cheeks. His shoulders shuddered. Home truths hit hard. Talk about tough love. Joe Hanlon's words were genuine, from the heart and possibly exactly what Steven Murray had needed to hear for a long time, but too many people were afraid to say.

"Sir, I fully acknowledge that we are all different." Hanlon then dropped an octave and proceeded cautiously with, "You know that I lost my beautiful, gorgeous, soulmate one year ago to cancer. And that, that has helped me recognise that happiness, acceptance and recovery are all journeys. I can't answer WHY you are not happy all the time; WHY you keep having panic attacks or experience depression during the beautiful summer months or WHY all the WHY'S?" Hanlon then threw his arms into the air in continued frustration. In a slow reassuring tone though, he finished with, "What I do know however. Is that it's YOUR journey… and YOU have to take ownership of it…and YOU have to seek help."

Hanlon's own personal recipe for happiness after the tragic death of his childhood sweetheart, was to let go of what had gone; to be grateful for what remained and to look forward to what lay ahead in the future. Nowadays he would often simply say to others, *"Just because some people are fuelled by drama - doesn't mean that you have to attend the performance."*

The rain outside had gradually ceased. In the neglected street, potholes the size of the Grand Canyon held their own private pool parties. A front drivers seat window in a car opposite had been rolled down and yet another empty cigarette packet discarded. The strangers eyes were once again focused on the main doorway. Not long now he reckoned. The driver stared carefully at the photograph in his hand. He then eventually scanned it for the umpteenth time that day, along with the detailed notes that accompanied it. Finally, he gathered them all back inside the envelope and replaced them cautiously into his jacket pocket.

TWENTY ONE

"I was the son you always had, tugging at your coat whilst you were sad. Don't cry, hold your head up high. She would want you to. She would want you to. I was the son you always had."

- Bear's Den

Whilst mentor and protégé were having their heart to heart. Nineteen miles east of the city lay a medieval fortress in the village of Dirleton. Barbra Furlong had not long ventured out for her regular evening exercise. She was accompanied by her tiny and often irascible Yorkshire terrier. The word 'irascible' stuck in her mind for a second - It's definition: 'Easily provoked to anger.' Could she ever be accused of that she wondered?

For the three years plus that she'd actually had the animal, its temper had gotten gradually worse. But then so had hers. Was she gradually following her pets example, or was her nature now rubbing off on the poor beast? It was not so much during her early morning walks, because those irate thoughts were mainly due to busy traffic heading off to work, commuters getting ready and irksome, early deliveries being made to a multitude of stores or local businesses in the area. No, normally the real angst and frustration was always guaranteed to be aired during her quiet, late night strolls. That was when a free-pass was given for those turbulent, reflective thoughts to enter into the fray. Pondering diligently on the day. Considering everything and nothing. Asking - How does that work? What if we did it another way? Why won't my mind stop throwing up new questions? And how do we get those animated cartoon numbskulls inside our heads to take a well deserved break?

All dog owners, walkers, cyclists and joggers must do it she thought. Well, all of the aforementioned who prefer to keep their ears free from playlists, motivational talks and the boom, boom, boom step to the beat sounds! For DCI Barbra Furlong, in the shadow of Dirleton Castle in East Lothian, she enjoyed the peaceful solitude. The chance to meditate, mull over and muse.   Irascible? Not me, she thought. It must be the dog!

Back at Trafalgar House, Murray dabbed his eyes with the only remaining dry tartan napkin on their table. Hanlon had remained silent. An old trick he also learned from Steven Murray.

"I told you earlier I was married and that we had three children."

"Thomas, David and Hannah," Hanlon remarked. "I was listening you know."

"Well, Isobel, my wife…"

This time it was the young apprentice's time to nod. A number 15 - 'A go on, I'm still listening!'

"Well, I was wholly responsible for her death." Murray had expected startled surprise, shocked silence or sheer disbelieve.

But 'Sherlock' shook his head vehemently. He was having none of it. "I don't think so sir. Latchford implied that it was a hit and run. Like that of his own dear wife. In reality, are you actually saying you feel somewhat responsible for her death?"

"Somewhat responsible? What kind of politically correct wording is that? What happened to the genuine honesty, the plain speaking, the…"

"Did you kill your wife?" Joe Hanlon voiced. "Is that plain enough?"

He maybe spoke louder than he would have liked. As a couple of those at the top table turned around sharply in a rather concerned manner. He gave them a defiant look and then flashed them his warrant card. At that, they swiftly and meekly turned away. The things his dining partner had taught him in the space of a year - Priceless!

"So did you actually kill Isobel?" He repeated.

Quickly sobering up mentally and physically, Murray responded - "Of course not!"

Hanlon noticed the edgy change in his tone. He felt him push back, regain his composure. He could sense the return of his mentor.

"I drove her to it though Joe. My gambling had gotten way out of hand. I was at the bank first thing that morning. I had already blown our life savings of over thirty thousand pounds."

"Thirty thous…" Hanlon gasped.

"I know Joe and now I was there to pick up another twenty thousand in cash. Partly borrowed against our home. The loan had been agreed the day before."

DC Hanlon was stunned. He sat shocked and speechless.

Murray paused and shook his head shamefully before continuing.

The guilt was beginning to surface in the pit of Joe Hanlon's stomach. What had he done? This man had only ever helped him. Had given him the opportunity to become a detective. Had been a friend, a role model and father figure to him. And now 'Sherlock, Holier Than Thou' Hanlon, had repaid him by dragging up all the heartbreaking memories of his late wife's final moments here on Earth.

"I was waiting anxiously, sitting outside of the casino Joe. I was out of control. Tens of thousands I had lost. Chasing the game. I was never going to win that back. Compulsion and desperation - are a highly toxic mix. I was a loser then and I am a loser now!"

Hanlon simply listened.

"They were due to open their doors at twelve noon and at 11.55 am, yours truly sat desperate, alone and addicted. I was in my car, furiously biting my nails with a sealed bank bag burning a hole in my pocket. It contained one thousand, fresh, crisp twenty pound notes."

If 'Sherlock' was still none the wiser as to how this fully involved the death of Murray's beloved Isobel. All was soon to be revealed.

"She had been tipped off. Tipped off that I was parked outside that casino."

"What!" Hanlon offered in genuine surprise.

"I know, right. To this very day Joe, I still don't know by whom." His pace in retelling the story increased. "Although at this point it didn't matter, she had figured out why I was there. She knew about my previous spending, the loss of our savings and had no doubt guessed that I had borrowed more from someone, somewhere or somehow."

His feisty young colleague now just shook his head. Feeling the pain and deep wounds of each chapter being recalled.

"Throughout all our married years together, she had continually asked me to get help. 'Begged' me actually would be a better word if we are sticking with the honesty theme. But I never listened and I lost everything that day. And Joseph, I mean... everything." His voice slowed. Speaking in no more than a whisper he added, "The roulette wheel never even spun... and my whole life imploded."

He turned gently to his friend. "Remember Sir Gerald Anderson's obsession with the comedian Robin Williams?"

Hanlon offered a fragile nod.

Through a voice raw with emotional contrition, Steven Murray concluded. "As that great troubled actor once said - All it takes is a beautiful fake smile to hide an injured soul and they will never notice how broken you really are." Murray pursed his lips and swallowed.

DC Hanlon looked deep into his eyes and felt his hurt, his tenderness, his bitter remorse and the relentless guilt he still carried with him twenty-four hours of every day.

"You don't have to finish sir. It's fine," 'Sherlock,' offered sympathetically.

"Don't you dare," Inspector Murray asserted. "Don't you dare weaken on me now," he repeated.

Various other Burns songs and poems had been offered during the twenty minute interval, but both colleagues had been oblivious to them.

Aggressively encouraged not to weaken, DC Hanlon then asked Murray, "Finish off your story then sir. I would like to understand fully and exactly what happened. And how we can both move forward from here."

With a brief rub of his nose, Murray continued. His memory of that dark day had never faded. "When my vehicle clock changed to 11.58 Joe, I opened the car door and headed for the casino entrance. I was quite happy to wait there until they opened. I was going to be a winner today I had told myself repeatedly. Only one bet. All on red or black, odd, or even! It didn't matter. For we'd only be ten grand or so down and we could live with that! Then in my head I offered up all the normal promises and platitudes at that point. Like obviously I'd never return - No more gambling from here on - It would be easy after this experience to give it all up - All the usual nonsense."

He paused. You could physically see him replaying each of those distressing events in his head.

"Only a minute could have passed, when suddenly Isobel drove up on the other side of the road. She obviously saw me standing outside, thinking I was heading straight in. Not fully realising they hadn't even opened yet. Undoubtedly desperate and frantic to stop me before I placed my 'winning' bet. It would only take a few seconds and... 'No More Bets' would be called... the money gone... our lives ruined. So no doubt filled with both dread and adrenaline, she suddenly drove her car up onto the kerb and halfway over the pavement. She then immediately threw open the car door and without hesitation or caution ran straight across the street to stop me. Initially Joe, the road didn't even appear to be busy. It was midday. But suddenly, as if from out of nowhere, a car struck her at speed. Her body was instantly sent scurrying over the bonnet, colliding with the driver's roof and eventually dropped lifeless, into the centre of the oncoming traffic. Horns sounded, tyres screeched and several small minor bumps and incidents occurred."

Hanlon looked at him gravely for final confirmation.

"Isobel was dead before she had even hit the ground. The T'inker carried out the postmortem. Her neck had broken on impact with the car roof."

There was another pause in the conversation before Murray asked his constable, "Can you really, truly tell me Joe, that I was not responsible for her death?"

Without any hesitation, which was maybe a mistake in itself. DC Hanlon responded tearfully and emotionally. "The driver was responsible sir. Not you. The circumstances were…"

"Do not go there 'Sherlock.' No one was ever caught. I've no idea if it was a man or a woman. The car was never traced. How they have lived with their actions all these years, I'll never know."

Another unconcealed, raw silence passed between them as Hanlon drank slowly from his glass and then delicately placed it back down.

"And that was why no doubt, Robert Latchford trusted you. It was like an identical case to his."

"I guess," Steven Murray responded slowly. "Although he at least still had his beautiful daughter to raise up. A purpose to continue on with life."

"But you had…"

Murray saved him the bother. "My children? You would think so wouldn't you? But sadly and understandably, they all in one way or another blamed their father. Our relationship soured. It never fully recovered and they all made lives for themselves elsewhere."

His raw, tender eyes once again moistened and he wiped away several emotional tears.

"My sole purpose for living died many years ago my young friend. So now I look upon every 24 hours as time added to my sentence. The executioner never arrives. So I have sought him out personally from time to time, as you more than anyone well know!"

It was now DC Hanlon's turn to shed a tender tear or two. Did he really have to ask that question. He was unsure if it had done anyone any good. But maybe in the cold light of day, it may prove worthwhile. Only time will tell. As a musician concluded his set, both men stood up and hugged. It was a familiar Burns love song finishing in the background. Murray, still standing, moved his head from side to side. It was a silent style of questioning that he carried out. Hanlon had become used to the technique. So he was personally delighted to see it rear its head in an evening that he had so far found totally soul destroying. It normally indicated that Detective Inspector Steven Murray was on to something and that was reward enough.

As the words, "Let's go Joe," exploded from his mouth, the famous lyrics continued to filter graciously throughout Trafalgar House… *"As fair art thou, my bonnie lass, so deep in love am I; And I will love thee still, my dear, till a' the seas gang dry. Till a' the seas gang dry, my dear…"*

TWENTY TWO

"Struck by lightning, sounds pretty frightening. But you know the chances are so small. Odds are we gonna be alright, odds are we gonna be alright for another night."

- The Barenaked Ladies

Once outside, Murray instructed Hanlon to follow him to Seafield Road. He needed to experience 'Thistle Do Nicely' for himself! Both cars indicated and took off. Several hundred yards behind them, unaware to either police officer, followed car number three. That driver also felt that he'd had a long night. But was now about to ensure that it drew to a satisfactory close.

Whilst travelling the short distance, Murray had reflected on Hanlon's honest words and counsel. With his stinging chastisement still ringing in his ears, he had tried several times in the last two minutes to contact Raymond Armour. Each time he had gotten the unobtainable tone. That number was dead and gone. It had ceased to be. Ray had been true to his word and severed links. There would be no further contact between the two men. Murray then had no way to pull out of his deal with the devil, except to visit Armour personally first thing in the morning. And that is exactly what he planned to do.

With their cars parked nearby, both colleagues walked contentedly toward the two surprisingly friendly and approachable security men on the door. As one of the tabard wearing stewards offered a cheery "Alright!" Murray seemed to be desperately searching around, specifically searching for something else!

Joe Hanlon threw his wrists into the air, in a gesture that clearly indicated - 'What's up?'

"Where is the boom, boom, boom? DI Murray asked. "Or, given it's a ceilidh, where is the diddly di, di, di, diddly dee, dee, dee?"

Hanlon smiled a teenage, self-satisfactory smile and pointed at the oversized hoarding outside the ex-car showroom. It read: Back by popular demand this Burns Night - The Thistle Do Nicely SILENT Ceilidh!

"The what?"

The DI's face was a picture!

"You'll soon see," Hanlon reassured him.

They showed both their warrant cards, followed by "official business," echoed in unison.

The two friendly doormen once again exceeded expectations. The slightly taller of the pair, waved his hand and indicated to carry straight on. Hanlon, thought that there was something strangely familiar about him, but couldn't quite recollect what. Possibly he'd seen him on the door at other events or locations in the city.

His shorter, bespectacled colleague even offered a genuine, "Enjoy officers!"

Steven Murray suspected those guys were in heaven and would hardly ever see any bother. It was the difference between being on duty at a hate filled football match or an 'all for one' rugby game. Ceilidh-sitting or on the door of a boozy night club? It was a no-brainer! Their bright, luminous orange rain jackets accompanied by their company name on the back, also added to the fun nature of their gig. The individual behind that particular name deserved a medal for originality Hanlon thought. Their logos read: 'You'll Get Kilt Security!'

After opening the inside front door, the two Police Scotland ceilidh dancers were greeted by a young female at the cash desk. She wore shocking pink rimmed glasses and had a hair colouring best described as 'the full rainbow effect.' Orange, green, blue and yellow were four colours to be going on with. It made you wonder if some shades were being washed out, with the others being recently added. Both men, wisely declined to comment. Again their official credentials were flashed. This time with no vocal accompaniment. So as Hanlon opened the third and final set of doors, Murray froze at the scene in front of him. Couples had their partners in the Gay Gordon's hold. 1-2-3 turn, 1-2-3 turn, spin under your partner's arm and a lively waltz to finish. All seemed normal. Except… the room was silent!

DI Murray looked steadily around in both amazement and astonishment. He had never experienced this before and it was surreal to say the least. It may even have resembled many of his strange, unique late night dreams. Each dancer wore wireless headphones. There was no longer a ceilidh band. They had been replaced with a DJ blasting out, or not as the case may be, the eclectic mix of traditional ceilidh tunes and some rather upbeat club versions. Not that Murray knew this, as he was experiencing total silence. Giving the effect of a room full of people gyrating, spinning and clapping to no accompaniment whatsoever. It made him smile actually. Shoes were being scuffed and the galloping sound of feet and heels stomping around was all he was privy to. Surreal or what!

Using their highly authoritative gravitas they beckoned a young lad that wasn't taking part over toward them. Hanlon pointed at his earpiece set, before quickly taking ownership of it. He listened for a second, then placed it at his Inspector's ear. Foot-tapping, Murray made a positive facial gesture, as 'Sherlock' handed them back to the disgruntled youth.

"Very impressive," Murray shouted.

A few palm down hand movements, partnered with a smile from Joseph Hanlon, reminded Murray the place was quiet. No sound - so no need to raise your voice.

"In a gentler quieter tone, Murray then offered. "A gentle tap on the shoulder and it would be real easy to get into a deep conversation without anyone overhearing."

"The killer got them all outside. Possibly, old style sir. He was maybe 'on a promise,' as they say."

Murray nodded and then shook his head. "I hear you Joe, but I don't think so. On a promise normally meant at the end of the evening. We know that at least on two occasions, the attacks happened and the victims time of death had been established, before the ceilidh had even finished."

"So the lure, the temptation or invitation, it was not sexual or physical?"

"I suspect not Joe."

Both men scrutinised the premises a bit more carefully. Checked out the various fire exits and continually showed pictures of the murdered females to those in attendance. Without any success. As they were sat side by side on the outskirts of the dance floor, Murray decided after half an hour of silent dancing to call it a night. To come at it fresh in the morning. He tapped Joe Hanlon on the knee to tell him as such, but no movement. He turned to look at him. Hanlon was oblivious, staring out into space. The silence had gotten to him Murray smiled. Again, with a little bit more force this time the Inspector kicked his ankle. 'Sherlock,' once again remained unfazed. His superior then chose to follow Hanlon's line of sight. A graceful duo were busy waltzing along with about forty or so similar couples. Detective Inspector Steven Murray suspected he never knew the names of the others. But the dance partner that had caught the unwavering attention of DC Hanlon, was none other than Mister Craig Jordan, fashion retailer extraordinaire!

"I see him Joe. But it's not a crime."

"But it is a rather strange coincidence, don't you think?"

"That he is out at a city ceilidh enjoying himself? Really? After what I put him through earlier?"

"You know what I mean."

"I'm off home. Are you heading out?"

"No - I'll continue with the photos and see if I can jog anyone's memory. And I'll keep a watchful eye on our buddy over there also."

"Yep. I thought you might say that," DI Murray added, as he offered the briefest of waves on his way toward the exit. "Interesting concept," he said encouragingly to the girl at the desk.

The two jovial bouncers were still smiling and game for a laugh, as two flirtatious females twirled several times around in their skirts to show off more fully their blue and green tartan tights. One leg was a bit more blue than the other.

Which, needless to say meant that the other was a bit more green.

"They're all the rage in Glasgow just now," she said in a rather clipped, west coast accent. "They are called 'The Old Firm.' It's a Celtic and Rangers thing," she added.

"It's all about promoting unity and getting rid of sectarianism, bigotry and the like," her tall, blonde haired pal piped up. Whilst still spinning around giving the two doormen an eyeful of tartan thigh!

"Goodnight," Murray cried in a friendly, parental manner. Which kind of said - 'And remember to put the lights out when you are done!'

The main road was deserted. An occasional, infrequent flow of traffic added the odd sound effect. His car was about 50 yards further along. He hit the key fob, the lights flashed and with his alarm off, he made his way toward it. The car behind his had its interior light on. Possibly a concerned parent still doing the taxi run at the end of the night Murray guessed. Even though wee Jenny or Johnnie are now nearly twenty-five! The Inspector had been so deep in thought that he never saw Joe Hanlon exit from the front door after him.

Within thirty brief seconds of Murray's departure, 'Sherlock' had remembered that his DI still had all the relevant photographs. So, hastily exiting from the ceilidh, he made his way past the two doormen and their new female pals. The fun loving quartet were now currently waltzing with each other to a tune on one of their iPhones. Outside Hanlon looked up and down the street. He quickly spotted that DI Murray was just about to enter his vehicle. The drivers door was parked kerbside. In fact most of the cars on that full stretch had parked on the right hand side of the road. It just made it extra handy for the drivers.

What Steven Murray could not see however was that his so-called 'concerned parent,' had hurriedly left his vehicle and was rapidly coming up menacingly behind him.

DC Hanlon, although still a good forty to fifty feet away, caught a glimpse of a shiny object. A blade, he immediately thought. A loud, impressive shout or two followed.

"Sir! Sir! Look out!" He yelled at the top of his voice.

Murray had no idea who had cried out. But on hearing a desperate scream, he'd adjusted his position. The blade severed clean through his jacket, shirt and tender skin. On turning, his jacket had opened wide. Red blotches instantly appeared on his shirt. But by the time the sharp edge of the blade had made contact, DI Murray had avoided the worst. The two inch of blade that had managed to break through though could still do some serious damage. Murray doubled over in both shock and wincing pain. He held tightly to both the outside and inside of his attackers jacket. Hanlon had shouted instructions to the bouncers to call an ambulance and police back-up. Immediately they had waved in acknowledgement.

'Sherlock' then began to up his pace, running energetically and at speed toward his friend and colleague. In that split second, overwhelming appreciation and gratitude for this man had just swept through him. The unknown assailant had broken free and then jumped hastily back into his car, but not before DI Murray had snatched at him. As he moved ever closer, Hanlon never heard any engine being turned over. It had obviously been left running and was ready and waiting for an ideal, instant getaway. The detective did get a partial plate. He also witnessed however, a large Hertz rental sticker on the back. So highly unlikely they'd get to trace the fraudulent hirer or it was probably stolen earlier in the day. Screeching tyres, the smell of burning rubber and an ever growing pool of blood were all waiting to greet Joseph Hanlon after his fifty yard dash.

He gently turned Murray over. His Inspector had passed out. Blood ran constantly down his left hand side. He grew paler by the minute. 'Sherlock' desperately tried to stop the bleeding. One of the doormen had once again exceeded expectations and had duly arrived with a substantial pile of towels. Joe Hanlon quickly grabbed one and pressed it firmly to Steven Murray's side. He then slowly focused up again at the helpful doorman.

"Alright!" the man offered. More by way of a greeting, rather than a question.

"Towels are always the most helpful, you know!" he added. "No matter if it's punches thrown, punters being sick, or knife attacks like this. A towel is always the best solution!"

'Sherlock' never heard a single word of the man's theory about 'the advantageous quality to using towels.' Because he had remembered in that very second, where he knew him from. There had just been something missing earlier. Now that was very interesting or maybe purely coincidence Yea right, he thought to himself. But all of that is for later.

Hanlon then peered across at the inside of Murray's jacket. A puzzled expression came over his face. He then looked from side to side to see how many people were around him. So far it was just the bouncer, although plenty more were now on their way. He deliberately asked the doorman to get him more towels and before other onlookers could arrive, he quickly dislodged the long envelope from Murray's bloodied fingers. As others came to his assistance, the collection of red stained literature was instantly hidden out of sight. Fellow officers and more importantly an ambulance arrived within six minutes. A few short months ago it was 'Doc' Patterson assaulted to within an inch of his life and being taken at speed to the nearest hospital. Tonight his close pal Steven Murray was about to give him a run for his money.

TWENTY THREE

"If all your dreams were on fire, which one would you save. When it comes down to the wire, should I be afraid?"

- Katie Melua

It was early morning on Tuesday the 26th of January. A few dramatic days had past and the Highlands of Scotland were this individual's next port of call.

The M99 was one seriously impressive piece of equipment. The mystery gunman had taken the unusual step of fitting a laser scope on to it. Which in most people's eyes was pretty pointless, because fifty calibre rifles were not normally geared up to target humans. And considering they are often fired from five hundred plus metres, they will still explode on contact with their prey. As the poor deer in his sights currently was about to testify to - or not as the case may be. Seconds later and sure enough, parts of the lifeless animal were to be found strewn across the remote, rural hillside. A picturesque, scenic location that had taken our 'nature loving' assassin nearly four hours to reach. Animals, isolation and Mr Barrett were all that was required. The special attachment of the laser scope was more about informing someone else of his presence. An advance warning. Even if only for that split second - it was an opportunity to instill fear and helplessness.

Back on the outskirts of Edinburgh at ten minutes before ten on a wet, damp and dreich, typically overcast Scottish morning, the body count had continued to stack up. Another victim had been discovered. Disposed of yet again in the rear car park of a pub. A drinking establishment close to Portobello swimming baths. Their bar manager had phoned it in on his arrival to open up. Five minutes later, Sergeant 'Sandy' Kerr had been given the call and was on her way. On her way she suspected, to firstly visit the licensed premises and then head onward to spend some time with an army widow!

DC Boyd's shift did not start until later that afternoon. She had already tried twice to get hold of him, but to no avail. On each occasion she left a voice message.

Across the city Joseph Hanlon had remained all night by Murray's side. After a brief trip into the emergency theatre on arrival, the Inspector was designated a room and 45 minutes later that was where he had spent the evening. By 10.00 am on the Tuesday morning, he'd already had seven or eight people all pop by to see him. Hayes, Curry, 'Doc' Patterson and even a lollipop man were included on the visitors roster. How the conscientious traffic enforcer had even found out, goodness only knows. Each one, without exception was unable to get past the unofficial gatekeeper. Although DC Hanlon's proffered reason that Murray was still out for the count and on medication, was one hundred percent valid and truthful.

Before he awoke fully, a strange concoction of drugs, dreams and paranoid delusions seemed to overtake his mind. As 'Sherlock' watched from the comfort of his chair only a few feet away, his Inspector was continually restless. Head movements, occasional words and garbled remarks all surfaced from time to time. Joe was certain that on a couple of occasions he clearly heard his own name get a mention.

Murray's chemically induced imagination ran wild - *In front of a train - effective but so unfair on the driver and his family. Pills - they never seemed like an easy option. Too unreliable with long term after effects if unsuccessful. Hanging may have worked - had it not been for his faithful 'deputy dawg,' Joe Hanlon! Car crash, wrists, from a cliff top - a plethora of other crazy schemes disappeared from his mixed-up, muddled mind as quickly as they appeared.*

A muddled mind! Ye right, that is a very generous, 'touchy feely' description Murray thought. *He couldn't quite hear the clinical psychologist offer the poor mother or parents of a child that one. 'Yes, Mr and Mrs X it would appear that little Stevie has a slightly 'muddled mind.' So no major worries then. Just give him a couple of these aspirins four times a day. They're soluble and they'll help dilute, refine and clear up the issue. Hey ho!'*

Plain, concise language worked best. But 'I just want to die' does not really do it justice or paint the picture very well. Rather than pills and medical help Murray *persevered with the laborious climb. However, he knew it had become a much more substantial mountain range to ascend in recent months. Over time it had gotten seriously dangerous. The peaks and troughs, the highs and lows they were filled with ever increasing extremes. He knew things were coming to a head. But he was still a '5th Dan black belt'....... in self-denial!*

So work it was then. May the (police) force be with you! He'd immerse himself even deeper into a case, or several at once. Even then, that was still the dark side. The Jedi knight seemed to be getting or was certainly less and less desirous to make an appearance. The goodwill gestures, the helping hand, the mentoring, cajoling and the supportive role was becoming tiresome. The individual was struggling to replace the daily grind with something fulfilling. The laughter and fun that once illuminated his life in so many ways was being slowly extinguished bulb by bulb, poor experience after another and minute by tiny minute. Again - just let me die he thought.

Many of those in charge were just silently biding their time. Waiting patiently for his resignation or death, whichever came first. They had no real time for the man. Their words applauded him carefully in public. But sadly, their combined actions said so much more. He could do his job and exceptionally well for that matter. But who cared? He did not play the political game. He would continually rock the boat and make those in authority feel uneasy by holding them to account. Those turkeys were not in the habit of voting for Christmas! When the floating vessel that you travel upon is already rudderless, without a Captain or compass and is leaking more water than Niagara Falls, then maybe the option to jump does become even more appealing with every gradual, passing minute. Time to grab a lifejacket he thought...... Oh wait. - Budget cuts. - They'd already gone!!

As the police vehicle pulled up in the Silverknowes area of Edinburgh for the second time in two days, the weather had dried up nicely. Sandra Kerr was surprised and slightly taken aback as she walked up the neglected path leading to the front door. There, larger than life was DC Allan Boyd working frantically to repair the roughcast on this woman's side wall. His pal from the telephone conversation the night before meanwhile, was busy energetically repairing her broken fence and shoddy garden gate.

"Detective Constable Boyd," was all 'Sandy' could think to say.

His friend made himself scarce and headed back toward his van.

"Sarge," Boyd responded with a rather embarrassed and flushed expression upon his face. "I just thought I could…"

Kerr held up her hand. "No need to explain. But I was trying to get a hold of you…"

"Oh, hello there. Good morning," came a hopeful voice from the open doorway. It's light female tone then turned toward Allan Boyd, his hands covered in shingle. "I thought you might like this?" she suggested, before offering him a large, freshly brewed mug of piping hot tea.

Sandra Kerr shook her head at Boyd before commenting, "I think we could all do with one of those Ma'am!"

Terri McKenzie's shoulders sagged as DS Kerr put a reassuring and comforting arm around her.

TWENTY FOUR

"Walk awhile, walk awhile, walk awhile with me. The more we walk together, the better we'll agree. Two miles down the road, Henry Tompkins wife. Three miles down the road and he's running for his life."

- Fairport Convention

It was mid-afternoon and Joseph Hanlon had just nipped off to get a coffee from one of the hospital's many vending machines. Murray had only just shut his eyes and was lying back against his wafer-thin, useless pillows. He had one foot crossed comfortably over the other - which was strictly against Doctors orders. It was then that he heard the familiar gruff, harsh tones. Thick and rasping they barked out from the frame of the doorway. It felt like they quickly reverberated, bounced and echoed off each participating wall surface - before escaping at pace from his single room and heading down the corridor to safety!

"Mr Murray, you were to get back to me! But unless I'm mistaken, it looks like you were rather indisposed."

"Just a little bit 'Bunny!'" Murray yawned.

The Detective Inspector forced himself to sit upright, wincing as he did so. The knife wound was causing him concern. Catching him between two ribs, it was agony when he tried to move his upper body in any direction. In a few days the excessive pain would be gone he was told. So for the next 72 hours he would complain as much as he could!

"I would invite you to take a seat Mr Reid but I know you won't be staying." Steven Murray realised as soon as he spoke the mistake that he'd made. Red rag - bull - etc, etc.

"Don't mind if I do," the uninvited guest growled with a smile. He then graciously helped himself to a grey, bog standard, NHS metallic chair. Flaking paintwork came as standard. As he perched himself alongside DI Murray he lowered his voice. Although still deep and hoarse, it appeared to have mellowed. As if concerned and talking cautiously about a sickly invalid in the room next door, 'Bunny' Reid spoke plainly.

"We are looking at two different killers you mentioned previously."

"Well, I'm basing that on you not having ceilidh dancers bumped off! Or leaving macabre clues behind 'Bunny.'"

"I think you know that you can trust me when I say…"

"I can trust YOU?" Murray shouted. Grimacing in pain as he did so.

A burly, alarmed, ugly head made an expected appearance at the doorway.

"Aye, I didn't think one of your glamour model henchmen would be too far away."

"There, there, Mr Murray. Keep it civilised. Simmer down Inspector. You can never be too careful. You don't always know who you can trust these days, know what I mean?" He offered a sly grin and a wink to complement those devious words. As if he had just sat down and enjoyed a succulent piece of sirloin, accompanied by an outstanding glass of Cabernet wine.

Murray resigned himself to a disgusted shake of the head and a timid… "My point exactly!"

"So how can I help?" Reid croaked.

"No retaliation 'Bunny.' That is what we need from you. Just for once, let us figure this out and allow the justice system to work its magic."

Murray then wondered if those words sounded as pathetic as he had intended. He soon got an answer to that query. The very one he expected.

"That's not going to happen Inspector." Reid made to stand up. Dragging each word slowly and precisely along the pristine, sterile floor he offered clinically, "I have a reputation to protect Mr Murray and this, this was made very very personal. Someone murdered. No sorry, let me start again more accurately. Some deluded individuals slaughtered my beautiful, innocent niece. Now mistakenly or not there will be repercussions."

He looked intensely at Murray, before continuing with his trademark voice and a hint of a knowing smile.

"There is nothing worse than losing a loved one, especially a family member. Wouldn't that be right Inspector?"

The concerned features on the face of the man in the hospital bed changed dramatically. His eyebrows narrowed and his lined forehead indicated worry. He was disturbed and mildly unsettled, specifically by that last remark. He knew 'Bunny' Reid well and was familiar with his mannerisms and vocabulary. He did not normally say things by accident. So what was implied in those words. The dilemma, he asked himself was this - Was he speaking in the past tense, present or maybe even in future?

"The justice system?" Murray offered.

"Aye, right!" Reid glowered. His dissatisfaction and contempt highly visible. "You just played me Murray, didn't you?"

"I'm sure I have no idea what you are talking about Mr Reid. But thank you so much for the visit…" Murray left it a few seconds before adding, "And the information!"

The burly minder outside glanced at his boss on hearing that.

"I - never - gave you any flamin' information Murray!"

"Simmer down, simmer down man. There, there Mr Reid." Murray was on dangerous ground, mimicking the man himself. Not just any man, but Edinburgh's number one gangland boss. A title he took on from the late Kenny Dixon. A title he had prepared for, for many years. A title he was not about to have taken away easily from his grasp. He was a ruthless, violent, evil individual who Murray hoped one day soon, would get exactly what was coming to him.

'Bunny' had become worked up. He had raised his voice and looked as if he was about to get physical with Steven Murray. The officer had just went too far.

The aged gangster raised his hand to strike, but it was grabbed just in time by his ever faithful thug of a bodyguard.

"So you are the infamous James Baxter Reid," the female voice eloquently stated. It was offered in an almost regal tone. She most definitely had that elegant, educated manner about her today. Dressed from top to toe in her official black uniform. Complete with three badges on her epaulettes and a silver band beneath her cap badge.

"Mr Reid, let me introduce myself. You may call me…"

"Detective Chief Inspector Furlong. Oh, I know all about you Missy. Don't you worry."

Furlong did not appear worried. In fact she held his stare without blinking. Reid being the first to give in. However, as the Edinburgh crime lord nodded at his loyal lieutenant to tarry with him. DCI Furlong couldn't resist.

"So tell me an interesting fact that you think you know about me Mr 'Bunny' Reid."

The Inspector knew that was a mistake. This would come back to bite her big time. Of that he was plenty sure.

Reid took a firm, confident step back into the room. Then at a very moderate pace, he began to run his eyes up the slender police woman's body. It was absolutely meant in a deliberate sexual, predatory, intimidatory way. But Furlong had experienced it all before. It was anything but new to her.

She smirked confidently. "So nothing then," she said impatiently. "That's what I figured."

This was dangerous territory. She had no idea what she was doing. Murray knew this man well. You simply don't goad him. At some point he would make her pay for his public humiliation.

Reid just stood patiently for several seconds. The room was hushed. His minder towered over his left shoulder. "So, does the fact that I know you walk three miles every day count?" he asked menacingly, in his familiar low, husky tone.

Furlong swallowed ever so slightly at that Murray noticed, and you can bet your life Reid spotted it as well. Although it was not always a good thing to bet your life when the Reidmeister was in your company.

The hoarse deep rasp continued. "However, I'm sure lots of your new colleagues will have been made aware of that fact also. So maybe it's not so surprising that I knew that," he shrugged.

"That would have been my assumption," Furlong said, from her moral high ground. "That would be very much in the public domain. So yes, much more surprised if you hadn't known that I think."

Wow! His DCI continued to take the opportunity to have a go at James Baxter Reid. She was a brave woman Murray mentally noted. There was no doubting that, fair play to her. He was continuing to recognise and appreciate many of her talents and character traits. Her elevation through the ranks to Detective Chief Inspector was becoming less surprising with every passing minute.

Unperturbed, Reid's glistening twinkle in his eye seemed to imply that he had just taken another mouthful of that most tender of fillet steaks, and was now about to wash it down vigorously.

"I wonder Chief Inspector, how many of your precious work colleagues," he deliberately paused for effect. "What precise number would know that 'Three Miles,' … is actually the name of yer dog, yer mutt, yer wee spoiled four legged pet pooch?"

Her eyes gave her away.

"Thought not. Have a nice day Detective Chief Inspector Furlong."

Exiting through the door he turned to Murray, clicked his heels and gave him a solid, self-assured Nazi salute. He then returned his gaze to the female in the room and parted with

"Or can I call you Barbra?"

Then as Little and Large made their way down the lengthy hospital corridor, Furlong collapsed mentally exhausted, into the vacated chair. DI Murray then threw his head back with an almighty and painful sigh of relief against the metal railings of his bed.

Recovering from the shock his DCI offered gloomily, "I think we may just have lost that particular bout of verbal sparring."

Murray never responded.

"Don't you think? Steven," she cajoled. Looking for some form of support or interjection.

The Inspector remained unfazed. Taking on board the conversation, processing the tone, the intimation, packaging and parcelling before delivery of the German salute. He briefly thought of his late father doing his Royal Mail duties at the postal sorting offices of old. It was an era where each postman by hand would place and position all the individual letters into their relevant boxes with corresponding routes. Now Steven Murray looked across at his DCI. A glimmer of a smile broke out upon his face.

"You noticeably missed the early rounds Ma'am. Because I think you will be pleasantly surprised to discover that we may just have won that match on points. But it was close, I'll give you that. Especially surviving the knockout punch - that 'Three Miles' was the name of your dog!"

The hospital room went silent. Expressions, glances and communication remained muted for several seconds. Furlong blushed slightly and Murray, well he was just being Murray!

"He's knows who did it Ma'am," the Inspector proffered. "He used the word individuals, plural. He already has something in place. Although I got the impression that seemed to be more directed at me, than at Cardwell's attackers."

"The Nazi salute?" Furlong offered up as a question.

"That was 'Bunny' telling us who it was and probably who he is about to go after. The volcano is about to erupt big style. I predict more fireworks than Princes Street at Hogmanay Ma'am!"

At that moment, returning to the doorway, Joe Hanlon piped up. "Am I hallucinating or was that who I thought it was?" Having just witnessed the mis-matched duo in the corridor.

"See you just got the one coffee then?" Murray observed. Ignoring the relevance of his question.

"You were still sleeping when I, wait a minute… What are you talking about? You don't even drink coffee," Hanlon remembered. "You're a freak of nature."

Murray held his side. He knew that he was going to laugh and even the mildest of laughter would result in severe pain. However, he did not get to see 'Sherlock' be opinionated enough. So bring on the rant he thought.

"You might want to take a seat Ma'am," Murray suggested. (To which she mouthed… 'Barbra')

"It is in our constitution," DC Hanlon started. "By law every TRUE Scotsman needs to be a coffee drinker!"

He then gave DI Murray a stern look and a little raised eyebrow. The eye movement indicated that what he was about to say would be slightly 'tongue-in-cheek' and should be taken with a 'pinch of salt.' He then continued to share his 'aroma' friendly thoughts!

"The Jacobite Rebellion, the dismal failure of the 1745 rising was ultimately down to the Young Pretender not knowing his constituents."

"I don't think he had con…"

"Don't interrupt me Ma'am." He began to raise his voice and up the pace. "Do you even know the story?

Furlong began to open her mouth…

"No, I didn't think so. So please, just keep quiet."

Her blue eyes grew wide in shocked amazement. Did he just speak to me, a higher ranked officer in that tone? She sat still and tried to comprehend what had just happened.

Detective Inspector Murray was struggling to contain himself. He had seen Joe Hanlon do this routine at an early social with the late 'Mac' Rasul. Machur had not long joined the team. 'The Rant' would go on to become 'Sherlock's' party piece. It didn't really matter about the subject. He just took the topic, ran with it and turned very quickly into a Scottish 'Mr Angry!' Steven Murray always found it hysterical. Although why he would encourage Hanlon, whilst trying to recover from a knife attack seemed rather crazy to say the least.

"Charlie did not like his coffee," 'Sherlock' continued. "In fact he hated coffee. So what real chance did he have of becoming Scotland's First Minister back then?

"First Min…" Furlong stopped herself just in time, as a wagging finger from Hanlon was heading her way.

"No chance, that's how much! He should have just taken a leaf out of that Ethiopian guy's book. What's his name? Sir, sir, Inspector - You know his name, what is it?"

Murray was desperately trying not to wet the bed at this point. He composed himself just enough to reply. "I believe it's Billy Bob, constable."

Hanlon shot him a look and screwed up his eyes nonetheless.

Without missing a beat he carried on with the show. "Aye, that would be right." He went with a slow highland drawl. "Billy Bob Costa. He was the African, 18th century equivalent to Microsoft's Bill Gates. He went on to create an unstoppable hospitality and leisure empire. He bought Del Sol, Brava and Blanca and turned them into the top tourist resorts that they are today. But chiefly, as we are all well aware, he was responsible for bringing his Costa Coffee to the world and we owe that man a massive debt of gratitude. They could be a bit cheaper like and not 'costa fortune!' But hey, whatever," he smiled.

By this point Furlong had twigged with a nod of approval and DI Murray felt his bedsheets for genuine fear of leakage. Ironically and cheekily, Joseph Hanlon then proceeded to walk fully into the room and join his two superior officers with a large Starbucks...... 'Hot Chocolate!'

TWENTY FIVE

"They seek him here, they seek him there. In Regent Street and Leicester Square. One week he's in polka dots, the next week he's in stripes. 'Cause he's a dedicated follower of fashion."

- The Kinks

As 'Sherlock' sat down, Murray's phone sounded by his bedside. The Inspector stared disapprovingly at Joe Hanlon. His ringtone had been unknowingly changed by some cheeky, anonymous culprit and was currently playing *'Mack the Knife!'*

A rather red faced officer mumbled a humble apology. "Sorry sir... I was bored!"

DCI Furlong had no idea what she had just experienced in the past two minutes. She shook her head in sheer bewilderment. The 'Keystone Cops' would never even get a look-in with these two she guessed.

Constable Hanlon, watching her uneasy body language closely, felt the need to point out: "We do get results Ma'am."

"That's just as well," she said quietly. Although her tone remained thoroughly unconvinced.

Yes, I didn't think she would remind ME to call her 'Barbra,' the young officer grinned to himself.

Murray saw the call was from Sandra Kerr. He had literally just text her before Reid came calling unannounced ten minutes previous. He listened carefully as he answered.

"Hi sir. How are you doing? How can I help?"

"Second one first," he insisted. "Got a road trip for you 'Sandy.' I need you and DC Boyd to travel down to Ayrshire for me and do a little bit of research. Gather some background info. Hopefully it may produce something worthwhile."

"Where are we off to?" Kerr responded with a mixture of intrigue and cynicism. Although ultimately more than happy to take on the assignment regardless.

"Well, this is where it gets interesting. There is a collection of 54 large paintings by the renowned Scottish artist Alexander Goudie being exhibited."

"I'm quite sure that's true sir," Kerr responded.

"The unique display depicts the incredible story of Burns' Tam o' Shanter poem. These paintings 'Sandy,' have only ever been displayed in full once before. That was here in Edinburgh back in 1996, two decades ago."

Kerr politely interrupted to ask, "What bearing do they have on the case sir? Is there something specific that you want us to look out for?"

"You know, I don't think so 'Sandy.' But I just had this interesting thought last night…"

"Would that have been before you got yourself stabbed sir?" She asked this in all seriousness. Aware that he would currently be all drugged up on medication, Kerr simply wanted to confirm it was not some random delusional thought that had just came to him. Although, he was also renowned for a few of those unpredictable long shots over the years. Which in fairness to DI Murray, the majority of them often paid off!

"It's probably just a silly gut feeling 'Sandy.' An inkling that I have, that it will be to our advantage to check out this display." He paused before adding, "Tam o' Shanter is widely hailed as the Scottish bard's finest work. If nothing else I'd expect you to come back better informed and educated about both Burns and Goudie. Isn't that right Ma'am?" Murray gestured to Furlong.

"Absolutely," she said politely.

"Who have you got there?" Kerr asked.

Ignoring her question, he also added. "You know what else Sergeant Kerr?"

"No. But doubtless you are about to tell me SIR."

"Goudie's son, Lachlan. He informs you in this article I read, about how his dad was obsessed with Tam o' Shanter and how he spent decades of his life creating those images."

"Fascinating sir!"

"Ye, ye, enough of the 'bored,' 'whatever,' backchat young lady."

Sandra Kerr grinned. He knew her only too well.

"But wait until you hear this. He then goes on to remind you that his father was a professional artist who needed to make a living, and how his mother would look at those terrifying huge canvasses and think, 'We are never going to sell those paintings.' Finally, and this is where I thought especially of you 'Sandy.'"

Kerr was bemused.

"He said his father was very 'theatrical, noisy, hilarious and sometimes terrifying,' and that is exactly what comes through in his paintings. It made me think that no doubt that is what

Constable Allan Boyd will also be like, during your prolonged three hour car journey together... Enjoy!"

Furlong had narrowed her eyes and was giving DI Murray an interesting look.

Murray cleared his throat. "Need to go Sergeant. Let me know how you BOTH get on. And just one last thing. The artist himself said, 'Viewing the cycle turns the black and white text of the poem into the most vivid fireworks that you can imagine.' And currently 'Sandy,' we need you to help us make sense of all these assembled notes, clues and theories. I've every confidence in you!" He hung up. Suspecting that so had Kerr several minutes previously!

A curious female voice from his side asked, "So why the sudden interest in Tam o' Shanter, Steven?"

"Not so much that poem Ma'am, more the 'Ploughman Poet' himself. Just an early theory at this stage," Murray assured her. "It was all about a song I heard sung last night at the supper I attended with DC Hanlon.

"I am genuinely intrigued," she said positively. "I look forward to hearing more and please," she reminded him, "Call me Barbra."

Murray was about to speak, but saw his Chief Inspector raise her hand.

"Your coffee loving, skinny, Ethiopian sidekick asked me to bring some things over for you. So here they are."

The Inspector shot Hanlon a worried glance.

"Crime scene photos, background info, etc, sir," 'Sherlock' felt the need to confirm. "I thought that when you awoke you would want to do some brainstorming, throw some ideas about. But I had hoped that Hayes and Curry, maybe even Sergeant Kerr and Boyd would have been around to spare us ten minutes or so. Never mind, we can do it another time. Maybe tomorrow morning would work better."

"No, no, that was a great idea," Murray agreed. Offering a large sigh of relief into the ether. For a second or two he'd thought Hanlon might have set him up and that Furlong was about to produce some spare underwear, pyjamas and toiletries.

'Sherlock,' on the other hand seemed to display a look that rather brazenly said - You doubted me sir, tut, tut!

With only Murray, Hanlon and DCI Furlong in attendance, they still agreed that it would be a worthwhile exercise. An opportunity to spend some time going over what information had been gathered up so far, including an updated selection of photographs. The locations, careers, lists of hobbies, clubs or organisations that the deceased were all members off - all was up for discussion. They had a trainee teacher, a librarian, a bank worker, a 'Jill' of all trades - and a fun loving student. No noticeable link or crossover.

Murray regularly asked… "Any thoughts?"

On one such occasion Barbra Furlong responded confidently with, "An inability to empathise, to consider validity in alternative views, to walk in someone else's shoes or to see the world through our own narrow myopic viewpoint - these are several of the things that restrict our ability to reconcile with others. 'Reconciliation' - the approach of the objectively good person."

Each of those in the room had a desire to be good, or at least be good at their job. But, both Hanlon and Murray had no idea at the pearl of wisdom just dished out by their well intentioned DCI. Or at least collectively, the pair had assumed it was wisdom!

The pictures of all the dead were female - no coincidence they agreed. Was it anything to do with their names? They now had several Mac or Mc's. They had all been found wearing blouses, trendy night-shirt style. A design that could have easily been worn on their own and been taken for a fashionably skimpy, short dress. Underwear had been removed in each case. Was that their attackers trophy? Witnesses definitely remembered seeing Gillian McLean at the ceilidh wearing a striped top earlier in the evening. Terri McKenzie had told Kerr and Boyd what her daughter was wearing and it wasn't the shiny blouse that she had on in her final photo shoot. Melissa MacLeod's tartan skirt was also found near her body, deliberately discarded. Her blouse was a shade of mustard and although no fashion guru herself, Furlong was certain there was no way that had been worn with a yellow tartan skirt on a night out on the town.

So it would appear their assailant not only took their panties, but he swapped their tops. As they further perused the photos that would appear to be borne out by the Debbie Griggs collection. The blouse she was found wearing had no buttons. So it would have been easy to throw it over her. Plus the vehicle that hit her, obviously collided with her at pace. Yet, there was no visible marking to her bright blouse whatsoever. The one she had on appeared to be fresh and new. Hanlon was also intrigued by the fact that both her shoes had managed to remain on her feet.

"No chance," Murray said. "She would have been thrown out of them. That vehicle had been speeding up on impact. They had been intentionally put back on."

"But why?" Furlong asked. Seemingly as confused at present, as her two fellow officers.

"It surely served no purpose," Hanlon added.

"It served some deluded person's purpose," Murray reminded them.

It would also be another interesting topic thrown in for discussion into the already crammed melting pot of conjecture, theory and gut feelings. They had all been at ceilidhs earlier in the evening. That fact had been established and certainly appeared relevant. A children's building block, a soft toy and compass were definitely meant as clues the trio decided - but had no idea as to what they fully represented. At that point there had been no obvious clue left with Laura McKenzie, but they were still scouring the area where her body had been found.

"Melissa MacLeod - both kidneys removed. What was that all about?" Hanlon enquired.

"It was the clear-cut exception to all the others," Furlong added.

Murray nodded in agreement. (It was a number 31 - No clue whatsoever!) They seemed to be getting nowhere fast.

At that moment the Inspector's phone lit up and sang merrily once again. This time Steven Murray, noticeably annoyed, accompanied it on vocals.

"Oh, the shark, babe, has such teeth, dear. And it shows them pearly white…" The Inspector's own pearly white fangs, now snarled menacingly in Hanlon's direction.

"Once you're finished the call, I'll change it," the constable meekly confirmed again. Offering a thumbs up gesture, as Murray answered.

"Ally?" Was all the hospitalised Inspector said.

"Christina Cardwell was an Avon rep Steven." Coulter having even less time for pleasantries than his ex boss.

"I genuinely thought they'd ceased to be in the late eighties," his old Inspector said.

"Me too, but not that you would notice. She's got plenty of stock. It is impressive. She could set up a fancy window display of all the stuff."

Murray kept quiet, because that was exactly what Christina Cardwell would have done with all the samples. She would have arranged them up on a table to exhibit them. Then demonstrated certain products, gave out samples and dispersed some smelly stuff. The whole shebang!

"Anything worthwhile?" The Inspector chided Ally.

A soft, gentle tap on his shoulder produced, "Where is Coulter?" Furlong whispered.

"There is really no need to check up on him Ma'am." Murray said, pulling the handset close to his chest.

"I would not think of it," her normal voice resurfaced. "But I get the strong feeling that a feminine touch may be helpful to him today. I did hear 'The Avon Lady' get a mention did I not?"

She was a smart cookie Murray acknowledged. She then made a flirtatious gesture with her hand, flicked at her hair and pretended to spray some perfume.

Murray got the idea and nodded reluctantly. "Suppose it couldn't do any harm. Here's one of his cards. Give him a phone and let him know you're on your way, Ma'am."

"Not a minute to waste and he'll be on the case!" she read aloud. "Really?" she frowned, obviously unimpressed by his tagline.

Murray and Furlong smiled.

As she went to depart the DCI once again encouraged DI Murray - "Remember it's Barbra not Ma'am. Oh, and just one more thing I wanted to add. Seeing as you seem to have this current fascination for Mr Burns. Interesting that!"

"What's that?" Murray asked.

"The fact that no one addresses him the way we would other people. There is never a prefix. It's always Burns. Anyhow, I have some trivia knowledge relating to Mister Burns for you."

"Fire away, Ma'am," Murray instructed.

"It's to do with one of his greatest known songs. And I told you, call me Barbra," she said. Now verging into sexual harassment territory Murray reckoned.

She continued in a very good Emma Thompson accent, "A Man's a Man for A' That, promotes both Burns' political and moral sensibilities."

Murray nodded (a number 63, I'm with you so far).

"But did you know that interestingly Steven, it was published anonymously in The Glasgow Magazine for fear of recriminations or even arrest."

The Inspector deliberately rested his head back against his pillow.

"It was thought that the emotive song was proof of Burns' support for the Revolution in France, and to this day it is often used as evidence of Burns holding 'socialist' ideals."

Steven Murray lay still, unsure if 'Barbra' was finished. As her posture began to shift, it would appear not.

"Just one last note on that," she said. "What seems beyond doubt is that Burns was influenced by Thomas Paine's 'The Rights of Man.' Both of them dealing with the idea of liberty, equality and universal human rights. With those themes to the fore it was interesting and hopefully prophetic, that 'A Man's a Man' was the song chosen to be sung at the opening of the devolved Scottish Parliament in 1999, don't you think?"

What Detective Inspector Steven Murray did think was, that she definitely never voted for that lone Tory MP last time around. However he was unable to share that or anything else with his DCI. His eyes were closed shut and he was pretending to be sound asleep. The words of Robert Burns often had that effect on many people in today's society.

"Let's leave him to rest," DC Hanlon suggested, as both officers departed the room.

TWENTY SIX

"What would you say, what would you do? Children and animals, two by two. Give me the needle, give me the rope. We're gonna melt them down to pills and soap."

- Elvis Costello

After ten minutes of shut-eye, the Inspector was confident his visitors would be well clear of the premises and thus allow him the opportunity to get back to operating mission control from his hospital bedside.

"Hi Doc," Steven Murray said on the third ring. "Anything useful?"

In his smooth Irish lilt Thomas Patterson responded with. "Sure I don't know about useful Steven, but 'Bunny' Reid's niece was never going to walk again. Even if she had survived."

"Really?" Murray gasped. "I knew she was in a bad way, but…"

"T'e telescopic wheel wrench t'at t'ey found at t'e scene was the matching culprit," the T'inker interrupted.

"Nearly two foot long. That's half a golf club cracking your knee to smithereens," Murray confirmed.

"Try knees, plural," the Doc continued. "Both tibiae were shattered. Easily struck twenty to t'irty times! Do you know what is t'e longest bone in t'e body Inspector?"

"Sure. It's t'e one in our t'igh," Murray joked. Instinctively patting his leg at the other end of the phone line.

"T'at is correct Steven. T'at would be t'e femur," said Patterson earnestly. Bringing some much needed sobriety to their discussion. "And you would do well to remember Inspector t'at Christina Cardwell's were smashed into t'in, tiny fragments of bone, such was the viciousness and continued momentum of her senseless attack."

Suddenly there was a prolonged silence. A quiet hush in the conversation. That was it Murray thought. It began to make sense. The clouds and mist began to lift. Sure that was it. It had been as simple as that. It hadn't actually been senseless at all. His mind leapt briskly into action. Scurrying like a well conditioned greyhound chasing an electronic hare. Or should that be a fast moving 'Bunny?' he smiled ruefully to himself. Thus far, after realising that it was the gangsters niece and aided by the SS message left behind, they had all assumed that this was simply someone lashing out or getting back at The Reidmeister. A deliberate power play by Fife's young pretender. A belief that a certain up and coming drug lord from across the water, had dispatched his trusted Lieutenants from the North to ensure that a clear message was sent - indicating that a new Sheriff was arriving in town and that he would take no prisoners.

However, "Thank you Doc," Murray affirmed. Feeling reinvigorated and vindicated he then continued, "This was not about taking over at all. I think the intent was all about taking back!

"Taking back?" Patterson quizzed.

"Of course," Steven Murray said with renewed clarity. "This was never meant to be a killing. Christina Cardwell was not just randomly beaten. She had been interrogated. Excruciating pain had been consistently applied. They were looking for answers Doc. They were desperately trying to find something. She had not been tortured for a specific item, but for information. Because she knew what it was or where it was. Or at least they thought she did! I'll need to go now Doc. Thanks again for that."

"You're wel…"

Murray had hung up!

Christina Cardwell had stayed at Harvesters Way in Wester Hailes. An often troubled and defamed suburb of the city. An easy five minute walk from the Scotrail train station, it had originally been a traditional Scottish council estate. But with that said, during the turbulent eighties and early nineties many of the tenants had taken advantage of the Government's 'Right to Buy' scheme. And as much as many of Scotland's non Tories may vent their disgust, fury and hatred over the years toward the late, departed, former Prime Minister Margaret Thatcher. For many working class people, they would simply never have been able to step onto the property ladder had it not been for her Conservative Party policy. Murray himself recognised the silver lining of her legacy and how it had enhanced his own early years.

Although a uniformed officer was at the front door of Cardwell's house and could have easily let his Chief Inspector inside. His DCI wanted Mr Coulter to answer the doorbell. So after it had rung twice, the retired officer duly arrived to open it. He was then greeted in an official tone that stated coldly:

"Hello, I'm DCI Furlong."

"Sergeant Robert Coulter," he heard himself say.

The raised eyebrows in surprise were enough of a correction.

"I'm so sorry Ma'am. Habit. I'm just Mr Coulter. 'Ally' to my friends."

She gave a polite nod. "Yes Mr Coulter and you can call me Barbra!"

"Since I phoned Steven... Apologies, Inspector Murray Ma'am... Sorry, Barbra. It's just I am not so sure that Christina Cardwell was quite the innocent party we all thought she was."

Furlong remained silent, but waited patiently for Coulter to compose himself and explain in more detail what he had since discovered.

Compose was probably the ideal word. Because these days the retired Sergeant always seemed to get flustered in the company of good looking woman. Especially those in power with an assertive, confident manner about them. In recent years Ally was always a ladies man. Mainly he enjoyed their companionship and the steadying influence they seemed to bring to a relationship. He enjoyed pleasant chat and laughter. And although himself and Steven Murray met regularly with those two character traits at the heart of their evenings, nothing could beat the companionship and conversation of an engaging, smiling and beautiful female by your side - at least in Robert 'Ally' Coulter's humble opinion.

"It's the small things Barbra."

Still Furlong remained unconvinced.

"Please work with me here Chief Inspector. Who owned this house? What age was she? What did she do for a living?

How old were her kids? And what bearing does any of this have on her death?"

Now DCI Furlong began to let her shoulders relax. She then began with a sigh. "So this is 'Bunny' Reid's niece and she lives in an ex-council house?"

"How do you know it is NOT still a council home?"

"Firstly it seems to have had fairly substantial renovation work carried out Mr Coulter," Furlong answered confidently. "Both inside and out. Some form of small conservatory added I can see from here. And on my way in I noticed a new driveway. Even the exterior roughcasting looked as if it had been done in recent months. These are not upgrades people tend to make unless they own the home."

"My thoughts exactly and after a few phone calls to some old contacts, I discovered Miss Christina Cardwell purchased the property several years ago."

"Okay - But you suspect something has changed recently that has enabled her to get plenty of work done in the last few months?"

"I would say so. But then this is when things get really interesting Barbra." Coulter was noticeably becoming more relaxed in her company. Allowing her christian name to flow freely from his lips. "I know you will probably not have had time to look at her file, so some of the questions…"

"She was thirty two," Furlong interrupted. "Had previously been a hairdresser. Her kids were aged 5, 4 and 1," she rhymed off without the slightest hesitation. "Oh and for full disclosure, I was also well aware before I arrived that she was the homeowner!"

'Ally' began to laugh. It was a sincere, appreciative sound. This lady had not only done her homework, but extra

229

revision also, he thought. I'll give her full credit for that. She also displayed an impressive level of humility, owning up to insider trading. He was not to know however, that her Cardwell education had come about by default at the hospital an hour earlier.

"In fairness retired Sergeant Coulter, I still don't have an answer to the bearing on her death."

"Well, current serving Detective Chief Inspector Furlong," Coulter added cheekily. "Let me take you… 'Through the Keyhole.'"

One wondered who was now flirting with who, as 'Ally' Coulter began his walking tour. Back in full police mode he stated:

"You were right Barbra about all that info. But let's strip the paper from those cracks. She's early thirties with three young kids and previously worked as a hairdresser. Most certainly that role would have been in the last half dozen years, and at best part-time, given the ages of her children. Agreed?"

"You would think so," the DCI replied.

"But even before that she could only have briefly worked for 4 or 5 years full-time after qualifying as a fully trained stylist say?" Coulter had meant this as more of a question than a statement.

Once again Barbra Furlong concurred.

"You mentioned the outside work you had clearly spotted when you arrived."

Coulter opened up the door to what appeared to be the main bedroom and Furlong's jaw dropped to the floor. So much so, Coulter physically stepped forward and with his workmanlike forefinger and index finger gently tapped it shut again. At his touch, the female officer's cheeks turned beetroot.

"I am sorry," Ally offered. "I really didn't mean to embarrass you."

She shook her head. "No, no, you're alright. I was just a little taken aback, that was all."

"Not as much as I was!" Ally confided.

They had been taken aback by a room that had a beautiful King-sized bed centrally positioned. Hand made oak furniture, including an exquisite set of dresser, drawers and wardrobe. There was a modern sink atop another solid oak unit, to the left of an inbuilt power shower. This was not en-suite. The shower and sink ran along a wall that had obviously been previously used as a walk-in cupboard. A dusky pink tartan covered chair hosted a rosy cushion with a highland stag on the front. And a range of expensive lamps, light fittings and a large screen, wall mounted TV completed the look. On closer inspection DCI Furlong confirmed the majority of the furnishings, bed covers and accessories were from 'Next.' No cheaper brand names like Matalan, Primark or 'George' from Asda were to be found. She was beginning to get onboard with Coulter's train of thought.

"I've checked the kids rooms as well, or room I should say."

"They all slept in the same one?" Furlong queried.

Coulter nodded, before continuing. "All the best quality items. Including it would appear, new wooden bunk beds and a child's cot. In the living room you saw the 'latest season' three piece suite and you'll be excited to see the 'little boy's room.' I'm leaving the best 'till last, trust me."

TWENTY SEVEN

"A river runs through you and me. Never reaches the ocean, never reaches the sea. You are the path, my hidden trail. You are the end, my holy grail. You are my mood, my sudden rage. You are my wit, my final stage."

- Oysterband

The bathroom was stunning. It was the interior's Holy Grail. Impressive in the extreme. Expensive Emperador Bianco polished marble tiles covered the sixteen foot long floor space. An Amari stone freestanding bath costing at least £3,000 was the main feature. Again fresh wall tiles, accessories, lights and fittings all finished off professionally came as standard! Consultant and Chief Inspector stood at the the linen cupboard. They shared a knowing look as they scanned the finest quality Egyptian cotton hand and bath towels stacked neatly in piles next to one another. An understanding female voice was the first to be heard.

"You think she had another source of income, other than her Avon commission I guess?" Furlong suggested. She further added, "You think that the extra revenue has been recent and lucrative, given the overhaul of her home." The Chief Inspector then proceeded to vocalise much of what they had just witnessed. She had gone from being a 'Generation Game' homemaker to 'Through the Keyhole' in one easy transition.

Her silky voice seemed to rise in pitch with excitement.

"New driveway. Lovely conservatory. Outside walls. Bunk beds. Bathroom. Bedroom upgrade, my goodness the list is exhaustive. She would need to sell one heck of a lot of smelly bubble bath Ally, just to pay for the light fittings alone!"

"Ironically there was actually a brand new 'cuddly toy' on the kid's bunk beds," Coulter added. But that reference went way over the Chief's head.

The only room they had not yet ventured into, at least Furlong hadn't. Because Coulter had reviewed them all before she arrived, was what had appeared to be the third bedroom of old. However, as Barbra Furlong opened the door it was clear that it was no longer used for sleeping in.

"You Dirty Big Pink Marshmallow!" Furlong exclaimed.

"Excuse me?" Coulter questioned.

"Oh, I'm sure your buddy, DI Murray will explain."

DCI Furlong then rubbed decisively at her eyes, shook her head and was completely gobsmacked. She had not been expecting that. What was going on? What in the name? This woman obviously sold more Avon products than the whole of the East of Scotland put together. Every wall in the room, a room which probably measured about eighteen feet by twelve had been kitted out from floor to ceiling in shelving. Even in the centre of the room, walk-around supermarket style units had been positioned. Merchandise was everywhere, the room had been…

"Filled to the gunnels," Coulter expressed.

Furlong smiled knowingly. "Do you know originally where that expression came from Sergeant?" she asked. Never once shifting her gaze from the impressive amount of body lotion, shower gel, shampoo and intimate creams on display.

Coulter was simply so chuffed just to hear her refer to him as Sergeant, that he didn't even feel embarrassed at not knowing.

"Let me bore you for 30 seconds."

"I don't think you would ever bore me Ma'am, Barbra," he quickly corrected himself.

With another slight reddening to her cheeks, she offered, "The word 'gunnel' is a phonetic respelling of the word 'gunwale,' which is a nautical term that refers to the topmost edge of the side of a boat. The phrase 'stuffed to the gunwales' means much the same as 'filled to the brim.' So there you have it."

DCI Barbra Furlong was beginning to grow fond of this rather slightly overweight ex-police officer. He was always in his own way very charming. Often happy to admit he was wrong or unaware of something. Yet experienced enough to turn things around and view things differently. Just a couple of hours ago he'd thought Avon had no longer even existed. Now he seemed to be quietly relishing the thought of demonstrating its products to her.

"Even selling all of this Ally on a regular basis, is nowhere near enough product sales to earn the cash she would need to do the work she has done, in such a short space of time," the DCI reiterated once again.

Coulter nodded. "Oh, I know Barbra. Because she didn't even host any Avon parties!"

"What?"

"Well, when you start up, who do you invite firstly to hold a party for you?"

She looked at him strangely.

"Please give me some credit. I do know how they at least

USED to work. And even these days, if it wasn't parties, where would you most likely distribute catalogues?

"So amongst family, friends, neighbours, work colleagues," the DCI suggested.

"Exactly. Even if we discount family, friends and work colleagues in her case and we are only left with neighbours. I checked with easily fifteen to twenty of those closest to the home. And?"

"No one got a catalogue," she guessed.

"Correct - In actual fact, no one even knew she was an Avon rep! Not one person. Two or three mentioned they would see her get deliveries. But had no idea she sold the stuff. One old biddy even asked me to order her two bottles of that." That, Coulter pointed out on the shelf was 'Skin so Soft.'

"It was a spray and her husband swore by it when he went fishing."

DCI Furlong's puzzled expression deserved a response.

"It seemingly keeps our Scottish midges at bay."

"But I suspect that is not why you have brought me into this well stocked and well fragranced room Mr Coulter? Not to impress me with some insect repellant?"

"Oh, we are back to Mister, Detective Chief Inspector? I am disappointed in you. Because I suspect you will want to call me Ally again in a second, maybe even sir! I wish I had put some kind of finders fee or recovery charge on my rates."

"Seriously, Sergeant. What are you now talking about?" Furlong grew concerned and sombre. "I'm guessing this is substantial?"

"As opposed to what I've already shown you?" he quipped,

before continuing. "When you said earlier that you knew she was the homeowner, I'm assuming you meant the mortgage payer?"

Barbra Furlong eyed him extra carefully, before nodding cautiously. "Yes, absolutely. It was no longer council property was all I meant. That it was now in private ownership."

"Sure and that would be most people's natural assumption. And sure enough seven or eight years ago Christina Cardwell did take out a mortgage to buy it from the council."

There was silence in the room. DCI Furlong moved her eyes in a certain manner and Coulter got the message.

"However, approaching three months ago she paid her mortgage off. Eighty thousand pounds - in cash!"

"How did you find that... No I don't want to know," Furlong said. Another pause between them. "But we still don't know..."

Again Coulter nodded. "Oh but we do!"

"We do?" She questioned.

"Trust me, oh yes, we do." Ally said. He then picked up a 'Skin so Soft' and tried to spray it. Nothing happened. Again he tried, and again nothing.

Barbra Furlong stepped forward slowly, lifted a bottle and began to unscrew the cap. As she lifted it off the bottle she could see that the miniature hose had been cut right inside the cap. It was 10mm long at most and never reached inside the stem of the bottle. Even if it had, it would have been of no use whatsoever. The bottle had been refilled with a white powder. And probably not Avon's best selling talc the two house sitters agreed. They would need it confirmed. But they suspected heroine.

Coulter pointed at a large wooden basket in the corner. It probably contained around one hundred open, unpacked bars of soap. The robust aroma overpowered the room and was no doubt intended to bring with it, a strong perfumed fragrance. One that would either hide or disguise other less than legal scents in close proximity. There also appeared to be more than enough room next to it, where Coulter guessed another basket had been kept previously. Based on the indentations on the carpet. Possibly even stacked at least two, maybe three high.

A scattering of fine, curly soap shavings adorned the bare carpet like tiny cake sprinkles. This also reinforced Ally's theory of excess baskets having been stacked there. The DCI lifted a bar, steadily manoeuvred it around in her hand, before carefully putting it up close to her nose. It was rich green in colour. A gold and black brand label curved over each end. Probably a combination of lime and coconut or thereabouts, she guessed. It was broad and thick. Too thick to break in two. Furlong never spotted anything untoward with the bar. She placed it back in the basket and shook her head.

"It's too big to hold in the bath or shower comfortably," she stated.

"Exactly!" Coulter agreed. Ally's large, oversized palms were certainly more suited to the task 'literally' in hand. He lifted the same bar up and handed it back to DCI Furlong for closer inspection.

With a mischievous glint in his eye and at a snail's pace, he asked her... "Why would they need brand stickers over both ends?"

Her gaze was sharp, as if lined with shards of glass around the edges. The calculating coldness at the centre drew Coulter in, yet they betrayed no feeling. She looked at him thoughtfully, peered once more at the soap then glanced back again at the retired Sergeant. Carefully holding the bar upright with her left hand, she began with her freshly varnished and manicured nails to cautiously pull back the little foil sticker at one end. Did those delicate acrylic nails signal affluence or vanity Coulter wondered. One, two, three small tugs and it came away smoothly in her hand. She then offered a dedicated and intense look toward the edge. But couldn't see it.

Plain old Mr Coulter stared at the DCI, willing her to figure it out. She returned the look, as if to say - What am I missing here? Coulter simply refocused his gaze at the edge of the green bar. Furlong's head movement became more investigative. She scrutinised it closely and put her nail back onto the surface of the bar. She looked up at Coulter. His raised eyes, indicating 'I dare you,' where the confirmation needed. Gently and with great care, she then scraped her right index finger at the area that had been covered previously with the Avon sticker. Fragments of soap crumbled and broke away. She began to notice there had been a small deposit, like a hole sealed over by remnants of soap shavings and these also were now falling away quite freely.

"You Buttock Busting Buffoon," she exclaimed as a 20mm diameter cavern opened up in front of her. Now animated and excited and certainly no longer caring about her fragile, fake nails. There was something in there, she realised.

"There is something…"

"I know," said Ally, holding up another bar in his hand which had previously had the mystery gift extracted from it. "They'll have used a small cordless drill and made holes all the way through. Afterwards they'll have put in their surprise guest and refilled the ends with flakes of soap. Finally they were re-sealed with the forged Avon stickers."

"That would certainly explain all the loose shavings," Barbra added.

The surprise guest which DCI Furlong had just invited to join her was a healthy roll of high denomination banknotes. Approximately ten, crisp, one hundred pound notes. One thousand pounds to be exact. Now that is an expensive soap! Coulter's contained ten, fifty pound notes valued at five hundred pounds. With around one hundred bars in total. They were looking at anything from between fifty to one hundred thousand pounds overall. The actual value of the drugs they reckoned would even outbid that total. And that did not include the assumed missing baskets!

A massive grin had broken out across Furlong's face. She looked admiringly at Mister Robert Coulter, gave him a celebratory hug and expressed sincere gratitude as she spoke. "Thank you Ally. You can once again call me Barbra."

Coulter, who had just dialled a number nodded gratefully. As his phone call was answered and before the patient at the other end could speak, a cheery voice next to DCI Furlong bellowed, "Hello Inspector, Avon calling!"

TWENTY EIGHT

"Yellow man in Timbuktu, colour for both, me and you. Kung Fu fighting, dancing queen. Tribal spaceman and all that's in between. Colours of the world (Spice up your life) Every boy and girl (Spice up your life).

- The Spice Girls

Chrissie Cardwell, Christina's mum, never discussed age. She seemed to have preserved her features, style and image in the 1980's. Her chosen look was heavy make-up, shoulder pads and a mass of hair gathered high at the back into a bun, although the greying strands were becoming more prevalent than ever. It was carefully held in place with several decorative hair-sticks. Each sturdy wooden stick measured six or seven inches long and featured a turquoise jewel at the end. This in turn made them stand out as a luxury fashion accessory.

The mother's face was hardened, round and creased. Like a well used ten pin bowling ball. A size 12 with two holes close together for your fingers, where her eyes should be! Visually, her face certainly portrayed her as the older of the two siblings. In more recent years her gangland brother 'Bunny,' had in turn experienced a fashion makeover. With his aged, straggling ponytail long gone. It give him a more mellow, 'trusted businessman' look. Fashionable, figure-friendly Italian suits were all he ever wore these days. However, one suspected that they were specially tailored, made specifically to embrace deep pockets. Certainly areas roomy enough to hold a Duracell bunny sheath. A casing that would safely host his infamous serrated blade.

As brother and sister, they grew up apart in the fractured Edinburgh council foster system. So although blood related, very few people were actually even aware of the relationship. Those in the know, fully recognised that there was a closeness with Chrissie's daughter, Christina 'Tina' Cardwell and her children. But no one dared ask questions about it.

Steven Murray himself had never even delved deeper into Reid's background. He had known him grow up as the faithful sidekick to Kenny Dixon and subsequently saw him as a bachelor, a single-minded career criminal. He noticed he would often have a spell of occasional girlfriends or hangers on. But there never ever appeared to be a long term, serious relationship. At least that was what Murray witnessed from afar in his various interactions and monitoring of Reid. He duly noted that the majority of female wannabes were discarded as regularly as the daily paper and often in a much worse condition.

Ten minutes later Murray had phoned 'Doc' Patterson once again. The T'inker had mentioned earlier via text, that he would pop by during visiting hours later in the evening. The Inspector had just wanted to confirm he was definitely coming, as he now had some follow up questions to ask him. At 8.15pm his colleague with the flowing Irish lilt duly arrived as promised.

Midway through the visit and after a few niceties were out of the way, Murray asked rather matter-of-factly, "So if the

Trainspotting gang were to land in today's Edinburgh drug scene Doc, would they still be using heroin?"

The T'inker observed Steven Murray's concerned frown carefully before responding. "Ah sure, I heard about t'e large cosmetics operation t'at you uncovered at t'e flat of 'Reid's niece. I take it t'e gear belonged to the man himself?"

"I doubt it 'Doc.' 'Bunny' was furious. He was driven by anger. He was absolute in seeking revenge. And there's no way he would have left those sums of cash hidden away in a flat. He would have had it laundered and circulating amongst his other businesses and earning him increased profits. No, this was separate. I believe this is exactly what Christina Cardwell's assailants were looking for."

"And she didn't give it up?"

"I don't think she didn't know it was even there Doc."

"In her own house?"

"My point exactly! I think it would be good to speak to our good friend Reid again and gauge his reaction to our sweet smelling haul though."

"Nice work by your new DCI. Word is it was actually her t'at discovered it. In the company of some poorly paid, hired consultant," he smirked.

"Aye, poor Ally. He's not going to be able to take the credit for what was probably the biggest find of his career. Anyway, getting back to my original question… Heroin?"

Dr Thomas Patterson once again paused before letting out a rather dismayed sigh. "Based on current drug use trends in deprived parts of our fine city, t'ey would still be likely to use heroin. Albeit alongside a cocktail of other drugs and sadly, all washed down with cheap booze and a bag of spice."

"Spice?" Murray questioned.

"That's for another time Steven," the Doc stated assertively. Muirhouse, one of the city's most deprived estates and Leith near the city's docks had between them Murray remembered provided a backdrop of iconic scenes, soliloquies and sounds to the cult film Trainspotting! He also quickly recalled that Laura McKenzie's home address was down as Muirhouse Parkway. In recent years he was aware that the estate's ugly post-war high rises had been replaced by less daunting low rises, and that the 'eyesore' shopping mall was about to get a multi-million pound revamp. Although he was also well aware of the mood of the people and in a community where many are dependent on food banks, residents doubt the window dressing will change much.

"Unfortunately," 'Doc' Patterson voiced, "For t'e real life Renton's and Sick Boys alive today, most are still using opiate drugs, living in social housing, on benefits, probably with hepatitis C and possibly with liver or lung disease."

Murray recognised fully that two decades ago, the 'choose heroin' monologue at the start of the movie was absolutely perfectly suited. He shook his head and ranted.

"The film was set in a time when heroin offered a way out of the grim realities of post-Thatcher Britain. It was seen as glamorous and extreme. It said what punk said: I don't care."

Patterson was unsure of his point.

"At the time, people felt that the old work opportunities did no longer exist. People questioned what was the point of slaving to be like your parents, whose values you despised."

The T'inker acknowledged that point with a faint shrug.

Murray then continued his mini tirade with, "But it's hard to run a smack habit these days. There are no squats and benefits are dreadful. They make you look for poor jobs that only exist because they are so awful that no one else wants them. Yet, will the most seductive drug in the history of humankind continue to seduce vulnerable and unhappy people in the future?"

"Of course it will," Patterson answered. "And t'e evidence t'at heroin is still locked into deprived communities is overwhelming Steven," he continued. "Drug deaths are continuing to rise fast in Edinburgh and not all are of t'e Trainspotting generation. From a purely practical sense, a lot of it is down to massive cuts to drug services in Scotland and is indicative of a Westminster government t'at appears to be walking away from t'e entrenched problem of heroin addiction in areas such as Muirhouse."

"Geez, 'Doc,' you sure know how to cheer a guy up. Why did you start talking about drugs?"

"Me???" He shrugged, as they both laughed heartily.

TWENTY NINE

"You gotta make your own kind of music. Sing your own special song. Make your own kind of music. Even if nobody sings along."

- Paloma Faith

Next day on the Wednesday, a partnership travelled together across the River Clyde in Glasgow via the endearing, half century old Kingston Bridge. Sergeant Sandra Kerr was conscious of the fact that her newly acquired sidekick had tapped, swiped and scrolled continually on his mobile phone since they had departed from Edinburgh. She never really took him for a game player or social media freak. So had been rather taken aback by his obsession with his phone. She had hoped that the drive would have given her a chance to get to know DC Allan Boyd a little better. A natural opportunity to find out about his likes and interests away from the day job.

There was no denying that she had been impressed by his people skills at Theresa McKenzie's home. He was very intuitive and capable of quickly empathising 'Sandy' had noted mentally. She was also fully aware of his follow up visit with a friend the next day. There he was carrying out a host of repairs and maintenance for the grieving mother. Well intentioned it may have been, but on the surface at least, it could very well be misconstrued. An ex-army widow already and now possibly extra vulnerable. She is currently devastated at the loss of her daughter and out of the blue this handsome, ex-forces, police detective comes to her rescue. Assisting and helping her out with no thought of gratitude or repayment in kind.

All Kerr knew was that he was setting himself up for a fall. She felt he was playing with fire unnecessarily. Again on first impressions Allan Boyd most certainly could come across as an arrogant, overconfident loudmouth. Quickly however, his Sergeant had witnessed a friendlier, supportive and gentler side to the man. But unfortunately not everyone is going to be privy to that and he will have to watch his reputation amongst the others. Once people had formed an opinion of him, it would be very difficult to change it. Kerr had already admitted to herself that he was handsome and although no temptation to her, he would have to be careful with his flirtatious manner. In some respects, in many ways he reminded her of a slightly younger DI Murray. Charming, kind-hearted and forever teasing the females!

Steven Murray in truth, would probably be mortified if he knew that she actually thought that of him. But he did it without even trying. He naturally oozed old fashioned respect and breeding. So generally speaking, because of that, he was able to playfully interact with everyone. Hardly anyone that he had worked closely with over the years had a bad word to say about him. Although in fairness, they never got to encounter the majority of his challenging bipolar episodes that he would experience from time to time. Having been his partner for several years previous to Joseph Hanlon and before her stint on maternity leave, Sandra Kerr had seen it all. She had been concerned about his car crash and the burns on his neck from last year. But she had remained quiet and watched from a distance as she knew that young

'Sherlock' had stepped more than adequately into her shoes.

"Sorry to disturb you," she said rather irritatedly. "But how did you cope with Army life and the experiences you spoke about with Mrs McKenzie?" Kerr asked sincerely.

"Did you know that Robert the Bruce was supposedly from Ayrshire?" he asked.

"What? Are you for real?"

"Well it is believed that he was born at Turnberry Castle!" Boyd stated, rather pleased with himself.

Kerr looked confused.

"There is the penicillin man, Alexander Fleming and John McAdam, famous for… "

"Tarmacadam on the flamin' roads we're driving on," his Sergeant yelled. Whilst giving him a piercing look. "What are you on about constable? Do you think we're all thick?"

He suspected he had insulted her.

"They were all Ayrshire men. Sorry Sarge, it's just I love to check out Google for dates, facts and statistics. I find it fascinating to get the story behind the headlines. So I had been getting up to speed with our Rabbie and it took me down the historical road of several other famous Scots over the years from Ayrshire. Apologies for that DS Kerr," he then added in a polite, acquiescent way. "Did you feel left out? Had you suspected I was checking out how many 'angry birds' I had, or how many 'candy crushes' I could…" He trailed off mischievously.

Kerr tried not to smile back, but she failed miserably. Although she also quickly recognised that her new partner had rather nicely avoided the original question.

"How you coped?" she repeated. Giving him both a nudge and a knowing, 'you don't get out of it that easy' stare.

A button was pushed, cruise control was set and DC Allan Boyd turned briefly to 'Sandy,' before allowing her to continue, fully focused on the road ahead.

Detective Sergeant Sandra Kerr was now driving on the M77 motorway, across the bleak, depressing, infamous Fenwick Moor. As the latest recruit to their investigating team pondered over his Sergeant's question. He would most probably have had no idea that this particular part of the Ayrshire countryside nearly three decades previous, 1989 to be precise. Was the focal point at that time of Scotland's lengthiest and most complex murder trial.

In summary, three men were convicted of shooting an English drugs courier. Vast, substantial acres of woodland scrub on the margins of the moor had been monitored, dug up and scoured thoroughly. However, the body of the victim, twenty-six year old Paul Thorne had never been found. Despite the labour intensive, costly police search.

Once again he avoided the question. "I hear you have two children Sarge. Is that right?" Boyd asked.

"I do Allan. One year old twins in fact. Carly and Stephanie."

The Glaswegian then added. *"A baby will make love stronger, days shorter, nights longer, bank account smaller, home happier, clothes shabbier, the past forgotten and the future worth living for! Pablo Picasso,"* he added.

"Mmm, I am actually familiar with that quote DC Boyd," Kerr said hesitantly.

"You are?" Boyd added in a rather surprised, yet impressed fashion. "I sense a BUT coming however and a major one at that," he said in anticipation.

"Well in an ideal world," Sandra Kerr said, "It would never

have been attributed to that man!" The emphasis was put fairly and squarely on those last two words - 'That Man!'

"Mr Picasso? One of the greatest artists ever. I guess you have some inside info on him Sarge. Some relevant Google facts, dead celebrity gossip or a recent Wikileaks scoop!" he added rather facetiously.

"Well as a matter of fact Mr Smarty Pants, I did a paper on him at University."

"Really!" Boyd expressed in an admiring and respectful way. "What are the chances? I would have never thought that you could remember that far back!"

After a much warranted punch in the direction of Boyd's shoulder. 'Sandy' Kerr added, "I only graduated last year actually. It was a History of Art distance learning course. Five years in total and Mr Picasso, as you so eloquently called him was not a very nice man when it came to females detective. In fact in the PC world we presently live, he would never have gotten away with half of his nonsense."

Boyd instantly grimaced. That educational revelation soon sobered him up. "Strictly speaking, what sort of nonsense are we talking about?"

"Now don't get me wrong Allan, I wasn't expecting him to be perfect and I suppose behind every great artist there is a muse."

Her current colleague shrugged his shoulders indifferently.

"Well 'Our Pablo' was certainly no different," the red haired mother offered. "Because he had plenty of them." She then continued in an animated and agitated manner. "His sexual appetite was irrepressible. Over the course of his life he had two wives, six mistresses and dozens, if not hundreds of sexual partners. His love (or lack thereof) led one mistress, one wife, one son and a grandson to suicidal deaths."

Boyd was dumbstruck. He had no idea. He felt foolish now that he was fully informed and educated of the relevant facts. He remained speechless for the next few minutes. Having then reflected on his recent utterance, eventually the silence between the two officers was broken and an impassioned response was offered up by the 'new boy.'

"You either get bitter or you get better. It's that simple," he said, offering his Sergeant a look of honest sincerity. "You either take the hand that has been dealt to you and allow it to make you a better person. Or sooner or later, you'll allow it to tear you down."

He continued his fervent declaration, "The choice does not belong to fate Sandra. It belongs to the individual - It belongs to you and I. Thankfully, I recognised that fairly quickly and chose from an early age to learn from my life experiences, and I allowed them to make me better. Hard and difficult as that may have been on many, many numerous occasions. In both peacetime and at war."

"Sandy' nodded. The private glance exchanged between them, acknowledged fully the fact that Allan Boyd never normally spoke about his military experiences. A bond was established that day.

Rozelle House and The Maclaurin Gallery was literally a 30 second drive away from the bard's cottage in Alloway. On their way to the small museum and exhibition, the officers drove past The Robert Burns Birthplace Museum. That commemorative site was a whole seven minute walk from their destination today. But it was here at Rozelle Park, that for the next six weeks, enthusiastic art lovers and aficionados of 'Oor Rabbie,' would be in awe at the work of the late Renfrewshire artist, Alexander Goudie.

Goudie had died in Glasgow in 2004, aged 71. Boyd had read that on a plaque at the entrance of the display room. Throughout his career the figurative painter held a fascination with Burns' narrative poem, Tam o' Shanter. Completed in 1999, the final illustrative cycle of over fifty, larger than life paintings retelling the story of the poem in visual format, would adorn the gallery walls until the middle of March.

Today Sergeant Kerr and her newly appointed, ex-armed forces sidekick, Allan (with a double l) Boyd would take the journey for themselves. No preconceived ideas or theories, but willing to play along with their Inspector's intuition, experience and gut feeling… *'A Man's a Man for a' That!'*

The words echoed around the whitewashed walls of the hospital room. "Tell me you've got me something worthwhile Joe?" The question was asked whilst Murray tried desperately to jiggle the handset and manoeuvre the two 'excuses' for pillows behind his back. "Flippin' things!" he said, hellbent on straining his neck rather than taking the time to adjust them properly by hand.

"Are you okay there sir? What are you up to?"

"I'm up to practising my DCI Furlong's 'non-swearing' techniques."

He suddenly pulled his free hand back over his shoulder, grabbed pillow number one and as he thrust it at great speed toward the toilet, shouted out at the top of his voice - "Fuddy Dumplin's!!!!"

A curtailed segment of brief laughter was heard from 'Sherlock.' Before he responded with - "Had them once sir. They went really nicely with 'Chinese Freckles!'"

There was a silence on the line.

"You're nuts," Murray exclaimed seriously.

"I'm nuts? You're the one that…"

"Never mind that Joe, just forget it and let's be moving on. What do you have for me? I am assuming you do have something considerably better than average."

"I think you will find 'considerably better than average' is my middle name."

At that remark, Murray could clearly picture his colleague with a smug, confident, self-satisfactory smile on the other end of the phone line.

"The barman at Wetherspoon's was able to give us a fairly good description of the two men that she left with. Unfortunately or with careful methodical planning, there was no security camera coverage at that area of the bar. Both men coming in and going out hid their faces. So they were certainly familiar with the location of those cameras."

"Not great then." Murray quipped. "Sounds like a needle in a haystack search required."

"So much for faith in 'considerably better than average' then!"

"Go on then Sherlock. Impress me."

"Well, it's not so much the visual description that Mr Knox the bartender gave. It's more the snippets of audio he overheard."

Murray had now dispensed with any pillows entirely and was sat hard upright against his bog standard NHS bed frame.

"Which was?" The Inspector asked with genuine curiosity.

"Which was sir, that one 'so-called' police officer was a Geordie, the other Scottish."

As Murray listened to those bland descriptions, his eyes darted from side to side. To most people, they'd think nothing of it. However to Detective Inspector Steven Murray those words were chilling. He instantly and deliberately crashed his head back several times, banging it furiously against the metal headrest.

"Sir, sir, are you sure you're alright?" 'Sherlock' cried. He could hear the distressed sounds departing swiftly down the adjoining corridor from his Inspector's hospital room.

Yet another round of silence took over. A few seconds passed. Joseph Hanlon knew that his boss was mulling things over. Pondering, considering options and deliberating THEIR next move.

"She never stood a chance Joe. As soon as she left with those two, she was dead. Reid told me as much yesterday at the end of his visit. His 'Heil Hitler' routine - he offered it up to us on a plate."

"So you know them sir?" Hanlon said in a surprised tone.

"Oh yes and so do you," Murray replied. "Well at least you know their recent body of work! Last year at Granton. The old retail park. Two males had their genitalia taken off with a blow torch and their throats sliced afterward for good measure. Their two female partners fared no better and that all transpired around last July."

"I remember," Hanlon squeamishly replied. "We found small traces of drugs at the scene. Gang related, right?"

"That was most certainly what we had thought initially at the time Joe. Then later in the summer you had those other

253

two individuals. A couple of Fife's top dealers that had been left to bleed out at Duddingston Loch during the last week in August."

"Each having been stabbed over thirty times," Hanlon added.

"Correct."

Another pause entered the conversation. A conversation that had suddenly turned perversely dark and stomach churning.

"I would be very surprised if there's still not a few more uncovered corpses lying in wait for us around some of the other squalid, neglected areas of this fine city in relation to that time.

"This fine city?" DC Hanlon left that question hanging in the air. Before adding, "However in all those cases they left the same identifiable tag sir. And we did reckon at that time that the murders were all drug and gang related. Someone trying to muscle in on someone else's patch."

"Exactly and unfortunately for us, I think we now know whose patch they had their sights on."

DC Hanlon shrugged with indifference at his end of the phone line.

"Although I do feel this has something more substantial to it Joe. They were desperately trying to retrieve specific information from that woman and yet as a mother to three children, she still never gave it up."

"Sheer stupidity? Or just sheer Scottish stubbornness and bravado?" Hanlon suggested.

"No actually - neither. In fact I suspect with hindsight, as I told 'Doc' Patterson, it was probably because the poor girl did not even know that she had it!"

'Sherlock' fully grasped and understood the parenthood angle. Although unseen, his currently tilted head and pursed lips would have confirmed it to Murray.

In a reflective, thoughtful and worried tone his Inspector then offered up a rather more honest and experience driven opinion.

"It was not a tall, brash, giant of a man moving into Edinburgh," Murray suggested. "But an angry and bitter woman that had swam arrogantly and determinedly across the Forth! She had openly traded in a certain Glaswegians territory. Right there on his doorstep, in the official Royal Fiefdom of Fife. It was purely a matter of time before he found out. And once discovered, he would then want to rectify matters. He would confiscate all her gear, take what he considered his rightful profits back and then, finally teach her a very painful lesson indeed. Alas, in theory," Murray's breath and speech pattern suddenly slowed. "His men went too far, too quickly and unfortunately for Christina Cardwell, it was with the wrong woman."

The phone conversation abruptly halted. It commenced again several seconds later though, when Joseph Hanlon humbly opined, "Because they seemingly had no idea of the 'Bunny' Reid connection?"

"That may well be true Joe. However I suspect you might find a bit of old fashioned skullduggery had transpired. Check with Furlong for the full definition of that word," he laughed.

Hanlon smiled. Wrongfully assuming that there was light at the end of the tunnel.

"I reckon you'll find that one of her assailants knew fine well who she was," Murray continued. "And that 'Bunny' just wanted a reason to start a war and shut down his rival before he could even begin to tread water over here."

"His own niece?" 'Sherlock' asked. "This sick, psycho was happy to have his own flesh and blood killed and in such a brutal, callous manner?"

"Well you know he's never been known for his warm, kind natured gestures Joe. But I suspect that it probably did go further than even he had instructed. But all is fair in love and war and it was simply collateral damage in Reid's book. Ultimately, who knows how much pain and punishment one person can handle. We are all different after all."

Joe Hanlon had listened intently. His pupils danced to the rhythm of every spoken word Murray had offered. His ongoing unofficial apprenticeship continued apace.

"I believe Ally stumbled onto it by surprise yesterday 'Sherlock.' Because I don't think it was 'Bunny's Avon order waiting to be delivered in the first place. My guess, as you'll have gathered, is that it belonged to another key player in the drugs world and that is why the 'SS' were in town."

The airways of the overly vocal Inspector then paused momentarily to take a much needed breath. After his lung-break, "Joe, check carefully for their signature," Murray announced. "We want to be hundred percent on this. Although based on the barman's description, we are already nine-tenths of the way there. They are certainly ruthless and ambitious, I'll give them that."

"Might one add, extremely foolish to that list sir?"

"Absolutely! I'd agree. Looking to possibly take over from James 'Bunny' Reid seemed foolish in the extreme I would say. Oh and Joe, one more favour. Get those remnants we discovered at Granton last year compared to our current Avon promotion."

His Detective Constable was surprised and taken aback at that last request. But with an inaudible mumble, positively acknowledged it. The receiver then went dead. Their conversation over.

THIRTY

"I don't mean to offend or add fuel to the fire. We are all stood in silence while the head count it gets higher."

- Gerry Cinnamon

The signature that The T'inker would be looking out for would be specific SS lettering. Those two horror filled initials would be marked, scarred, etched or even tattooed in some way, shape or form onto Tina Cardwell's body. In all of the other vicious, atrocious beatings that those two 'Auld Alliance' partners had carried out, they had made sure that they'd left behind that vile symbol of hate. Foreheads, thighs, buttocks and breasts had all previously been used as suitable templates.

Under Adolf Hitler and the Nazi Party, the Schutzstaffel literally stood for 'Protection Squadron.' Today, in Scotland's capital city, it stood for Scullion & Scott. They were no fancy lawyers, architects, or chartered accountants. Nor in fact were they even a handy gas central heating company. No, Messrs Shaun Scullion and Paul Scott worked for and were the 'Protection Squadron' to the young pretender. The new kid on the block when it came to the future of crime in Edinburgh and surrounding districts. His visionary protection scheme that he currently ran for companies would not generally involve old-style bully boy tactics. His ultra modern enforcement, involved one delicate click of a mouse and your firm's security was down. With that, your firewall was breached, numerous viruses installed and he could and would, kill your business stone dead! No threat of physical violence whatsoever was required. Although muscle was always on hand to deal with any last minute snagging! Next on his impressive rota of schemes was his VIP package - Virtual Incredible Prostitution. A range of virtual reality, interactive opportunities geared at those with no real desire to travel out-with their own (normally expensive) four walls. Even that pales into insignificance, compared to his recently expanded and highly innovative 'Triple D' service. Which in all its deluded grandeur, stood proudly for a pretty self-explanatory resource… Drug Delivery by Drone!

Only weeks before on Christmas Day, four fully stocked, pilotless mini aircraft deposited their respective white loads over Saughton Prison in Edinburgh during break time. Hundreds of tiny packages were delivered free of charge for the inmates. No names on them from Santa mind. But the several dozen inmates involved in the ensuing 'free for all,' guaranteed disruption and chaos in the prison over the festive season. Merry Christmas to all his loyal customers was the message sent out loud and clear by this enterprising, law breaking impresario.

This individual was a forward thinker. He was a University graduate and was in line to become the Mark Zuckerberg of 'Auld Reekie's' criminal underworld fraternity. Having initially made a name for himself throughout the rural, picturesque settings of Perth and Kinross. His ambition and natural money making abilities brought him ruthlessly into the Kingdom of Fife. Numerous torched buildings, lorry hijackings and the brutal slaying of the previous two drug barons that ran the area, enabled his growth and expansion plans to continue unabated.

Heading like a mighty, unstoppable behemoth toward the Forth Road Bridge and the ripe territories for the taking of James Baxter Reid. The entrepreneurial CEO of this impressive strategy and vision was a west of Scotland man. At 6' 5', nothing fazed him. He was used to literally looking down on people and getting his own way.

It lay seven winding miles southwest of Glasgow City Centre. It was an affluent suburban town and the largest settlement in East Renfrewshire. Surely the history books in years to come would also make mention that Newton Mearns had also been the schoolboy home to one of Scotland's most notorious gangland criminals, and one never referred to by his initials alone… Andrew Robert Scott.

As Murray's eyes gazed upon the two pathetic, chunky, yellow potato mounds. He watched in trepidation as a bubbling flow oozed between them. Floating gently upon the darkened river of grease was a poor immigrant family of minced beef. They wore bright fluorescent lifejackets. DI Murray due to his advanced detective skills soon realised they were in actual fact, diced carrot survivors!

Hell! Torture! Boak! Were the first three suitable words to enter the Inspector's mind.

Never mind fear of infection Murray instantly thought. Hospital food itself, was still the biggest threat to life in the medical arena! Thankfully he wasn't hungry. This was probably in no small part, to trying desperately to vanquish thoughts of the 'new' guard and their current plans from his mind.

Paul Scott was Andrew's younger, unfortunate brother. He always carried himself with a rather mournful hangdog expression. Browbeaten, shoulders down and a good foot shorter than his older sibling. Realising at an early age that he did not have the academic capabilities often required to succeed in life, his parents encouraged him to build up and strengthen his body. So from 14 years of age this academic delinquent had a regular gym membership. Now in his mid-thirties he had struck a fine work-life balance. He was built like the Incredible Hulk, but had the brain power o' a 'jeely piece!'

Shaun Scullion on the other hand was indeed a true Geordie lad. Born and brought up in the town of Heaton, on the outskirts of Newcastle. If truth be told, which was not like Scullion. It was only two miles east of the city centre. A curly haired, wayward individual from his teenage days. He was always destined it would seem for a life of illegal activity. His academic report card had him graduate from petty theft, malicious damage and GBH. To earning his PhD in 'Applied Rape!' On release from Durham Prison near a decade ago he travelled to Perthshire, got in tow with a couple of Andrew Scott's foot soldiers and worked his way up through the ranks ever since. Obviously proving himself more than capable time and again to become part of his trusted protection squad, aka the SS team. Why aye man, canny lad!

Back in Edinburgh, a gentle buzz broke the silence in the quiet of his hospital room. Accompanied by a stirring vibration and his phone was quickly given his full attention. It was 'Sherlock.'

The brief text read: *Another body discovered. 5 mins from Princes Street!*

In the heart of the city. Murray was alarmed by this. Things were escalating swiftly. He knew what he had to do and was in the process of texting back, when:

I know. I'm on my way to get you!

It looked like he and Hanlon were in perfect synch after all.

The medical staff attending him were none too happy. But Murray, although drugged up to the eyeballs and still experiencing extreme pain from time to time was adamant. He was off.

"Adios amigos," he would submit to all, as he dressed and walked simultaneously. Then waiting at the front door pick-up point for Hanlon. He duly sat on an unoccupied, complimentary wheelchair. All around him smokers got their daily fix whilst still attached to fine wires, pumping tubes and other medical paraphernalia. Graffiti artists had taken great pleasure in altering the hospital sign. The new alternative graphic involved three fingers, two blackbirds and a rather large baseball bat! The Police Scotland patient hurriedly checking out made a few other calls to find out further information about the latest discovery. Fortunately for him, he had gotten hold of PC George Smith at the station. The willing constable knew Steven Murray well and was able to provide him with the briefest of details.

The Inspector was told it looked to be a female in her mid to late thirties. That it had happened about only half an hour ago and although less well known, it was in a busy city centre thoroughfare right enough.

North of Princes Street and south of Queen Street, lay North St. Andrew Lane. A rather obscure and random location. Mainly office suite premises, it was part of the bustling one-way traffic system if Murray recalled correctly. How did someone manage to do this and go unseen he immediately questioned to himself. However his potential solution aroused his curiosity. I wonder if the… he began. Just at that Joseph Hanlon arrived and duly screeched to a halt.

They had no sooner lurched and crunched over a couple of 'traffic calming measures' near the exit, when an intrigued 'Sherlock' handed over to Murray one recently opened, blood stained envelope.

"What's this?"

"It's a photograph of you that I came across in the past few days. Taken during the Edinburgh Festival I'd guess."

DI Murray was taken aback as he looked at the likeness on the snapshot. "How did you know that Joe?"

"Well, it wasn't really a guess sir. You had written it on the back along with the date."

As he turned the picture over, "So I did," Murray began…

Then a rather intense stare was shared between the two men. His curious DI realising quickly that he'd been set up. That he'd been caught with his guard down. 'Sherlock' knew his handwriting and unless this image had been stolen during some previously unreported theft - The only way our hitman would have it in his possession was because he had been given it directly or through some third-party intermediary.

And the latter was DC Hanlon's preferred notion at this point.

As each man slowly began to second guess the other. A heavy, uncomfortable silence prevailed throughout the remainder of their short journey to the crime scene.

On arrival the traffic was heavily congested. The inside lane of the thoroughfare had been cordoned off. The area was crammed with police vehicles, a forensics tent and a multitude of officers with torches had begun to scour the surrounding area. As a chilled air of heavy darkness fell, horns were being repeatedly sounded, angry voices raised and a mass of heads shook in frustration. Pedestrians on the opposite pavement crooked their necks and walked at a snail's pace. A hybrid of cars, lorries and vans all tried to merge anxiously in turn at the busy road junction.

The officers were soon signed into the crime scene and lifted the police tape which sealed off the busy area.

"Why here sir?" Hanlon hesitantly questioned. "It's pretty random don't you think?"

Murray said nothing.

"Although to be fair, it may have nothing to do with the other bodies," Joe said. "There's nothing glued to her or…"

"I think a five minute walk will give us that answer," Murray interrupted, whilst tenderly pulling back the sheet from the lifeless corpse. "And although we have only just arrived constable, the fact that the only item of clothing she has on is a blouse. Makes me pretty confident that she is one of ours." Joe Hanlon blushed, observed the scene, studied the surrounding area and then watched diligently as his commanding officer raised his eyebrows high into the cold air. Indicating - let's go! Currently they were setting off from the back of an impressive red sandstone building that had been built in the late eighteen eighties.

"Are we at the back of a museum sir?"

"Do you not know what building this is 'Sherlock?'"

"I'm afraid not sir."

"When I heard where the body was discovered, I was fairly confident then it was one of ours."

"How do you mean sir?"

Murray said nothing.

Both the officers had now casually meandered around two heavily populated street corners and found themselves on the busy Queen Street. On this side of the building the windows were in carved pointed domes and the main entrance was surrounded by a large gabled arch.

"Ah, The Scottish National Portrait Gallery," Hanlon exclaimed. "I should have known that's what it was. I've been along this street plenty and I know that a distinctive feature of the gallery is its four octagonal corner towers. I just didn't recognise them from the back." There was then a brief silence before the rather confused Detective Constable felt brave enough to ask, "But how does this help us sir? How does it confirm or deny the connection?"

Once again Murray said nothing. But at least this time he felt the need to point.

"She will be Maxine McDonald."

"The girl that's been missing from the ceilidh on Sunday night?" Hanlon questioned.

"The very one 'Sherlock.' And there is the clue," he stated. This time gesturing toward the large, impressive advertising banner hanging vertically outside the main entrance. It read:

For 3 weeks only: The Black Burns!

THIRTY ONE

"Diet coke and a pizza please, Diet coke, I'm on my knees - Screaming, Big Girl you are Beautiful!"

- Mika

Two hours later and the dishevelled girl, youth or young adult that answered the door wore very little. The ageing Inspector sadly had no idea which of the first three she was. But he was fairly confident at least, that she fell into one of those categories. The female face when accompanied with make-up was not one of his strong points these days. She was a rather large individual and her black ski pants were everywhere, except covering her backside Murray felt. In his often 'grumpy Scottish old man persona,' he would rant, rave and step feverishly onto a hypothetical soapbox to vent his rage and despair until his heart was content. His father would often say, "dress for the weather." And this 'well upholstered' female had obviously taken no heed of that inspired counsel! Advice that Murray thought very apt, wise and practical. It was January for heaven's sake. However, with that said, he would much rather be a ferocious and fervent advocate for - "Dress to suit your size!!!!!!!!!"

We are all very different. So the Inspector has no real issue with someone's actual size, their physical appearance, warts and all. But when you are the weight of a small car and choose to wear figure hugging, micro thin ski pants no thicker than tights - He would rather see you put down and put out of your misery! And he was not being sexist. Steven Murray would apply that same rule for both sexes. No discrimination whatsoever!

"We should have fashion police," he would regularly offer up. "Give them stun guns and jolt people to come to their senses."

However, he also believed beauty was no longer in the eye of the beholder. It was in the hands of social media savvy experts. They would decide what offends and whose lives they would choose to ruin in an instant. You may think that the lady that just walked past you was a beautiful looking woman, had a terrific hairstyle and smelled wonderful. But don't you dare express those thoughts - You sexist, deranged, chauvinistic stalker. Pay a compliment? Don't be so stupid.

This particular girl's modern, calf high, Doc Marten style leather boots were partly laced. With the exception being the upper three ringlets - it must be a fashion statement Murray figured. Up top, her bright red tousled hair was shaved down one side. The remainder was gathered up tightly at the back and bound in place with a *'black velvet band'* into an impressive ponytail.

Murray pondered on the lyrics of that old Irish folk tune and wondered if *'her eyes really shone like diamonds?'*

Warrant cards were shown and it was approaching 7pm as Murray and Hanlon broke the tragically sad news. Found at the rear doors of the National Portrait Gallery, twenty-six year old Maxine McDonald was openly described and in a positive manner as being free spirited. She had distinct auburn hair. Well at least it was this month according to the three out of her five flatmates that were actually home. She had a highly individual and unique attitude, lifestyle and imagination. She was your typical nonconformist, the trio of friends offered in unison. The sisterhood of six all shared the trendy, modern loft conversion near Leith Docks. Tears were shed and texts were sent to the remaining pair of tenants. Tributes were shared on social media whilst the officers were still present. Sharing the shock through the retelling of the individual's life was something Murray had witnessed regularly over the years. In many respects it helped tremendously with investigations. As often, information and background details were offered up more freely and frequently, without the real need to dig or pry at what was always a very sensitive time.

Waitress, barmaid, part time model and tele-sales operator, were all listed on her current CV. In recent times she had even carried out pizza deliveries on her 90cc moped, one of the friends informed them. It was a career choice inspired by a recent trip to the 'Vespa' capital of the world… Rome.

"What happened to her?" Veronica, the taller of the three girls asked through mascara clad tears.

"We cannot give you any specific details at present I'm afraid," Joe Hanlon routinely answered. "But if you have any idea where Maxine spent yesterday and last night, that would go a long way to helping us at this moment in time."

Nods of understanding were offered and again it was left to Veronica to speak. Her cheeks were flushed and her eyes still puffy and red from the continual rubbing over the past few minutes.

"She was with Cindy yesterday."

The third girl in the room then held up her hand, as if to acknowledge 'that's me!'

"They were both off work during the day and hung out together until about seven o'clock. Which was when I returned home."

"That's about right Inspector," Cindy chimed in.

This girl had a rather low, raspy, harshness to her voice. Quite possibly a heavy smoker Murray guessed. Or at least, something very similar based on the aromatic smell in their chic, funky premises.

"I was getting ready to go out to work and Maxine was heading off to the dancing," she croaked.

Murray and Hanlon glowered at each other. Murray nodded (a 74), go ahead it counselled. Hanlon duly did so.

"Ceilidh dancing?" he piped up.

Three female heads all turned in his direction.

"At 'Thistle Do Nicely' by any chance?"

They were dumbstruck at his knowledge.

The small, intimate group of close friends then went on to share more upbeat stuff about Miss Maxine McDonald. How she was a happy, clappy, church goer. Her goal being to visit a different venue each week. They also informed the police officers of how she continually found new charities and causes to support every month and then became their fundraiser extraordinaire. Although interestingly by omission, no one knew anything about any parents, extended family or siblings. That was how the officers had found themselves here in the first place. Her plastic driving license, which was discovered inside one of her new shoes, gave this address. Deliberately, once again placed there for her to be identified quickly, Murray concluded.

Ski pant girl - whose name was actually Kylie (Of course it was thought Murray) was desperately sobbing into the stretched waistband of her dark polyester, transparent bottoms. The elasticated item of clothing was now being used as a makeshift handkerchief. At this sight Murray felt nauseous. But in a bid to calm down he walked swiftly toward the distraught teenager, who at this point was as mobile as a one-legged hippo! He generously handed her a packet of his never to be without, pocket-sized tissues.

The police officers then gathered up all other basic information in relation to the girls. Their own whereabouts, jobs and contact details, etc, etc. With the blonde, curly haired one, Cindy - extra keen to ensure Joe Hanlon had her correct number. Getting him to repeat it back to her twice, as she smiled intimately.

Steven Murray had always with hindsight wanted to switch career every three or four years. Something in the city at first and then he would have possibly moved on to more rural and remote. He had grown to love the past. How products and ideas were developed and how they were ever changing. So nowadays modern, cutting edge technology fascinated him also. What must it be like to experience all those different facets of life? To be a schoolteacher, a farmer, a dairy technologist or miner? In forty years to have sampled the hustle and bustle, the quiet solitude, the wide open spaces and the inner city congestion. Ten or more occupations throughout your working lifetime. Sure, it had always intrigued and enchanted him. But it had never been or would ever be... a reality.

Policing was all he'd done for over three decades now, yet here was the free-spirited Maxine McDonald putting all that to the test. In one short decade after leaving school, she had immersed herself fully in that hectic lifestyle and experienced so much in her brief life. Murray as he often would and was his want, shed a few emotional tears at this point. And thus began his inner turmoil for another period of time. He watched his dark canine friend stroll up to his side and sit. He knew then that his four legged buddy was about to accompany him for at least the next twenty-four hours. That was his life. His coping mechanism began as soon as he returned to his car and hit shuffle on the iPod!

Home, home is wherever I'm with you…….

THIRTY TWO

"Some people never come clean, I think you know what I mean. You're walking a wire between pain and desire and looking for love in between."

- The Eagles

As the busy Wednesday was drawing to a close. It appeared as though a gloomy, misty haze had descended across the whole of Scotland's capital city. On an average night the iconic castle, historic rooftops and peaked spires had the natural ability to create a memorable, picturesque silhouette. Normally, gloriously crisp and clear. Tonight however that picture postcard image was badly out of synch. As it arose it emerged broken, distorted and significantly out of focus and unbalanced. Similar in character to a certain person of interest to the police at this moment in time.

A typical Winter's evening had taken hold. Sensible, busy commuters had not wasted any time in their quest for home and the warmth and comfort of indoors. Pavements and streets were generally deserted. Infrequent, powerful winds had gathered in strength like a ragtag posse in a western movie. And they were now champing at the bit, ready to impressively chase down their threatening prey.

Ding-ding-ding-dong; A short dramatic burst of *'Danny Boy'* chimed eloquently from Murray's front door bell and the Inspector rose painfully to answer it. An evening bout of pain killer medication would be required shortly. It was approaching ten o'clock in the evening. Who would call around at this time of night Murray questioned. As he looked cautiously through the small peephole before answering, a certain Miss Melanie Rose came into his reflective mind. She was the lovely accountant from a year ago that whilst answering her door and peering through her security viewer, had had her face unceremoniously blown off by a mystery assailant with a gun. And as much as they knew 'Bunny' Reid was responsible, proving it had been a different story!

Tonight it would appear that Murray was about to be needed as a friend, counsellor and confidant.

"Sir," the meek voice offered.

At that, Murray wanted to cross himself and say - 'Come in my Son,' using his best Anglican tone. With great restraint and a wry smile he resisted. He then simply ushered his guest through to his sitting room with a more gentler arm gesture.

His rain soaked, confused and rather disconcerted visitor sat quietly on Steven Murray's sofa. His Inspector pursed his lips and remained silent. He could not, and had no intention of, making this part easy for his young constable. At twenty-three years of age, Andrew Curry had amassed two solid year's worth of experience and training under his belt.

Partnered and tutored by Detective Constable Susan Hayes they made a fine team. Murray knew he could depend upon them. They were diligent and proactive. With lots to learn, they were both keen to develop and progress in their respective careers. Little subtle changes had crept in though. 'Hanna' Hayes had probably noticed them, but did not want to report on her partner and was no doubt trying her best to see him through his difficulties or challenges.

However Detective Inspector Steven Murray had been here before. Over his long, illustrious and interesting career path he had witnessed many fine prospects throw it all away because of silly, initial indiscretions. Issues that if handled more sensitively and thoughtfully could have enabled some wonderful individuals to have still been serving, and serving well! Men, women and lives dismantled and destined for the scrapheap in an instant. Bureaucracy gone mad! It was boxes ticked and officialdom kept happy, whilst families were torn apart at the imminent fallout. Their legacy soon became one of disgrace and shame. Labels were printed and duly given out. Numerous bankruptcies, repossessions and suicides followed. Many of which, possibly the vast percentage, could have been avoided. But first you had to care and that was the problem - No one did. For the majority of officers in the force looking to get ahead, it was all dog eat dog.

At 5' 10" in his bare feet, Andrew Curry would normally always be close to looking his 6' 1" boss square in the eye. Tonight however, seated and with his blues eyes filled with moisture, he currently had no intention of trying to engage with Murray's gaze. His recently purchased and expensive pure new wool suit of only a few weeks appeared lifeless, crumbled and dishevelled. A little like its present owner! Fingernails that were always previously well groomed - Were now dirty, ragged and bitten. And as a fully paid up member of that exclusive club, Murray could easily testify to the fact that nail-biting can often be a source of guilt and shame in the biter.

The uneasy silence remained. Eventually broken by the humility of a man seeking freedom, relief and some edifying form of solace. What that may look like - remained to be seen!

"I am currently overdrawn I'm afraid sir. I've made way more personal withdrawals than deposits," the quivering voice stammered.

Murray gestured that he understood. His body language was non-judgemental, slow and at ease. No questions were asked or concerns raised. Although the slightest arm and eye movement, coupled with a small circling of the head did offer up - 'Anything else? Would you care to elaborate on that? We ultimately need the whole truth!'

"Judy, she left me sir. Or to be more strictly accurate - She flung me out," he cried in the real Scottish vernacular. With emphasis being placed mainly and squarely on the FLUNG!

"I gathered that young man," Murray confirmed. Slightly amused at Drew Curry's choice of words. "What was the cause? How did things get to that stage? Why would Judy ask you to go?"

DC Curry became uncomfortable. He blushed slightly and moved his head awkwardly from side to side. He simply didn't know where to start.

"How much did Reid give you?" Murray quickly followed up with.

Shocked and already taken aback, 'Drew' Curry was about to deny any wrongdoing. But the penetrating, piercing scowl of disapproval he received from his 'Father confessor,' soon corrected that course of action.

A disguised mumble was heard instead.

"And that excuse for English was what?" Murray brazenly questioned.

"Five thousand pounds sir," his chastened officer replied with perfect clarity. His chilling response was accompanied with a multitude of guilty tears running down his face.

"How did you know sir?'

"Years of experience constable."

Curry sighed, before Murray's honest caveat.

"And I looked up your phone contacts when I borrowed it the other day. You could have at least changed his name and gave him an alias!"

'Kid' Curry groaned, shook his head and berated himself.

"How could I have been so stupid?"

There is always a road back Andrew," Murray told him."

"I doubt it," he said, continuing to shake his head.

"You are here aren't you? And listen to one that knows." Murray spoke whilst pointing at himself. "There is always a way," he reassured him. "The secret of your future is hidden in your daily routine young man. So absolutely, it may be a long path and in your case, one that is exceptionally arduous and rocky at times, but it can be done son. And again Andrew let me be at pains to remind you - You are here now and that is the first step. You may not be in Alcoholics Anonymous, but today, this is most definitely a recovery program - And don't you forget it. This is a lifeline that hundreds of good officers before you were never extended."

This time as their eyes locked, 'Kid' Curry was reminded yet again by Murray.

"The key is - You will not be alone in the journey."

Curry curtly nodded, wiped away more tears and brought his chin up and down a few more times, determined assertively once again.

"How did it begin constable? What have you done for him and what does he expect? Because moving forward we could turn this to our advantage."

Overwhelmed by DI Murray's handling of the situation, his emotionally challenged colleague went into his crumbled jacket pocket to retrieve an envelope. As he struggled deeply to remain composed his weary shoulders began to spasm as he spoke.

"I've written a list of times, details and amounts down here for you sir. It contains the sordid details of everything that I have divulged to Reid or have been involved with."

Murray held up a hand. "Before I read it son, I just need a few curiosities to be satisfied vocally. A few i's dotted and t's crossed. If you don't mind, I would be grateful."

Already vulnerable Andrew Curry took a sharp intake of breath, closed his eyes and pursed his dried lips.

"It was you that escorted Reid from the casino?"

'Kid' Curry was intent on maintaining eye contact. He blinked once, swallowed and nodded.

Murray sighed. "Just three days ago you then told 'Bunny' about Tina Cardwell?"

Another positive assignation was offered.

"Holy moly 'Kid' - you certainly didn't do things by half. Furlong's background, walking 'three miles' every day. That would have been down to you also?"

Momentarily ashamed, the disgraced constable's gaze fell to the ground.

"So whilst I am asking," Murray decided. "You wouldn't happen to know who the officer was that reckoned he saw me gently encourage Gerald Anderson to leap to his death?"

The young man's sorrowful eyes said it all. He shook his head in an apologetic manner and handed over the unsealed envelope that contained all the relevant information.

THIRTY THREE

"Heroes and heroines are scarcer than they've ever been. So much more to lose than win. The distance never greater. Way back when you made history by flying planes across the sea. Embarking on your odyssey - you put away the danger."

- Mary Chapin Carpenter

Next day, back in the city centre away from the hustle and bustle of the busy overly populated Princes Street, sat one of the country's top Art Museums. The Scottish National Portrait Gallery was situated at the east side of Queen Street. The street itself had a rather unusual claim to fame. It was noted as the longest parade of 18th Century architecture in Edinburgh and was named in honour of Queen Charlotte of Mecklenburg, the consort of George III.

Currently at a side lane and to the rear of the premises were a large gathering of police and forensic officers. Each diligently working hard to position and line up the pieces of the puzzle that they presently had to work with. Steven Murray had given Hanlon the assignment to follow up at the Gallery and unearth something to move them forward. And even having spent half the night with young Andrew Curry, the Inspector was in no mood to sleep. He had arrived sharp, bright and early playing the 'official police' business card.

Douglas Gordon's dramatic destruction of Robert Burns at the SNPG is - 'An act of love, admiration and possibly envy!' Or at least that is what a prominent pull-up banner advertising the new exhibition screamed vehemently at Murray on the outside steps of the premises earlier that morning. The Turner Prize winner Gordon's new major commission, was in fact a response to the John Flaxman statue of Robert Burns in the Gallery's Great Hall. This was the impressive white marble figure that Joseph Hanlon had aptly described. However on DI Murray's visit in person to the location, something very fortuitous happened. He had been lucky enough to have stumbled across a Q & A breakfast session with the acclaimed, Berlin based, Scottish artist. Gordon's early morning appearance was obviously scheduled to help publicise and create an awareness of his latest work, which was only being displayed for a limited period. It was a promotional VIP gathering of press and photographers, of Art correspondents and writers. Murray though, magically waved some accredited ID and was ushered in accordingly. He stood at the back of the room and was on his best behaviour - listening and learning. Something that had become a favourite pastime of his in recent years.

The new piece was appropriately called: The Black Burns. It was a solid black replica version of that in the Great Hall. The project/artwork lay scattered in numerous pieces in front of the John Flaxman original. Murray as a supposed detective, was intrigued.

A former student at The Glasgow School of Art, Douglas Gordon's work on this occasion was "full of doubling, alter-egos and doppelgängers," he himself explained. "For every

Jekyll - a Hyde; For every white marble figure - a matching black one."

One broadsheet columnist commented on, "How the broken pieces made him think of the fervent, jubilant crowds that pulled down various statues of Saddam Hussein."

"Very Interesting," Douglas Gordon had responded. "Because I am trying not to say 'breaking.' I'm trying to convey 'opening.' I think all men – mankind – should be opened. It's kind of what Burns did. Poets and songwriters naturally seem to do that. They open themselves. I try to say to my kids (Murray learned he had a daughter in Berlin and a son in New York from previous relationships): be open, be open, be open."

The Inspector thought that remark in itself was very open. It was a very humbling admission from an artist at the top of his game. Two decades ago, Gordon won the Turner Prize for '24 Hour Psycho' – Hitchcock's original movie slowed down, frame by frame, to last 24 hours. It was the moment many still recall as the birth of the so-called, 'Glasgow miracle.' A miracle that oversaw many artists based in the city win an impressive string of awards. Other prizes followed for Gordon: the Premio 2000 at the Venice Biennale in 1997 and the Hugo Boss Prize in 1998. He found himself under commission for some of the top galleries and museums in the world. His work combined a conceptual rigour with an ability to connect with people, drawing on a common cultural language: movies, books and football. He is the master of the beautifully encapsulated idea you wished you'd had yourself, but never would have.

He then finished by adding, "I suppose it's a bit like that with myself and Burns. When people ask, 'What is the icon of Scotland?' For me, it's Robert Burns. And here, lo and behold, I go and break him." He paused and then gently laughed. "You should speak to my therapist."

Having been given a free hand by curators to respond to any work in the Portrait Gallery's vast collection. He surprisingly, to them, chose Burns. "I could have done something really nasty with Queen Victoria," he joked, briefly.

He is, by turns, jocular, confiding and profoundly serious Murray gleaned from these brief soundbites of his life. Burns was important to Douglas Gordon.

His late father shared a birthday with the bard. He recited Scots poetry at school for his Burns Society Certificate. "I still have it. It's a very emotional thing for me," he said. "And I love the Flaxman sculpture." Briefly, he looked very sad, before once again smiling brightly, "But I had to break it!"

Early on in his life, this so-called genius, understood that creativity for him was fuelled by being around other people. "I think one of the great things that I learned from my parents, my brother and sister and my teachers, was to go out. I don't believe in the ivory tower. I picked up on conversations, films and images from other people in bars, planes and trains. I got everything from other people. I'm a professor at an art school in Frankfurt, and I say to my students: Pick up everything, throw nothing away. There's no such thing as litter. To be 'literate,' you have to have litter!"

Murray loved that particular quote. In fact he had become so enthralled with the whole experience that he began to confidently raise his hand. "Is this work in a way then, a collaboration with Robert Burns?" He quickly followed that up with, "And if so, what did you admire most about the ploughman poet?" The artist's response, very much kept with his self-promoting image, Murray thought.

"Burns certainly had his feet on the ground," Gordon began. "He was seduced and abandoned. And the great thing that stood out for me was that not once, or even twice, but three times he chose not to go to the West Indies. I think Burns was a great example of choosing NOT." Before departing the limelight, the tattooed maestro grinned, "Robert Burns was a punk. He would be a modern day, rebellious punk!" The creative genius, then swaggered off as quickly as he had appeared.

As Inspector Murray looked upward, at the original white masterpiece, the sculpted man held a scroll! As if Burns used parchment for his poems? Also Murray observed his plaid had become a classical toga. This was an ideal man, or so John Flaxman's famous statue would have us believe back in 1824.

But times have changed, the world has moved on. Now, nearly two centuries later, look down at the surface and find his dark and troubled double – His exact inverse, lying broken and twisted on the floor. It had been carved out of rich black marble that came from the exact same mine, all his pristine aspects and attributes had turned to night. The national poet had been brought down to earth and ruined.

Today, this was Douglas Gordon's tribute. Here lay: *The Black Burns*.

It was a shattering sight, not least because the monument was now unrecognisable. Head and body parted, Burns was a divided self. From the balcony above he looked like a fallen angel. At ground level - mangled body parts jutted disturbingly from a trench, with one foot still polished like a dead soldier's boot. The inner man was revealed as dark and flawed – literally, a fault line running through the stone defined the way the figure cracked. At the same time the innards of a marble sculpture were exposed in all their dark and twinkling beauty. Hidden Gems: both statue and poet.

Doppelgängers, doubles and divided Jekyll-and-Hyde selves, Murray could absolutely relate with. As an artist, the Scotsman had long been heir to his compatriots James Hogg and Robert Louis Stevenson. But here today, Douglas Gordon had gone further and had fully liberated Burns, even as he appeared to have destroyed him. His confident, tremendous, anti-monument had found tragedy in the life that Flaxman's statue altogether ignored. It was as if Burns had not died young and poor, a drinker and serial adulterer. And a man, moreover, once so desperate that he booked a passage to Jamaica with the aim of becoming a bookkeeper on a slave plantation.

THIRTY FOUR

"It's been a while since I walked the streets and I can't remember where to go. And the warm sunny side of a Glasgow street, passed me by some time ago."

- Tide Lines

Sycamore Avenue was part of a quiet, residential, leafy suburb of East Renfrewshire. Only six prime houses occupied the exclusive address. The white sandstone buildings appeared both important and imperial. They had an awe inspiring, majestical feel to them. Through the bleak winter clouds high in the sky today, streaks of vibrant sunshine broke through and shone directly upon those impressive buildings. Each with their own distinguished stone turret. Reminiscent to being singled out by a higher power, they were akin to a select, half dozen, expensive sparkling gems being set delicately onto an everyday ring.

Number Two - The Avenue, as people referred to it, experienced it's rich mahogany front door being gently closed over. The homeowner, an attractive brunette in her late sixties, had just returned from a morning of much needed retail therapy. Home was this modern, five bedroomed property that she and her husband had only moved into four short years ago. For the past three, however, she'd lived alone. Her husband's sudden death nine months after moving in, had turned her whole world upside down.

Now within the confines of her luxurious abode, she was about to break the beautiful, peaceful, solitude and silence with the slightest touch of her recently manicured finger.

The digital female voice announced - 'You have four new messages.'

"Hello mum. It's Tess here. I'll be popping by shortly. Probably be there in the next twenty minutes or so. I really do wish you'd get yourself a mobile! Love you!"

Bee...... eep.

"Hello - It's Lisa from 'Nailed It,' beauty salon. It was just to let you know that you left your scarf here this morning."

She touched her neck to confirm her forgetfulness. Then she smiled a reassuring smile as the bright and breezy Lisa finished her remarks.

"We have put it aside for you and you can pick it up when you are back in for next week's scheduled appointment. See you then, bye."

Bee...... eep.

"Mother where are you? What's going on? Your youngest granddaughter is missing her sister. We are on your front step. No darling don't touch…"

Her poor mum, rather confused, listened intently whilst beginning to remove purchases from her range of designer bags. She then began to unbutton her coat.

Bee...... eep.

"Sorry, some little minx got hold of the phone. But what's going on? Where is Leah? I don't know where your car is or what we have done to upset you. But I can hear you moving about upstairs. I know you are in. I can see your shadow behind the curtains. Answer the door please and let's talk."

The woman's slender hand immediately froze on her coat's

top button. For all of two seconds her finger began to encircle the ridged pattern. Her mind started to immediately process the information at greater speed and clarity. That last message had been left roughly an hour ago. But she had been out all morning. Her daughter though had confirmed to her, that her car was not in the driveway. But even more alarming, she was adamant that someone else was most definitely in the house.

Rooted to the spot, apprehension and fear filled her stomach. A thousand small drummers began to play simultaneously. At this dreaded point, only one question burned deep into her mind - Should she make for the front door or the kitchen drawer?

It was early on that Thursday afternoon before Murray eventually caught up with Hanlon on the telephone and asked with a smile.

"How did you get on at the Gallery?"

He was confident that Joe Hanlon was about to yet again exceed expectations.

"Have you ever been sir?" The young detective enquired.

As DI Murray started to shake his head, he was about to say... Just this morning!

"Me neither," 'Sherlock' quickly jumped in and confirmed, catching Murray off guard.

The Inspector made an interesting, yet slightly inquisitive, negative eye gesture toward the phone.

"I've since taken the online virtual reality tour around the whole place and remarkable it is too," Hanlon said. "I have literally walked for miles and miles, yet never broken sweat!

The Scottish National Portrait Gallery," Hanlon proudly announced with arms and hands venturing into theatrical mode. "It has a very impressive and regal sound to it. Don't you think sir?"

"Indeed I do Joe, indeed I do. However in all honesty, I think I am more concerned with…"

"Why another girl wearing only a blouse was dumped on their back doorstep? Yes I get it," Hanlon accepted. Holding up both hands in mock surrender. "So let me begin by firstly informing you that the Gallery had been closed for over two and a half years sir. Since early April 2009 in fact and I tell you that for good reason, which I'll come back to shortly."

Murray was becoming more and more impressed each day with DC Hanlon's style. A delivery which certainly seemed to be modelled very closely on his own. So he knew full well if 'Sherlock' mentioned something these days that it would very likely have significance at some point. He ran a nervous hand across a day's stubble and listened more intently.

"The Museum itself features portraits of famous historical figures such as Mary Queen of Scots and Prince Charles Edward Stuart, as well as more contemporary names. According to their promotional material, must-see literary portraits at the gallery include those of Sir Walter Scott and Edinburgh's very own Robert Louis Stevenson."

Murray had his hands deep in his pockets. His feet tapped anxiously on the floor. You could see he was desperately trying to refrain from telling Joe 'to get a move on.' Mainly because his boss fully recognised at times that it was important to get some of the background details, so that you could really appreciate what was about to follow. Patience though, never came naturally to Steven Murray, as his white knuckles testified to on this particular occasion.

"When it was eventually opened to the public in 1889," Hanlon continued. "It was the world's first purpose-built portrait gallery. Without question, it was designed to be a shrine for Scotland's heroes and heroines. The numerous portraits exhibited currently, show men and women whose lives and achievements have helped shape Scotland to be the country it is today."

"And what was the relevance of its closure that you mentioned a minute ago?" the Inspector now asked.

"It made me ponder and consider something sir. And it has been niggling me ever since."

"And again I ask…"

"The fire at the Jordan's home sir. Mrs Jordan's death. The cause and circumstances behind it. Something just doesn't feel right."

Steven Murray looked at him with thoughtful surprise.

"After being closed for a comprehensive refurbishment and repair the National Gallery reopened on the 1st of December 2011." 'Sherlock' continued, "As you enter and step excitedly inside, a large white marble statue stands tall and majestic. Dominating the great hall, it is a visually stunning representation of…"

"Robert Burns?" Murray added, with a touch of educated guesswork. Mainly based on the fact that he had been there several hours previous! Although he had stated it confidently, it was uttered with a healthy dose of curiosity. "We must be getting close Joe?"

With a renewed verve Joseph Hanlon added, "I think if we revisit, reopen and re-examine her death. Those third degree burns will get us even closer still."

"A gut feeling?" Murray offered.

"And then some," 'Sherlock' said, with a crisp passionate edge to his voice.

"Then get moving on it!" Murray instructed. "I'll need to go Joe, I've got a call waiting." By the time the Inspector had hung up, he had missed it.

Joseph 'Sherlock' Hanlon's mind was always filled with curiosity. As a young lad it was more with mechanical and engineering challenges that he would be determined and excited to overcome. He blamed it on the vast array of boxed Playmobil and Lego sets he received for birthdays and Christmases growing up. As he gradually grew older, his father would constantly have him at his side learning from and working on a variety of cars in the family garage. So that character trait of dogged determination and perseverance, of seeing things through to the end and completing the task, was inherent throughout those early teenage years. That morning as DC Hanlon sat at the computer and was about to patiently scroll and click his way through numerous police files, that fitting attribute would be greatly required.

From a grieving widower just over twelve months ago, Joseph Hanlon was exceptionally grateful for the autonomy and trust that DI Murray seemingly placed in both him and the rest of the team. And as much as he was sure it was deliberately to allow them each to grow, to confidently run with ideas and hopefully get successful results. There was always a niggling, slightly cynical part of him wondered if it was also because it allowed his team still to function. Even when their boss was occasionally posted missing for a day or two at a time. The fact was that they got on with the job and covered so well that nobody would even realise he was off sick. On those rare occasions when they were left in the dark. It was more than likely, that he was literally at home in the dark. Usually wrestling with unruly demons and villains of a more highly personal nature.

Five minutes had passed before the caller rang Murray back. The Detective Inspector had just entered DCI Furlong's office and she nodded anxiously for him to answer it.

"It could be important," she said optimistically.

Murray reckoned a number 36, 'Barbra' would have had no idea! The glass screen always displayed the callers name. So it was clearly The T'inker, Doctor Thomas Patterson. But the Inspector intended having words with Joe Hanlon nonetheless. The misguided 'Sherlock' had obviously, yet again been messing about with his phone. Because ringtones had been allocated to individuals. On this particular occasion *'The Rambling Irishman'* was belting out as Murray took the call. Very unprofessional, he thought. But pretty funny.

"Hi Tom, how can I help you?"

"Your Nazi sympathisers were being noticeably lazy Steven."

"Let me put you on speaker-phone. I've got DCI Furlong with me. So how do you mean Doc?"

"T'ey didn't even try to make it original. As soon as Miss Cardwell was on my table. T'ere t'ey were, right t'ere in front of me. On t'e soles of her feet, two amateur slice and dice marks. One on each foot. Angled mind you in such a way

Inspector, t'at when you overlapped them, you got the sign of the swastika. Nasty and evil Steven. Go get t'ese guys."

"Thanks for that Doc," Murray offered cautiously in front of Furlong. "Was there anything else?"

Tom Patterson hesitated, before asking, "Are you feeling okay?"

The Inspector paused ever so slightly, and although still on speaker-phone he recognised he should be appreciative. "Mentally I am doing okay Doc. Thanks for asking. My black dog seems to have taken a couple of well deserved days off!"

You - You have a dog? Furlong mouthed to him silently.

Murray's complexion blushed slightly.

"Well, sure I'm glad to hear t'at," the Doc said. "But I was actually meaning physically? Because we have now had at least t'ixteen officers come down wit' food poisoning, and all of t'em were in attendance at our Burns Supper t'e other night."

"Oh! Really?" Murray pondered. "Any idea of the cause or common denominator?"

"No, not yet. But t'at is far too much of a co-incidence Steven. An outbreak like t'at needs proper investigation. I believe some of our lads visited the hotel officially t'is afternoon, so hopefully..." Patterson broke off momentarily. "Someone's just came into my office Inspector, I'll need to go. I'll keep you up to speed."

"No problem and thanks Doc."

"Sure, you're welcome. Bye."

"Bye."

Both parties appeared to take a few moments to consider what had been said.

"The symbolic swastika. That's a solid and mighty robust trademark to be associated with. Especially if you are threatening, nasty and evil," Murray concluded.

Steepling was a powerful nonverbal behaviour. It normally occurred when the fingers were pressed towards the sky in an almost church-like or prayer position. Actually, almost exactly like how DCI Furlong's fingers were positioned right now. Murray knew full well that it tended to be associated with a sign of confidence. When an individual believed that they had a truth worth sharing, and Murray's wait would soon be over.

"Coca- Cola used it. Carlsberg also, on their beer bottles," she began. "Heck, the Boy Scouts adopted it and the Girl's Club of America even called their magazine Swastika!" She informed a dumbstruck Inspector.

"Really?" he said. Where and how did she learn all this stuff? Hanlon and her must hang out together at the weekends and surf the same websites he figured.

"For 'Furbies' sake, they would even send out swastika badges to their young readers as a prize for selling copies of their magazine," she continued.

Then his Chief Inspector seemed to stop for a moment to ponder and consider. She very carefully observed Murray before asking -

"Do you ever wonder where that badness in people comes from? Is it the 'nature/nurture' debate?"

She then raised her voice in a rather alarmed manner. "Whoever is committing these murders, these brutal killings Steven, these barbaric SS attacks. They themselves were once young, small and innocent. Hopefully back then, they were filled with laughter, joy and smiles. So how, how…" she slowed. "How did that extreme change come about? What horrible experience did they suffer, put up with or go through, to enable that seismic shift to take place?"

DI Murray thought that those words definitely seemed to come from her heart. At this moment in time he felt impressed to acknowledge it best though, through a respectful silence.

"And just for the record Inspector, the swastika was also used by American military units during World War One and could even be seen on RAF planes as late as 1939."

Steven Murray could not help but be intrigued. "So what changed there Ma'am?"

"I thought you'd never ask Steven and remember call me Barbra," she smiled. "It was because the Nazi use of the swastika stemmed from the work of 19th Century German scholars translating old Indian texts. In the ancient Indian language of Sanskrit, swastika actually means 'well-being.' The symbol has been used by Hindus, Buddhists and others for millennia and is commonly assumed to be an Indian sign."

The Inspector was transfixed, listening intently.

"They'd noticed similarities between their own language and Sanskrit. They then concluded that Indians and Germans must have had a shared ancestry and imagined a race of white god-like warriors they called Aryans. The Nazis then turned it into the most hated symbol of the 20th Century."

Murray, baffled and bemused, simply shook his head!

THIRTY FIVE

"Like a small boat on the ocean, sending big waves into motion. Like how a single word can make a heart open. I might have only one match, but I can make an explosion."

- Rachel Platten

In East Renfrewshire, the kitchen drawer had decisively won the 'where do I make for first' competition. And as a tall, masked figure appeared from the darkened shadows of her sitting room, it may initially have been thought to have been the wrong decision. But that was of course before the Matriarch of the home had reached inside her hidden drawer within a drawer, and in dramatic fashion, produced an impressive looking semi-automatic pistol. A .45 revolver with a camouflage coloured handle. One which seemed to have been deliberately purchased with her notable colour coordinated fashion sense in mind. This Kimber Super Carry Pro matched her expensive gold trouser suit, and calf length, cinnamon and walnut Burberry coat beautifully.

As she carefully raised the gun, there was no sound of panic or alarm in her rich voice. She had with forethought, weighed up her options very carefully after listening to her daughter's concerned remarks on the answering machine. Having quickly sussed that things were amiss and that a potential intruder or attacker was in her property - it was either flight or fight? And this housewife was far from desperate. She had no intention of flying anywhere. Except First Class with a glass of champagne, to exotic, sunnier climes. She had never once shirked a fight in her life. Her family of two boys and a girl were always encouraged to stand their ground, to face up to bullies and never be intimidated. And as for her current trespasser, it was indignation in her voice he was about to hear, not fear!

"Have you any idea what you have just done you foolish man? How dare you make this personal? What outfit are you from? You will never survive this and there is no going back now you know."

Her invader remained surprisingly unfazed.

One minute she was a good looking, friendly, fashion conscious widow. The next, meet the notorious, gun-toting Bonnie Parker. Half of the iconic crime duo: Bonnie and Clyde.

"My son is a good man," she said in a refined, rather pronounced, upper-class brogue. She stared at him intensely. A further ten seconds of unbroken eye contact passed between them. Becoming harsher and much less ladylike, she reiterated, "But I suspect he will slice you into tiny pieces and feed you to his pet fish." Raising the level a further notch and with a far more sinister and disturbing tone, she then added, "Actually, it's odds on he'll quietly feed you to his pet fish, and THEY will tear, gnaw and devour you into tiny pieces. That's piranha for you, don't you know!"

"Yor laddie doesnae aan any fish!" Was mumbled aggressively in a distinct accent from beneath the mask.

"True," she said with a satisfactory grin. Then without hesitation she added, "Ah well!" Arm raised and extended, she swivelled quickly, pointed the gun and pulled the trigger.

"Now that's interesting," 'Sherlock' mumbled aloud. He had searched for and found the incident report detailing the fire that Mrs Jordan had died in. It had been signed off as ARSON. But not only that surprised him, but the actual date that it had occurred on. "Nobody thought that worth mentioning," he again vocalised. Although two colleagues at a desk just a few feet away did give him a rather random joint stare.

"What! Can't you see I'm on a call," he insisted. As he held a single finger up to one ear.

They nodded, were appeased, and went back to chatting.

She died in a fire that was deliberately set alight and at a very specific time of year, especially for Scots! For some reason that dogged determination and need to be satisfied kicked in. So 'Sherlock' then cross referenced the date of that fire with other deaths in similar circumstances and in recent times. Wasn't modern technology wonderful? For before he could even finish that thought, a half page of results had filled the screen.

How many man hours did it take in the recent past to just look through piles of paperwork, to even begin some process of cross reference? And that was just within a local area, never mind results for various other parts of the country. How many killers, rogues, vagabonds and thieves constantly got away with a multitude of crimes? Vagabond - now there's a nostalgic word, a blast from the past. Hanlon's overactive mind had once again gone off at a tangent. How easy would it be or had it become to set up others? He stared intensely at the screen. "Really?" was put out there once again. Murray's catchphrase was infectious. This time, Hanlon's two work-shy colleagues completely ignored him. It was now his vast volume of internal thoughts being mulled over continually. Roads travelled, dots connected and a gamut of clues just waiting to be discovered.

In the last four years, forty-five months to be precise. Either just before or after the 25th day of January. In Burnley, Carlisle, Inverness and Newcastle, all close enough, yet far enough away. And only in that one Scottish area would the time of year possibly even register, or come into play.

Again this individual's desire to understand, to dig deeper, to investigate more fully had become apparent. He spoke at length to the HR department at a certain retail store. Plus he knew that some phone calls to fellow officers down south and up north would be insightful. That was yet another sound, helpful tip learned from DI Murray. His Inspector had constantly reminded him, 'that the information in the file was cold and clinical, very black and white. And although that was great in many ways, it offered no assistance with the on the ground vibe and feel, or with the multitude of complicated variables and suspicions.'

Those considered words of wisdom from a few months back, had taught him that a colleagues intuition and experience can be invaluable at bringing those dormant facts back to life! It looked like 'Sherlock' was in for an exceptionally busy afternoon.

Click, click, click - three dull clunks. No thunderous shots rang out, no bullets emerged at great velocity. Just the lonely, desperate sound of an empty, pathetic, and hollow gun chamber.

The masked intruder shook his head and let out a brief, psychotic laugh before his North East accent burst fully into life.

"Wot d'ya think ah wes searching yor kip fo'?"

He then held out his almighty gloved hand and slowly, one at a time, released six silver bullets. Each metal cylinder parachuted softly onto the plush Saxony carpet underfoot.

"Bedside cabinets, coffee table drawers an' kitchen units are elwis the most popular places people choose tuh conceal their illegal weapons or firearms. They nivvor asked yee that queshtun on Family Fortunes did they?"

Now it was his turn to produce a surprise. For whilst Grandma was busy deciding to rush off to the kitchen to locate her hidden pistol. Her young granddaughter Leah, had been involuntarily introduced to a Geordie gangsters knife. And this was no ordinary, bog standard - 'let me butter your sandwich' knife! Not unlike 'Bunny' Reid's preferred weapon of choice, this was a travelling backpackers dream. With an orange and black handled Gerber fixed blade, it had been made consumer friendly by having the intrepid adventurer Bear Grylls' logo on it. It was a deceptively daunting, dangerous and deadly weapon, and it was currently being held within an inch of an innocent young four year old's throat. A tender, yet exuberant child. One, that earlier that morning had been playfully attending nursery class. Then afterwards headed out and about, shopping happily with her Grandparent.

There she was, not a care in the world. Her enthusiasm and zest for life temporarily stilled. Silent and frightened, her lengthy, braided pigtails hung like two cascading golden waterfalls either side of her lilac anorak's hood. As if shy, protruding nervously from each sleeve were two matching woollen mittens.

'Neeo, neeo, ha abyeut yee an' ah hev sum fun? What d'ya sa?"

The grandmother stood frozen to the spot.

"Firstly tek off yor bloose please pet. Maybe wuh gan frolic abyeut."

She may well have struggled with his Geordie accent. But she understood fully the consequences implied if she didn't obey, as the jagged blade ran smoothly up one of her granddaughters rosy cheeks.

"Or wud yee leek wor tuh carve up this hinny?"

"No, no," she cried. "Whatever you say," was followed up quickly by her designer top being unbuttoned.

"Hoy it owor heor."

She had no idea what he had just said.

His circling arm gesture though, intimated toward him. He pointed the knife at his feet, and the blouse was soon thrown in that direction.

He took a step forward. She immediately raised her arms across her ample breasts and let out a short shriek.

"Calm doon, calm doon. That's neet the kind iv fun aa'd in mind."

Sniffling and the small shuffling of feet could just about be heard over the recent exchanges.

"It's alright my love don't fret. There is no need to worry. Things will be fine," her grandmother tried to reassure her.

The bulky Geordie thug was impressed by her comforting voice and her optimism. But he also knew that she was sadly mistaken. It was rather disappointing to hear grandparents lie to their grandchildren he concluded.

"Gan throo thor," he instructed.

With a rather dismissive shake of the head. Thinking her captor had chosen the wrong door, she arrogantly and regally exclaimed, "that's the door to the garage you imbecile!"

It was out and said before she realised fully what she had done.

His anger was instant and obvious. Without hesitation, he furiously lifted the knife and in a fuming rage thrust it down violently toward Leah's cute, unblemished face.

A wild, repentant scream bellowed from her grandmother's lungs. "No-ooo-ooo!!"

The razor sharp edge sliced, scissor like, through her impeccable hair and a tousled pigtail landed imminently at her Gran's feet. Much to her relief that was all it was.

"Ah knar wheor the door goes. Neeo open it pet. Nae mair o yer lip."

He knew it led to the integral, twin roofed garage and he couldn't believe his luck when she had returned home and parked her car inside it. By that point he had still not decided how to end things. But with the car inside the house, it was now perfect. Although it had to be said, not for everyone.

The young infant was in shock. A combination of tears, frightened laughter and crying echoed out in equal measure. Her captor was a stereotypical bad guy. Was he ever hoping to look inconspicuous in his current getup? He wore dark loafers, charcoal trousers and a polo neck jersey in 'criminal' black. Even the chunky, heavy, fake Rolex added to the whole stereotypical scenario. All that he was missing was some extra bling around his broad, muscular wrists and tattooed neck!

He quickly lifted the key fob from the kitchen worktop and followed his semi clad female guest into her spacious two car garage. The red BMW X5 was a beast of a car. Easily fifty grand plus, and hers was still warm to the touch. A gentle press on the door handle and the supermachine burst into life. Grand-sized indicators flashed, wing mirrors the size of rugby balls flourished and beautiful interior lighting system welcomed you. At this rate, the local cabin crew would be through shortly after take-off with drinks and refreshments. At present though it was just a sobbing child with grubby mittens and a single pigtail, that was placed carefully behind the steering column.

"Just let her go. I'll do whatever you want. Please, I beg you don't harm her. I'll give…"

At that she was bundled head first onto the back seats.

"Lie thor, face doon an' keep quiet. Put yor hands ahint yor back."

"Please, please," she pleaded. "Let her go!"

"Don't yee worry, she is ganin wi' yee. Neeo yor hands."

A pair of aged, wrinkled and regularly suntanned and manicured hands soon travelled around to the back of her body. A plastic restraint was put in place and they were secured. The man in black then opened the passenger door and pushed the seat as far back as it could go. Then he walked around to the driver's seat, pushed a button and lifted out the terrified youngster. He proceeded to repeat the same action with that seat. He had now tilted both backward, easily to about 45 degrees. Making it near impossible for the female in the back seat to turn around, never mind try to raise her body up.

The experienced matriarch grew concerned by this though.

He had said, if her understanding of the Geordie dialect was correct, that her grandchild would be going with her. But nobody is driving this car in those seating positions she figured, and that in itself worried her. Another button was then pressed and a small click sounded. The woman recognised the sound, but couldn't quite place it initially. He shuffled, pushed and slightly dragged the little girl around to the back of the vehicle.

"Will she be rites in heor?"

Stupid, thick Geordies, she thought angrily to herself. What is he on about? She soon realised that the boot of BMW had been raised. A shadow hung over her. 'Will she be alright in here?' They had been his words - and they made sense now!

"No please, don't! She'll suffocate."

Silence. Although the vehicles tailgate remained opened. During all this time Geordie boy had carried her blouse with him. She had never figured out why. Just some weird perverted fetish she had reckoned. A sleazy form of voyeurism she guessed.

But just how wrong she was!

For the bold Shaun Scullion, his next action had become something of a trademark over the years. But not one he could openly own up to on social media. Well, especially if he wanted to remain a free man!

The lady of the house now deliberately lay still and tried desperately to hear the slightest of movements. She recognised something was being unscrewed. That's what the click had been. It was the petrol cap being opened. There was no need to put fuel in though, she had just filled it earlier that morning. Where were they heading off to? Was he syphoning or possibly adding something to the tank? She could hear the slightest of ruffles, accompanied with occasional tapping sounds. But ultimately had no idea what was going on. Although it most certainly wouldn't be her blouse again. That expensive, silken apparel was going down, deep down - In fact, all the way into the depths of the fuel tank. It had been twisted and swiftly encouraged with a long metal rod, hence the tapping sounds. All that was left over, deliberately, was one dry sleeve. It had remained, hanging temptingly down the outside of the oversized vehicle.

"Sleep teet wee yen."

Sleep tight wee one or little one - she understood those words that time. But again not necessarily the connotation. The meaning however, very quickly became very clear and very apparent. Firstly, the car boot was firmly thrust back down. Her heart sank. The garage door then gave a gentle, vibratory rattle as it was activated. On hearing this, the panicked and anxious grandmother cried out, "Leah… Leah! Are you okay sweetheart?"

A cigarette lighter was perilously flipped open. The small, seemingly innocent orange flame, flickered dangerously close to the edge of the petrol soaked blouse.

With her heart in her mouth the aged woman let out one final, terror-stricken scream, "L - e……….a - h."

The electronic door was over half way up when the costly, twisted fabric caught alight. Scullion never hung around. He picked something up and ran at speed straight out into the driveway. When the key fob in his pocket was out of range, the lights flashed, the doors instantly locked and the chilling screams could be heard for several seconds.

That was, until the almighty explosion ripped apart the quiet, exclusive neighbourhood and time stood still.

THIRTY SIX

"The pain of war cannot exceed the woe of aftermath, and the drums will shake the castle wall."

- Led Zeppelin

Back at the station Joseph Hanlon put his finger back up to his ear. He knew expectations had been more than exceeded in the past few hours. A satisfactory, yet mischievous smile crept menacingly over his smug face.

"Thank you mum. I'll keep putting the cream on at regular intervals," he bellowed positively.

This time, nearby colleagues ceased all work and shocked eyebrows were raised! Like an American Secret Service agent, 'Sherlock' strode past them at speed. An earlobe was covered and the wrist of his suit jacket was getting all the juicy intel.

Hanlon's quartet of treasured discoveries had taken him right up until last year in Inverness. It was there, where the victim, a 32 year old female was found on January 23rd with her throat ruthlessly slashed. She was discovered in bushes just off the narrow pathway at a church. It was on a common route for those leaving the popular Eden Court Theatre on the banks of the River Ness. The word 'Borrowed,' was written with lipstick on the inside of one of her shoes. The other fashionable stiletto sat next to her discarded body. The expensive footwear contained a severed ear belonging to the deceased.

In Tyneside the previous year, the body of a young 17 year old girl had been discovered outside a Government office block in Newcastle city centre. She had been a local 'Big Issue' seller in the area, was a familiar face and well liked. The local community were devastated at her brutal death. Her mouth had been clamped open, a funnel inserted and a vast quantity of assorted coins slid down her throat until she had choked, passed out and ultimately died a cruel, callous death.

Then Hanlon had discovered that back in January 2013, a Carlisle family run bed and breakfast had two girls booked in under assumed names. They'd only discovered this subsequently, when on the next morning, the 26th, one of them was found slumped on the rug at the foot of her bed. The bed itself, along with the mattress and quilt had each been ripped and torn ferociously, then saturated in blood. The other girl to this day, had never been found, traced or located.

The furthest back match that the computer had eventually flung up was for 2012. Again, January the 25th itself, and it was in the English market town of Burnley in Lancashire. The victim, a social worker by the name of Tracy Phelps, had been discovered in the early hours of the morning by a council clean up team. She had been abandoned at the rear of the century old Burnley Town Hall, where a busy function had been held the night before. Lipstick was again used. Only this time it was a date written on the victim's forehead - '1st July 1999.' Needless to say, Joseph Hanlon did some more arduous digging - and surprise, surprise! They would not have been so aware of the significance in Lancashire, but again North of the border relevant, very relevant indeed. It was the opening of the Scottish Parliament.

The female HR director that he had spoken to about an hour ago, was worth her weight in gold. Especially after Hanlon had said that the only way to keep this out of tomorrow's newspapers was to make him aware of holiday rotas, absences and scheduled days off. In fairness, he had only wanted the details on one particular individual. He was pretty certain that with that information forthcoming he would be able to keep the company name out of the hands of the tabloid press, and thus maintain the anonymity of his employers. The accuracy of that particular statement was, as his role model and mentor would say - 'Piffle! Absolute piffle!' But it worked.

Wow! Joe Hanlon thought aloud. 'What were the chances?' Based on Craig Jordan's employment record he had had 3 days holiday at that time of the year, in each of the previous four years. One day either side of the dates when the girls were killed to be exact. Now that could be no coincidence. Not only that, alongside the use of lipstick, messages in shoes and garrotted throats were the pictures of the victims. If anything, on first viewing those themselves should have clinched it for 'Sherlock,' before he knew the dates or anything else. Why? Because each female accompanied her footwear with only a blouse, no other clothing! This was it. That was enough. They were closing in. They had him.

Hanlon's query at this point, was this particular year. Why suddenly the spate of bodies? What had changed? And Craig Jordan had requested no days off his work this year. The young Detective Constable had already confirmed that fact in his earlier chat with HR. Now that in itself was a slight anomaly! This time though Hanlon figured, it was on his doorstep, he wouldn't need the extra time off. So that could and should account for that. But why then, so close to home? Why take the chance? Again he questioned, what had changed?

DC Hanlon knew his talent lay in the discovery, in the dig and the unearthing of the facts. His strength was not in the reason why, the clues, the background or what linked the newly discovered valuables. For what they all had in common? He had no idea.

Not one of these historic deaths had ever been resolved. All the cases still remained opened and 'Sherlock' had unwittingly stumbled head first, into murky and dangerous territory. He was now entering a troubled hornet's nest and delving deep within to explore a series of improbable situations. However, in DI Murray's Solutions Handbook, each, although brilliantly disguised would present itself as a 'Great Opportunity.' One that as yet has to be unraveled. Hanlon, without doubt on this sublime occasion, had even exceeded his own expectations this time around!

As his further enquiries, reading and research continued uninterrupted back at his own desk, Joe discovered that the husband (Max Jordan) had started an illicit affair. Seemingly his wife had never actually forgave him. Although on the surface when the investigating officers at the time questioned him about the rumours, he strenuously denied them. His wife still loved him deeply and she then reportedly went after the other woman instead and warned her off.

Could that be the key? Hanlon wondered. The father's unfaithfulness was certainly the catalyst for him to speak to the son Craig. As the eldest child he would most probably have been old enough to have picked up on his dad's schedules and any unusual shift patterns or extra curriculum items on his agenda. As 'Sherlock' read on, indeed, there were two mentions given to Craig Jordan's recollections of his father's workload at the time. But the key observation recalled was that his dad was doing 'ongoing bits and pieces of work on a regular basis for someone called Jean.'

Whilst informing Murray of Max Jordan's gallivanting during a brief phone update. His Inspector praised him profusely. Then his instruction to Joseph Hanlon was to search for any deaths around that time of young females with the surname...

'Sherlock' finished the sentence for him!

"Brilliant work once again 'Sherlock.' After that, go pick up our elusive Craig and give him a free ride to the station. Let's get this all wrapped up and put to bed today. See you soon!"

At roughly three o'clock in the afternoon his mobile sounded. Murray could plainly see it was from 'Barbra.'

"Ma'am," he politely answered.

"We have trouble Inspector."

"Ma'am?" he repeated. This time in the form of a question.

"Another dead female!

Those three words were like a soaring punch to the gut for DI Murray. He'd genuinely felt they were getting close, things were falling into place and coming together. Surely the guilty party would choose to cease and rest up for a period of time, he had thought. They also must have figured that the so-called 'long arm of the law' would soon be descending upon them.

"Leith, Portobello, City Centre, where are we to find this poor girl?" Murray asked.

"Well that is the thing Inspector."

He didn't like the sound of that.

"No. It's just that she is no youngster Steven. I also somehow suspect, that she is no ceilidh goer either."

Murray was confused.

"And for that matter, she was discovered a few miles away from of our most recent series of deaths."

Silence. Murray pondered on her words. Unable to join up the dots in his mind.

"Are you still there Inspector?"

"I won't be for much longer Ma'am. Out with it. What are you not telling me?"

"Well she is of pensionable age."

Murray said nothing.

"She lived near Glasgow."

"And..."

Several seconds passed.

"And?" Murray once again encouraged. "Just spit it out Ma'am!"

"And her son is...!" She then went on to explain exactly who he was, in case Murray was not familiar with him.

The DI had heard none of that though. Because during the past 12 months Inspector Steven Murray was fully aware of who this man was and what he was capable of. It was Furlong he suspected that genuinely needed updated and upgraded with regards the wealth, clout and strength of this criminal deviant.

"Move over Arthur's Seat, there is a new volcano in town," Murray garbled down the line.

"Thank you for those inspired words DI Murray, but…"

"It's erupted," he then broke in. "Like I said it would. He's took his revenge to another level."

"He being?"

"He being? You can't be serious Ma'am? You must know who. He knew everything about you. Including the name of your flaming dog!"

"Reid! Reid? You think this was down to 'Bunny' Reid?"

"Oh, I don't think Ma'am. I know so."

A muted silence prevailed. This time it was Furlong's turn.

"I hope you have a healthy supply of 'expletive substitutes' at hand Ma'am, because I suspect you are going to be needing them. The Reidmeister, one James Baxter Reid has started a war and not just here in Edinburgh. The repercussions of this, the remnants of the slow burning volcanic ash will lie scattered throughout Scotland and beyond!"

How Steven Murray had the appetite for any humour, who knows. But he mustered up enough charm to ask one pertinent question to his new Detective Chief Inspector.

"How well do you feel your first week has gone thus far then Ma'am?"

"**#€+!! ¥€**#? *#%!"

She went with the real thing. Substitutes were not required!

THIRTY SEVEN

"Because I once wrote you love songs, you never fell in love. We used to fit like mittens, but never like gloves."

- Frank Turner

There can be few experiences more relaxing than driving an S-Class Mercedes. In fact, just about the only thing that would top it, is if you were in the back seat being chauffeur driven! With its modern technical advancements the S-Class had always been the car that showed the way forward for Mercedes' design, which meant you were guaranteed sleek powerful lines and a superbly finished, well equipped cabin.

The black, high spec, executive model that had just avoided strewn debris throughout the street, screeched to a shuddering halt only ten feet short of the mono-block driveway. Its 'cabin' door was opened almost instantly by an irate, local policeman.

"Off limits I'm afraid sir. You can't park there. Did you drive through our cordon?"

"I need to speak to the officer in charge," he said authoritatively. The anxiety in his voice was clear. His accent and manner, clipped and brusque. Behind the leather steering wheel, the gentleman had the finely defined features and chiselled good looks of a Hollywood heart-throb. Nevertheless his dark, sinister stare was a cross between that of a Tasmanian Devil and Jack the Ripper. Even although the Whitechapel assailant was never caught and we have no idea of his actual appearance.

"And you are sir?" questioned the rookie gatekeeper.

"I am the man constable that is going to make your life hell by tracking down those responsible for this and cutting out their…"

"I'll stop you there sir. Before you get yourself into deeper trouble."

"Trouble! Trouble!" A good lung filled volley was to follow. "I suspect you'll be the one getting into trouble my good man, if you do not go and get me whoever is in charge and pronto!"

The concerned officer, sensing a serious situation developing, retreated a step and spoke quietly into his police radio.

The reality and shock of the scene he had found himself at, was only now just kicking in. Tugging at his coffee coloured Harris Tweed waistcoat, the Mercedes driver announced without warning -

"The homeowner is my mother officer." With a high level of authority, but this time with much more respect. "My apologies for my earlier outburst."

That seemed to work.

"That's okay sir, I understand."

The young officer then moved closer to get some further relevant details and uttered the extra information down the line. This time his words seemed like a pleading, a request to help and assistant a member of the public, rather than have him carted away!

Dressed exquisitely as ever. The elegant, elevated, slimline figure of one Andrew Scott, watched desperately as his mother's luxury home continued to burn gradually to the ground. The garage doors and roof were gone. A skeletal framework remained in place. Wheels, tyres and a parade of assorted furniture lay scattered across neighbouring gardens and lawns. Every single window throughout the house had been blown out. Glass camouflaged the street. Scorched and blackened debris lay interspersed throughout. How could remnants of the old vintage piano end up on the large, modern island in the kitchen? A toilet seat hung on a hallway bannister like a game of toasted 'hoopla!' Fireman had arrived quickly, but one whole side of the house was gone. The ferocious, tiger and gold flames had been gradually tamed and were now simpering off in retreat. Large black plumes of smoke were first on the scene, due to the car being the initial incendiary device. By the time of her son's arrival, the cloud of smoke was a dirty grey …… and Andrew Scott was worried.

Where were his mother and young niece? Don't tell me they were… He never finished that last thought. Two fire crews and appliances that had helped bring the ravaging flames under control, three Police Scotland vehicles, including an unmarked C.I.D car and a lone ambulance made up the total contingent of emergency services in attendance.

Scott's timed arrival during this destruction was purely coincidental. He had actually left Perthshire earlier, after a worried, tearful call from his anxious concerned sister had alerted him to a potential problem. There had been no response from her mum to her repeated messages. So she had no real idea if her daughter was still with her Gran or not. Andrew Scott then had no advance warning as to what to expect, but it was most certainly not this. This, being a smouldering, blackened, charred shell of a building. The smell of death hung in the air and a respectable neighbourhood were in complete shock and fear for their lives.

As a plain clothed police officer approached him, the tall, toned figure slumped back into the driver's seat. The detective held out his gloved hand. He was delicately carrying something. Balanced over the middle finger of his left hand, hanging by a lone piece of wool - were what appeared to be an infant sized pair of scorched and slightly singed, child's mittens.

Angrily, Scott lashed out violently at the steering column. He was devastated, silenced and numb. An emotional tidal wave of tears were unleashed. The actual realisation of what had taken place was only now beginning to kick in. How could this happen? Was it an accident he pondered? The continued turning and tossing of his head seemed to be his immediate response to that query. He needed answers and somebody needed to pay. And who, if anyone - Was in that ambulance?

'Kid' Curry's named flashed up on the Inspector's mobile.

"Sir, I'll have to be brief. Turns out Scullion now actually works for Reid," the low whispered voice announced. "I've went out on a bit of a limb here and pulled a few favours. But it was the least I could do for you. I hope this helps."

Murray said nothing.

"He was told to ensure the dealer was killed to intensify the heat on Andrew Scott," Curry continued. "At that point they had no idea that she was Reid's niece. She was simply destined to be a casualty of war."

"Yes, with the lying, scheming Chrissie (her mother) being the actual rogue dealer," Murray spat out disgustedly. "How did this happen 'Kid?' Because it should have been a non-starter. And where are you? Who told you this?"

Andrew Curry's voice was still low and measured, but grew more nervous with every passing minute.

"Where are you Detective?" Was once again repeated.

Inspector Murray could quite clearly hear shouting and raised voices close by in the background. He had instantly become concerned for the safety of his young officer. The naive 'Kid' had no idea what he'd done getting involved with 'Bunny,' and was certainly no match for the devious James Baxter Reid.

Curry, carefully, yet casually ignored the question, but continued to murmur under his breath. "So initially, Scott's drugs had been carefully sourced and supplied from Newcastle. And still with his close links to Tyneside, Scullion got wind of this and saw the opportunity to move up the chain," Curry paused, as if about to be overheard.

A heartbeat or two of estranged silence filtered through the airwaves.

"Andrew are you okay?"

Curry carried on, once again disregarding the question.

"No time sir, listen up. The highly ambitious and ruthless Geordie thug in exchange for a territory to run, then happily informed 'Bunny' Reid of the full details regarding shipment quantities, dates, etc. Alongside being given some 'overtime!' Which included a few more physical tasks and assignments. Scullion needed no persuasion. He willingly accepted the deal, took the money and swapped sides and allegiance in an instant."

Like many old traditional values in society, loyalty amongst thieves had long gone.

"Greed, wealth and power now rule the roost 'Kid,' you should know that by now," Murray confirmed to his young foot soldier. "And since the demise of Kenny and Sheila Dixon, the Reidmeister was ensuring his reign for the foreseeable future by continually extending and strengthening his empire's foundations." He then ended his brief communication with Andrew Curry. Adding some simple, yet sincere words. "My house. Tonight, eight o'clock. Everyone will be there. And wherever you are 'Kid,' be careful!"

THIRTY EIGHT

"There's just one thing that I forgot to mention. What have you got to lose when you know - you're guilty 'till proven guilty. Isn't that the law - Guilty 'till proven guilty, that's what we saw."

- *The Boomtown Rats*

" ……… I'll let him know Jim. He's busy in an interview right now, but thank you again for the update."

Barbra Furlong hung up. The call had been from her west coast equivalent, DCI James Cavanagh. Chief Inspector Cavanagh wanted to inform DI Murray personally, that they had been made aware of a certain Mister Andrew Scott now actively on site at the Newton Mearns wreckage. Both his mother and young niece had been presumed killed in the devastating explosion and unsurprisingly, he was now threatening severe repercussions. Murray was right, she thought. His personal experience with Reid had taught him that there would be a major backlash. A volcanic eruption or some such terminology he had used. Her mind began to race. Where will it all stop Barbra Furlong questioned. Cardwell. Jean Scott. An innocent child. Who's next? And where?

"This time you've been cautioned Mr Jordan. You have a lawyer at your side and trust me, if you thought the walls in the last room were closing in, you ain't seen nothing yet. Because by the time we are finished with you today young man, you'll be wearing your clenched buttocks as bright, rosy red earrings!"

DC Joseph Hanlon tried rather unsuccessfully to holster his smile. Murray appeared back on form. Twenty minutes earlier the constable and a colleague had arrested Craig Jordan in front of his workmates at their Ocean Terminal retail store.

"I thought we were past all this," Jordan continually repeated. "That earlier in the week we had sorted everything?"

"Sorted everything Craig! Oh, I apologise if that was what you read into your release a few days ago. If I appeared to offer you false hope."

Jordan looked confused.

The lawyer offered, "Inspector?"

"What? We just never had enough evidence to proceed against your client then. But now we have and you can thank Constable Hanlon here for that Mr Jordan!"

Hanlon blushed for a multitude of reasons.

"What new evidence? I keep trying to tell you both - I've not done anything wrong?"

"I never said we had new evidence Craig, just not enough. Now we have facts, figures, days and dates that have been apparently uncovered and brought to light. Fascinating! And DC Hanlon here, is our star tracker and archaeologist. He loves a good exploratory dig. And this time he has unearthed one or two rather spectacular gems for us to consider. Feel free to sit back and give us your input," Murray encouraged. "Constable, he's all yours."

Jordan's eyes closed. His bony elbows that were swallowed up in a trendy woollen jersey, rested firmly on the desk. The tips of his manicured fingers rubbed feverishly at his brow. Here we go again he thought. In perfect syncopation as his fingertips came to a stop, his thumbs began massaging carefully on his temples.

"We ascertained the last time," Hanlon began. "That you attended the same ceilidhs, purchased the blouses that the dead were found in and recognised their photographs."

The sweating palms of Jordan's hands now fully supported his forehead. The frequent, non-stop, left to right movements had begun again. Muted sighs and groans could be heard, but nothing coherent.

"We have your fancy camera remember Craig? Complete with traces of blood. Your tennis racquet strings are a definite match for two of the victims."

When Max Jordan's son had been brought in, he had been wearing the latest plimsoll shoes and no socks. His skinny tight, beltless jeans were all the rage. And his loose fitting, dark brown v-neck sweater with one large singular white hoop, completed this seasons fashion statement on behalf of Top Shop.

"This room is definitely shrinking Constable Hanlon. So maybe we should get to the juicy bit a little quicker. The new... sorry... the old evidence... that you just recently rediscovered."

"Apologies sir, yes, right now," 'Sherlock' said nervously. "We are going to go back about four years Mr Jordan."

The DI then made a bold, audacious gesture with his two hands, holding them eighteen inches apart, before gradually and slowly, closing them together. "People like you disgust me!" He yelled from nowhere. His hands continued to shrink the room.

Beads of sweat ran involuntarily down the accused's cheeks. What did the Inspector mean by 'People like me?' He then frowned dejectedly as Hanlon began to recite specific days, dates and places. Craig Jordan's eyes narrowed in recognition. What was going on here? Genuine worry and concern were now etched upon the mans face. His swallowing became more intense and much more frequent.

Newcastle, Inverness, Carlisle, Burnley he was aware off. Those dates sounded right, but he would have to double check. That though, was were his accurate recollection of those events ceased. Hanlon had went on to mention - Lipstick, the Scottish Parliament, a bloodied bed, coins in a throat and a severed ear. Several other horrific descriptions were offered up, but Craig Jordan had fully switched off by that time. Protestations had resurfaced and now he was once again desirous to fight his corner.

"Those dates that you mentioned, they sound correct. The locations, absolutely I was there, but so was my father. He accompanied me."

A look of confused intrigue was briefly shared between the two officers.

"But the deaths, the killings, the names of the females - No, no, no, no, no! That has nothing to do with me. We were at shows, having meals, celebrating the New Year together. They were Christmas gifts."

"Was it just meant to be abuse Craig? Maybe you simply took it too far? What about the clues? What significance part did they play?" Murray persisted.

"You are not listening to me. Either of you. What clues? I have no CLUE what you are talking about Inspector. What is all this about abuse?"

"The child's building block! The tiny compass! The red flower and the soft toy!" Murray expressed wearily. "Ring any bells?"

Silence - That familiar shake of the head was coupled this time, with a look of undeniable incredulity. Disbelief in other words.

The Inspector seemed somewhat off his game. Frustration and pettiness appeared to have crept in. It wasn't like him Hanlon thought. But then again, 'Sherlock,' fully aware of the evidence he himself had built up and uncovered against Craig Jordan, still felt something, no idea what, but something just didn't seem to fit. Gut feeling was a very real experience altogether.

Both he and the Inspector recognised and were fully confident that Jordan had not even known anything about the blouses being purchased on his credit card, until it had been pointed out to him. With that said, Hanlon had also agreed with his boss that Craig Jordan had been hiding something from them from day one. And the continued abuse of his sister would still seem like the outstanding candidate.

"Listen son," Murray pleaded. "I deeply suspect you are going away for a very long time. Because innocent or guilty, we have no one else! And all the overwhelming evidence points clearly to yourself." Murray gave him a wave of his hand and then offered further instruction to 'Sherlock.' "Alright DC Hanlon, take him to a cell."

Hanlon turned abruptly.

Jordan sat upright, "What? No! You can't be serious?"

"Deadly serious Mr Jordan. Do you think we've just been messing around with you all this time? This is all getting wrapped up in the next twenty-four hours and you're going down for it!" he then confidently declared. After which, he looked again at his young protege and uttered, "Alright Joe, he's all yours."

That was twice now Murray had used that word in a matter of seconds and it triggered an idea in Hanlon's overactive mind. A little bit unorthodox, but it was one last shot worth taking for all the parties concerned.

"Do you mind if I try something sir? Hanlon asked cautiously. "I think it may provide us with a few answers. I just need Craig here to assist me in one particular task."

DI Murray said nothing. But his fervent curiosity had certainly been piqued. He smiled, nodded decisively and waited with interest.

The nervous tension in the room was palpable. This was a risk worth following through on 'Sherlock' had hoped. The inexperienced legal aid brief Craig Jordan had, was way out of his depth and feeling under extra pressure by the minute from all the relevant parties concerned. DI Murray sat rather smugly at present. He had long held a particular view with regards to this man's guilt. So it would be interesting to see what his noble lieutenant came up with!

"Craig I need you to do me one favour. It's a pretty unusual ask. But if I am proved right, I think this precise action may clear you of all charges."

"What! Are you being up front with me here? Is this genuine? For real like?"

Joseph Hanlon stood up, bit on his lip nervously and with sincerity stated - "I believe so!"

"So what do you need me to do? Jordan asked more excitedly than at any other point in their interview. "Of course I'll do it, if it proves my innocence. What do you need from me? "

"Remove your shirt and trousers please sir," Hanlon then requested in a firm, yet professional manner.

"Wow! Whoah." Jordan cried, pulling his body backward.

"Constable?" DI Murray echoed. Slightly concerned at this turn of events.

"Trust me here sir. And Mister Jordan help me. Don't back out on me now."

As the anxious young man went to undo the top button of his jeans, he noticeably flinched. His eyes darted momentarily toward Joseph Hanlon. It was a look of recognition. He now knew that he knew. His hands stopped instantly and returned, palms down, onto the top of the desk once again. And once again he began to visibly perspire.

'Sherlock' shook his head. "It's over Craig. It's time to open up and admit it. To be strong and accept it. To rid yourself of any guilt, dark secrets and heavy burdens that may well go hand in hand with it. Remove your clothes," Hanlon again rallied. This time his voice was forthright and persuasive.

Jordan then exchanged a quick, concerned glance toward his lawyer. Possibly looking for some wise counsel or support. Sadly for him, the man in the pinstripe suit, pursed his lips tightly together and shrugged!

"Do the right thing son," Murray encouraged. Having no idea where Hanlon was going with this.

"For goodness sake, look to save yourself Mr Jordan. And let us get on with finding the real killer!" Hanlon expressed impatiently.

Murray looked anxiously across at 'Sherlock,' opened his fingers wide and brought down both palms from chest high. "Calm yourself Detective," he quietly expressed.

Throughout those verbal exchanges, buttons were being revisited. The older brother's long sleeved, navy blue shirt had been laid flat on the small table that sat in the corner of the room. Murray's eyes carefully scanned over the upper torso of the man with growing unease. He still was not quite sure of the relevance.

"Constable?" Again the one word echoed out clearly as a question.

"All in good time sir. All in good time."

THIRTY NINE

"Love when you can, cry when you have to. Be who you must, that's a part of the plan. Await your arrival with simple survival and one day we'll all understand."

- Dan Fogelberg

"There is enough there in that report to at least suspend him sir, if not charge him."

The investigating DCI listened carefully to Mare offer up his rather irrational and somewhat biased recommendation. But David Cleland bit down heavily on his lip, contorted his face and sighed for the umpteenth time that day.

"If this becomes public knowledge we'll get slaughtered," the angered face of Inspector Mare felt the need to re-emphasis.

"I won't throw him to the wolves," Cleland stated. "Others may have that as their agenda, but I'll not be the one to do their dirty work. He's been an invaluable officer throughout the years. Sure, he's been a little unorthodox at times. Even gone close to the line on numerous occasions," he offered a wry smile to himself at that last comment. Knowing full well, that Steven Murray had veered well across it several times. "But he's a good man, an honest man. He has dedicated the best part of his life to locking up the bad guys and I'm sure not going to be the one that takes away his badge."

"But…"

"No buts man, I hope he continues to stir it up for another decade at least. Long may he continue to ruffle a few more feathers with the brass upstairs - Hell mend them and good on him. It's more than I ever had the courage or bottle to do! Let's get out of here and head home Jim. This is over."

Inspector James Mare looked a worried man.

The accused Top Shop manager stood upright, slipped off his shoes and allowed his skinny, cream denim jeans to snake gradually to the creaky linoleum floor. Feeling somewhat embarrassed and self conscious and with only the skimpiest of briefs covering his modesty, Craig Jordan then went to sit back down.

"No, apologies Craig, but please remain standing just for one more minute sir. Difficult as it may be. It will allow DI Murray and myself time to ascertain exactly the extent of your injuries. We are also going to have to get a doctor in to take a closer look at you shortly."

Craig Jordan began gradually to slowly and nervously turn full circle. Mr James Campbell-Smith his inexperienced lawyer, appeared to study the floor more intensely at this point. Simply unable to witness for any length of time his client's damaged body. Even the more experienced Inspector held a hand over his mouth in shocked revulsion. A cultivated tear or two began to run down the humiliated man's shallow, lank cheekbones.

From his badly scarred chest down to his tortured thigh, this man's body was a street map of affliction and agony. The various shades of blues represented motorway connections. Expressways and private tolls ran from discoloured midriff to shredded buttocks. Dual carriageways travelled east to west, from imperfect testicles to the groin area. Scattered intermittently throughout this region were blackened motorway services.

With intense swelling complementing the fading green and yellow bruising, it was obvious to all that it must have been exceptionally painful to get around. Mobility was bound to be a serious problem.

Joe Hanlon nodded. It was exactly what he had guessed. But ten times worse.

Mr Jordan grabbed at his dishevelled clothes and this time sat back down.

"Joe?" Murray questioned through gritted teeth.

"Remember the very first night we visited with him sir? How we got a flash of more than we expected?"

Steven Murray grimaced. The merest shoulder movement acknowledged that particular memory.

"Well, I guess I never turned away as fast as you did that night," Hanlon remarked. "Because I noticed then, the substantial bruising around his abdomen and genital area. I've since watched this relatively thin and fit thirty-something," he pointed at Craig Jordan. "Limp around, continually hindered, each time we've met with him. That, along with small, barely audible ooh's and aah's, made me suspicious that he was always in some form of constant pain."

Again Steven Murray went to question the whole point of this conversation.

"Detective Hanlon, will you please…"

"He is gay sir!"

Silence.

If looks could kill - DC Joseph Hanlon was a goner and

flowers for the graveside would be arriving later that day. As Jordan continued to stare daggers at Hanlon, Detective Inspector Murray seemed rather taken by surprise.

"I tried to give you the opportunity to come clean several times," Hanlon remonstrated. "I pleaded with you to own up Craig. You had ample time. But you chose to remain silent."

Rubbing thoughtfully at his mouth and chin, DI Murray spoke in a quiet and considered tone. "So you were not doing the abusing son. You were the one being abused." He then raised his voice slightly and groaned, realising his massive error in judgement. "I am so sorry Mr Jordan," he continued. "Truly I am," he offered in the most humbly apologetic manner.

"It all changed after our mother died," Craig Jordan sighed. He then slumped forward after hearing Murray's admission of remorse. His head buried deep down in the folds of his two bare arms. Arms that cleverly and carefully had been kept free from any beatings.

"Earlier sir, twice when you said - Alright! It clicked with me. I remembered when you were stabbed. The kindly doorman that supplied us with towels that evening, he said it also. But I had heard him utter it one time before. Last week in fact."

He then paused for effect. Taking another invaluable tip from his Inspectors training manual.

"Go on then," Murray insisted, "Enlighten us."

"It was our initial visit to their flat last Saturday night," Hanlon enthused. "As we ascended the stairs, a man - complete with trendy beard at that point was making his way downwards. He used the same expression and cordial greeting then. Later, the next week when he assisted with the towels, he was clean shaven. But the same man, definitely. Of that I have no doubt. Ain't that correct Craig?" He mischievously threw into the interview.

Jordan junior looked up, but remained silent. He then proceeded to re-dress, pulling back on his crumbled jeans and shirt at least.

DI Murray felt comfortable enough to toss in a couple of possible observations. "So your buddy was leaving your flat Mr Jordan. Because your father was due home? Possibly, because he was never in London that day was he?"

Jordan again failed to speak. This time he was busy replacing socks and shoes.

"That would be the often drunk father," 'Sherlock' added. "The often drunken father that had been arrested years ago for being a homophobic thug!

Craig looked at him in amazement.

"Oh, I read all about it, earlier today sir. Not the most forward thinking of people your dad? Eh!"

On Murray's side of the desk, an immediate rethink was required. Craig Jordan was now outed as gay. His father homophobic. That was not a good combination. The son had tried reasonably successfully up until that point, to keep his private life secret. No wonder he was always on edge and nervous. He was simply continually trying to disguise things. Desperately trying to hide his sexuality, his parenthood, his beatings and his possible involvement in any of those deaths!

He'd panicked when his boyfriend or one night stand had only just left the family flat minutes before the police had first visited. His agitation caused by the thought of his father returning home early Murray guessed. Especially if he'd had a skinful. Because when his dad got drunk or never came home until the next morning, it was Craig Jordan that seemingly had been the one getting physically abused.

The four corners of the jigsaw were once again needing rearranged. Surprisingly, they seemed to be falling nicely into place better than ever before. It was the mismatched, slightly askew, outside edges that DI Murray and his team later that evening were now going to have to seriously revisit.

FORTY

"Sometimes you tell the day, by the bottle that you drink. And times when you are all alone, all you do is think. I'm a cowboy, on a steel horse I ride. I'm wanted dead or alive, wanted dead or alive."

- Bon Jovi

Outside the beautiful detached bungalow that nestled in the Campsie Hills on the outskirts of Kirkintilloch, Detective Chief Inspector David Cleland had just arrived at his garage. Before he could even exit his vehicle, a call came through on his mobile from the ACC - Assistant Chief Constable Robert Beckett. What now he thought to himself. Had his whinging colleague already complained about his decision regarding DI Murray to those in authority. Whatever it was, he ensured he took an impressively large intake of air before answering. After only thirty seconds he was deflated!

"Twenty minutes ago sir?" he questioned with alarm in his voice. "I was only with him less than two hours ago. I stopped to get some bits 'n pieces on the way back…" he hesitated. Cleland's face had gone chalk white. "At Riverside Drive you say. He could only have been ten minutes away from his Dundee home."

"That would appear to be accurate," the distant voice on the line relayed to him.

"Stationed outside sir? Okay, I'll look out for them. But I don't really think… Oh, okay for the next few days. Thank you sir, if you feel that it is necessary. Sure, I'll hear soon. Thanks again for the heads up, I appreciate it. Yes, absolutely. Bye for now."

The experienced officer remained upright, still and motionless in his driveway for the next ten minutes. A multitude of thoughts, images and remarks from that morning played out on his mind's loop system. It had been an average working day up until then. Nothing out of the ordinary. They asked questions, conducted interviews, sought out the truth as they always did. Tried desperately to decipher fact from fiction. It really had been an average day he concluded. That was until now. Less than an hour ago, DI James Mare was found in a compromising position in a lay-by on Riverside Drive, Dundee. They had no CCTV, no witnesses and no initial leads. But the position he found himself in was - behind his steering column, with a deadly gunshot wound to the forehead.

He'd obviously had every right to be worried earlier!

After what had been an exceptionally busy day all around for everyone, the 'Doc' was searching for his coat and scarf to head off. Steven Murray stood, hands in pocket at his sitting room window and looked out thoughtfully into the winter darkness. A disturbing assortment of dark questions, depraved thoughts and theories worked overtime in his mind, as he awaited the arrival of his fellow colleagues. He watched with interest as several runners in their bright, luminously attired athletic frames, jogged steadily by. Immediately he looked down at his ever increasing midriff and smiled contentedly. In that precise moment, he had just realised how much those keep-fit fanatics had inspired him...... to close his window blinds!!!

It was shortly after 8.30pm when the rather dated, white, UPVC front door to the Inspector's house was opened and his visitors filtered in. Did you hear about DI Mare seemed to be the consensus of the discussion. Murray had been busy texting the troops all day to rally their support for another late evening 'brainstorming' session. With the lone exception being Andrew Curry. The 'Kid' having been invited during their mysterious *'cloak and dagger'* phone call. Hearing of the demise of DI Mare was disconcerting. For not only did Murray take an instant dislike to the man, he felt for sure he was corrupt! It was just something in his manner. The things he was concerned about. The questions he asked and his overall aura. Murray had been around enough bent coppers over the years to recognise certain little tell tale signs. Surely, David Cleland had his suspicions the Inspector questioned to himself. No doubt there was lots about to come out in the coming weeks. I suspect they'll have plenty more to worry about than me, he smiled to himself.

"Sure, I'll leave you all to it," Doc Patterson shouted, whilst exiting Murray's sitting room. He had arrived at seven o'clock for his catch up and to add his tuppence worth!

"T'is is your t'ing, all t'is investigation malarkey," he sang generously as he disappeared back down the corridor. "Goodnight all!"

Walking in briskly to take the T'inker's place had ventured officers Kerr, Boyd and Hayes. They had even brought a specialist consultant with them. Although this one was not from the medical profession - Robert 'Ally' Coulter (Private Investigator) was the penultimate body through the door. He was soon followed by a pretty weary looking Joseph Hanlon. It was he, who after everyone got seated was about to begin the discussion.

Noticeably absent was DC Andrew Curry. This concerned Steven Murray gravely, although just as he began to think the worst, the doorbell rang.

"Sorry folks, I got caught in traffic," uttered the dulcet tones of the individual, lovingly referred to as 'The Kid.' A reassured Detective Inspector offered a silent sigh of relief of his own and proceedings then got under way.

"Was there a natural link between the two hostelries that Melissa MacLeod and Laura McKenzie had been found at folks?" 'Sherlock' enquired. Doing his best to accurately recall both girl's names, because that had always been a pet peeve of his Inspector. There was no way that we should forget the names of those assaulted, raped or murdered, he would regularly state. If it meant referring to a notebook or whatever, he had no problem with that. But at least make the effort to show and treat those people with the respect due. For in the vast majority of cases, they and their families had genuinely gone through complete hell.

"Different parts of the city," 'Hanna' answered. "Separate ownership altogether. One was part of a large multinational group. The other, a small family run concern," Hayes further confirmed.

"The Starbank Inn and Cup of Kindness. Both corny names if you ask me," Curry aired. "But all to their own."

"So, no dance or ceilidh links?" Hanlon reconfirmed.

Eyebrows narrowed all around. What was he getting at?

"I was thinking more touristy," he said. "Like maybe they ran a small shuttle bus to our favourite ceilidh once or twice throughout the night."

Hayes and the others then soon nodded, having a much better understanding of what 'Sherlock' was now alluding to.

"We never even asked," 'Hanna' said. "Though we can easily double check, but I would doubt it. We certainly never saw any coaches or minibuses at any of the premises. Also, if they did run such a service I would think it would be more likely at the height of the tourist season, than the chilly, baltic depths of January!"

"No, bus service!" Boyd shouted, holding aloft his phone. "I've just checked."

"Why no clue for this one?" Hanlon once again piped up. Deliberately changing the focus.

"Yes, 'Hanna' and I were both thinking that exact same thing," 'Kid' Curry added. "During our drive yesterday that actually was our main topic of conversation. It wasn't the norm."

Joe Hanlon then confirmed this with his Inspector. "That was right sir, was it not? So far nothing glued to her body or left by her side? No soft toys, children's plaything or any other helpful item discovered?"

There was a brief, noticeable silence. Sandra Kerr who had not spoken thus far, had witnessed this on numerous occasions past. Having spent several years previously at Murray's side as a hard working constable. Now all six curious heads turned in the direction of their commanding officer. He smirked, scratched repeatedly at his cheek and twitched his nose in a rather 1970's 'Bewitched' manner. They all recognised, the all too familiar pose.

DI Murray started slowly - with the slightest of American accents... in talking mode initially... before steadily increasing the pace and volume slightly. For his trusted minions, it was a sight to behold. It was always an indication to - A major breakthrough!

Their DI opened his mouth - *"Raindrops keep fallin' on my head. And just like the guy whose feet are too big for his bed, nothin' seems to fit. Those raindrops are fallin' on my head, they keep fallin' - Nothin's worrying me."*

Cries from various sources all bombarded him at once.

"How come?"

"What gave it away?"

"Raindrops! What's the clue? Really!"

He tried to placate them. He gestured for peace and quiet. But another wave of questioning lashed over him.

"From what?"

"Did you already know?"

"There was nothing said! Help us here!"

This time DI Murray shook his head, pulled his hands shoulder high and lowered them gently. Hushing his colleagues into the bargain.

"Thank you."

Silence then re-entered the workplace or living room to be precise.

"Kid, you are probably too young for it to have any significance," Murray stated and smiled.

"None taken," came the reply, Hanlon, Kerr and Hayes shouted in unison.

"But it was your polite pronunciation that alerted me."

Andrew Curry looked at him intensely, with one eye closed and a squinted mouth.

Nope, he wasn't getting it Murray realised. Some extra help was required.

"Remind me. Where was Laura McKenzie found?"

"Outside of a pub in the middle of the night," he replied cagily. "I don't…"

"The name of the premises?" Murray encouraged.

"The Cup of Kindness!"

"Yes, exactly." Murray nodded. "That is precisely what you said the first time. But looking at the images here in front of me on my phone, that is not strictly correct is it?"

Allan Boyd was once again quickest of the others to react. Whipping out his mobile, Boyd confirmed, "Cup O' Kindness the outside sign read."

"Not OF?" 'Hanna' Hayes queried. "What difference does that make sir?"

"Absolutely none," Andrew Curry jumped in. "Because the apostrophe stands for an F, we all know that. So, OF is exactly what it stands for," he re-iterated passionately and firmly.

DI Murray remained quiet. Once more his group of six troubled 'troubadours' turned toward him with humbled, ambiguous faces.

"Go on then," Curry eventually said disappointedly. Knowing full well when he was beaten. His shoulders sagged, "Enlighten us!"

"You are right of course 'Kid.' Normally the missing 'F' would be of no real consequence. But sadly, when we have been up to our necks in Burns Suppers, ceilidhs, shortbread and haggis! This time, I think it is absolutely significant."

"And Raindrops Keep Falling on…" a female voice offered up.

"That, alas 'Hanna,' has no link to anything," he smiled. "However, the line - *'Nothing seems to fit,'* came swiftly to my mind. Because now lots of other little inklings, vague notions and a rather tentative hypothesis that I had been playing with, do seem to come together quite nicely."

"You're saying I read it too poshly?" Curry quizzed.

Murray took another sharp intake of breath, before beginning with a familiar song chorus. *"For auld lang syne my dear, for auld lang syne…"*

His eyes darted quickly to Hanlon. A number 14 nod was clearly given and 'Sherlock' responded smoothly in a slightly higher key with…

"We'll tak' a cup o' kindness yet, for auld lang syne."

"He did a great job in making us believe that it was his son," Murray put forward.

"You are telling us that it's not Jordan?" Curry exclaimed. "But I thought the evidence was overwhelming?" he continued.

"It is," said 'Hanna.' "The dates, his days off, all of the purchased blouses, etc!"

"You would think. But mainly circumstantial," Joe Hanlon reminded those gathered.

"So not Mr Jordan?" Andrew Curry repeated. This time shaking his head for good measure.

They all looked for a final time at Detective Inspector Steven Murray. He duly smiled, shrugged and added, "Oh, absolutely - A Jordan… Just not Craig! You two cowboys mount up," he said staring at 'Hanna' Hayes and 'Kid' Curry. "Take a posse with you if you have to. But make sure you bring Max Jordan back to the station in the next half hour and leave him to stew overnight. Because he is most certainly wanted!"

"Dead or alive?" Hayes asked.

Smiles all round at that one.

As the western pairing rode off into the sunset via a standard Police Scotland motor vehicle, Joe Hanlon threw his head from side to side and declared - "I don't get it sir. I mean I knew the ending to Auld Lang Syne. But the overall significance, Max and not your favourite *'piddly feel.'* Nope, I'm at a loss."

"I've every confidence," Murray smiled. "Neither do they! They just drove or rode off delighted to get their man. But I'll bet you all that by the first set of traffic lights they'll stare at each other, look back to the road and drive on in silence to Max Jordan's flat. Each thinking the other knows. When in actual fact - none of them are any the wiser!"

All those that remained in the room laughed heartily, as they pictured that wonderfully humorous scenario playing out in their respective minds.

As Steven Murray began to share some thoughts, he firstly addressed his long term colleague Detective Sergeant Sandra Kerr.

"'Sandy,' do you remember from your brief visit to the exhibition in Ayrshire any of the lines from that epic poem Tam O' Shanter?"

Both Boyd and Kerr looked quizzically at their superior, before heads were nodded.

Their helpful DI added, "In particular, where the witches are dancing as the music intensifies and upon seeing one particularly wanton witch in a short dress, he loses his reason and shouts, 'Weel done, cutty sark!'"

"Well remembered," Kerr offered. "You certainly got some beneficial study done in that hospital."

Murray nodded acceptingly. Although having studied that poem in his 4th year at High School also helped.

Allan Boyd then added, "But that surely wasn't talking about or referencing any boat at that time, was it?"

"The fully renovated vessel located now in Greenwich was built nearly one hundred years later," Murray voiced. "So safe to say a definite NO to that DC Boyd."

"In the poem, from what you just said, it would seem to be referring to an an item of clothing," 'Ally' Coulter added with uncertainty.

"It would 'Ally' the Inspector confirmed.

'Sherlock' had interestingly remained completely silent up until that precise moment.

"Is this going where I think it is going?"

Punching out his next few words as broken questions. Half in excitement, half in sheer disbelief! Because he was just figuring it out.

"The - witches - top? The - alluring - garment - that - she - wore?" he said patiently and deliberately. As he continued to vocalise, a realisation and dawning came over him.

"It was her night shirt!" he exclaimed.

"Of course it was," Murray nodded.

He continued with. "For each of the victims it was a night gown - he dressed them in a short blouse - In true Robert Burns terminology… a flamin' Cutty Sark! We have been surrounded with all the Burns references," Murray suggested. "Unsure of their relevance. Fact or fiction, purely coincidental or what? But now, most definitely, they are very much the crux of the investigation. I'll need you to take the lead on this tomorrow Joe." Steven Murray then stated firmly. "'Sandy' you and DC Boyd will be travelling to pick up Lucy for assault and battery. And of course 'Ally' will…"

"I'm no longer a cop remember Steven."

"If you had let me finish Mr Private Investigator. And of course 'Ally' will be too busy flirting with our new DCI."

As winks, nudges and smiles were offered throughout the room. Coulter himself initially screwed up his eyes at that supposedly cutting remark. Then as he appeared to ponder on the words, he shrugged, grinned and offered a gracious, accepting nod. Thinking that not a wholly unreasonable proposition.

"Speaking of which 'Sherlock,' his Inspector added. "See if our 'Barbra' will sit in with you whilst you chat to Mr Max Jordan. If the rest of you want to go, I am just going to bring DC Hanlon up to speed on a little conjecture I have in relation to Craig Jordan's father." No one moved. Not one inch. They all wanted to hear this.

"Well, let us begin with that simple Cup o' Kindness."

DC Hanlon lowered his chin and offered a clenched movement of his mouth as he proceeded to close over the room door fully. And although no words were verbally exchanged, it clearly said - That will do nicely sir. Thank you very much.

FORTY ONE

"We'll drink a drink, a drink - To Lily the pink, the pink, the pink. The saviour of the human race. For she invented medicinal compound, most efficacious in every case."

- The Scaffold

By next day, DCI 'Barbra' Furlong had agreed to 'babysit' Joseph Hanlon in the interview. 'Sherlock' had been well briefed by Murray the night before and had taken plenty of notes. Let's just hope I can remember most of it, he thought to himself.

The middle aged man was still reasonably mild mannered, considering he had been kept in custody for the last twelve hours. He had been quietly confiding in his lawyer. Although as soon as Furlong and Hanlon entered the interview room, Max Jordan asked boldly, "Why am I here? What has happened? Surely there was no need to keep me in overnight? Where is your boss? Murie or Moray, or whatever he calls himself?"

"Detective Inspector MURRAY was in hospital sir. Someone attempted to murder him…" Hanlon offered politely.

"No way," Mr Jordan instantly exclaimed. "That wasn't me! You can't pin that on me." He then added desperately, "I was at home. I was with Craig. Speak to him. He'll vouch for me."

"No need sir. We know that you didn't do it. That is not why we've brought you in. However…" At that, Joseph Hanlon paused.

"Thank goodness," Max Jordan said in a relieved voice. "So why am I here?" he then added, more confused than ever. "What is this all about Detective?"

It was time to hear the graceful, sweet, reflective female tones that belonged to the station's newest Chief Inspector.

"Murder sir. It's all about murder. Or rather, a series of murders to be exact."

When Detective Sergeant Kerr and her colleague arrived at the Afton Drive premises, Lucy Jordan had just coloured her hair. She was in the midst of towel drying it when the doorbell sounded. The bright, fluorescent pink now matched perfectly many of the art student's bedroom accessories - lamp shade, wall quote and pillowcase to name but a few.

Shocking pink may even have been how Allan Boyd described it. He had only seen snapshots of Max Jordan's daughter previously. But the high cheekbones, pale complexion and brand new candy floss finish, did not seem to do her justice. Other photographs definitely portrayed her as a well toned athlete, someone more familiar to regular exercise and gym workouts. Boyd then began to wonder - just how recent were those images? On the other hand, maybe it was the rather worn, loose fitting beige sweatshirt and bottoms that did her a disservice!

When arrested by DS Kerr, there had been no angry remonstration, no instant denial, no physical reaction whatsoever actually. Certainly not the expected response of a sister being charged with assault on her brother. 'Surreal,' would appear to be the unspoken word exchanged between the two police officers as they positioned the young girl into the back seat of their patrol car.

She offered nothing - No resistance - No sound - No emotion.

As Boyd drove he adjusted his rear view mirror and viewed Lucy Jordan regularly. As he watched her throughout the journey he was struck by her focus to stare out through the rain spattered windows with intensity. Every street, house and storefront - Every blackened lamppost, tree and bus stop seemed to require a second glance and further inspection. Childlike - as if it was all brand new to her. Had she suddenly reflected on her father being taken the previous night? On the days, dates and places that she was intimately aware off? Thoughts that maybe he was never actually where he said he was at times? But, back in that moment, at home, she was just delighted and happy to have at least one parent return to her.

As they dutifully arrived back at the station, they knew things didn't quite feel right. But they had no idea just how much of an understatement that would turn out to be?

Max Jordan had quickly sobered up as the list of women he was being charged with murdering was read out to him by Furlong. As his victims were named aloud, he gave the impression of a beaten man. He initially grimaced, but after that brief show of contrition he showed no further emotion whatsoever. He had seemingly no desire to discuss the events and saw no merit in hiring a defence lawyer. Although one had been provided nonetheless. His recent past, a decade of grief and angst had taken its toll and he was clearly at a tired, burnt out stage where he just wanted to accept the consequences of his actions. His body language said as much. Over the next twenty-four hours he would hear the various allegations and theories behind his crimes repeated, reworked and regularly reviewed to ascertain a more accurate pattern. But ultimately to get the real truth of what genuinely happened and why - they would need Max Jordan to confess all.

"That is a lot of bodies Mr Jordan," Joseph Hanlon stated. "A lot of violence, a lot of pent up rage and anger."

DCI Furlong listened carefully, watched his response. Of which there was none. But more importantly, she kept her own counsel.

"What had brought it all to a head in the last few years?" 'Sherlock' asked. Not really looking or expecting an answer. But by way of trying to simply engage him. "More so in the last few weeks to be precise? Why suddenly so many girls? You were well organised and methodical. The clues were obscure and dubious, without being totally concealed and hidden. But they were at least contained annually."

Jordan shrugged.

"You wanted us to find them this time, didn't you? Ultimately you wanted us to find you?"

Still nothing.

"Inverness, Carlisle…"

"Burnley and Newcastle," the frustrated Jordan finished. "I know, I know, I heard you the first time son. What's required? Where do I sign?" the broken builder shouted. "You lot should have locked me up years ago," he bellowed. "Never mind asking me why. How come it took you guys so long to figure it out?"

'Sherlock,' nodded. Interesting he thought, before continuing with, "It all stemmed from your house being burned to the ground ten years ago didn't it?" Hanlon began. "I discovered in the last twenty four hours that the Fire Brigade signed off on it as arson. But your poor wife died in that fire by allegedly falling asleep smoking a cigarette. So there was no way the police were going to pursue it any further, if everything seemed to check out. Which it did! Because they could never prove whether your good lady set it alight deliberately or not. Whether she was fully alive or sleeping at the time? And there were no other witnesses to corroborate or deviate from that version of events."

That made Hanlon look up. "She was asleep," he insisted. "I was always told she was asleep."

"I'm sure you were sir. But when I asked Doctor Patterson to take another look at her files, he told me in no uncertain terms that the results indicated that she was very much alive and possibly moving about. That was based on the smoke inhalation in her lungs. If she had been sound asleep, there would have been substantially less damage to her vocal chords and upper respiratory areas."

Jordan appeared alarmed for the very first time. This was news to him. But you could see he did not quite understand what it meant.

"She was alive Mr Jordan. She had not fell asleep on the chair at all. She was trying to stop someone else and ultimately was pushed onto or collapsed into the chair, overcome by smoke and fumes."

A single tear of self pity, regret or genuine remorse began to steadily make its way down Maxwell Jordan's flushed cheek.

"Is that what you meant when you said we should have locked you up years ago?"

Jordan's aching eyes were firmly sealed shut. Hanlon was convinced he could see the tiniest vibrations under his eyelids flickering away, replaying all that night's tragic events in his head and asking: Why? Why? Why? Why?

This time it was DCI Furlong's turn to purse her lips and try to remain calm. She had desperately tried to remove the mental image of that hard working housewife being burned to death. But had failed miserably. High definition pictures flashed into her mind. She could feel her thumping heart pound at the initial fear and scorching pain. The emotion of sudden helplessness. The inability to escape and then to be rapidly overcome by smoke. Finally, 'Barbra' Furlong envisioned the poor woman being fully engulfed in flames and passing out - never again to regain full consciousness. The cuff of the DCI's blouse, briefly met her moist eyes.

"It would appear that everyone survived, except your wife sir," Hanlon offered tenderly. "With hindsight, that probably seems incredible."

Jordan swallowed hard. He glared up cautiously at the young police officer as he walked around the room Steven Murray style. Then the direction of his gaze changed and he observed DCI Furlong. As yet another solitary tear embarked on a mission toward the neck of her collar.

In turn, she noted that this man seemed to take everything Joe Hanlon threw at him. She found this slightly disturbing. In all her years of experience those who sat in that seat always had something to say. They may well have held their hands up and admitted to a variety of misdemeanours and heinous crimes. But they liked to correct you on certain things and strenuously deny others. They needed you to understand, to empathise with them, to see the bigger picture and what their role really involved. It was a type of 'Big Man' syndrome, Furlong figured. They would want you to know - Why this was different and unique. Nothing like all those other cases! Just listen and wait until you hear my story - my background - my justification!

And that in itself, is exactly what made this slightly more intriguing, fascinating even to Detective Chief Inspector Barbra Furlong. Because their deeply fragmented Mr Jordan, was not interested in entering into or expressing any of that kind of dialogue whatsoever.

For currently he just sat impassively with his elbows arched tightly on the desk in front of him. His chin rested steadily on the interlocked fingers of his raised, calloused hands. A workman's hands, a stonemason's hands, the hands of a master tradesman!

'Sherlock' stated confidently - "From that day forth you set out also to be a Master Freemason!"

Again, Jordan seemed surprised that Hanlon had managed to accrue such knowledge.

"Having been an actual stonemason it didn't take you too long to make the leap. By all accounts, your study and desire to learn came before anything else, including your grieving family Mr Jordan."

Max momentarily felt the need to speak up. But at the last moment reigned himself back in and remained silent.

Joe Hanlon nodded toward Furlong before continuing. So he had recognised his vocal omissions she thought. Good for him.

"You'd been an apprentice mason for twelve months previously according to your son. And your daughter then informed us that you succeeded in becoming a Master Mason, just nine months after the fire. How about that? Within a year of your wife dying from 'Third Degree Burns' you became a fully qualified 'Third Degree Mason.' That is what they are called right? A Master Mason or Third Degree Mason?"

The slightest of heads movements offered confirmation of such. 'Sherlock' grinned. He had every confidence that Max Jordan's personal pride would ultimately kick in and that he had to acknowledge his elevated rank and position.

"Freemasons have long since been regarded as a secretive society with arcane rituals," Furlong interrupted. "Does that sound about right to you Mr Jordan?" She then added pleasantly.

DC Hanlon could see that she had a desire to continue her comments. "Please..." he offered. "Feel free."

"Well," she paused. "Some dismiss it as a club full of funny handshakes and raised trouser legs, but to others it is the heart of the establishment that pulls strings and wields real power behind the scenes. I mean at one point, probably more lawyers, judges and police officers were Masons than fully paid up union members!"

Anne Thomson, his legal counsel in the room tried desperately to stifle a laugh at that remark.

Furlong continued her fine form with, "Did you know Mr Jordan that Sir Robert Moray - a Scottish soldier, statesman, diplomat, spy and natural philosopher - joined a stone mason's lodge and many consider that to have been the moment when the freemasons began."

The other three heads in the room all shook in awe at the sheer wealth of trivia knowledge this quirky woman so obviously possessed.

"Just saying!" She announced.

Now, feeling rather unqualified, DC Joseph Hanlon tried his best to continue. "Coupled with the status progression within your fraternity and again according to your family and the enquiries we made. You soon developed a deep rooted passion and fascination for the Scottish poet and lyricist Robert Burns, better known throughout the world as The Ploughman Poet - Rabbie Burns."

Hanlon paused for any further acknowledgement. But Max Jordan had returned to his sombre, silent ways. 'Barbra' Furlong simply closed her eyelids in unison, Hanlon took that as - 'Well Done!'

"You'll be aware sir, often in this line of work we get to wear many hats." Hanlon gestured. He intimated taking off one piece of headgear and replacing it with another. Furlong gave a slight scowl, but she had guessed from whom he had taken that little piece of showmanship.

"This is my wacky psychologist's cap. Do you like it?" the detective asked.

Jordan's expression hardened. It portrayed that he was less than impressed.

"It allows us simple policemen to speculate. To revisit the events and offer our theories on what we think happened. But I would be more than happy for any input or correction you would like to offer Mr Jordan."

Again, nicely dealt with DCI Furlong thought.

Hanlon had noticed the slight upturn at her mouth. The mere hint of a smile helped his self confidence no end as he continued on.

"Possibly suffering with your guilt as well as grief and remorse, you decided within six short months to move home. Surely then, after being inspired by your new found love and admiration of the Bard's work, it was no coincidence that you moved into your current home on Afton Drive."

"Speaking of coincidences, I have one I think you'll like Max."

Hanlon glanced at her in a slightly surprised, taken aback manner. Using the man's christian name seemed a tad unusual to say the least. But in fairness, he had not heard the coincidence yet.

"It's rather sad," the Chief Inspector continued. "The Bard's youngest son was born on the day of his father's funeral, 25th of July 1796."

Jordan's scrunched up face obviously indicated that he could not see any connection to anything.

"Oh, sorry," DCI Furlong explained. "That's not the coincidence. It's the fact that the child's name was Maxwell!"

Hanlon had certainly done his homework also. For without any written notes or a prompts, he continued with - "*Flow gently, sweet Afton, among thy green braes. Flow gently, I'll sing thee a song in thy praise.* The opening lines of Afton Water Mr Jordan. By a certain Robert Burns no less!"

Jordan's eyes offered a modicum of respect.

By the time Detective Inspector Murray had arrived to interview Lucy, the loan agreement to lock up Max Jordan and throw away the key had been signed, sealed and delivered. The Procurator Fiscal was happy to proceed on his confession and the relevant evidence that they currently had. And they were also convinced of a lengthy sentence being handed down. A good day all round the prosecuting legal team seemed to think. As an added extra, they were also confident that in the coming weeks they would be able to procure a deal with Craig Jordan into providing and giving evidence against his murderous father. Thus, making their case even stronger still.

Barbra Furlong was admittedly impressed by DC Hanlon's style, poise and manner throughout the interview process. However in fairness, the accused Max Jordan, did make it a fairly straight forward 'slam dunk,' by finally admitting to the crimes and being willing to 'fess up. Even more striking though to DCI Furlong was the impressive fact that Detective Inspector Murray had so much confidence in his fellow subordinate officers. How magnificent was that she thought. She knew she'd been told in advance that not only was HE a character, but that it was also an invaluable trait that he possessed. So it was lovely to witness it first-hand, even if it was second-hand so to speak.

Hanlon concluded their questioning with, "Either in poem or song, you immersed yourself fully in the works of that great man. Furthermore, sadly, you continued to drink heavily. Coming home drunk most evenings. That is of course, if you came home at all."

Maxwell Jordan's 'Respectometer' seemed to be lowering again!

"That would have been when you first began to do lots of voluntary work on an old, historic, clipper ship. The very one that had been damaged by fire while undergoing renovation work in 2007. The vessel had been one of the last tea clippers to be built on the River Clyde in Glasgow. And of course its name now resonated with your new found passion."

Quickly mimicking the catchphrase of the long running BBC television quiz show, Mastermind, Hanlon said: *"I've started, so I'll finish...* The life and works of Robert Burns!"

FORTY TWO

"Thank you for the days, those endless days, those sacred days you gave me. I'm thinking of the days, I won't forget a single day, believe me. And though you're gone, you're with me every single day, believe me."

- Kirsty MacColl

This past week DCI Barbra Furlong had certainly hit the ground running. Nevertheless she never managed to get to her rank in the force without being prepared. So in the last 48 hours she had taken a crash course in the deeper intricacies of the case and DI Murray's thoughts, feelings and hunches. As she sat across from Maxwell Jordan she found herself pondering on a few observational thoughts.

Without fully realising it, she reckoned that this seemingly gentle man had grown estranged from his two children. Both Craig and Lucy with a decade between them in ages, felt abandoned by him after their devastating house fire. They had lost their mother and up until those tragic circumstances befell him, by all accounts their father had doted on his children. Further investigations had shown that he had been a naturally generous and loving man. As a family they would regularly go for walks, venture along country trails and head out on exhilarating weekend adventures. They would excitedly visit parks and museums and generally spend time together. Fun and laughter was always high up their priority list.

Life can be oh so cruel at times Furlong considered. The hopes, dreams and ambitions we may have for our valued loved ones can be dashed in an instant, and not just figuratively speaking - But literally go up in flames. When the Chief Inspector mentally rejoined the proceedings DC Hanlon was still in full flow…

"… it was easy enough to avoid Craig, knowing he was at those ceilidhs and that they were always jam packed. Even if he had bumped into you, you could have made up any lame reason to have been there. Such as: You were heading down south on a job, or you just wanted to drop something off for him… a plethora of valid excuses could have been used. Initially you used your business card with the ripped edge that you had scraped on that poor dead girl's fingernails, to make sure we visited your flat. Because you were still in Scotland. Your phone locator sir, told us that half of your so called English visits didn't even happen. Modern technology, don't you just love it?"

Max Jordan seemed to have aged by a decade or more in the last several minutes.

"You even had full access to Craig's credit card details. But why then would you not take advantage of his staff discount if you were buying from your own store? We found that interesting." Hanlon made a puzzled face, before adding. "Although, why buy them online or in-store at all and leave a paper trail. A paper trail you would think even the dumbest of police could easily trace and most certainly then ask questions about! Sorry, if I were the manager of that store, I think I could have easily just taken a few items home with me without anyone even noticing.

DCI Furlong also seemed to spot something in Max Jordan's eye. But she thought it was it was puzzlement. He had no idea where 'Sherlock' was going or what was coming next. Neither had she to be fair.

"Like I said, you became obsessed in renovating The Cutty Sark. Not only was it a world renowned clipper ship - but in Burns' Tam o' Shanter - the cutty sark was a night shirt or night dress. In modern terminology even, we would describe it as a blouse." Hanlon slowed, his voice defaulted into whisper mode. "That Sunday evening when you offered us a drink, it was Cutty Sark whisky." He regained and upped the volume control with, "This has all been about Burns. Redemption for both you and him I suspect! That framed picture in your home that DI Murray much admired - 'The Ancient of Days,' I believe Craig told us it was called. The figure with the large compass at his hand. Stunning imaginary there sir. In fairness, it was Detective Inspector Murray that finally twigged to the symbolism in the clues. The oldest Masonic symbol is the square and compass. It is also the most recognised. How well you managed to meld the Ploughman Poet and Freemasonry and in truly spectacular form give us - Third Degree Burns!"

A finger in the room was raised. "I actually know that work DC Hanlon," Barbra Furlong interjected. "The image was used as the cover for Stephen Hawking's book *God Created the Integers.*"

"Really? Ma'am," Hanlon heard himself state.

"Yes constable, and there is no need to sound so surprised" she said. "Did you know Mr Jordan that it draws it name from one of God's titles in the Book of Daniel?"

The design by William Blake, who many of his contemporaries considered mad for his idiosyncratic ways, showed Urizen (the man Murray mistook for God) crouched in a circular manner with a cloud-like background. His outstretched hand held a compass over the darker void below.

"In the complex mythology of William Blake," Furlong continued. "Urizen was the embodiment of conventional reason and law. He was usually depicted as an older, bearded, caucasian man. Sometimes he held architect's tools, thus explaining the compass on this occasion. That was to enable him to create and constrain the universe. Were you trying to constrain the universe Mr Jordan?" Furlong then asked flippantly, disgusted by his refusal to co-operate vocally. "One young woman at a time?"

Hanlon offered a few seconds respite. They seemed to be digressing. But he certainly could not fail to be impressed by his DCI's knowledge of the arts and culture. He then mentally gave himself two further minutes to draw some form of reaction or connection from this dangerous, deluded man.

"The soft toy glued to the hand," he said. "On first viewing we all thought that it was a rat Mr Jordan."

Still nothing.

"On further reflection, we deduced that it obviously represented Burns' *To a Mouse,*" Joe Hanlon declared. "The Cup o' Kindness pub, very good sir, that was impressive. It could have been easily missed, but we got there. It of course, was part of the lyric to the Bard's worldwide anthem - *Auld Lang Syne.* The kid's cube was a square - it went with the compass and those two combined were symbolic of freemasonry. The fraternity to which our Rabbie was also a part of. The beautiful flower in the hair? Again a Burns favourite - *My Love is like a Red Red Rose*."

Hanlon kept it coming hard and fast. His voice firm and accusing, filled with a passion for justice and a knowledge of what he spoke.

"Then of course - Newcastle, Burnley, Carlisle and Inverness. All of those New Year jaunts that coincided with Craig being off on holiday. So yet again we thought that it was your son who was the culprit. Why did you feel the need to frame him? To set him up for all those crimes? What kind of MAN was he?" Hanlon prodded.

But no takers. Still nothing. Just a beaten, aged male. One that had dramatically grown old in front of the two officers in the last ten minutes.

"This time however," Hanlon continued. "We quickly recognised the Burns stamp of approval connected to each of those deceased girls."

At this point, Furlong herself was intrigued. For this was the first time she had heard about those old cases. This would be a major feather in the cap for everyone if they were able to wrap up not only, all these brutal deaths, but also a number of other unsolved murders into the bargain.

Hanlon continued apace. "Burns was an exciseman, a modern day tax collector. And it was outside the Inland Revenue offices that a seventeen year old was discovered in 2014. She had choked to death after being forced into swallowing a bucket load of coins. Ring any bells sir?"

Barbra Furlong swore she briefly spotted a tear well up in Max Jordan's eye. Why was that she wondered.

"Last year it was Inverness. Two years before that Carlisle. Thankfully there at least, one of the girls managed to escape your evil clutches at the bed and breakfast."

Maxwell Jordan dipped his head. His shoulders fell and his upper body creased onto the desk in front. A faint yelp could be heard. Gradually it developed into a sob. But Hanlon, as much as it pained him, had learned from the best and was unrelenting.

"A few belated tears doesn't make up for it Mr Jordan. You were at it even as far back as 2012, where I found a visit to Burnley. The same brand of lipstick we've ascertained was used throughout the years. It would have been probably the only occasions you used it. So no surprise it had lasted a few years. That was enough of a connection in itself, to say at least that murder and the one in Inverness three years later were linked. And coincidently once again, it was during one of your road trips with your son! What were the chances? The date on the victim's forehead read: 1st July 1999." Hanlon then felt rather daring with this one, but had belief and every faith in the recipient of his invitation.

"Ma'am?" he asked. Nodding over toward his superior officer.

Detective Chief Inspector Furlong inwardly applauded his bravado, cheek and possibly even his misplaced confidence. She then pondered on it for a second or two before giving it her best shot.

"Mr Jordan, I would assume our clever detective here, is referring to the official opening of the Scottish Parliament. Which if memory serves me right was opened by traditional folk singer Sheena Wellington, giving us her rendering of

Robert Burns' - *A Man's a Man for A' That*. Now was that what you were looking for DC Hanlon?"

"Absolutely Ma'am. I never doubted you for a minute."

His boss smiled at that.

"Burns, Burns, Burns and more Burns. You certainly developed a very unhealthy appetite there Mr Jordan. But what if we leave Ayrshire for a moment."

'Sherlock' paused. He had only just realised that the man had stopped crying and had once again looked up to concentrate on his words. Interesting he thought. But I'm not sure how he'll like this?

"You had an affair sir, is that right?"

That certainly got a reaction from Max Jordan. His eyes intensified. They followed DC Hanlon as he took two paces forward and immediately sat down opposite the master mason.

"When your dear wife died in the fire, the death certificate stated smoke inhalation. Even although the official Fire Brigade findings were arson. At that time you were going out regularly with another woman, correct?"

Still a wall of silence. Both officers could see he was desperate to share something, but he just would not or could not commit.

"Like I said previously, that doesn't necessarily mean that she was asleep at the time. I personally have no doubt that she suffered greatly. That she would have been experiencing unbearable pain. Desperately and anxiously fighting to survive."

Jordan sat upright. You could literally feel his heart thumping at the walls of his chest. His giant hands turned white as he gripped, first the desk and then the chair beneath him, fiercely trying like crazy to stay in control. Hanlon was getting to him. This time, now, eventually brick by brick, he was infiltrating his faltering defences.

"Do you think she was trying to stop you from setting the place ablaze?" he continued. "Or was she trying to stop someone else? Maybe we'll just never know. Never get to uncover the actual truth. I'm certain someone knows it Max. In fact, I think that someone - is you! I believe you know the truth Mr Jordan. But you are just too scared to share it, or possibly admit it. To shed light on those poor girl's deaths, to resolve the mystery of why, why, why?"

On that note, it looked like DC Hanlon had decided to have a break. A decision which was merited DCI Furlong thought. It would be good to regroup, speak to Murray, get an update on any other information received and let Maxwell Jordan stew just a little longer. In which time, maybe he would come to his senses and co-operate. She also thought that was interesting terminology or phrasing that Hanlon had just used... *'or possibly admit it.'*

"Oh, and just one more thing Mr Jordan," Hanlon said. "I managed to track down your old flame."

Jordan's eyes opened wider than 'the Golden Gate Bridge.' A combined look of horror, resentment and or guilt took over his contorted facial features.

"Sadly it appeared she died not long after your wife," 'Sherlock' continued. "Her name was Jean. Jean Armour you'll recall. Which unsurprisingly, given all the other symbolic gestures you have managed to embrace... was also the name of Robert Burns' wife."

Tears now readily flowed down the accused's reddened, gaunt cheeks. Joseph Hanlon's parting shot before ceasing the interview, was a simple historical question he had unearthed on his explorations earlier in the week.

"Did you know sir, ironically, that Jean Armour's father had also been a stonemason! Strange how often life can come full circle don't you think?"

FORTY THREE

"Chestnuts roasting on an open fire and Jack Frost nipping at your nose. Yuletide carols being sung by a choir, and folk dressed up like Eskimos."

- Nat King Cole

Standing in the nearby corridor at a water cooler, the Chief Inspector extended her smooth and finely manicured hand to young 'Sherlock.'

"Swinging excellent." she said.

"Thanks Ma'am... I think."

Suddenly he remembered her current predilection for avoiding swear words and immediately got her meaning. He then quickly added a more upbeat and confident response.

"I really appreciate it Ma'am. That means a lot to me."

Whilst nodding, "Just one small thing however," she whispered. "Your daring invitation part?"

"Yes," he smiled.

"Just so as we are crystal clear. If you ever pull a stunt like that on me again DC Hanlon, you'll be the one swinging from a chestnut tree without any CONKERS! Understand?" Her sweet, innocent beam, disguised the no doubt real threat from any interested work colleagues. She then walked ladylike, calmly and serenely back to her office.

DC Joseph Hanlon blushed profusely, put his hands in his pockets for reassurance and scurried off for a quick sandwich.

In her recently acquired office Barbra Furlong sat contemplating. The once impressive bouquet of flowers that DI Murray went to great length to deny sending, were now wilting and past their best. She spotted some remnants of the old broken vase glisten up at her from the edge of where the carpet met the skirting. New photographs had been firmly established on her desk. She was gradually marking her territory. It would take her a while however to get things just the way she would like, she knew that. But she was also a bit of a neat freak. She liked order, everything in its place and total preparation. Those were a winning trio every time for her. Yet today, in that interview, as much as she was impressed by Hanlon's knowledge and preparation, as much as she was happy with the order that he'd laid out things to Maxwell Jordan, the last piece of her 'success triangle' was missing. For her, everything did not seem to fit in place. He had offered no resistance and showed no remorse. There was no recognition in his face when Hanlon threw an almighty barrage of points at him, one after the other. If anything, there was surprised revulsion and shock.

It was only at the very end, when the older atrocities in Inverness and England were mentioned, when his affair was brought to light that even a spark of emotion and sentiment broke through. He was still keeping 'it' well under wraps. Although, what 'it' was, remained to be seen. Both him and the son were holding something back she had no doubt about that. Did they possibly carry out those awful deeds between them? Was the wife his, or their first victim? Whatever it was, it was most definitely something personal. Something so important that neither one of them was willing to give it up. As she looked over the photographs of the dead girls for easily the sixth or seventh time, suddenly the hazy mist began to lift and a much welcomed lightbulb moment descended upon her. She would have to check this out further, but...

Gillian McLean... Eureka!

Melissa MacLeod... Eureka!

Debbie Griggs... Eureka!

Laura McKenzie... Eureka!

And finally in Maxine McDonald's high definition coloured image there it was! Right there in plain sight all this time. The lure, the hook, the deadly inducement. As a woman DCI Furlong got it. Oh my! Without pursuing lunch... she got started making further enquiries.

Within forty five minutes, she had summoned DI Murray to her office.

"Steven I hope you don't mind, but when you spoke to me about Lucy Jordan initially and shared your fear about her being abused by her brother, it made me pursue some further enquiries of my own. Quietly and discreetly behind the scenes, you understand."

Oh I understand perfectly 'Barbra,' the Inspector thought. Since that first unannounced arrival at the Starbank Inn, I knew right away - You like to have a finger in all the pies!

"Absolutely," though was the word that he shamefully, actually offered up.

"Well, I've just sat in on DC Hanlon's interview, which went very promisingly by the way."

The Inspector nodded humbly. He had already heard that from the rather chastened, undisputed 'conker' champion himself.

"However, it reconfirmed to me one thing. The need to re-examine the photographs of all the dead girls again." Thus explaining why a selection of multi-coloured prints lay strewn across her desk.

At this Murray said nothing.

"You still have Miss Jordan in custody downstairs awaiting interview for numerous attacks on her brother, right?"

A cautious nod was offered by the DI.

"The thing is Steven, as I carefully studied the enlarged copies that I had requested, I spotted something definitive. This was from a definite female perspective I hasten to add."

The cautious Inspector Murray remained silent, but grew more interested.

"Are you still…"

"Oh yes, I'm still listening Ma'am. There is no need to worry on that score."

"You know that she recently graduated from Glasgow School of Art of course?"

"Some sort of textile, craft and design studies I believe," Murray answered.

The Detective Chief Inspector anxiously offered, "Well, I felt impressed to take a closer look at her coursework Inspector. I was curious and intrigued."

Again Steven Murray remained silent. This time he was taken aback by her beauty. He found himself entranced, carefully admiring her strong cheekbones and dark eyelashes. He had, for the first time only just realised what a good looking woman DCI 'Barbra' Furlong actually was. Was it her taking command of the situation, acting authoritatively and exerting her power that seemed to excite him? Murray had no idea. What he did know though, was to let it go immediately and refocus.

"I think you would have been impressed Steven," she commented. "Lucy Jordan's final year presentation included putting together a charity fundraiser - an exclusive fashion show. It was entitled: The Sneeze."

"The Sneeze?" DI Murray felt the need to reconfirm. "And you feel this is relevant how Ma'am?"

"Because it had an unusual subtitle Steven." Her eyes then furrowed in anticipation.

Not wishing to fully disappoint. Murray reluctantly obliged with, "Which was?"

Barbra Furlong grinned. "Well it was rather curiously subtitled: Ring-a-ring-a-Roses."

"As in: A-tish-oo, A-tish-oo, they all fall down?"

"That is the very sneeze in question," Furlong confirmed. "The gallery where it was performed said that every performance went down a storm. It was one of their most successful student events ever held. Each of its three nights were sold out!

Again, nothing from the normally, naturally inquisitive and talkative Murray.

"Thankfully, the fact that it was so impressive and memorable, made it relatively easy for me earlier to garner lots of facts and info about it."

And still no productive input from her beloved Detective Inspector. This wasn't like him and he was now feeling rather defensive.

"You haven't yet sussed out why this is relevant have you? I can hear it in your extended silence, the unspoken question. What the heck does this have to do with anything?"

"Maybe not quite that bluntly Ma'am, but I was indeed wondering."

Slowly the DCI continued. "She was very specific in her promotional literature Steven. Let me explain that she used a very clever and fashionable play on words, and her models were given an extreme minimalist look."

It was now DI Murray's turn to make big-eyed gestures.

"They wore no underwear, they had no visible panty line," she continued.

Murray did not like the direction that this seemed to be heading in.

"They only wore trendy tops with their heels."

The Detective Inspector then continued the minimalist theme with - "Ma'am?" He spoke only the one word, but it was offered up as a fully fledged question.

"A-tish-oo, A-tish-oo they all fall down," she said warily. Before adding sternly, "We've got the wrong person Steven!"

Initially Steven Murray failed to respond as he took in the enormity of her statement. Then a gradual dawning came over him as he pondered over her stunning words. Slowly he began to whisper.

"DCI Keith Brown got rid of his used... but she used an E didn't she?" His volume increased. "At the end of shoo... she used a flippin' E."

"She did indeed Steven," well deduced. "A-T-I-S-H-O-E Furlong stated. Pronouncing each letter clearly. Then she slowly turned each photograph on the desk around to face the Inspector fully.

"Aaaaaaggghh!! A-tish-oe," Murray grumbled to himself. "All the other clues were secondary. They were like I always said, extras to throw us off the scent. To distract us and take us scurrying in different directions. Mainly all the Robert Burns stuff pointing us firmly in the direction of her father and older brother. Although very clever nonetheless. Alas, it was never about the blouses Ma'am, the so-called cutty sarks. It was all about…"

" ……the footwear!" Furlong finished off for him. "She had worked part-time in a shoe shop for several years remember. What better product to entice impressionable, fashion conscious, dancing girls outside with. It would be every female's dream job to model or pose in certain exclusive, designer brands. Especially with the promise of stock in lieu of payment. Well now her relatives were circling the wagons and trying to protect her. The father - his daughter, and the brother - his sister. It was obvious now, that had been the dreaded, shameful secret that had been troubling them, that they'd been painstakingly guarding all this time. It wasn't an IT after all, that they'd been protecting. They had been safeguarding a WHO!"

Furlong's need to vocalise continued. "That was why on occasion, Max Jordan seemed so surprised and disturbed in equal measure. He literally was only hearing about many aspects of this case for the first time. But his regret at not being a better father had kicked in. For not being there for his children first time around when his wife died. Not this time though. That was never going to happen again he had decided, especially when he realised how serious things had become and the level of charges she would face. This time he would be a proper father and protect her to the end. Hence the silence."

"But from what young Hanlon said, it had obviously become too much for him. He'd had no idea at the seriousness and severity of her vicious, murderous attacks or any inkling that they had been going on since 2012."

"I would concur one hundred per cent with those thoughts Inspector."

Steven Murray's active mind began to throb incessantly. It promptly went into full DJ mode as the devil cavorted with the twisted demons in his mind. His black dog, which had been relatively quiet of late had ran for cover earlier in the afternoon. Yet this troubled man could sense the fiddle player's tune was far from over. Just then in his head the Irish arrived. Christy Moore sang, *'Howsitgoanther, everybody!'* And Van the Man belted out the *'Brown eyed girl!'* For an *'encore,'* they all joined forces and fearfully *'Danced to the reel in the flickerin' light!'*

FORTY FOUR

"Remember times when you put me on your shoulders, how I wish it was forever you would hold us. Right now I am too young to know, how in the future it will affect me when you go. You could have had it all - You, me and mum you know... anything was possible."

- Glasvegas

Finally, ten minutes later, once all the main players had gathered their thoughts and gotten their head around this startling series of events and revelations, the Inspector breezed in in spectacular fashion - like a drunken cast member of '42nd Street!'

High kicks accompanied the graceful running of his long, narrow fingers throughout his short, greying locks. Murray's soothing singing voice then began to gently circulate around the small, rather cramped, although acoustically enhanced interview room.

"At the age of thirty-seven, she realised she'd never ride through Paris in a sports car, with the warm wind in her hair."

'Sherlock' had become well accustomed to his senior officer's unconventional antics and was well aware of DI Murray's often outlandish interview techniques. Today however, he was partnered with DC Hayes, and 'Hanna' was gobsmacked. It was her, more than Lucy Jordan that had been caught completely off guard.

Now in the station for the second time, the young girl seemed somewhat different to Steven Murray. It wasn't just her bright, unmissable hairstyle, but her manner, persona and character he reflected. Based on the substantial evidence DCI Furlong had turned up, he wondered if she was a straightforward schizophrenic? Or in the politically correct society that we currently live, did she suffer from - DID?

Dissociative Identity Disorder was also known as multiple personality disorder. It was a mental illness characterised by at least two distinct and relatively enduring personality states. In fairness, before Murray's analytical brain could put that particular theory to the test or ponder on those specific thoughts any further, Lucy herself spoke up - with a sermon no less…

" …Before you speak to me about your religion Inspector - First show it to me in how you treat other people. Before you tell me how much you love your God - Show me how much you love all his children. Before you preach to me of your passion for your faith - Teach me about it through your compassion for your neighbours. In the end Inspector Murray, I am not interested in what you have to tell or sell - As in how you choose to live and give!"

Her innocent, simplistic and naive smile which followed her comments, made her seem like an extremist. But Murray's own personal faith regularly reminded him that whenever he found himself in a tough situation, he just had to keep being his best and continue to honour his God. He had personally realised a long, long time ago, but had continually struggled to accept, that you have to let go of the ideal picture of what you thought life would be like and learn to find joy in the story you are actually living!

His black dog continued to make frequent unscheduled and unwanted appearances in his life and he still regularly stumbled and faltered. But his God had already given him the strength, wisdom and favour to not only make it through, but to come out better than he had ever been before! So if she wants to go down a philosophical or spiritual route, then let's see where it leads, Murray thought.

"There is a piece of God in all of us Miss Jordan, don't you think?"

She played with her newly coloured hair, wrapping it tightly around her tiny, right index finger. Curling, twisting and chewing on its ends for several seconds. All of which seemed to allow her time to think before responding to the officer's divine question. The five words she replied with though, were unexpected and about to silence the room.

"So is Melissa Margaret MacLeod!"

"What?" Murray exclaimed.

DC Hayes looked desperately at her superior for guidance. Murray sat rigid, frozen to the spot. A multitude of recent interactions were being frantically replayed, fast forwarded and rewound at supersonic speed in his already overloaded mind. The time ticked slowly by. Within four seconds he had it!

ONE - The Sunday night - when he first met her - he thought he'd seen her before.

TWO - What are we investigating - Jordan case - key clues.

THREE - Burns related - time of year - Burns suppers - Haggis.

FOUR - That was it - the Police Burns Supper - the girl serving the haggis - the enticing sign - the triple MMM - Melissa Margaret MacLeod.

What did she mean...........*'So is Melissa Margaret MacLeod?'* Doc Patterson. The spicy haggis. The food poisoning. Her missing kidneys!!!!!

"Noo-oooooo!," Murray vented. His disgust and rage obvious. His fists slammed down, aggressively hammering the desk top. He immediately felt nauseous. "You sadistic psychopath," he continued. "Stay with her 'Hanna,'" he instructed DC Hayes as he slammed the door firmly behind him.

The female officer offered a flurry of rapid eye blinks. Trying desperately to clear her tear ducts which had filled suddenly on the full realisation of what poor Melissa MacLeod must have gone through.

Meanwhile Murray considered wiping yellow remnants of foul tasting sick from the edge of his pale, chapped lips. But gargling his mouth with the tepid, unhygienic tap water in the Gents toilet would have to suffice. The DI now had some serious questions for our quote loving, twenty something female. Instantly, a thought-provoking Buddha reference came to his mind. Lucy Jordan would do well to add this to her collection. Maybe an ideal one for her prison wall...

Our life is shaped by our mind; we become what we think. Suffering follows an evil thought as the wheels of a cart follow the oxen that draws it. And it is a man's own mind, not his enemy or foe, that lures him to evil ways.

As Murray exited the tiled floor of the bathroom, his mind at that moment hastily bade farewell to the spiritual Buddha and waved in Irish braggart, Sir Bob Geldof - *'And then the bullhorn crackles and the captain tackles; With the problems and the how's and why's.'* For instance - How did they never see this coming? And why was this female student able to elude capture for so long?

His crazy and rather erratic machine-gun laugh cackled and shot through the air in wild abandonment on his eccentric reappearance into the interview room. Small droplets of water still ran off his chin from where he had splashed at his face thirty seconds earlier.

"You are most certainly a character Miss Jordan, I'll give you that." A brief thought came into his mind. He rubbed his hands together, excitedly turned toward Hayes and offered. "You took plenty of photos at Blackhall House constable, did you not? I seem to remember you trying to keep DC Curry in check all evening. You probably have some pretty decent material for blackmailing purposes in the future I'd guess."

'Hanna' got the message, produced her mobile and began scrolling.

"Consciously and intentionally setting up both your brother and father. You would have been happy for one or both to have been charged and locked up no doubt. In fact… " Murray continued. "They both were. You so nearly had the perfect result."

'Hanna' Hayes was currently tapping her screen, choosing an album of photos, enlarging them and handing her phone across to her Inspector.

"Is this what you were looking for sir?"

DI Murray manoeuvred the image slightly, adjusting and centring it. "Fantastic DC Hayes that one works for me," he said, swivelling the iPhone around in his hand to show Lucy Jordan.

A knowing smile crossed her face. There was no trace of remorse or wrongdoing whatsoever as Murray pointed to the enlarged image of the girl working at the hotel that evening. Different hair colour, but same good looking girl who had been flirting with all the officers throughout the evening.

"That first Sunday evening both DC Hanlon and I thought we knew you from somewhere. But neither of us could recollect from where." Murray zoomed in on the name badge on her blouse. "Inventive alias, Katie Price - nice choice."

Quickly, Hayes interrupted, "Katie Price! That is the name of…"

"The ex-page three, topless model Jordan. Yes, I am not too old to have known that 'Hanna,' thank you very much."

"I think Jordan or Katie Price as she is now, prefers to be known as an author these days sir."

Murray's quizzical glance at the female detective conjured up a magical little speech bubble on his shoulder which quite clearly said… 'behave yourself!'

As DC Hayes took receipt of her phone back from Steven Murray. The officer then managed a rather disconcerted look of her own. A furrowed brow, pursed lips and an over-active tongue searching both cheeks, signalled some form of alarm with her boss.

"Hanna?" he asked. "What is it? What is your concern?"

"Let me double check something sir." She again began scrolling and tapping on her device.

Inspector Murray considered Susan Hayes to be reliable. She was always particular and thorough. She was probably a generation older in her thinking, manner and dress sense than those of a similar age. If she was concerned about an issue, it would be with good cause. He would value her counsel on return.

"Fire killed your mother," he began. "I figure you blamed your father for that. The cutty sarks, the blouses, very good young lady. Clever. But ultimately we had the wrong accessory. It wasn't their tops or lack of sexy briefs… it was their shoes, their high end footwear - Atishoe, atishoe and they most certainly all fell down."

Katie, Lucy, Miss Jordan, Price or whatever name she cared to go by, was still oblivious to life.

"Tha neart teaghlaich, mar neart arm, na laighe na dìlseachd dha chèile," she spoke.

"For those watching on the video feed, get me a quick translation of that please. It sounds like Scots Gaelic," Murray added.

In a nearby room, DCI Furlong had nodded to George Smith to get on to that right away.

Once again in a soft tender voice the young girl repeated, *"Tha neart teaghlaich, mar neart arm, na laighe na dìlseachd dha chèile."*

Murray shook his head. "That was never Craig's fancy camera. You were obviously the official owner of that fine piece of equipment. You had signed the prints in your hallway, emotive stills from your successful fashion show, your graduation piece. Sensual close-up images of the shoes, teasing pictures of their abdomen and chest areas. Thinking about it now, I guess artistically - that was all about their *heart and 'sole.'*

"Sir," Hayes chirped up. "Speaking of cameras." Thinking that this time, everything was finally sewn up, she was more than a little trepidatious in broaching the subject. However, with a sharp intake of breath she duly returned her phone to DI Murray and pointed out slowly and gradually the time frame that accompanied those pictures of Katie Price, aka Jordan!

"Are you sure these are accurate 'Hanna?' Murray asked, desperately hoping that she would be unsure. But she wasn't. In fact she was one hundred percent confident that her phone settings were all correct.

"That's what I was double checking sir."

"Of course it was," Murray said knowingly and dejectedly.

Both officers stared at each other. Furlong watching nearby on a monitor had figured out exactly what was going on and added a few new expressions to her ever growing vocabulary. *'Ya Greenwich Village Toffee Twiddler'* and *'Turkey Muffling Sandwiches,'* being just two to be going on with! George Smith had returned just as the 'turkey muffling' was at an end. He at least had a smile on his face.

Murray did not do silence. It was by far his least favourite approach. But even he recognised he needing some breathing space. This was not for anyone else but him. What was going on here? It wasn't the dad. They had already ruled out her brother. They had both been protecting her, of that they felt sure. The four corners. The outside edges. Nine hundred and ninety-nine pieces out of the thousand all fitted in place. But alas, she could not have been in two places at one time! There she was in all her glory serving up bowls of 'kidney' enriched haggis at the Burns supper. Whilst the body of Gillian McLean had been abandoned and the fatal attack on Deborah Griggs had taken place. He was at a loss. He looked to his right, DC Hayes sadly shook her head also none the wiser. A knock at the door and surprisingly, in entered DCI Furlong.

"I thought I would deliver this in person and wait and see if it helped."

No extra pressure then Murray thought. His Chief Inspector took four short steps across to his side. He had then expected his commanding officer to hand or pass him a note. That did not happen. Instead he felt the warm breath of 'Barbra' Furlong venture ever closer to his left ear. From about only one inch away, her words were clear, unhurried and concise. Struggling to contain himself from blushing fully, he nodded gently to register receipt of the brief message. DC Hayes took a flustered moment to view the carpeted floor tiles, as her Chief Inspector took up a prime position in the corner of the room.

Murray allowed a stillness to come back over proceedings before asking, "Would you do me the favour young lady of delivering your Gaelic quote once again for us?"

Lucy Jordan looked at her legal counsel, who shrugged and nodded dismissively. She then delicately parted her pink fringe with both hands before reciting confidently: *"Tha neart teaghlaich, mar neart arm, na laighe na dìlseachd dha chèile."*

Steven Murray's response surprised her. "The strength of a family, like the strength of an army, lies in it's loyalty to each other."

"Well done Inspector. That couldn't have been easy via Chinese whispers with your intimate partner there."

This time, both he and DCI Furlong blushed fully at that comment. There was no disguising it.

"By Mario Puzo, author of The Godfather," Murray felt the need to quickly add. "I saw a copy of the book on a shelf in your home. Quite an eclectic literary collection you guys had there I must say."

Why use that quote? And why now he wondered. Unless, he considered, but surely not? Unless it was a cleverly disguised clue - a subtle cry for help. With that now at the forefront of his mind. Slowly, Detective Inspector Steven Murray stood up. He then delivered the translation one more time.

"The strength of a family, like the strength of an army, lies in it's loyalty to each other."

He paused for two further seconds and then openly aired, "I think I am going to put that to the test Miss Jordan."

That remark was met with confused faces all around. He suddenly proffered his hand for Lucy Jordan to shake. He then stood far enough away from her to ensure that she would have to stand up to make contact. As she rose to her feet, DI Murray unexpectedly withdrew his invitation. She appeared totally confused. Murray seemed very certain. He looked her up and down very carefully, before offering...

"I wonder..."

"I'm telling you Lucy has confessed to everything," Murray adamantly declared.

"No she can't have," her older brother responded rather protectively.

"Oh, but she has. Although don't fret Craig, you will still be charged also if that's what's worrying you?"

Having anxiously risen to his feet when Murray burst in through the door, the bruised and battered body of this waif like individual now collapsed back into his seat. The accompanying PC that had been babysitting Mr Jordan had no clue what had just happened.

"The very last piece," the Inspector cried with a distinct level of urgency in his voice. "Give me the final, remaining piece of the jigsaw Craig. Otherwise she is going away for a long, long time."

The patchy, stubbled chin of the crumbled figure in front of Steven Murray slowly looked up. Words began to form, but made no sense.

"You're too late, she's done her time. She'll be well gone!"

"Explain yourself. What are you telling me?"

Through his painful tears, once and for all the broken body of Craig Jordan, broken both mentally and physically, finally revealed the hidden truth.

Ten minutes later and at long last, Murray was eventually in possession of that solitary missing piece. It made him feel lousy. Had he been too distracted not to have spotted it sooner? To have made the connection? Thankfully it did ultimately complete the puzzle. He quickly made a few frantic rushed calls and dispatched several text alerts to colleagues. However, even he felt deep down it would possibly have been too late.

On his way back to DCI Furlong and DC Hayes in Interview Room 1, Murray called 'Sherlock' and instructed him to join them. He then had Craig Jordan escorted there also, whilst he made a slight detour next door and duly invited the lying father to be part of this intimate family reunion!

By the time the disheartened Murray returned with Max Jordan in tow, all the others were already present. Or perhaps, 'crammed in' was a more apt description.

As if beginning the start of a joke, Hanlon felt impressed to share, "How many police officers can you fit into a telephone box?"

Murray sighed. "Patience 'Sherlock,' patience. All in good time."

"He has a relevant point," DCI Furlong was at pains to agree.

Feeling more than a little irked by this, Murray turned sharply toward 'Sherlock.'

"Put aside your poor comedic skills for a minute DC Hanlon and help me out here. Do you notice anything strangely different or perplexing about our young female guest?"

Max Hanlon's eyes turned to his son, but Craig ensured he stared straight at the floor. Lucy for the moment sat impassively. When both her brother and father had been brought in, even her ever-present smile seemed to evaporate momentarily. But surely by offering up that Mario Puzo quote she had hoped that Murray would reunite the family once more. Again the body language experts would have had a field day. They were definitely not comfortable together. They knew they were vulnerable, that something was about to bring their seemingly iron-clad defences clattering down around them, and then the most significant of prices would have to be paid.

Joe Hanlon did not wish to upset his DI any further by stating the obvious, regarding her new outlandish hair colouring. But given her posture and how she was sitting, 'Sherlock' struggled to detect anything noticeably different. Possibly her clothing made her appear slightly wider and her makeup gave her puffier cheeks. But those were just cosmetic touches, they lacked depth and real substance. He knew that Murray would have wanted more than that. He would have been looking for a response that was very specific and unique. And even more importantly than that, he would having been looking for something that was worth bringing this motley crew back together for.

DI Murray could see his young protege was struggling. "No joy DC Hanlon? he said. "Need a little helping hand?"

He gave it a deliberate second or two. Leaving everyone wondering where this was going and what he was about to do next. Craig Jordan still refused to meet his father's burning eyes. Anger, maybe tinged slightly with disappointment was the latest emotion being displayed on the face of the family Patriarch, Murray noticed.

"Miss Jordan can I get you to stand again please, if you would be so kind." His polite tone and cordial way slightly flummoxed the young girl. But then, Detective Inspector Steven Murray more than most, was well used to fluctuating Jekyll and Hyde mannerisms, tantrums and mood swings!

As she calmly got to her feet. Murray could instantly see Hanlon's mouth open in surprise. He knew young Joe would spot it immediately and from his current gobsmacked facial expression, he had done so. Words eventually formed and DC Hanlon exclaimed -

"I couldn't tell sir, because she was seated."

Murray nodded in agreement. "Me too."

"But how is it even possible sir?" Hanlon asked. While the others all looked on in bemusement.

Craig Jordan had finally found the courage to lift his head, just as his father dropped his. Maxwell Jordan knew from that moment on that his family's decade long charade was at an end. In the following few minutes truth and reality and their accompanying consequences were about to kick in.

Failing to restrain herself any longer their new DCI addressed Hanlon directly with, "How is WHAT even possible Constable?"

'Sherlock' - firstly looked at Murray for the okay. His number 43 nod indicated, proceed!

"Well Ma'am, both myself and DI Murray would be wondering - How can that young lady possibly have grown in height since we first met her a week ago?"

Audible gasps echoed all around the tiny room.

"Everyone," Murray announced without further ado. "Let me introduce you to Katie Jordan. That's right not Price, but Jordan."

The room fell silent.

"She is Lucy's identical twin sister - Only taller!"

FORTY FIVE

My evil twin, bad weather friend. They always want to start - when I want to begin. It scares me so - like I scare myself, with that book of Nostradamus up upon my shelf."

- They Might Be Giants

Craig Jordan had earlier unburdened himself and told Murray the complete story, or at least as much as was required. Both father and son would doubtless be charged on several counts for various offences. But the police would still have to figure that out, after having spoken with the Procurator Fiscal.

Although there was no real proof at the time, apart from the Fire Service listing the fire as arson. Her immediate family had been certain that Lucy's younger sister, by all of ten minutes had been responsible. Lucy had seemingly taken the box of matches and cigarette lighter away from Katie just as her father and brother had emerged from their respective rooms out into the flame engulfed hallway. By which point the heavy, dense smoke had blocked any possible rescue path to Max Jordan's wife.

Only weeks after her mother's death, Katie Jordan had been admitted and incarcerated at The State Hospital (also known simply as Carstairs). The hospital is the only one of its kind within Scotland and is located near the rural, picturesque village of Carstairs itself, in South Lanarkshire. The facility accommodates individuals with mental disorder who cannot be cared for in another setting, on account of dangerous, violent and criminal propensities.

For allegedly causing the death of her mother, Katie most definitely fell into one of those categories. Or did she? Both her father and brother over the years, especially Craig, had become more and more convinced that the most violent, dangerous and deranged of his two sisters was actually the one that was still able to roam about freely and unhindered. With the numerous cruel attacks on him personally, he began to seriously doubt the events of that fateful evening had played out the way Lucy had described them. During the intervening years, Max Jordan could not even bring himself to think like that. It would have destroyed him fully if he had thought Katie was innocent. But even with his stubborn head in the sand, given everything that had come to light in the past few days, even he had to finally recognise that rather than confiscating lighter and matches from her sister that evening a decade ago, possibly Lucy Jordan was in fact setting her up.

When Murray had heard Katie quote that Gaelic line a second time. Something registered with him that it was a clue. A desperately disguised, hidden cry for help. Not only had the two sisters lost their mother in that tragic fire. But they had also both lost a sister! 'The strength of a family, like the strength of an army, lies in it's loyalty to each other.' He had instantly recalled the Margaret Mead quote that he had witnessed in 'their' bedroom. *'Sister is probably the most competitive relationship within the family, but once the sisters are grown, it becomes the strongest relationship.'* Once the SISTERS plural, it had read. When he had her stand up, he was ninety-nine percent convinced then that his hunch was right. He just needed Craig to confirm things and put in place that final missing piece. Sadly though that was exactly what Lucy Jordan had become - Missing!

Her brother explained his earlier mumbled ramblings and they began gradually to make sense to the Inspector. And as much as, 'She's done her time,' was clearly in relation to Katie. 'You're too late, she will be well gone,' was his humble opinion in regards to the true murderer in their midst. Or not, as things currently stood.

During his most recent conversation with Craig Jordan it had transpired that both female siblings up until that point, had been the best of friends. As twins they did everything together. They shared in games, fun, laughter and smiles. They confided in each other with childhood secrets, private thoughts and dreams for the future. However, once Katie had been locked up, things changed. Her sister had fully expected to rekindle her close relationship with her father. To be reassured, loved, hugged and spoiled as once before. Lucy had expected things to go back to normal. But in fact, very soon recognised that sadly, she had lost him also.

Her complete nature changed. Puberty and hormones kicked in. Adolescence, social media, literature, boys and a host of other major outside influences began to impact on the cognitive behaviour of the troubled teenager. That was when the resentment toward her brother first surfaced. Craig's life seemed to be going well. His University studies were near completion. His relationship with his fellow band of students seemed to be flourishing. It was then that his young, easily influenced and ultimately vulnerable sister, first saw a mature couple intimately embrace. And although it involved her older brother, no female was on the scene. That had disturbed her already troubled mind. She found it disgusting. From that moment on, her brother repulsed her.

Lucy was growing up. Developing close affinities toward certain groups. She was following movements, forming strong opinions and harbouring firm views on a wide range of varying issues. Eventually though, she was always seeking to get some form of justice and revenge for the devastation of her perceived lost childhood! Her frustration and angst soon found a suitable outlet. Her early artistic leanings enabled her to quite literally create her first body of work! Pounding the defenceless sibling whose sexuality she detested.

Her older sibling, physically took it on the chin at times. At first he thought that it would just be a temporary thing, a young girl's way of coping with her loss and grief. However, it continued and as time passed it became thoroughly relentless. His body would be battered, bloodied and bruised on a regular weekly basis. Lucy Jordan had become stronger, fitter and more capable over recent years. Her part-time job that she had since aged 14, had allowed her the finances to pay for a regular monthly gym membership. Again Craig Jordan had hoped that her frequent visits there would have allowed her the ideal opportunity to vent and release her pent up anger and hatred toward society and less on him. It never worked. Neglected fully now by her once loving father, who in his own way was trying desperately to come to terms with his loss. Lucy had quite obviously in recent years become a deeply troubled and dangerous individual.

Murray had let many clues slip through his grasp on this case. He had become distracted, but that was no excuse and he knew it. On his drive homeward once again the circuitry of his mind changed gears. This time, and even without the encouragement and accompaniment of his black dog his pensive thoughts were wistful and reflective. Depending on how you looked at it, or through whose eyes, Robert Burns had been the hero, the villain, the protagonist, the antagonist, ally, foe or supporter. He was involved every which way, right from the start and on so many levels. Steven Murray remembered some of the biographies he had read in his hospital bed. One informed him unceremoniously, that by the end of his short life Burns was to have fathered fourteen children by six different mothers. Including two sets of twins by Jean Armour. Was that in itself a clue that had been overlooked? When Hanlon and himself had realised that the father was having an affair (another Burns character trait Jordan had innocently or deliberately embraced) they had wisely checked for a Jean Armour. Maybe that was when they should have checked her family tree, found she'd given birth to two sets of twins and thought about that as a possible line of enquiry.

His head was buzzing. There were so many tenuous links. They would never have and could never have second guessed all the obscure Burns references. Many had been build up over the intervening years and were innocent tributes at the time. From Afton Drive to Tam o'Shanter, Cup o'Kindness to Auld Lang Syne. Now only five minutes from the indoor safety and refuge of his house and the futile deaths of loved ones and family relationships hit home. Robert Burns had experienced it two hundred odd years ago, but what about those currently left behind in this great maelstrom of tragic events. All three remaining Hanlon's would face charges. Whilst an intensive search would be ongoing to find the real culprit, the elusive Lucy Jordan. However nothing could compare to the devastating loss and break up of Max Jordan's family. We would never envisage or choose certain routes or future paths for our own children Murray reflected. The stonemason's wife, a young mother burned alive in her home. Allegedly by one of those that she tenderly loved and nurtured on her knee since infancy. But which one, they would never know!

A seriously deranged daughter responsible for the most chilling series of murders witnessed in Scotland in the last half century. In her wake she had left behind family after family. Each one distraught, fractured and eternally damaged. From bank tellers and librarians to loving teachers and carefree students. No longer able to add to their incredible, unique story. The hope of new adventures, memories and treasured moments that would now never be created. Murray himself had witnessed the violent death of his wife and been through the heartache of not only being blamed by his family, but by being ostracised by them also. They gave up on him and his ability to change. Close friends, like 'Ally' Coulter and 'Doc' Patterson had remained loyal and supportive. And even with Joe Hanlon covering his flank these days, all three men often could only watch and spectate from a distance as occasionally, every once in a while, Steven Murray would allow his inner demons to get the better of him and he would self-destruct! As he turned his attention to the well heeled Andrew Scott, Murray briefly pondered on what he may consider suitable retribution? The man had lost a mother and a brother. He had come close to losing a beloved niece. How would he react? What impact will this have on his sister and both her daughters? Disruption was inevitable Murray concluded, but what did the future hold for the Scott clan? On the final approach to his driveway the Inspector had only the briefest of time to dwell on James Baxter Reid. His estranged sister Chrissie was on the run with a basketful of heroine and cash! Would she resurface, maybe for her daughter's funeral? Not a chance Murray surmised. 'Bunny' would have people on the case and she would be held responsible for Christina Cardwell's death. Even although it was her Uncle that ultimately sanctioned it. Now the employer of one Shaun Scullion, the death of Paul Scott was an added bonus in the cleanup of his Newton Mearns mother!

FORTY SIX

"I've got bipolar disorder, my life's not in order. I know I'm not the only one who spent so long attempting to be someone else. Well, I'm over it. I don't care if the world knows what my secrets are…"

- Mary Lambert

Later on his arrival home, Steven Murray reviewed that morning's startling newspaper headline. It began with a big, bold font stating: **'Burns in Bipolar Shock!'**

Murray then read with great interest about recent research that had taken place. It said, *More than 800 letters and journals written by Robert Burns were studied in an attempt to analyse his mental state. The project, which started in 2015, also looked into his personal relationships and day-to-day life. Now a Glasgow team believe they have evidence to suggest Burns' mood cycled wildly between depression and hypomania. They say this might explain the writer's periods of "intense creativity, temperamental personality and unstable love life.*

Aye, all us creative types, definitely have a cross to bear Murray grimaced to himself, as he read the next few paragraphs.

The research, which had initially been published in The Journal of the Royal College of Physicians of Edinburgh, looked at blocks of letters across four separate time frames from 1786 to 1795. The first covered a three-month period around December 1793. This time was specifically chosen by researchers as it was a known period of "melancholia or depression," identified by Burns in his own writing. At this time, Burns' letters show him feeling "altogether Novemberish, a damn'd melange of fretfulness and melancholy...my soul flouncing & fluttering." Two of the letters met the criteria for clinical depression.

Only two, Murray thought. What would they have made of him? What if Hanlon had handed over his last group of A4 documents? He had paid good money to take a hit out on himself! Needless to say it failed, like many things in DI Murray's warped judgement of his life. But our modern day researchers and analysts would have had a field day with it!

He continued with the article.

Moira Hansen, the principal researcher on the project, said: "During his lifetime and since his death, Burns has often been viewed as a tortured poetic genius which helped to explain his reputation as a lover of life, women and drink. But it is only in the last two decades that it has been mooted he may have suffered from a mood disorder." She added: "This project is using modern-day methods to track and categorise the bard's moods and work patterns. The work published in this article shows that we can use Burns' letters as a source of evidence, in place of having the face-to-face interviews a psychiatrist would normally have."

A sudden, solitary teardrop appeared from nowhere and fell gently onto the inky, grey tabloid. A brief shiver came over him. Was it a lightbulb moment or simply the reality of the situation dawning upon him. In the past two years, Detective Inspector Steven Murray had no less than three times tried to take his own life.

Nature, nurture, upbringing and experiences. Who knows, who can say Murray smiled.

"I'm just a creative, big, jammy beggar!" he vocalised out into the ether.

He then paused and considered the politically correct society we currently live in. Could he even make that statement these days he asked himself. Maybe one should really say: "I'm just a gifted, tall, lucky traveller without work!" A cat outside on a nearby window ledge seemed to tilt his fuzzy head to one side, peer in and ask - Is he for real?

Having read the article thus far, he scanned the last few lines in relation to his fellow sufferer's fate.

Prof. Daniel Smith, professor of psychiatry at the University of Glasgow, said: "Carefully assessing the mood and behaviour of one of Scotland's iconic figures, using both medical and literary expertise, is a new approach that helps to paint a picture of his mental health and how it affected both his life and writing. Obviously it hasn't been an easy task given our subject has been dead for more than 200 years. We hope that the possibility that Scotland's national bard, a global icon, may have had bipolar disorder will contribute to discussions on the links between mental illness and creativity. This work might also help to destigmatize psychiatric disorders such as bipolar and depression."

The Inspector closed over the article and carefully placed the newspaper on top of a nearby desk. He silently thought to himself - Bipolar and depression... that Burns chap is in some good company.

With an important day ahead tomorrow, he was just settling down in bed when another call caused his mobile to gently vibrate. Murray had forgotten to take it off silent from earlier in the day. It was his colleague George Smith. He was on front desk duty at the station.

"Sir, sir, we have just had a Detective Sergeant Lennox from Glasgow on the phone."

Murray shrugged dismissively at his end. The name rang no bells. "I don't know…"

"It's the granddaughter sir," Smith interrupted. "She's fit and well. DS Lennox just wanted us to know that a small child, fitting her description, had been left alone at a convenience store earlier tonight on the outskirts of Newton Mearns. Leah is alive."

The much relieved Inspector simply beamed from ear to ear and hung up. George Smith would understand. A huge smile of genuine happiness and relief engulfed his whole face. Although his emotions were also instantly tinged with sadness and regret. Not unlike Christina Cardwell and Melanie Rose before her, young Leah Scott and her older sister Chloe had no control over being born into an underworld dynasty. No one wanted to marry Tracy Scott when they found out that she was Andrew Scott's sister. Her two girls were fathered by different men. Both of whom had scarpered each time, when they discovered who her notorious brother was. It had never bothered Tracy. She never loved any of them anyway. She just longed to be a mother. But being raised in such a world definitely guaranteed an abnormal life. Potential riches, power and influence for sure. But the other tainted side of that coin brought danger, deception and almost always early death. Constantly looking over your shoulder. Keeping yourself alert to the possible threat of kidnap or ransom. It was, as most normal folk recognised - a different world. A world that DI Steven Murray would never have wished on anyone. Leah and Chloe Scott would need all the luck in the world to survive unscathed. And with Chrissie Cardwell on the run with a basketful of soap, the ongoing territorial war between

'Bunny' Reid and the currently grieving and seething Andrew Scott, would continue to escalate, devastate and divide Scotland's capital city.

Meanwhile at the same time across town at Edinburgh's Waverley station, a young girl was heading out of town by boarding an overnight train to London. It consisted of old-style separate apartments. Each one capable of seating between six to eight people comfortably. That was an unexpected bonus for one particular traveller. She herself, had made her choice and was seated comfortably.

"Would you mind if I joined you?" the middle aged man asked in a distinct brogue, as he slid open the door.

"No, by all means," came the polite response.

Having placed a small, solitary item of hand luggage above his head, the cheerful stranger then felt the need to offer up a compliment. "That's a lovely smile you have there young lady."

As she graciously nodded with a blushed complexion. It took all of three seconds for the natural reciprocity process to kick in this time, and the compliment to be returned!

A radiant beam responded with, "And I really admire your boots sir. I have a strong penchant for shoes and footwear." Excitedly she added, "In fact, as part of my student portfolio for University I produced a fashion show. It involved designing, modelling and photographing shoes."

"Really? How interesting," the man said. "Do you mind if I pull these curtains across? The older I get, the more privacy I prefer." He tugged gently at the window shades"

"No not all," she replied, without even giving it a second thought. "In actual fact, in recent weeks," she added brazenly. "I've even had several people model for me once or twice."

"You have?" he asked.

"I most certainly have," she confirmed proudly. At that, the cheery twenty-something sat back and relaxed. A large satisfactory, reflective grin, spread wide across the fullness of her young nubile face. The glowing whiteness of her skin was in stark contrast to the worn, aged blue and purple carpet running along the floor-way and vertically up the wall of the dated carriage. Thoughts of her future travel plans ran rampant in her mind. Currently she fancied London to France via the Eurostar, then on to either the North or South. Countryside or coastal? She was still undecided, but was looking forward to the adventure.

"My name's Lucy," she continued confidently.

"Pleased to meet you Lucy," he nodded. Before adding in his strong Irish accent. "I'm Raymond."

She reached out and gestured to shake his hand. The genial Irishman grasped it firmly and smiled.

As she went to release her grip, his surprisingly tightened. His voice suddenly turned cold and menacing. He then stated with conviction.

"I believe your father knew my sister."

Lucy Jordan instantly recoiled on hearing this.

"In fact, he dated her, dumped her, broke her heart and discarded her," he added.

It was now the turn of the deranged, female psychopath with the newly dyed red hair to fear. As he began to relax his grip, through yellowing gapped teeth he hissed with contempt.

"She took her own life you know."

At that, the young fugitive from justice pulled free. Her expression of utter astonishment, seemed to clearly indicate - I have no idea what is going on or who you are.

Freedom would have no direct alliance or correlation with the deranged psychopath Lucy Jordan in the foreseeable future. If captured, it would be more than likely that her remaining years on earth would be spent behind bars. Cruelly, she herself, had been badly damaged and traumatised by her abusive upbringing.

The stranger in front of her swivelled his hips flawlessly and forcibly delivered one almighty fatal kick to her forehead. Crack! The knockout blow dispatched with his 'admirable' steel toe-capped boots on, ensured that *'the morning sun would no longer touch lightly on the eyes of Lucy Jordan.'*

"Although people call me Ray," he stated satisfactorily as he stood over her still, lifeless body. "Ray Armour."

EPILOGUE

"May you always be brave in the shadows. Till the sun shines upon you again. Hear this prayer in my heart and we'll ne'er be apart. May you stay in the arms of the angels."

- Maggie Siff

The unpredictable Scottish weather was currently dry, with a heavy layer of moisture bristling on the ground. Blue skies overhead were interspersed with pockets of arctic white cloud. Patriarchal trees stood tall, proud and still as they welcomed yet another momentous day to their lengthy ring of memories. Blinding golden rays of splintered sunshine attempted at regular intervals to brighten the morning in this near forgotten northeast suburb of Glasgow.

The sprawling car park was mostly deserted, with two notable areas of exception. One being Murray's own trusted Volvo S40, which sat isolated in the confines of ten empty disabled bays. At a supermarket or retail park the thoughtful Inspector would never normally occupy a disabled spot. This morning however, at literally the dawning of the day and with no one else around, he felt comfortable enough to pull up there for a short period of time. The fact that it was located a very manageable forty yards from the front door, on this occasion also made it a very attractive proposition. A further group of around twelve to fifteen vehicles all parked up on the southwest corner, would take ownership of exception number two! That recently resurfaced area was specially designated for employee parking, so the tight grouping was understandable.

On his frequent visits over the past few years, Murray had become familiar with the dated plaque on the outside wall just before you entered the fully modernised reception area. The iconic premises, initially opened for business way back in 1882. And in the intervening 130 years since, very few other prisons had gained such notoriety as Glasgow's Barlinnie had in its long and murky history.

The Maze in Northern Ireland. Alcatraz in San Francisco. Possibly even the Bangkok Hilton and a few others had actually reached similar infamy. The monolithic H.M.P Barlinnie in the battle hardened district of Riddrie, was once again releasing one of it's finest back into society. He was by all accounts, ready and rehabilitated!

Adapting, that was always the key. How would or could an individual look to rebuild their life, set their sights on the future, hopefully re-establish their family connections and fully appreciate freedom once again? Support would be offered - absolutely! But the system was badly fragmented and flawed. The more likely scenario was every man for himself! And that would be why a high percentage of those exiting through these very doors, would sooner or later, re-enter via the back entrance in the near future.

The murderous feud between 'Bunny' Reid and Andrew Scott had escalated and would continue to simmer. Erupting at regular intervals with volcanic consequences, as neither man would be willing to step down from taking overall control of Edinburgh's less reputable tourist attractions!

Murray's evening assailant had had his chance, prepayment had been made and the Inspector had been assured that there would be strictly no sale or return. It had been a one-off price. A second attempt would not be repeated and Murray was now free to go about his daily business unhindered.

His daily business… would bring us nicely back as to why Detective Inspector Steven Murray was waiting outside this century old prison at 7.30am on a weekend morning. As if paying homage to many American movies the troubled Scotsman sat perched on the bonnet of his vehicle. As a non-smoker, a piece of mint chewing gum was inserted between his nervous lips in place of a cigarette.

Nearly a quarter of an hour had passed since his arrival. In that time he had managed about twenty clockwise circuits of his beloved Volvo. As well as thumb drumming on the car roof to a couple of quirky tunes playing in his head, he also routinely checked out his tyre pressure - allocating each wheel several heeled kicks. Firstly from his left, then quickly followed by his right! Whilst waiting, walking and whacking… he also wailed a few lines of *"I hear the train a comin', it's rollin' 'round the bend. And I ain't seen the sunshine since, I don't know when. I'm stuck in Folsom Prison and time keeps draggin' on…"*

Finally at 7.32am from behind a solid metal door at the front entrance, activity could be heard. In the silence of the still morning, several bolts being unlocked echoed in the air. A final double chink, followed by a high sounding clang and there was definite movement. A few delicate inches at first. Then gradually it became a foot or two. Eventually the gateway to the outside world sat fully opened at ninety degrees.

Forty feet away, a shape emerged from the morning shadows. Brown leather cowboy boots that had last seen daylight several years previous, were now covered by heavy duty denim jeans. An impressive belt buckle tightened around a less impressive figure. One that at first glance appeared to be slightly under nourished. His loose fitting, red checkered shirt would not allow you a glimpse of his upper body strength. However, the man currently carried no jacket and his cotton sleeves were turned back to his elbows. He began walking stiff and rigid toward the lone figure who was now rising from his car. Distance wise, they were now probably about thirty feet apart.

Murray had patted down his knees and stood up excitedly and abruptly when the door had first burst into life. His heart pounded rapidly. Wariness, apprehension and jubilation were strange bedfellows. He instinctively spat out the gum and his chest tightened as he swallowed continually. Trepidation and pent up energy had taken over. His fingers again began to drum, tapping continuously on his thighs. He bounced nervously from foot to foot. Whilst inside his black, lace up shoes, his sweating toes curled and stretched like a drug enhanced selection of mini Olympic athletes on rowing machines!

With only a short distance of twenty or so feet now separating them, the younger man paused. He adjusted his hair, scratched gingerly at his freshly shaved chin and then continued to amble forward. His face was understandably slimmer than the DI remembered, but he looked good and there was much talking to be done. At less than ten feet away, Murray could now clearly see that those once dynamic blue eyes, lacked the energetic sparkle and personality of before. Although that fire and passion could be rekindled and would gradually return over time he quickly hoped and figured. The detective, twitching, shaking and rubbing his hands anxiously, then stopped suddenly in his tracks. He was preparing to talk, to clear his throat and to hopefully offer up an appropriate and relevant greeting.

However, it was his counterpart who summoned up the vocal strength first as he stood absolutely still. In the openness of the large, isolated parking facility, the American style lumberjack nodded, bit his lip, looked across from only five feet away and offered nervously.

"Inspector."

Easily three seconds elapsed as they faced each other. Several intense moments that were crammed to breaking point for Murray with a selection of nostalgic memories. The infectious sound of a child's laughter in his mind opened the floodgates to grandparents, schooldays and birthday cake. Each clambering for space within a short allotted time frame.

'Inspector' was certainly not the word an emotionally anxious Steven Murray had longed to hear after all this time. He was disappointed and saddened, but knew that they had their work cut out and a long arduous road of bridge building ahead of them. Once again before he could respond with a careful, considered reply and in advance of anything proffered, he looked more carefully and curiously at this man's face. Across his taut, sallow skin, the Inspector wondered if it was it a mere trick of the light? Was his eyesight possibly deceiving him? Or had the combined sunshine and haze blurred his vision?

Was this what he......

Suddenly his stomach crunched and ached, instantly wrapped in shreds of barbed-wire. Within a millisecond, Murray's eyes suddenly bulged at the realisation at what he was witnessing. With a sharp intake of breath, his heaving chest throbbed and pounded with pain. 'Bunny' Reid's cryptic clues and veiled threats immediately resurfaced. Alarm bells, klaxon horns and sirens all sounded at once as he began to recognise and understand fully, the significance of the distinctive red dot on the forehead of the man facing him. Initially paralysed with dread and fear, he simultaneously heard what sounded like the almighty 'boom' of someone lighting a small scale cannon.

Five hundred yards away in a dank and miserable tenement building, glass, brickwork and window frames shattered into tiny pieces as the experienced finger squeezed firmly on the trigger. Everything from that moment on proceeded in slow motion. Murray began belatedly... to frantically reach out... stretching and twisting desperately... to push his youngest beloved son to the ground. It was too little and far too late!

In an instant, in the simple blink of an eye. The deafening explosion and its thunderous exultation, whipped the deadly five inch bullet clean through the air, piercing and penetrating its target.

A full half-second later...... David Andrew Murray lay dead!

THE END

Dedicated to my friend:
David Burns

A man that lived his life with determination, laughter, love and dignity.
In his own wise counsel, David encouraged others to always be kind, always be respectful and to always love your family.
A true gent. God Bless!

Printed in Poland
by Amazon Fulfillment
Poland Sp. z o.o., Wrocław